YOUNG NED

A Novel in Four Parts

By

Brett Ross

Young Ned

Copyright © 2013 by Brett Ross

Thank you for purchasing this book. You are welcome to share it with your friends. This book may be reproduced, copied and distributed for non-commercial purposes, provided the book remains in its complete original form, with the exception of quotes used in reviews.

Your support and respect for the property of this author is appreciated.

*****

*****

'Are we alive or dead?'

'Alive, but.... not'

'What do you mean?'

'We're both alive back where we are, here we're not alive because we haven't been born, but we're not dead either, we're just existing for a brief window of time. We appeared here but we weren't born here, we can't die here, we're like living ghosts. I'm still at home right now and you're wherever you were before you came here, we're outside time.'

*****

Part 1

(All dressed up with nowhere to go)

Ronald had lived next door to the Roach's for as long as Ned could remember. From the kitchen window Ned had an unobstructed view into Ronald's backyard. He could see him bringing sections of sheet-metal down the side access and into the yard, adding it to a large, neatly stacked pile that, judging by its size, must have been growing for several weeks. Over the years Ned had often gazed over the fence, watching Ronald's family, noting the great many differences to the family life on the other side of the fence.

Ronald's parents were nice people; they seemed to be older than his own parents. Ronald was the same age as Ned's older brother. Until a few years ago, Ned would see Ronald's father leave the house early every morning dressed in a suit heading off to work and wonder why his own father would be sitting on the couch watching golf. Ronald's mother was forever in their backyard, gardening or relaxing in the sun and they were always having friends over for dinner. Ned's mother hadn't set foot in this house for years and even when she did live here, she only ever went into the yard to have a cigarette or empty the shit out of the cat's litter tray. Ned can't recall visitors ever coming to the house. Ned's mother's social life had almost exclusively consisted of visits to the gaming lounge at the Binnara Point Hotel, that is, until they acquired a computer. After this memorable purchase, she socialised enthusiastically with all manner of distant and mysterious online lothario. Ned wasn't sure if his dad had any friends. He couldn't remember the last time he saw him talk to anyone on the phone or leave the house for more than 20 minutes. Since Ronald's father retired a few years ago, Ronald's parents were regularly going on cruises or taking their caravan for weekends away. The Roach's have a caravan too, it's in the far corner of their yard but it doesn't go anywhere. The Roach's caravan is a permanent dwelling; it's where Ned's brother lives.

Ned considered all this as his eyes steered from Ronald's yard back to his own, across the shin-high grass, dotted with flattened dead-patches resembling sad little crop circles, created by apathy rather than aliens. Some of these crop circles have very specific shapes, allowing one to identify the item that has brought them into existence. There are two distinct patches left by children's bikes and another that is unmistakably a shovel. Others are more abstract, such as the shapeless patches by the fence which were likely made by items that had fallen from the clothes-hoist and then neglected to be picked up, spending several days soaking up rain before being kicked to the back door and thrown back into the washing machine unworn.

The largest of these dead-patches lay beneath the caravan that sat in the corner of the yard furthest from the fence that the Roach's share with Ronald's family. It was on the caravan that Ned's gaze rested. He knew Shane was inside. Ned and Shane didn't have a great deal in common aside from a surname. Ned wasn't even sure that they were actually brothers given the vast physical differences between the two and the fact that even when still together, his parents relationship was little more than one of mutual disinterest. Ned noticed that a track had been worn into the lawn while he had been away. It led from the back door of the house to the caravan and was bisected by an upturned skateboard which had been consistently stepped over, rather than moved, for the several weeks it would have taken Shane to have worn such a mighty trail. Ned also noticed a second, shorter track that lead from the caravan to the adjacent paling fence, on which a large, pale patch resided. Clearly Shane had taken to pissing on the fence rather than walking the 20 yards to the house. It came as no surprise, Shane was not one for walking far to use the toilet. For years, prior to his move out to the caravan, he had kept an empty juice bottle under his bed which he used as a makeshift chamber pot.

    It was 8am and Ned was alone although the house was full. He had just arrived back from a trip down the coast. He'd spent a month driving from place to place with a surfboard and a tent and only his car stereo to keep him company. He regretted that he was back amongst the Roach's. When he was younger, Ned thought other families weird when they went on outings together, ate dinner at the dining table and spoke to one another, all things he was entirely unaccustomed to. By his early adolescence he figured out that it was actually his family that was in the most part odd. And these days he considered them to be a boil on the neck-fat of humanity.

*

    It was the youngest permanent member of the household that first disturbed the serenity of Ned's reluctant homecoming. Ned heard the toilet flush, followed by the slap of bare feet down the hall and into the kitchen. He knew it was a child approaching as the footsteps were not accompanied by vibrations reverberating through the floor and into his chest.

'Where have you been?' asked Little Jake in his subtle Auckland lilt, his left index finger two knuckles deep into his right nostril.

'I went on a bit of a road-trip mate' replied Ned.

'Oh yeah' sniffed Little Jake as he waddled over to the pantry to burrow for Pop Tarts or some other similarly sugary shit.

'Why don't you have a banana or some Weet-Bix Jakey?'

'Nah, I always have these' Jake replied, his little belly jiggling as he rummaged deeper in to the pantry. 'You'll have to borrow clothes off your dad soon if you keep eating that junk mate'.

Jake paid no regard to Ned's comment as he waddled over to the toaster with his frosted booty.

*

Little Jake's dad, Big Jake, lived in the house too. Big Jake was a delivery driver for Newman's supermarket and would have left for work a couple of hours before Ned arrived home. Big Jake was the partner of Ned's older sister Jodie. Big Jake came over from New Zealand 9 years ago. He and Jodie had met at Newman's back when she was a chubby, 16 year old check-out chick. Jake was 23 when he started seeing Jodie but this didn't seem to bother Ned's parents, he had a job and a car, things neither of Ned's parents had managed for quite some time. Ned was 12 when Big Jake moved in; it was after Jodie fell pregnant a few months into their relationship. Ned liked Big Jake, he was the only one in the family he really got along with and he made the Roach household slightly bearable. Big Jake and Ned went fishing every few weeks and watched the footy together on weekends. Big Jake was a gentle giant and contributed the most to the family. He and Jodie had taken over the running of the household when Ned's mum left, which allowed Ned's dad to while away the days without having to think too much.

Jodie still worked at Newman's too; she was in charge of fruit and veg these days. She didn't work on Sundays though, and wouldn't emerge from her room for a good few hours. Jodie was not a big fan of being upright for longer than was absolutely necessary, particularly on weekends.

*

Ned picked his bag up from the kitchen floor and carried it to his room to unload his clothes which were sporting several weeks' worth of accumulated dirt. He dumped the contents of his bag onto the bed and then headed to the toilet to dump the contents of his bowels onto the unsuspecting porcelain; it would be his first shit in 4 days. Ned had always loved camping but he'd never grown fond of outdoor movements.

The half-week back log would take some moving and Ned settled down for a long haul. Ned wasn't opposed to spending some quality time on the shitter, it was *his* time and he could get lots of thinking done, indeed, it was where he got his best thinking done and it was the one place in the house where he could have some quiet time.

When Ned emerged from his contemplations he returned to the kitchen to sort out breakfast. He took the Weet-Bix from the pantry and built a small tower of four bricks in a bowl before joining Little Jake, who was into his fourth chocolate Pop-Tart, in the living room.

'What are you watching mate?' 'Dragonball Z' replied Jake, maintaining his focus on the television which was only a few short inches from his face. Ned sat on the couch and watched the snippets of the cartoon that were visible around Little Jake's afroesque head mop.

Ned looked into the beige mush in his bowl and noticed that it was almost the same colour as the couch he was sat upon. This couch had not always been the colour of soggy Weet-Bix. Ned could remember when it was pristine, eggshell-white with salmon pinstripes, but always covered in a bed sheet to keep it clean. He never understood his mother's logic when it came to this, sure the couch was clean but it was covered in a grubby bed sheet so it looked old and dirty anyway. He would sneak an occasional peek underneath, just to see how clean it was, and one of the sheets on the rotation was worn-out enough to be able to make out the stripes that lay underneath. Ned had mentioned this bizarre Catch-22 to his mother who had never given a better response than 'it's to stop you bloody kids from getting your grubby handprints all over it'. It had embarrassed Ned when he was young and his friends would ask why the sheet was there and he couldn't give a sensible answer. Now, looking back, Ned thought that his mother had probably never bought many nice things and knowing that under that bed sheet was a lovely, clean couch gave her a sense of pride - however small. After a few years she stopped caring much about the state of the house and the sheets stopped appearing. At this point the couch began its transition to the stain covered monstrosity that it now was, covered in sweat stains and cigarette burns, and smelling like a chain-smoking, wet-dog's bath-towel.

The strip of sunlight that crossed the lounge room every morning and made it impossible to watch the TV between 8am and 9am was no longer shining on Little Jake's back and was now resting on the buffet and hutch that was gathering dust in the corner of the room. The air had warmed up in the hour that Ned had been home and he was keen to get out of the house. He took his bowl to the kitchen, picking up Little Jake's plate of remains on the way and rinsed them quickly before heading out the front door and into the sanctuary of his car. Ned backed out of the driveway and headed down Scarborough Street toward the north end of Binnara Beach. As his Nissan Pintara approached the end of the street Ned saw a familiar figure lumbering along the footpath in the direction of his house. It was his younger sister Krystal making her way home with shoes in hand and make-up streaked down her face like a chubby Alice Cooper. Her right arm was gesticulating wildly, flailing the shoes about whilst her left hand held her mobile phone in front of her face as she yelled indecipherable obscenities down the line. Ned had often noticed people yelling at phones in this manner, perhaps it made them feel that they were yelling into the persons face, emphasising their rage. Ned, to his great relief, ghosted past her unnoticed.

At the end of Scarborough Street Ned turned left onto Ocean Parade just where it straddles Binnara Creek. The creek empties into the ocean halfway along Binnara Beach, dividing the north and south ends. Ned followed Ocean Parade north, towards town until he reached number 22. Number 22 was a single story weatherboard house, resplendent in its cracked and flaking lemon paint, its unpolished wooden deck, covered in a forest of splinters. Its windows were thickly crusted with salt and the tin roof was a subtle shade of rust. To Ned it was a palace. Once upon a time all the houses along the beachfront were like this one. Over the years they'd all changed - renovated, extended or knocked down altogether and replaced with designer monstrosities owned by rich professionals from the city who come up to visit on the weekends and during the school holidays. Number 22 was the last of the original houses built in the 1940's for the miners who worked in the pits behind Bulwarra Bay.

Number 22 is where Andy Dobson lives. Andy and Ned have been mates since they were in the Under 6's together at Binnara Surf Club. Andy's grandparents had lived in the house for fifty-three years up until his grandfather died two years ago, Andy's Nan had since moved in with his parents. Andy moved in after he finished school and he made it his castle.

Ned strolled up the driveway and could just make out, through the crusted up glass, Andy standing in the kitchen. As his foot hit the first of the two steps leading up to the deck the flimsy screen door flung open with a hiss and a bang.

'Hello dickhead' greeted Andy in his nasal twang. 'How was the trip?'

'Yeah, it was good mate, good to get away for a bit y'know' replied Ned smiling.

'Well I reckon you're a weird prick' laughed Andy, 'going away by yourself for a month just when all the tarts from the city are up here slutting about. They were loose this year mate, very loose'.

'Yeah right...... well I'm sure they'll be back next year mate, it's always the same'. Andy nodded in agreement.

Ned stepped up onto the deck and propped himself up against the wooden railing - there to protect the unwary from the hefty one-foot drop to the grass below - being careful not to get a back-full of splinters, and looked across the road and over to the beach.

'Did you get some waves while I was away or were you too busy gettin' amongst the birds?'

'We had a few good days Neddy but I've had a fair bit of work on, been doing a job up in Bulwarra Heights. Big place up the top of the hill.'

'Good to hear mate, you been putting the pennies away?' Ned asked, flicking ant off the railing.

'Yeah mate, the funds are piling up nicely, might have to treat myself to a trip away soon.'

'Yeah cool, I might have to join you.'

'Always welcome Neddy, always welcome. You been home yet?'

'Yeah I dropped in for a shit and a feed, only Little Jake was up. I saw Ronald dragging some tin out to his yard.'

Andy chuckled, 'Ah Ronald, that dude is top shelf'. 'I ran into Shane up the top-pub on Friday, being a menace like always.'

Ned nodded with a wry smile on his face.

'He cornered me for a few minutes… told me he'd been speaking to the manager about him DJ-ing up there.'

Ned and Andy both let out a burst of laughter. Shane regularly came up with awesome money making ideas in the heat of intoxication that faded into the ether once any actual effort was required.

'I guess it's the next logical step after his rap career died', chuckled Ned.

'Yeah, I don't know how he failed, all those quality tunes he wrote about smoking bongs and fingering chicks behind Newman's' laughed Andy.

'The world wasn't ready for him man' suggested Ned sarcastically. He glanced up towards the headland, 'You wanna go for a wander up the lookout?'

'Ahhh…yeeeah, ok. I've gotta go up the jobsite at eleven-thirty but it should be sweet.'

'Cool'.

Andy went into the house to grab his wallet and then the two headed out onto the road and followed it towards the north end of the beach where it split, one arm heading west toward the town centre and the other continuing up onto the headland where the lookout was. The walk to the headland took them past the surf club and the caravan park, both places that they had spent plenty of time while they were growing up, keeping themselves amused and getting up to mischief.

With little else to do in the town, the local kids spent most of their time down around the beach and when the holidays came around they all looked forward to seeing what new kids would turn up to the caravan park and the strip of holiday houses to break the monotony. A lot of the guys still did this, well into their twenties. As Ned and Andy walked along the footpath they had scratched swear words in when it was freshly laid 10 years ago, they passed the rows of wooden benches on the foreshore reserve which had become the favoured daytime drinking venue of a lot of the boys they had grown up with. Already some of the fellas were claiming their places for the day, exchanging their versions of events from the night before while they waited for the bottle shop to open at half-past ten.

'The boys are on it early today, what a life they lead eh' said Andy, nodding his head in the direction of the bench.

'Living the arseholes dream' Ned replied as he delivered a nod of recognition in the direction of the bench hooligans who had now spotted the boys and were waving them over.

'Maybe later lads, got a few things to do...' shouted Ned as he and Andy continued on their way up to the lookout.

In recent years some of the bored youth of Binnara Point had made an uninspired attempt at notoriety by creatively calling themselves the Binnara Point Thugs and playing the part of gangsters. They went and had shirts and hoodies printed up, got bad tattoos of the local postcode and invented rivalries with the neighbouring communities whose own young men were happy to play along in order to break their similar boredom. The BPT boys made a habit of accidentally bumping into groups from the neighbouring towns on nights out and starting brawls, this would give them something to talk about for the following week until the next brawl-night. There was even a short lived BPT girl gang which resulted in a few bad tattoos and unwanted pregnancies but little else.

The boys continued quietly up the headland road for a few minutes before they reached the lookout. Ned sat down on the grass on the wrong side of the safety rail where he could see over the whole beach, the reserve and across to the row of shops that hugged the main road.

'It's busy down there today.'

'Last day of the school holidays mate, everyone's cramming it all in. And all the blow-ins are bailing back to the city' Andy expertly explained as he joined Ned on the grass. 'Back to school for you too hey?'

'Yeah' replied Ned, bereft of any enthusiasm. 'I'm not keen though, I'm a bit over uni..... I was thinking about it a fair bit while I was away'.

Why's that?'

'Don't know, just...... it's all a bit bullshit I guess. I'm hanging around a bunch of nerds who've wiped their pasts and are trying to out-cool one another with made up stories.' Ned plucked out a piece of long grass and started peeling it apart. 'I don't really know what I want to do, but being funneled into some shitty job at an engineering joint doesn't really appeal to me. I don't want to be kissing some rich blokes arse all day just so I can buy a new car every 3 years and pay for all the stupid shit I've filled my house with to distract myself from the shitty life I have.' Ned gestured at the group they had passed earlier sitting at the bench, 'I might as well go hang with those fellas if I'm going down that path, it would be just as shit of an existence, at least this lot get to be around people they like'.

'Fucken hell Ned, just kill yourself now' replied Andy, trying to hold back a grin.

'Sorry mate' said Ned 'too much time on my own lately, too much thinking.'

'That's why people go on holidays with *other* people; you lose your shit when you're on your own all the time. Solitary confinement is a *punishment* in jail mate, they don't give it to the crook with the cleanest bedroom.'

'Cells' replied Ned.

'What?'

'Prisoners have cells not bedrooms.'

'Fuck you' laughed Andy, shaking his head. 'What's the time?'

Ned pulled his phone from his pocket, 'it's…. quarter to eleven'.

'I gotta head off mate, don't wanna upset the boss' said Andy rising to his feet.

'You work for your dad.'

'Yeah, he's a good bloke, but he's a cunt of a boss'

'Righto mate' said Ned still sitting, his right hand gripping his left wrist, hugging his knees 'I'm gonna hang here for bit longer'.

'Sweet mate, well I'll talk to you later' said Andy turning to straddle back over the lookout railing.

'Ok mate, later'. Ned stared out into the ocean watching the waves, thinking of very little.

A minute after he left, Andy came into Ned's field of view down by the foreshore reserve. Ned could see the gang on the park bench calling out to Andy, beers in hand, then Andy waving them off as he continued back to his seaside palace.

*

Ronald MacDonald's name was acquired through family tradition. His uncle was named Ronald as was his grandfather. Going back to 1858 the first born male of each generation of the MacDonald family has been named Ronald. The first Ronald MacDonald, after whom all the others are named, received a Victoria Cross for 'bravery beyond the call of duty' during the Crimean War. He had been killed holding off Russian troops while other members of his section retreated to cover.

*

Ned spent the next hour chewing on grass stalks, watching the comings and goings of Binnara Point from above. This spot - in front of the lookout railing - has been Ned's other quiet place of contemplation, for when his need for thinking time and bowel movements didn't correspond. From here he'd seen the town change over time, fancy new houses going up along the beachfront and the shops on the main road changing names and locations and closing down. Ned remembered the pet shop that used to be next to the old Newman's moving 4 times around the town centre before disappearing altogether. Newman's too had moved from the east end of the main road near the beach to a big new building at the far western end next to where it joins the Pacific Highway. He remembered Jodie being rather upset that Newman's was moving to the other end of town, away from the takeaway joints where she gorged during her lunch breaks. Ned looked over at the entrance to the beach car park where he was hit by a car as a six year old; the council had built a concrete island in the middle of the entry to slow down the cars going in and out after that. Ned barely remembered it now, just a long scar running down his left shin where he had to have his broken leg pinned and another one, more faded, on his upper lip where his teeth went through the skin were a lasting reminder. The Roach's had arrived in Binnara Point in 1986 after Jodie was born. The birth of their first child meant they were entitled to an upgrade from their 1 room council flat to a fully-fledged council house which they later purchased. Since that arrival only Ned's mother had managed to leave.

*

Every morning Ronald gets up early and walks to the newsagent at the end of his street to pick up the newspaper. He has done this every day since he was 11, the only exception is when he and his parents go to Murrays Inlet for two weeks at Christmas and one time when he had his wisdom teeth out and had to stay the night in hospital.

*

It was getting on for lunchtime and Ned was starting to get hungry and decided to make for home. He hopped back over the railing and made his way down the slope of the headland and towards his car. Along the way Ned observed several of the proud owners of the holiday beachfront behemoths cramming all of their seasonal shit into their weekend cars for the trip back to the city suburbs and real life. The dads going back to their offices to yell at underlings and fuck their secretaries and the mums going back to a bottle and a half of wine between dropping off and picking up the kids from school, or so Ned's cynical mind imagined.

Ned pulled his car into the driveway and took his camping gear out of the boot and carried it up the steps to the front door. The door was wide open and from the lounge room Ned could hear the Sunday Sports Wrap-Up blazing from the TV. Little Jake must have been relegated to the portable tele in the back room by one or more of the adults. Ned bypassed the lounge to his bedroom and dumped his gear on the floor.

'That you Ned?' bellowed a voice from the lounge room, barely audible over the blaring TV. Ned's reply was lost amongst the random nouns coming from the deafening horseracing commentary.

Ned walked down the hall and into the kitchen to make lunch, 'Fellas' he said as he walked past the archway that linked the lounge and kitchen, a wholly acceptable greeting in the Roach household. When he glanced in he saw Shane reclined on the sofa, belly exposed, ankles 5 feet apart and a plate of bacon and eggs resting on his crotch. Ned's dad was sitting in the armchair next to the front window sitting with a slightly more modest posture but with his plate of food in the same relative position. Ned made himself a tuna sandwich and went to join his elders in front of the TV. He stood in front of Shane and blocked his view to show that he required some space to be made on the sofa, as was the family custom.

'The cat pissed on your bedroom floor while you were away' announced Shane as Ned squeezed himself on to the end of the sofa.

'Awesome'

'I got Little Jake to spray some deodorant on it'

'Thanks mate' Ned replied, the sarcasm lost on Shane.

'There's bacon and eggs in the fridge if you want' said Ned's dad motioning toward the fridge and glancing at Ned without moving his head from its position on the headrest of the armchair.

'Nah I'm alright thanks'.

'Did you see the cricket while you were away?' asked Shane between mouthfuls of bacon.

'I listened to it on the radio, wasn't too good'.

'They're shit! I'm better than some of the myths in that team' declared Shane without a hint of hyperbole.

Ned let out a short burst of laughter, 'you'd better dust off your kit bag mate, get ready for the call-up'.

Shane's attempt to retort Ned's doubt was foiled by a full mouth of food and his haste resulted in him inhaling a chunk of bacon. The ensuing coughing fit projected the half chewed contents of Shane's mouth back onto his plate as well as onto the carpet around his feet and a few stray pieces onto Ned's bare foot.

'Ah!...ya grub' snapped Ned as he shook his foot flinging the regurgitated bacon to the floor. Shane managed to gather himself after a minute, washing down the obstruction with the breakfast cola he had on the floor beside the couch.

'Rooster!' Shane bellowed, 'Rooster! Get in here.'

Through the open front door slunk Rooster, the Roach's patchy mongrel dog. He approached cautiously, unsure if he was going to be kicked or fed.

'There you go' said Shane, pointing to the mess at his feet. Rooster sniffed at it for a few seconds before eating it up. Rooster licked the carpet briefly before Shane nudged him away with his greasy foot. Rooster wandered to the centre of the room and plopped himself down, he then proceeded to chew at the bare patch of skin at the spot where his tail joined his rump.

The three Roach men sat in front of the TV watching the sports updates silently aside from the occasional remark about one of the overnight scores or presenter's choice of tie. A bang from outside motivated Ned's dad to move his head from the armchair headrest and peer out the window to see what had caused the disruption.

'Just crazy Ronald' said Ned's dad before returning his head to it's indentation on the chair.

'Is that spastic bringing more shit home?... Fucking idiot,'sniped Shane.

'Leave him alone, he's alright' interjected Ned.

Shane continued, 'I was talking to a bloke who works at the welding joint on Nightingale Street up at the pub the other day. He told me 'Dickhead' next door put in an order for some stupid metal box he'd drawn with his pencils. Bloke said the things the size of a fucken shed. Reckons they'll have to deliver it in parts. Silly prick.' Shane then produced the high pitched maniacal snicker that he uses to emphasise any statement he believes to be hilarious.

'Good on him, at least he's not sitting on his arse all day like you.'

'Fuck off Ned, I'm a busy man, I run a business.'

'Since when was selling weed to high school kids a business?...Or are you talking about the DJ-ing career I've heard about.'

'Whatever...... he makes us look bad, creeping around and stealing people's garbage.'

'It's not Ronald making you look bad mate.'

Shane chose not to continue the discussion and refocused on the motor racing highlights that were being shown on Sunday Sports. The next half hour passed in silence aside from the sound of cans of Newman's Own brand cola opening, the associated burps and the wet, smacking sound of Rooster chewing himself. After the cricket highlights had been shown the third time round Ned's dad decided it was time to change the channel. He brought up the program menu and he and Shane engaged in brief debate regarding what to watch. Shane emerged victorious due to his father's lack of will rather than any oratory or persuasive skill. Shane decided that MMA cage fighting was the order of the afternoon. The idea of watching two sweaty, semi-nude men locked in an aggressive and prolonged embrace didn't appeal to Ned and he took this as his cue to leave. Ned didn't imagine that it was likely to be to his father's taste either but realised that moving from his armchair and doing something that required effort or thinking was substantially more unappealing to him. Ned went into his room and grabbed what was probably the cleanest towel in the house and exiled himself to the backyard. He moved the wet washing off of the dirty, sun-weakened deckchair that resided on the back patio and dragged it out into the yard. Ned draped his towel over the deteriorating cushions and popped himself down with one of his sisters 'That's Life' magazines.

*

Each morning Ronald goes through the same routine to which he has become accustomed. Ronald only drinks soup, no other liquid has passed his lips since he was 8 years old, he has a bowl of soup and a cup of soup every morning. Ronald then showers, washing all over, including his hair, with a bar of Sunshine Soap. He brushes his teeth for 1 minute and 20 seconds before going to his bedroom to get dressed. Ronald is always dressed impeccably; he coordinates all his clothes from head to toe, always matching his tops, bottoms and socks by colour with the exception of his underpants, which are always white. When he leaves his house at 8.05am Ronald exits his front gate, swivels to the left and walks one thousand three hundred and sixty eight paces East-South East to the newsagent. The walk takes 13 minutes 28 seconds which is rather slow, due to Ronald's gait. Ronald walks on his tip-toes; it looks as though he is at all times walking on hot sand. He's always walked this way.

*

Ned vainly attempted to take an interest in the self-penned articles of hardship and recipes for the 'perfect pavlova' that constituted the magazine but his attention was drawn elsewhere. He was curious as to what lay behind the walls of Shane's caravan and decided to sneak across the yard to gaze upon the wonders that were contained within. Ned kicked a stray basketball behind the caravan to use as a step so he could peer in through the port window. It certainly wasn't a well-lit space; Shane had taped a Frisbee over the skylight which gave the inside of the van a red, brothel-like hue. There were a few pictures on the wall that Ned could make out, one of Shane with the Jim Beam girls that visit the pub every so often with a Polaroid camera, another which appeared to be Shane and a friend at the pub, dressed as pirates, both men comically holding their plastic swords like a shiny, curved phallus and below this a photo of Shane's ill-conceived children Kobe and Shakur sitting on Santa's knee in Bulwarra Plaza. (Kobe and Shakur were the result of Shane's relationship of mutual laziness with the across the road neighbor Tenille. Shane and Tenille spent much of their late teens sitting on her couch eating, farting, screaming and apparently, at least once, fucking. Kobe and Shakur were named after two cool black guys Shane had heard of, in spite of their gingerness and total lack of melanin. Now they acted as go betweens for their parents abuse). There was a mattress directly below the window with a sheet that was loosely spread across it, on top of which rested a dirty plate and a shoe. Stuck to the wall besides the bed was a birthday card decorated with crayon which read 'To Daddy' and in the corner nearest the door was a folding table that held a small TV and a box which recently contained a new laptop computer. The caravan was quite cluttered which was understandable as Shane had downsized considerably. His previous abode was the garage, which had never been used for its intended purpose as neither of Ned's parents had ever driven. Now though, Jodie had reclaimed the garage as both her and Big Jake had their own vehicles and with Ned's car in the mix parking spaces of late, were at a premium. With his curiosity - for what was in the caravan at least - satisfied, Ned wandered back to his deckchair and reclined in quiet contemplation.

After looking up at the sky for a little while a particle of fluff or dust came into Ned's field of view. He'd always enjoyed trying to control the direction of the particle as it slid across his cornea, steering it around with subtle eye movements, he hadn't had one for ages and made the most of this opportunity, amusing himself for quite some time with this challenge. He remembered as a kid laying down on the sand after a swim and staring directly up into the blue sky, he would wait for a minute or two and there it would be, sometime more than one, floating gracefully across his eye. If it started to slide to the right a quick glance to the left would bring it back to the centre where it would rest for a time before it again began to slide towards the edge of his vision. He could keep this up for a good while, until something would make him blink suddenly or circumstances necessitated that he use his eye in a more conventional manner. A fly was buzzing around Ned's head and was threatening to end Ned's game. He swatted at the fly, still maintaining his focus on the eye-fluff, keeping it at the peak of its slippery slope. The fly distanced itself momentarily but it was persistent, quickly returning to rest on Ned's top lip. At first he tried to ignore it, hoping that it would get bored and leave, but it waltzed about in no particular hurry spending a short eternity in Ned's philtrum. Ned started blowing bursts of air out of his nostrils but to little effect. The fly's meanderings took it perilously close to the inside of

Ned's left nostril and at once he sat up, slapping and nose-puffing wildly and, of course, irretrievably losing the wandering fluff to the corner of his eye where it would be picked out in the morning, fossilized in his morning eye-crust.

Ned was thirsty from his time in the sun and headed back into the house to get a drink. He'd planned on just having some water but a stack of dirty plates piled to within millimetres of the tap-head put an end to any such plans. Instead Ned surveyed the fridge and was greeted with all variety of Newman's Own soft-drink cans - cola, lemonade, orange, tropical, ginger beer and one interestingly, called sars. The selection was broad but curiosity won out and Ned grabbed himself a can of Sars, mainly because it shared its name with the virus that caused a panic when he was in high school but also because he could add it to his list of tried items. After the first sip Ned immediately regretted his decision, it's tasted old-fashioned, something that people considered a treat in days gone by when anything sweeter that water was considered delicious and sugar was worth more than gold. Those bad-boys would be ageing in the fridge until the next time Ned's grandmother came for a visit and her old-fashioned taste buds could assist with their disposal.

The television was still blasting in the lounge and Shane and his dad were still frozen in recline, eyes glued to the one-day cricket game on the TV. Ned continued past and went into his bedroom with his Sars. He placed his drink down on the bedside table and flopped down onto his bed. It was now that he noticed the large white patch where Little Jake had given the carpet a whores-shower to mask the cat piss. Ned turned on his clock radio and listened to the cricket, occasionally downing a pained mouthful of Sars. The early start to the day was catching up with him and Ned caught himself drifting off a couple of times. He was normally a big fan of an afternoon nap but Ned wanted to make today last as long as possible. The thought of having to get up tomorrow morning a go to the university campus filled him with dread.

The sound of the bedroom door rattling against its frame snapped Ned from his slumber. He could tell from the dampness of the bedspread and the sweat around his neck that he'd been lying still for a while. A glance to his left confirmed his suspicions, the glowing red digits on the clock radio read 18:47. Outside his bedroom Ned could hear talking, and it didn't seem to be scripted or accompanied by a laugh track. It meant that one or possibly both of his sisters were back. Big Jake should be about as well, he would almost certainly be cooking dinner by now. Ned emerged sheepishly from his room and headed toward the kitchen.

'Hey bro, long time no see.' Ned looked up to see Big Jake standing in front of the oven, stirring the contents of a saucepan, with a big grin on his face. 'Been having a little kip mate?'

Yeah…. I hit the road early this morning, took it out of me I guess.'

'It'll do that mate, you want some food?' asked Big Jake, turning his body to give Ned a view of the various foodstuffs awaiting their fates on the cook top.

'Aww, I won't say no mate.'

'Sweet should be ready in five. Me and Jakey are gonna eat out the back mate, if you're keen…? '

'Yeah mate, sounds like a plan'. Ned stuck his head around the corner into the lounge where Shane had been replaced on the sofa by Jodie and Krystal. His dad remained in state, the armchair in full recline.

'Decided to come back to us Ned?' squawked Jodie in her aggressively sarcastic manner.

'There's no place like home' replied Ned, mirroring Jodie's sentiment. Krystal looked across at Ned but remained silent.

'What have you kids been up to all afternoon?'

'We went up the Bulwarra shops t' get some school stuff for Jake, 'n Krystal needed some stuff for her course too.'

'Oh that's good, what course you doin' Kryssie?' enquired Ned. Both he and Jodie looked at Krystal expectantly. Jodie jabbed Krystal with her elbow to extricate a response.

'Childcare' muttered Krystal, withholding eye contact.

'Oh, cool' replied Ned in an enthusiastic a voice as he could manage. As he said this, a wave of anticipatory empathy washed over him, he could imagine the discomfort of the toddlers left in Krystal's charge, running around for hours in piss-soaked nappies while she buried her hangover vomit in their sandpit. Luckily for the under five's of Binnara Point the likelihood of her finishing the course was minimal, particularly if regular attendance was a requirement.

'Dinners up!' Big Jake bellowed from the kitchen. Jodie and Krystal struggled out of the sunken couch, both requiring a couple of practice thrusts and significant leverage from the wobbly arm rests. Ned's dad snapped the armchair into is upright mode and followed the girls out. The three of them schlepped past Ned into the kitchen where a row of plates, piled high with food, awaited them on the counter-top. There was an unspoken order to the distribution of meals, Ned's dad always took the plate closest to the oven and the others collected their dinner along the line by order of birth. Ned took the last plate in the line next to Little Jakes cow print plate; he didn't often eat with the family and had lost his place in the pecking order. Jodie and Krystal returned to the lounge and buried themselves back in the sofa with their dinner, Ned's dad retreated back to half recline mode in his velour chrysalis. Ned and the two Jakes took themselves out to the back patio to enjoy some alfresco dining.

'Looking forward to school tomorrow Jakey?' asked Ned, brushing dirt from the outdoor setting.

'Nope' replied Little Jake testing the temperature of his food with his right index finger.

'Me neither mate.'

'You told me you liked school Jakey.' Big Jake interjected, 'You change your mind?'

'Yeah, I'm up to level nine on War Commander 2 now. I wanna stay home.'

'What?' asked Ned quizzically.

'Bloody video games……. they'll rot your brains kid, I'll throw that thing away.' declared Big Jake, strangling a smile well enough to scare Little Jake.

'Well I wish I was back at school, I reckon you're lucky Jakey' assured Ned. The comment was meant in jest and he didn't expect Little Jake to believe it, but upon saying it Ned realized that he wasn't really joking at all. When he was there, Ned couldn't wait to leave school but having experienced the alternative he missed it.

'Me too, I'd rather be hanging out with my mates and finger painting all day instead of getting up at five in the morning to drive a van around for 12 hours'

'I'm in year 4 now Dad, we don't finger paint!' asserted Little Jake, stabbing a sausage with his fork to emphasise his seriousness.

'Ok buddy, chill out' replied Big Jake, palms up in mock surrender.

Ned could see a red glow emanating through the darkness from across the yard, 'Shane not eating tonight?'

Big Jake let out a girlish chuckle, Ill-fitting his robust physique, 'Shane's feeding himself these days mate'

'Why's that?'

'Jodie told him he had to start chipping in and stop bein' a freeloader. That's why he's out in the van, Jodie kicked him out of the garage, plus she wanted it for the car….. He's got himself a microwave in there; think he's just eating pizzas and dim-sims every night.'

Ned chuckled to himself quietly, 'I saw him getting stuck into some bacon and eggs this morning, I don't think they were microwave jobs.'

'Cheeky prick' muttered Big Jake through a mouthful of mashed potato, glaring at the caravan.

Little Jake licked the remaining gravy from his plate and headed toward the back door.

'Oi!' shouted Big Jake, 'Enjoy that video game tonight; I'm throwing it in the bin tomorrow.'

Little Jake paused and looked back at his Dad, scanning his face for a sign that he was just kidding. He swung open the screen door and ran inside, satisfied that his Dad wasn't serious.

Big Jake got up and walked over to the beer fridge next to the back door; he picked two bottles out and motioned to Ned that one was for him if he wanted it.

'Yeah, thanks mate.'

Big Jake opened the beers and sat down at the table sliding Ned his drink. 'So, what's the latest bro, back to uni tomorrow?'

'Yeah I guess.'

'You don't sound too keen.'

'Nah....I think I'm over it'

Big Jake took a swig from his bottle, 'Quit then.'

'Aww I don't know, I've already done a fair bit, seems like a waste,' replied Ned picking at the label on his bottle.

'Seems like a waste to keep going if you're hating it.'

'Yeah, I dunno…..I'll give it a chance, see how it goes.'

'I can sort you out with some work if you decide to pull the pin mate' assured Big Jake.

'Thanks mate'.

Ned and Big Jake carried on drinking their beers with their feet up on the table, looking up at the clear night sky.

'We should go fishing one arvo this week' suggested Ned.

'Yeah bro, sounds good to me,' Big Jake downed the last few drops of his beer. 'I got a few nice flathead while you were away, took Jakey down to the creek.'

'Nice' replied Ned nodding in approval.

'Yeeeah' exhaled Big Jake, 'you wanna go shake up the caravan before we head in?'

'Yep.' Ned and Big Jake put their bottles on top of the fridge and snuck up to the van, their conspiring whispers masked by the Eminem CD that Shane had cranking inside. They each took a side and began pushing on the outside walls of the van; Ned was surprised by how loudly the metal siding popped with each shove. He could hear objects starting to slide down the wall and hit the floor inside.

'Fuck off dickheads!'

Ned could hear Big Jakes high-pitched giggles in between the shouting and pinging of the tin walls.

'Well you shouldn't eat my bacon!' yelled Big Jake before scurrying back to the house with Ned in tow. Ned picked up the two plates still sitting on the patio table and carried them to the sink.

'Thanks for dinner mate, I'll get the dishes tonight.'

'You sure mate? I was gonna get Jakey to do it.'

'Yeah mate, I got it'

'Alright bro,' Big Jake gave Ned a thumbs up before disappearing down the hall.

Ned surveyed the mountain of dishes in the sink before him and piled everything on the countertop; this load was going to require at least one water change.

He did battle at the sink for 45 minutes, having to drain the dishwater and refill it twice before the pile subsided completely. He dried his wrinkled hands on the damp tea towel that hung from the cutlery drawer and reached into his pocket to check the time. It was nearly nine o'clock and Ned decided to call it a night. He followed the well-worn path down the hall and into his room. He quickly assessed his wardrobe and felt confident that he would be able to put together a clean ensemble for the morning. Ned tuned his stereo to the National Radio science program and lay down to contemplate the mysteries of the universe as he went to sleep. He felt less anxious about going to university in the morning than he had earlier in the day, but he could still think of plenty of things he'd rather be doing.

*

On his morning constitutional Ronald passes 67 houses on his side of the road. Once a month the council trucks come by and collect large unwanted items from the street. In the lead up to the monthly council clean-up day the neighbourhood's unwanted wares begin to accumulate on the roadside, some households put items out weeks before the designated day. Over the years Ronald has brought home a lot of items left out for collection by the council. The first thing he ever brought back was a broken Walkman; Ronald took the Walkman apart to see why it wasn't working. Ronald took apart his father's functioning Walkman and compared the two. After a process of trial and error Ronald was able to replace the broken part with a part taken from his dad's Walkman. After that Ronald continued to bring home interesting items from the kerb-side. Ronald couldn't believe his luck when DVD's usurped videos and people started leaving their VCR's out for collection. In the April of 2002 Ronald brought home 13 VCR's and he ended up with 44 by the end of that year. He has a shed in the backyard that's full of all sorts of found items; TV's, toasters, computers, microwaves, gaming consoles and vacuum cleaners. 2007 was a particularly good year for TV's, big flat-screens had become much cheaper and everybody seemed to be throwing out their old rear projection sets.

*

The bus ride to the university was not doing Ned's motivation any favours. It was a long journey, an hour and a half on a busy day. The first bus took Ned from Binnara Point thirty minutes up the highway to the Swansborough Plaza Shopping Centre on the southern outskirts of the city. From there he caught the 108 which weaved its way through the outer suburbs of the city for almost an hour before passing through the University of Eastern Australia campus.

Ned, in the main, shared his journey with two types of public commuter, the elderly and the unemployed. There were always lots of pensioners on their way to and from shopping centres, RSL clubs and doctors' appointments, all going about their daily business calmly and quietly. Ned liked to listen to the conversations between the elderly passengers, discussing the way they saw the world, their bafflement at the modern young, their distrust of all things new and confusing and the decline and demise of their friends with their various ailments. The way they spoke of things done better back in the day always made Ned pay attention. Ned saw himself as old fashioned in many ways, the disdain he felt for his own generation mirrored that of the old timers on the bus. He had never been a dedicated follower of fashion, he liked what he liked and everything else was for other people to worry about. Ned admired the way most of the old guys on the bus were little concerned by the opinions of others, they wore what was comfortable, they did what they enjoyed and they said what they thought, he felt it a shame that it took people so long to free themselves from the shackles of other people's perceptions. So much energy was wasted by people worrying that others might have noticed the hole in their shoe or the out of place hairs on their head, oblivious to the fact that others are themselves too caught up worrying about the exact same thing to take any real notice. Ned thought it to be the greatest hindrance in life, concerning one's self with how one was perceived by others. Ned was of the view, if you're trying to be good, that's good enough. Not giving a fuck was the key to success.

The other type of passenger Ned encountered on the bus also didn't give a fuck, but they went about it all wrong. Instead of not caring what others thought, they didn't care about how they affected other people. Along its meanderings the bus would collect tracksuit clad ratbags on their way to job centre appointments or the betting shop or carrying home their supplies of cigarettes, cheap soft drink, chips and cut price booze. These commuters usually rolled in packs, strutting down the aisle like puffed up roosters, their loud, profanity laced boasts drowning out or bringing to an abrupt halt, the conversations of the old folks. They screamed their private conversations into mobile phones for all to hear. Ned had seen young couples finding great humour in the curse words being parroted by their infants who were too young to feel any shame.

When Ned had previously doubted his commitment to his studies, seeing these people on the bus would remind him why he was there, he was determined to avoid such a future, not wanting any part of this lifestyle that so many of his peers and family members had resigned themselves to. But after two years at university, amongst the motivated and educated, he was beginning to feel that he had no real desire to join their ranks either. Growing up, Ned's greatest fear was that he would end up like his father and brother, now he was concerned that he would end up as someone who was financially secure, living in the nice part of town, and then all too late concluded that he had traded his best days in for a fancy house he was rarely in and a swimming pool that he never used, no longer getting any satisfaction from the fact that at least people thought he'd done well.

On this particular bus journey Ned sat behind an elderly couple who, by way of subtle eavesdropping, he knew to be going to the bank and then the barber and then to the bowling club raffle. On the way out of Swansborough the bus passed a row of newly constructed townhouses.

'Look over there Jack,' said the elderly woman pointing out the window to the townhouses. 'They've put some houses in where the old upholsterers was, they look nice don't they?'

'Mmm,' the elderly gentleman replied.

'We got our armchair covered there, you remember?'

'Mmm.'

Ned looked through his class timetable, like last semester, it was shit. He'd gotten up early on the online enrolment date and logged on only 20 minutes after the site went live but he might as well have waited 20 days, again he was left with the crumbs. Almost without exception he was enrolled in the tutorial classes that nobody wanted, early starts and late finishes with nothing in-between. Today, after the morning lectures, Ned would have to wait four and a half hours for his 5.00pm Fluid Mechanics tutorial. Without the option of going home, like the greedy campus arseholes he so loathed who snapped up all the midday classes, Ned would have to come up with some new time-killing measures. Previously he'd tried spending his afternoon in the library reading every newspaper available, sleeping on the grass outside the chemistry block, hanging out in the student bar, walking to the local shops and occasionally studying. None of these were particularly wonderful ways of spending an afternoon.

'Do you remember when that used to be the drive-in pictures?' asked the elderly lady as the bus passed a multi-storey parking lot.

'You're a fucking dog Jamie, if I see that slut out in town I'll smash her fucking head in. You've got a kid and you spend all day smoking bongs with your mates and fucking around with that slut…….. Whatever Jamie you're a dog and you've got a thin dick and I hope she gives you AIDS….' Ned turned around to see a greasy haired girl of about 17 slouched on the back seat of the bus shouting into a sparkly pink mobile phone. She had the gaunt appearance of someone whose diet consists mainly of cigarettes and chips and beside her was a little boy who'd heard it all before. Ned could imagine Jamie on the other end of the phone, resplendent in his tracksuit and wispy goatee, video-game controller in hand and a faint trail of smoke pluming from the juice bottle bong sitting at his feet. Ned thought Shane had probably been on the receiving end of similarly charming phone calls from his own 'baby mama', Tennille.

The elderly lady, doing her best to ignore the goings on at the back of the bus remained focused on what was going on outside her window.

'They've done these gardens up nice Jack, we should get some of those hydrangeas for the front yard', she distracted, as the bus pulled into the university campus.

Ned hit the button and made his way to the front, braced for the long day ahead.

*

'How was the first day back mate?' asked Big Jake, sliding a half frozen prawn onto a hook.

'Long,' replied Ned, winding in his line to reveal a soggy and sad looking bit of prawn meat draped in creek weed, 'How about you?'

'Same old shit bro' Big Jake flicked his line out into the middle of the creek. 'A lot of dickheads on the road today.'

'On the bus too mate, can't escape 'em.' Ned cast out a fresh line and sat down on the bank. 'Sounds like we could both do with a change of scene.'

Big Jake flashed a thoughtful smile and nodded his head. 'Maybe.'

'You ever thought of leaving, doing something else?' asked Ned.

'Plenty of times mate...... I didn't think I'd still be here at thirty two. I shit myself when your sister got pregnant; I was ready to do a runner back to NZ.'

'Really?' Ned was shocked, he'd always thought of Big Jake as a stand-up guy, certainly not one to shirk responsibility.

'I was fresh off the boat mate, just a young rat looking for a good time. I definitely wasn't thinking about kids.... I was still a kid myself.' Big Jake was focused on the creek, his eyes hidden behind a pair of wrap-around sunglasses. 'Yeah... time's got away from me a bit, been busy looking after Jakey and working, it flies past mate. I want us to get our own place but Jodie reckons we should stay. She's running the show there anyway, she's just waiting for the rest of you to fuck off.' Big Jake flashed Ned a grin before lifting a foot out of the creek and flicking a fat footful of mud at him.

Ned jumped up, dropping his fishing rod, 'Oi! Watch it buddy. I'll have to come over there and sort you out.' Big Jake let out a shrill cackle as Ned repositioned himself back in his divot on the bank.

*

When the MacDonald's returned home from Stewart Inlet was the best time for collecting. After Christmas there was always a goldmine of electrical items glittering on the kerbs just waiting for Ronald. He would always spend the afternoon of their return trawling up and down the street bringing home all manner of electronic and mechanical treasures. In his shed he would stack the items in like piles; kitchen based items on shelves along the left wall arranged by type and size, the component parts of dismantled items arranged on labelled shelves, TV's, gaming and audio equipment are kept against the back wall and miscellaneous items are stored on the shelves above his workspace on the right side of the shed. His work bench has several rows of drawers containing his tools, all immaculately maintained and stored in perfect order. On the wall is an itemised list of all the parts he requires for his master project. Ronald has spent countless hours in his shed/lab dismantling his bounty, studying the inner working of the everyday items we all use without giving any thought to the intricacies of their innards. He had gotten exceptionally good at repairing out of action gear and making it work like new. Ronald could almost always turn 3 broken items into 2 functioning ones and make something useful from the leftovers, like the MacGyver of household electronics. A great many of the treasures Ronald picked up were not-wanted rather than not-working especially those picked up during the post-Christmas bonanza. Ronald had begun experimenting with his gadgets a little while back, changing parts from one object to another, adding parts, changing the function and making new, though not always practical Frankensteinian machines.

*

As the bus drove down Beach Street, the road that constituted Binnara Point's modest CBD, Ned peeled his forehead from the window where it had been pressed for the past half hour. Outside he had spotted Shane sitting in front of Charcoal Chicken and on his lap was sat a plump young lady wearing a Bulwarra Bay High School uniform, Ned hoped against hope that this young lady was on her way to some sort of fancy dress party, but he knew this was unlikely. Ned stayed on the bus past the corner of Scarborough Street and alighted at the headland corner where the bus turned around to head back to the depot. It had been a long and drawn-out day; he had waited 4 hours between his Fluid Mechanics lecture and Theory of Structures tutorial at 5.30pm and found little to be thrilled about during either. Ned threw his backpack over his shoulder and headed south along the beachfront toward Andy's house. As he walked along, Ned left a trail of security lights glowing behind him from the now vacant beach houses. The first smile of the day spread across Ned's face as he stepped off the footpath and walked across the lawn towards Andy's verandah.

'Hey buddy, what's the latest?' Andy was sitting in one of the old car seats that he'd turned into patio furniture.

'Just kicking back Neddy, beers are in the fridge mate.'

'Sweet.' Ned opened the screen door and made a bee-line for the fridge.

'How was school, did you learn lots?' Asked Andy as Ned pushed the door closed with his foot, holding a beer in each hand.

'Oh yes, I learned about the application of the general form of the Navier-Stokes equation for the conservation of momentum,' recited Ned, echoing the sarcasm of the question. He planted himself down beside Andy on the bench seat and handed him a beer, 'When do you wanna head up to the pub?'

Andy wobbled the beer bottle between his thumb and index finger 'After these ones.'

'Sweet,' Ned took a moment to stretch out and absorb the freedom he felt having seen off the week. Across the road he could see the waves breaking, the whitewash looking like it was glowing under the moonlight.

'Saw Shane out the front of Charcoal Chicken when I was on the bus…. looked like he had himself a bird.'

'A delicious barbeque bird, with chips and gravy? That's a nice dinner' joked Andy.

'I wish…. it was a fat little one in a school uniform.'

'Serious?!' Andy shrieked, before bursting into laughter upon Ned's mournful nod of confirmation. 'Well she's a lucky girl Ned, you can't deny it. With any luck we'll see them up at the pub.'

'Maybe…..He'll have to leave her in the kiddie area with a couple of packets of chips and some red-drink,' reasoned Ned. 'And some change for the Street Fighter machine.'

'Classic,' laughed Andy, 'I need to start following him around with a video camera, "The Fucked-Up Adventures of Shane Roach", it'd win an Oscar.'

'Hopefully you'll get it finished before the cops take it for evidence when he finally gets busted for benefit fraud'.

'Benefit fraud?... I had him pegged for a minor drugs conviction', Andy retorted.

'Yeah,' Ned nodded in agreement, 'I haven't seen him all week, don't know what he gets up to out in that caravan.....I mean a ton of masturbating I'm sure, but what else.....' Ned shrugged his shoulders.

'Probably for the best mate,' said Andy in a tone of mock comfort.

Ned peered into the top of his beer bottle to check the depth, 'How's the job going?'

'Yeah, alright. Been smashing out the hours, did sixty this week.'

'Shit!' replied Ned in acknowledgement of the feat.

'I reckon I might go away after the next jobs finished, I'll have plenty of coin by then.'

'Are you gonna go to Bali again? You could get your hair braided and go silly on a bunch of pseudoephedrine tablets eh, good times,' Ned asked with friendly cynicism.

'No mate, those days are behind me. I'm keen to go to L.A and then down to Mexico, get a few waves.'

'Hmmh'. Ned was surprised. 'That would probably be pretty awesome actually. A proper overseas trip, you're growing up mate.' Ned accompanied the statement with a congratulatory pat on Andy's back.

'You should come mate, we could both go. I don't really want to go on my own, I'm not a freak like you.'

'I'd go in a second but, it's expensive man,' Ned stated with a pained expression.

'You're sitting on that payout from when you were a kid, you've hardly touched it.'

Ned had received a nineteen thousand dollar payout from the Bulwarra Bay Council after his childhood car park run-in. Since he was able to access the money when he turned eighteen Ned had bought his car and some textbooks for uni but had been keeping the rest, assuming he would use it for something grand and mature in years to come.

'Yeah, I s'pose, I've always thought of it as a bit of a safety net, put away for the future….'

'This is the future,' said Andy.

'Thanks professor….. you finished your beer?'

Andy tipped the dregs from his bottle on to the decking, 'Yep, let's hit it.'

Ned and Andy jumped up out of the car bench-seat and lobbed their bottles into the wheelie bin next to the front gate before heading off north towards the top pub. The pub was the last building on the main road before it meets the intersection with the foreshore road. There was a bottom pub at the opposite end of the main road closer to the highway junction, it was the domain of the less desirable members of the community, not that the top pub had an especially high-brow atmosphere, just less glass crime and herpes.

As the pair came within site of the pub car headlights cast their shadows on the footpath in front of them, as the car drew near it let out a short burst of siren squeal and blue and red flashed light up the night. As the police car approached a voice came from the open passenger window.

'What are you two ladies doing out at this hour?'

Ned glanced over his shoulder and saw the officer leaning across the passenger seat, 'Hey Chris, busy night I take it?' Chris Bastoni had been friends with Ned and Andy at school; he had recently taken the police residency at Binnara Point after spending his first year out of the academy in Coonabarabran. Chris's dad had been the sergeant at Bulwarra Bay prior to his retirement and had pulled some strings to get Chris the job.

'It's a scary place mate, you boys off to the pub?'

'Yeah, we're heading up for a few, nothing too special,' replied Ned.

'I'm knocking off at ten, I'll meet you boys up there for beer.'

'Righto mate.'

'Make sure you save some sluts for me, I've already saved a few for Andy,' Chris gave Andy a wink before sitting up and speeding off.

'What was that all about?' asked Ned, as he and Andy continued on their way.

'How the fuck did they let that bloke become a cop?' replied Andy, tactically ignoring Ned's question.

'Cops don't get paid enough mate, smart people work where the money is. You pay peanuts you get peanuts, and Chris is certainly a peanut.'

'Isn't the saying, 'you pay peanuts you get monkeys'?' asked Andy.

'I think that's racist.'

'Is it?'

'I don't know…. better to be safe than sorry, anyway, what was Creepy Chris on about back there?'

Andy hesitated, 'I'll let Chris explain, he's going to tell you anyway.'

Ned could hear the music from the pub and the rabble from the beer garden as they approached the intersection. When he was in his mid-teens Ned would see the people packing out the pub, swaying and shouting, they seemed to be having the time of their lives. After he was finally old enough to join in on the fun the novelty wore off fairly rapidly, seeing the same drunk dude's sleazing on to the same drunk chicks every week and hearing the same stories on repeat got very boring very quickly. This would be his first visit in months. As they walked in Ned saw the same faces he'd always seen, it smelt the same too, a mixture of smoke, piss, sweat and perfume.

'What are ya having?' asked Andy rising on to his toes and craning his neck to get a look at the bar-queue depth.

'Whatever you are mate, I'm not fussed.'

'Alright, well I'll head over to the bar, you wanna grab a table out in the beer garden?'

'Righto'. Ned started wading through the crowd, making for the back door as Andy made his way toward the bar, maneuvering himself around beer glasses held with varying degrees of firmness. Ned made it to the beer garden without incident or acknowledgement and found a recently vacated table next to the fence overlooking the main road, still sporting two half eaten serves of calamari and chips. The glass doors dividing the indoor and outdoor drinking areas served as a real-life live movie screen through which Ned could watch a silent movie full of exaggerated actions and responses with a soundtrack of 90's pop/rock being dished out by the house band.

After a few minutes Andy backed his way through the glass doors with a schooner of beer in each hand.

'You score us a feed mate?' said Andy pointing at the remnants left by the previous occupants.

'Yeah, they're both for you.'

'You're a sweet man Ned.' Andy placed the beers on the table and slid across the bench so he could lean up against the fence.

'I saw Chris' dad and grandpa in there; it'll be a real family affair when he turns up.'

'I reckon most days of the week there'd be three generations of a family in this joint' replied Ned. Ned's mother had been a regular here for years, back when she was still a resident. She didn't drink all that much, but her arseprint was embedded in the stool in front of the 'Queen of the Nile' poker machine which still held pride of place in the far corner of the gaming room, next to the emergency exit.

'Speaking of family affairs, guess who I can see lurking over near the car park.'

Ned turned around and saw Shane unloading a tall tale on some of his local acquaintances who were swaying, with what Shane would assume was interest.

'He's gonna spot us eventually mate' warned Andy.

'Hopefully Chris is here by then, they can shit-talk the night away' Ned replied, willing himself to blend into the scenery. Due to the relative infrequency of his visits compared to the majority of the pub patrons, Ned always spends a good deal of time returning nods of acknowledgement and exchanging details of recent events with people he went to school with and with friends of his sisters. These exchanges usually resulted in a few free drinks which helped to make the experience more pleasant. Ned, without directly enquiring, had become fully up to date with the recent events of people who hadn't troubled his thoughts for a couple of years.

*

'You're up mate' said Andy tapping his empty beer glass on the pine table-top, rattling the cutlery that remained uncollected on the table.

'Same again?' asked Ned, sliding to the edge of the bench. Andy nodded his head and Ned set off for the bar. As he pulled open the glass doors the hot pub odour filled his nostrils. Ned led with his left shoulder and cut his way through the crowd with a sideways shuffle. There were several spots along the way where the carpet stuck to his shoes like flypaper.

As he made his way back to the beer garden Ned could see through the doors that Shane had discovered their location and was thrilling Andy with his podgy presence.

'Sorry Shane, I would have got you one too if I knew you were here.' Ned placed the schooners on the table and maneuvered himself into his seat. 'Looks like you've got plenty left in that one though' he said pointing at the drink Shane was cradling.

'Shano's started training as a cage fighter' Andy informed Ned, managing to maintain a serious demeanour.

'Really... how did this come about?' Ned motioned for Shane to regale the story.

'I met a bloke at the greyhound track on Tuesday who runs a mixed martial arts club in Bulwarra Bay. He told me I had a good build for it.'

'Sounds promising mate, when does that start?'

'I'm gonna start next week, he's giving me the first weeks training free'

'Bonus!' said Ned enthusiastically.

'So who's this girl I've heard about Shane?' asked Andy.

'What do you mean?'

'A little bird told me you were down the chicken shop tonight with a young lady.' Andy gave Shane a wink and a nudge.

'Oh' Shane hesitated, 'I met her down at the greyhounds too.'

'What was she doing there?' asked Andy already smiling in anticipation of the answer.

'Her dad had a few dogs racing there….. he owns the Charcoal Chicken shop too.'

'So she's an heiress!' Ned piped up, 'you'll have to hang on to her.'

'Yeah, imagine all the chicken' added Andy. Shane smiled the smile of a proud man.

'So what's her name?'

'Melanie' replied Shane.

'How old is she?' Ned chimed in, as innocently as possible.

'Umm, like sixteen I think, or fifteen….. I'm not sure' Shane sheepishly replied.

'Oooh' Ned and Andy responded in unison, bouncing it out through a laugh that made it sound as though they were on the receiving end of a vigorous massage.

'That's pretty young buddy' Andy stated while Ned was still winding down his 'oooh'.

'It's not that bad' insisted Shane.

'You're twenty four dude' said Ned, taking on a serious tone.

'Yeah, but I'm a young twenty four'

'I don't think that'll hold up in court mate.'

'Whad'ya mean, court' asked Shane dismissively.

'You can't go around playing silly buggers with fifteen year olds mate, it's against the law' insisted Ned.

'What if they're into it?'

'We can ask Chris when he gets here, he should know' suggested Andy, who was finding the debate immensely amusing.

'Because he's a cop or because he still tries it on with fifteen year olds?' asked Ned, not entirely joking.

'Hopefully the first one, but probably the second one' answered Andy.

The conversation had clearly made Shane a touch nervous, 'I'm going to get another drink' he said, and with that he marched to the door and disappeared inside the pub.

'Have you seen much of Chris since he's been back?' Ned asked Andy.

'Not really mate, I've been trying to lay off the booze and stay out of trouble so I can save more, he wouldn't make that easy.'

'Yeah, you're not wrong.'

Inside the pub the band started up again after their drink break, continuing their pattern of Matchbox 20, Bon Jovi and Maroon 5 covers and soaking up the affections of the over forty divorcees. The music level briefly rose each time someone opened the beer garden door, temporarily muting the conversation. Midway through a passable version of Bon Jovi's 'It's My Life' the volume increased and above the music Ned heard Chris shout 'what are you faggots doing out here?!' He was carrying three beers delicately with both hands, in the standard triangle formation.

'I just had your dickhead brother in there, asking me some bullshit about fucking fifteen year olds' said Chris nodding in the direction of the pub as he lowered the drinks on to the table.

'Yeah, he's met himself a schoolgirl' said Ned.

'Well he needs to take what he can get, looking like that.' Chris took a seat at the table and shook hands with Ned and Andy 'good to see you boys again'.

'Yeah mate, it's been a little while' affirmed Andy with a smile. 'How ya finding being back?'

'It's alright mate, been fun stirring the locals up, I've given a few of the boys a fright.'

'Yeah right, have you banged anyone up?'

'Not really. I give the drunk little tarts a lift home when the pub shuts, laying down the groundwork.' Chris drummed the top of the table, 'so Ned, has Andy told you about his date he went on the other week?'

'No mate, I think he was waiting for you to tell me' replied Ned, looking at Andy for confirmation. Andy gave a resentful nod.

'Remember years ago' Chris started, 'I smashed that bald chick I met on MySpace?'

Ned did remember this. Chris had always been a creep, and unsurprisingly he was one of the pioneers, at Bulwarra Bay High at least, of social network kerb crawling. He would send requests of friendship to every tarty looking chick between the ages of fourteen and twentyone who lived within a forty kilometre radius of Binnara Point. While thankfully the majority was wise enough to reject his advances there were a few - naïve, lacking in self-esteem or otherwise - who reciprocated. One such girl invited

Chris to her house in Bulwarra Heights for what he correctly assumed would be some action. This particular girl had failed to inform him that since her posted photos were taken she had been receiving chemotherapy for a malignant tumour in her femur and as a result she was quite bald. Needless to say Chris still made the most of the opportunity and took great joy in telling and retelling the tale afterwards. He assured everyone that 'she would have been hot with hair', and 'she was way more into it because she thought she might die'.

'Yep' replied Ned.

'Andy, I really think you should take it from here' said Chris offering him the story on an invisible platter.

Andy sighed, 'Righto…well I met this chick at one of the fellas from work's birthday party up at Bulwarra Heights. She seemed pretty cool so we organised to go out for a feed and a few drinks in Bulwarra Bay the next night…' Chris began laughing loudly in anticipation, 'do you want me finish or what?' asked Andy.

'Sorry mate, go on' said Chris.

Andy continued, 'so we went out and she was chirping away about whatever and then she started talking about how she really appreciated life because she'd had cancer. Next thing she busts out her mobile and shows me some pictures of her in hospital with no hair'. Andy pointed toward Chris, 'so first thing that comes into my head is this dickhead with his creepy story, and she lived in the right area… but I stuck it out, didn't say anything just carried on with dinner and whatever, I didn't want to be a prick. I messaged Chris the next day to ask what the chicks name was…'

'Rosie Mackay' chimed in Chris, nodding his head and staring into the middle distance as though lost in a memory.

'So it was the same chick?' asked Ned, finding the exchange quite amusing.

'Yep', Chris answered on Andy's behalf, glowing with some sort of misguided pride.

'So you're not going out with her again I take it Andy?'

'I can't have anything to do with a bird who's let this grub anywhere near her' replied Andy, pointing his head in the direction of Chris, 'that dirt never washes off.'

'I think that's fair enough' replied Ned.

'I was right though wasn't I Andy? Hot with hair' reiterated Chris.

'Yes mate, you were right' responded Andy, willing the conversation to end. Chris sat back with his arms folded, finally satisfied that his claim was proven, though long after everyone had stopped caring.

'What's the plan for tonight then?' Chris asked, 'you boys heading up to the Bay after this?'

'Not tonight mate' replied Ned 'pinching the pennies'.

'Yeah same here' added Andy, delighted that the discussion had moved on.

Chris shook his head disapprovingly, 'what happened to you boys?...Well, next Saturday my cousin's having her twenty-first at the bottom pub, you fellas need to be there. The place is going to be full of drunk sluts, it's going to be loose.'

Andy questioned the choice of venue, 'Why is she having it there? That place is a shithole'.

'It's the perfect location mate, no rules. They don't give a fuck!' Chris declared.

'Sounds like it might be worth a look haven't been to party for a while' said Ned, looking at Andy for agreement.

'That's the way' Chris said excitedly, 'it's a costume party too; you gotta dress as your favourite movie character'.

Ned and Andy were both partial to a good costume party; they'd compiled quite a collection of charity shop oddities over the years. Andy was already rubbing his chin, contemplating the possibilities.

The three boys remained at the table for a little while longer, discussing the events and inanities of their recent pasts until Chris decided it was time to head for the bright lights of Bulwarra Bay to get his creep on.

'Alright boys I'm out' Chris announced, planting his glass firmly on the table before standing up and issuing a salute. 'I shall see you boys next weekend'. Chris turned and wandered towards the car park to score a lift out of town. As he was about to disappear around the corner he spun around and shouted 'Meet me at my joint before and we'll walk down together, I expect some kick arse costumes boys'. Ned and Andy both signaled their agreement to this proposition, and then Chris was on his way.

Shortly afterwards Ned and Andy finished their drinks and vacated the beer garden. They cut through the car park and around the corner, heading back along the foreshore and towards home. Andy took his leave as they approached his house while Ned continued along the creek until he reached to top end of Scarborough Street.

*

Since he started working at the Bulwarra Council Recycling Centre, Ronald has had access to the cast-offs of not only his neighbours but of the entire council area. At the end of each week his manager Mr. Richards drives home via Ronald's house with his trailer loaded up with Ronald's selections that were too large for him to carry home during the week. Since he started work on his big new project Ronald has also started stockpiling batteries, the space under his work-bench is now filling up with all sorts of batteries, 9-volt, mobile phone, car, truck, boat and laptop arranged, like everything else, by type and size. Ronald is building something new, before now he has always built things that already exist but this one he's thought up himself. For this project Ronald has had to have some parts specially made. For many months he has been saving his money from the Recycling Centre to pay for the manufacture of his parts.

*

It was the second Wednesday back at university and Ned had taken to attending random lectures in the building around the engineering department to pass the hours between his classes. So far during the week he had attended lectures on Number Theory, Midwifery Clinical Practice, Oral Pathology and Applied Ethics.

As he waited at the bus stop at the bottom end of Scarborough Street, in front of the newsagent, Ned saw Ronald approaching. Ronald was clad from head to toe in bottle green, aside from his black work boots. Ronald stood to attention beside the bus stop sign facing the road, his thumbs hooked inside the straps of his backpack. Ned moved forward to stand beside him.

'G'day Ronald.'

'Hello.' Ronald's reply was monotone and unenthusiastic.

'You off to work?'

'Yeah.'

'I noticed you've been pretty busy out the back mate.'

'Yeah.'

'What are you building?'

'Time machine' Ronald replied, maintaining his focus on the approaching traffic, waiting to spot the bus.

This unexpected answer brought a smile to Ned's face 'wow, that's pretty cool mate'.

'Yeah' replied Ronald, who had started to lean out over the kerb having spotted the Bulwarra Bay bus slowing towards the stop.

'I'll see you later Ronald.'

'Ok' said Ronald as he stepped on to the bus displaying his bus pass at arm's length.

Later that afternoon, inspired by his morning encounter with Ronald, Ned attended lectures on Quantum Mechanics and Electromagnetism during the three hour break between his penultimate and last class. Ned found the time-killer lectures far more interesting than the classes he was enrolled in. On Thursday and Friday Ned didn't attend any of his own classes; instead he attended lectures on Linear Algebra, The Neurobiology of Pain, Metaphysics and An Introduction to Astronomy. He had also used his time to decide upon a get-up for the upcoming themed party.

*

Ned stood in the kitchen watching Ronald working on his time machine through the window. Behind him he heard Big Jake's van pull into the driveway followed by Jodie's shrill orders muffled by the closed front door. Two dull thuds were followed by the sound of the front door handle turning and the rustling of plastic shopping bags.

'…and close the door behind you Jake', directed Jodie as she shuffled through the front door towards the kitchen. 'I'm getting that bloody dog put down Ned!' she announced as she dumped two bags of groceries on the kitchen floor.

'What?' Replied Ned, requiring clarification for this seemingly out of the blue statement.

'Rooster the little shit, he dragged a great, big, dead fucking possum in here this morning. The thing was soaking wet and rotten and fucking disgusting.'

'Hey bro, nice cardigan! You off to pick up some old duck down at the bingo?' asked Big Jake as he strode into the kitchen with the rest of the shopping. It was Saturday afternoon and Ned was dressed for the costume party.

'Yeah mate desperate times…'

Big Jake let out a little chuckle.

'I'm off to a twenty-first at the bottom pub, this is my costume.'

'Jake, tell Ned about that fucking thing Rooster brought in this morning,' demanded Jodie.

Jake began laughing uproariously, 'He was so proud mate, sitting there with this big bloody possum in the middle of the lounge room, you should have seen him. Jodie gave him a kicking, he couldn't believe it. But mate, this thing was rotten, all the skin was eaten off its head and it was stiff and bloated. I saw it floating in the creek a few days ago.' Jake shook with silent laughter, 'ahh Rooster' he exhaled, as he wiped a tear from his eye.

'It's not funny Jake; I'm taking him to get put down.'

'C'mon Jodie, he's already ancient' said Ned, 'he'll take himself under the house soon enough.'

Jodie shook her head, her brow straining to furrow against her tightly pulled ponytail, 'well I'm not happy.... Jake!' she shouted, 'come and help your dad put the shopping away!' she then waddled off towards her room, swivelling her large backside out of the way as Little Jake slingshot around the corner toward the kitchen.

'You fellas up to anything tonight?' asked Ned.

'Nothing spectacular mate, me and Jakey might go for a fish', replied Big Jake stacking cold groceries on the countertop.

'You think you might catch a few Jakey?'

'Yeah, I always do, I'm good at fishing' Little Jake assured Ned as he hunted through the shopping bags for treats.

'Good at eating them' came Big Jakes comment from behind the open fridge door. 'So is it going to be a wild one tonight?'

'Might be' replied Ned, who had turned his attention back to the goings on next door. 'I'm heading over to Andy's in a minute to warm up.'

'Yeah right.'

'Been watching Ronald for a bit' said Ned.

'Yeah, he's been busy over there' replied Big Jake who joined Ned in his observation.

'He's crazy' announced Little Jake.

'He's not crazy mate, don't listen to what Shane says.'

'What's he building?' Big Jake thought out loud.

'It's a time machine' replied Ned. Big Jake let out a high pitched burst followed by wide mouthed, mute convulsions of laughter.

*

Ned stopped in at the bottle shop on his way to Andy's to pick up some road beers, in the shop were Rambo, Alice and Austin Powers browsing the liqueurs.

When Ned pulled up, Andy was on his front porch clad in only a pair of board shorts and a hat.

'That's a shit costume mate' he called out as he grabbed the beers off of the passenger seat.

'Hey, it's 'The Dude'' Andy shouted in response to Ned's 'Big Lebowski' themed garb.

'Glad you recognise it mate, I think most of the people down the street thought I was a bum.'

'You are' replied Andy.

'I grabbed a few warm-up drinks for the walk' said Ned, holding up the plastic bag containing the beers.

'We can polish-off a couple here and then head down to the cop shop' suggested Andy.

Ned took the beers in to the house and wedged them in to the narrow space between the over-frosted walls of the freezer while Andy vanished himself into his bedroom. Ned cracked open a can, sat up on the kitchen counter and flicked through the local paper: 'Record Haul in Summer Fishing Classic', 'Bulwarra Bay Council Elections' and 'High School Student's Art Exhibit A Success' were the riveting headlines.

Andy came strutting around the corner and gave a swaggering twirl. He was donning a particularly good costume, Lloyd Christmas, in a powder blue suit with a ruffled shirt and a front tooth half blackened with permanent marker.

'That is sweet mate, where did you score that 'Dumb and Dumber' gear?'

'My dad got married in this fucker' Andy replied holding open the suit jacket to emphasise it's splendour.

'He's a stylish man Andy, he's been rocking that handlebar mo for twenty years and now it's gone full-circle, they're cool again.'

Andy kicked open the fridge door and scanned the contents, 'where are the tinnies?'

'In the freezer' replied Ned, Andy opened the freezer and excavated a can. 'Have you heard from Chris this week?'

'Yeah' Andy replied, 'he messaged me a couple of times during the week, I think he was worried we weren't gonna turn up'.

*

The police residence was next door to the station on Market Street which ran along the southern parallel of the main drag. As they approached the top of Market Street in all their finery, Andy called Chris to let him know that he and Ned would arrive shortly. As they made their way down the street they could see Chris cutting a solitary figure against the brick wall in front of the police station. As they drew near they were both slightly taken aback.

'*What* the *fuck* are *you*?' asked Ned haltingly, emphasising the peculiarity of what he saw.

Chris glanced down at his costume and stood up to better display his attire. He had attempted to dress himself as Marilyn Monroe, wearing a flimsy and revealing dress that was clinging to him in the worst possible way.

'I just spewed into my mouth a little bit' announced Andy.

'Boys, I look good' insisted Chris.

'You really don't' replied Ned, 'you want a beer?' Ned held up the plastic bag containing the beers.

'Yep.' Chris reached into the bag and pulled out a can, 'you know the chicks are going to be all over me in this boys, it shows I'm confident, they love that shit.'

The three boys made their way down Market Street amusing the passing motorists and pedestrians with their garb. Chris was taking pleasure in lifting his dress and flashing his jocks at the passing cars, seemingly confident that his blonde wig was sufficiently disguising the fact that he was the local police constable.

As the three approached the end of the street they needed only to round the corner to the main road to reach the bottom pub. There was still a single can of beer remaining in the bag so they opened it up and each took a scull to finish it off. As they stood on the corner waiting for Chris to squeeze the last few drops out a maxi-taxi pulled up a few metres ahead of them. Filing out of the taxi and into the pub were a troop of girls dressed as sexy Harry Potter's with the exception of one who was dressed as sexy Batman, which Ned found especially perplexing.

Chris threw the empty can under the taxi's kerbside back wheel and the three boys followed the Harry's and Batman inside. There was a sign on the door alerting any would be customers that the bar was closed for a private function. Inside the walls were emblazoned with balloons, streamers and banners announcing Shelley's 21st. Amongst the disposable decorations were photographs of Shelley at various stages of development with the standard spattering of photos meant to embarrass the birthday girl.

'Sweeeeeet' Chris hissed, taking in his surrounds.

'Jesus Chris, you're the most modestly dressed woman here' said Andy noting the abundant flesh on display.

'Go and grab us some drinks fellas, I'm gonna go and find Shelley. There's a tab, so you won't have to pay.' Chris wandered off into the crowd leaving a wake of pointing fingers and unflattering comments while Ned and Andy ambled toward the bar.

'All these birds must have gone to boarding school with Shelley' commented Andy, 'they sure as shit didn't go to our school.'

'No they did not' replied Ned scanning the guests. 'It's amazing what characters these girls are able to tart up, that slutty Batman is just confusing.'

'Tidy rig though.'

Ned nodded in agreement, 'it's true'.

As more guests arrived and moved in and out of the bar area Ned and Andy discussed the various costumes and spotted the familiar faces. Ned's younger sister Krystal arrived in an unflattering and unimaginative military themed ensemble, accompanied by an oafish looking fellow who was too cool to participate in the costuming. Ned was fairly sure his sister would have come across this champion at the Thursday night Newman's car park gathering, where the local car enthusiasts met weekly to stare at each other and rev their engines menacingly. A similar engagement takes place on Sunday afternoons along the foreshore road; participants often bring a picnic blanket and sit by the roadside watching the cars drive past and inhaling the carbon monoxide. The men who frequent these events require their females to have big hair and big enough sunglasses to divert attention from their more obvious flaws. Since they display their females mostly from the passenger seat of their cars, the male car enthusiast cares little for the somatotype of his lady. Krystal fit these criteria perfectly and was therefore rather popular with the car crowd.

Chris came bustling through the crowd towards Ned and Andy 'where's my drink dickheads?! I've been waiting out there for ages'.

'We've been waiting for you, you didn't tell us to go searching' Ned snapped back, 'there's your drink', pointing to a sullen looking beer sitting on the bar. Chris picked up the glass and the three stood in a line with their back to the bar, silently observing.

A voice blasted from the P.A. system in the function room announcing that the night's entertainment was to begin, a three-piece band called 'The Handsome Brothers & Friend' would be providing the entertainment, followed up by a DJ who would play until the early hours. The boys ordered two beers each and carried them in to the function room to check out the sights.

The band played enthusiastically, if not entirely competently and managed to keep the crowd fairly well entertained. Ned found himself in an increasingly one-way conversation with one of Chris' aunties for an uncomfortably long time. She was already quite drunk and described in intimate detail how she met her husband in this very pub 24 years earlier and how they'd spent some personal time under a piano which once stood where the DJ's rostrum was now located. Chris' aunt assured Ned she was quite a sort back then and that all the blokes around Binnara Point wanted to fuck her, a lot of them still did. Admittedly Ned did think that she didn't look too bad for her age, in spite of her drinking several litres of Pinot Grigio a week and sunbaking with coconut oil for twenty years. Every so often her left boob, which was wobbling about in her top like half-set jelly, would press against Ned's arm. Ned pretended not to notice and hoped that she wasn't doing it deliberately. Over her shoulder Ned could see Andy chatting intently with Sexy Batman, he'd already demolished his two beers and looked to be heading to the bar with Sexy Batman to load up with some more. Before the awkwardness reached crisis point, Ned was reprieved from his torment when a stray elbow knocked the fuller of the two beers from his grasp and sent it crashing to the floor. Ned excused himself in order to remedy the mess and legged it to the bar area.

'You looked like you were having a good time in there chatting up Aunty Tracey', Chris was leaning against the wall next to the door that linked the bar and function areas.

'She's a menace mate. You better keep your eye on her, she's pretty pissed.'

'How about Andy over here' Chris pointed to the corner of the bar where Andy and Sexy Batman had been joined by one of the Sexy Harry Potter's, 'A couple more beers and we might be joined by Carlos'.

'Yeah', Ned grinned 'it's been a while since old Carlos was let loose'.

(Carlos lives inside Andy. Dormant deep inside, he emerges when Andy's blood alcohol reaches a certain saturation, at which point he is unleashed to terrorise all and sundry. Carlos has caused a lot of trouble over the years, getting locked up on several occasions and being banned from numerous late night venues. This has been to the detriment of Andy as very few people can tell the difference between he and Carlos.)

'We better smash down some drinks before the tab runs out' said Chris, grabbing Ned by the arm and pulling him toward the bar. Chris enquired with the bar staff as to how much of the tab remained. His head snapped around 'there's only eighty dollars left mate, we're gonna have to load up'. Chris proceeded to order ten schooners of beer and four shots of tequila, he thrust two shot glasses at Ned, 'let's do this shit!'

'Fuck mate, this is going to get sloppy'. Ned downed the shots and then followed Chris's lead, sucking back the schooners at a hefty pace.

By the time the final schooner was drained Ned was struggling to go fifteen minutes without having to piss. He left Chris propping up the bar as he hastily made his way to the gents just as the band was packing up. As he stood gently swaying at the urinal Ned could feel the froth of his last mouthful bubbling away in the back of his throat, undecided as to which way to flow. In the cubicle beside, Ned could hear vomit splashing into the toilet and slapping against the tiles. As he emerged from the toilet he could already feel his bladder brewing up the next trough load as he focused on keeping the drinks down. Ned knew he was drunk, but he wasn't sure how drunk. He checked and memorized the time -11.49pm - and made a mental note of the song that the DJ was playing. Ned decided he would retain this moment to see if he could remember it in the morning. The results of this experiment would be a gauge for future benders he thought, maybe he would discover the blackout point, where memory ends and blackness begins. Genius. His inspired musings were interrupted by a rush of people towards the front doors. Ned was involuntarily ushered to the fringe of the crowd where he could hear Krystal screeching profanities from somewhere near the epicentre. He rose-up on his toes and could see it was Krystal's plain-clothed companion in battle with a Jedi which had drawn the throngs. His sisters' lummox had removed his shirt to enhance his toughness by putting on full display the ill-conceived tribal and BPT postcode tattoo's that adorned his chub.

'Smash him Nath!' Krystal was screaming, like a redneck at WrestleMania. To Ned the fight resembled that of a couple of five year olds grappling over a toy far more than a pair of proud pugilists, though he was sure both combatants would tell otherwise tomorrow. It wasn't long before Indiana Jones and Austin Powers stepped in to end the fracas, dragging the Jedi inside and informing Nath that he could fuck off. As the crowd began filing back inside Ned walked toward the roadside where his sister was standing, 'Krystal!'

Krystal was holding Nath's discarded shirt while he strutted and postured in front of the pub doors like a rutting arsehole gorilla.

'Krystal!' Ned repeated, Krystal turned her head and looked at her brother, 'what the fuck was that about?'

'That dickhead was giving Nathan shit about not being dressed up,' Krystal replied.

'Who is this bloke? Where'd you find him?' asked Ned pointing at the oaf pacing the sidewalk.

'He's my boyfriend.'

'Seriously? Seems like a pretty massive wanker, you need to be a bit more selective Krystal.'

'Fuck off,' Krystal replied, she then called out to Nathan who was still huffing shirtless by the roadside. 'Let's go somewhere else' she suggested, handing Nathan his shirt 'this place is full of wankers anyway.'

As his sister led her boyfriend away Ned called out, 'Krystal…you can do better than that prick,' Nathan swung around and gave Ned his best menacing glare. Ned responded with a middle-finger salute as his sister dragged Nathan up the street.

Ned was now feeling the full effects of his binge and wobbled back into the pub. Ned pressed himself into the wall and scanned the room, looking for a familiar face; this was proving to be difficult as he struggled to steady his focus. Ned felt as though his head was floating a metre above his neck, he needed to sit; he slid along the wall until he reached a vinyl sofa. The sofa was occupied with a pair of amorous couples who were too busy to notice Ned squeezing himself onto the arm. His less than pristine condition was helpfully hidden by his costume sunglasses for a time until a sudden uprush of imbibed beverage made its way out of Ned and onto the floor beside the tastefully cheap sofa. Ned was fairly confident that his indiscretion had gone unnoticed but still felt it best to vacate the immediate area. It wouldn't be a problem, the floor was wooden and the furniture was vinyl upholstered for a reason. Ned waded through the crowd hoping to spot Andy, or at least Chris, the floor was now a sea of wet, dirty paper, broken glass and discarded costume items. He could feel another king-tide rushing up his oesophagus and managed to contain it inside his mouth. With his lips shut tight as possible and his cheeks bulging like an autumn squirrel Ned managed to discreetly deposit his load at the base of an indoor plant that was located more conveniently than the men's room. He took this as his cue to leave and abandoned the party. He found his way to the front door and marched up the street towards the beach, head down, eyes focused on the ground immediately in front of him, giggling occasionally at his own thoughts and sporadically stopping to take on water from accessible garden taps along the main road.

*

'Ned! Ned! Wake up mate!' Andy was gripping Ned's nose and pulling his head from side to side. 'Ned!' Andy shouted directly into his ear. Ned opened his eyes and was greeted by Andy leaning over him dangling Ned's car keys in front of him. Ned looked down and saw that he was lying on the car seat on Andy's front deck, the sun was low in the sky; it must have been quite early.

'We need to drive to the hospital mate' said Andy, who was wearing just the powder blue trousers from his costume.

Ned struggled to his elbows and blinked painfully, 'What? …Why?'

'Chris' Andy replied, 'we've got to go pick him up'.

Ned sat up on the car seat and held his head in his hands, 'how'd he end up there?'

'He cut himself up somehow, had to get some stitches. I'm just gonna grab a shirt and then we'll go'.   Andy headed inside and Ned checked himself over, he seemed to be in decent nick aside from a few stains on his cardigan and the absence of the sunglasses he'd worn to the party. He looked at his car which was parked on the road in front of the house, the day was clear and the sunlight was bouncing off the car roof and stinging his eyes. Ned struggled to his feet and gathered himself. Andy came out of the house still pulling down his t-shirt, 'you ready mate?'

'Yeah I guess' answered Ned, still rather surprised by the whole situation. Andy threw the car keys at Ned; they hit him in the chest and fell to the ground. 'I don't know if I should drive mate' said Ned looking at the keys resting between his feet.

'Well I can't, I only finished my last beer fifteen minutes ago' said Andy stepping off the deck and striding towards the car. Ned patted himself down and located his wallet and mobile phone. He pulled out the phone and checked the time; it was a quarter to seven.

'How long has he been in the hospital?' Ned asked across the top of the car while he unlocked the door.

'Dunno, couple of hours I s'pose' replied Andy. Ned flopped into the driver's seat and leaned across the gear stick to unlock to passenger door.

'And why are we picking him up?'

'He said he didn't want his folks finding out'.

Ned noticed some blue paint on Andy's arm and neck, 'what's all this' he asked, pointing at the splotches.

'Ah nothing really, there was this chick dressed as one of those blue things from Avatar' replied Andy.

'That's risky mate, could be anybody under all that paint that you're getting stuck into' joked Ned. Andy smiled and nodded his head. 'So what's the story with Chris anyway' Ned asked.

'He rang me about half past six and said he needed picking up from Bulwarra Bay, I told him to get a taxi and he said that he didn't have his wallet and he was in the hospital. He didn't want his old man blowing up at him so he asked us. Said he was waiting to get some stitches.'

'Is he still wearing a dress?'

'Dunno, probably'. Ned and Andy both had a laugh, imagining Chris sitting in the emergency room in his dress and makeup, trying to explain himself to the nurses.

'I don't remember seeing him after me and him downed that ridiculous pile of drinks he ordered' said Ned, 'it's all a bit blurry after that anyway'.

'Yeah last I saw him he was clowning around on the dance floor, but he wasn't about when they turfed everyone out at three'.

'Where did you go after that?' Ned enquired.

'Some blokes invited everyone back to their place a couple of streets away from mine. I saw you crashed out on the deck when we walked past my place on the way'.

'Yeah right, I don't really remember much of the walk home' replied Ned, 'you slept yet?'

'Nope' said Andy.

Ned's car rattled through the town disturbing the idyllic surrounds. As they rolled through Bulwarra Bay they passed joggers and people eating breakfast in cafes, enjoying rather different starts to the day than Ned and Andy, not to mention Chris. Ned was all dried out from the previous night's indulgences and his thirst had reached a peak as he parked his car opposite the hospital.

'I need a drink mate, I'm dying' announced Ned as he and Andy exited the car and started crossing the street, 'I'll meet you in there'. Ned sprinted across the street and through the hospital car park desperate to abate his thirst. As he streaked through the door he notice, out of the corner of his eye, a vending machine and slid to halt on the polished laminate floor. He rushed over and poured his coins through the slot. As he lowered the bottle from his mouth after gulping down half of the contents, Ned spotted Andy ambling through the hospital doors. Ned walked towards Andy and met him in the middle of the entry foyer, 'so where is this ridiculous prick?'

Andy puffed out his cheeks, indicating his uncertainty, and looked around the foyer. 'Not sure, maybe we should just go over to the emergency room'. Ned and Andy headed off down the hallway beside the vending machine and followed the signs to emergency. After several wrong turns they arrived, there was no mistaking it, the room contained several young men in their Sunday best nursing head wounds they'd acquired overnight.

Ned made his way to the front desk where he was greeted by a nurse who seemed even less pleased to be there than he was. 'Um, hi. I'm here to pick up a guy... Chris Bastoni?' Ned knew he didn't look particularly well and there was no telling if the hospital smell was adequately masking the boozy stench emanating from his pores. The nurse hammered at her keyboard for a few seconds and the details that presented on the screen caused her to raise an eyebrow and then look Ned up and down once before replying.

'Is that the young man in the lovely dress?' asked the nurse with a half-smile.

'Ah… yeah, that would probably be him' replied Ned.

'He's getting cleaned up now, he'll be out shortly. Take a seat.' The nurse said, motioning to the rows of chairs being occupied by crying children and bleeding hooligans. After he and Andy sat down Ned noticed the nurse say something to one of her colleagues and then point with her head in their direction, obviously Chris's arrival had been quite an event. Ned grabbed a couple of 'That's Life' magazines from the communal pile and gave one to Andy, who was fighting to keep his eyes open. Ned took a swig from his blue Gatorade and flicked through the magazine, settling on an autobiographical piece about a woman who'd lost her hair after a car accident, a topic close to both Chris and Andy's heart. The next time Ned looked across, Andy had fallen asleep in his chair, he was slowly sliding downward, his chin pressed hard against his chest and his knees spreading further and further apart.

Chris popped his head out from behind the triage door and looked sheepishly about trying to spot his friends amongst the casualties and companions. Ned nudged Andy who snapped back into consciousness with a jolt and pointed silently over to the triage door where Chris still hadn't located them. Andy wiped his mouth which had leaked during his short nap, 'I s'pose we better put him out of his misery' he said before raising his arm to alert Chris to their location. It took a few seconds for Chris to spot Andy's waving hand and scurry over, clad in a white hospital gown.

'Did you bring me some clothes?' whispered Chris, crouching down beside Ned.

'No mate, was I supposed to?' replied Ned who was staring at the bandages wrapped around both of Chris's wrists.

'Yeah!' Chris snapped, though maintaining a whisper, 'I told Andy I needed some clothes…what am I supposed to do?' Chris scuttled across the floor and grabbed Andy's thigh, 'give me your pants!' he hissed through gritted teeth.

'No!' Andy replied, standing up from his chair and prising Chris's fingers from his trouser leg.

'You can have my cardigan mate' offered Ned. Chris glared at him, unimpressed.

'Where did you park?' asked Chris, who was growing increasingly frustrated.

'Across the street, next to the park.'

'Bring it over here, I'll be in the shit if anyone sees me' demanded Chris who it seemed was motivated as much by fear as embarrassment.

'Righto mate' agreed Ned, 'but you'll have to be ready at the door, I'm not paying a fine'.

As he and Andy reached the doorway leading out of the emergency room Ned looked back to see Chris still crouching amongst the rows of seats, eyes darting around like a prison escapee.

'Those bandages looked a bit suss didn't they?' said Ned as he and Andy strolled across the hospital car park.

'Yeah, looks like he's tried to top himself' replied Andy with a smirk.

Ned pulled the car up in the ambulance bay; Chris was standing just inside the emergency doors. As Andy reached around to unlock the back door Chris dumped his hospital gown on the ground and sprinted to the car wearing only his navy-blue underpants, he flung open the door and dived onto the back seat. 'Go!' he yelled as he swivelled himself into an upright position.

'Chill out buddy' demanded Andy, 'this isn't a bank job'.

'You look like a gladiator in your undies and bandages' commented Ned, much to his own amusement.

'Yeah well, whatever…' replied Chris, 'this is a very fucked up situation'.

'What happened?' asked Ned, 'I didn't see you after you got that ridiculous round'.

'I was just partying, you know, getting amongst it' explained Chris, 'I was pretty pissy, I went into the disabled shitter for a spew and I got stuck'.

'What?!' Andy interrupted 'in the toilet?'

'No dickhead, in like, the room, I couldn't get the door open. I tried to bust it down and banged and shit but no cunt came to help me so I ended up punching the glass out of the window to try climbing out that way'. Ned and Andy were both laughing hysterically at Chris's tale of woe. 'It's not that funny fellas' Chris insisted, hunched forward with his head between the front seats.

'It is mate' Andy assured him between fits.

'How did you end up in the hospital?' asked Ned after composing himself.

'The window was too small and high for me to get out I guess, I ended up just passing out on the toilet floor. One of the bar staff found me after the party finished and freaked the fuck out. She thought I'd tried to off myself', Chris held up his bandaged wrists in lieu of further description. 'The ambo's came and brought me here. They thought I was some suicidal trannie, they were acting real weird, asking me some fucked questions…until I explained what happened'.

'Well you're safe now', Ned sarcastically reassured Chris.

'I'm fucked if work finds out about it though' said Chris looking out the window, surveying the roadside, 'I'm gonna have to borrow some clothes before I go back home, if that's cool?'

'Yeah mate, you can grab something from mine' offered Andy, who was now resting his eyes in the passenger seat.

'So how did you boys end up?' asked Chris, hoping to hear something that might make his own evening seem slightly less ridiculous.

'I just ended up passed out on Andy's deck, nothing spectacular' replied Ned, 'but Andy here partied on, he hasn't been to bed yet. Got himself a little piece of blue alien too I believe'.

'Aagghh' Chris bellowed, 'I saw her!' This news had brightened Chris's mood. 'We'll have to give you shit about that. I remember you boys gave me plenty of grief for hooking up with that chick in the clown costume that time'. Chris finally sat back in his seat, rejoicing in this revelation.

Ned pulled up in front of Andy's place and let the boys out, as he drove away he saw Andy waving in the rear-view mirror, he was holding up Ned's sunglasses which it seemed, had spent the night in Andy's letterbox. On the short drive back to Scarborough Street, *Single Ladies* by Beyoncé came on the radio, it was the song Ned had committed to memory the night before at 11.49pm, both facts he could remember remembering. His experiment had been a success.

*

Ned was in other people's Neurobiology of Pain lecture when he received a text message from Chris. It contained only two words but it carried a lot of weight. It simply read, 'I'm fucked'.

When Ned arrived home from university there was a particularly stupid looking car parked behind his own. Its exhaust resembled the muzzle of an anti-tank gun and it was covered in all manner of bold embellishments signifying that it was the vehicle of a massive douchebag. Ned did a lap of the car taking in all of its grotesque glory, the icing on this shit-cake was a bumper sticker that read 'fuck off, we're full' beside an Australian flag. Ned went into the house and dropped off his bag before heading to the kitchen for a drink. As he passed the familiar rogues gallery in the living room Ned noticed an additional fat belly nestled on the couch. Krystal had brought her new boyfriend Nath home to meet the family. Ned had a hazy recollection of their meeting on the weekend and was thoroughly unimpressed that Krystal had brought this turd into their home. Shane and Nath seemed to be getting along royally which came as little surprise to Ned, they would be able to bond over shit cars, shit tattoos, shit music and racism. Ned's dad waded through the lounge room ennui and came into the kitchen to get a can of soft drink.

'Krystal's boyfriend seems like a real winner' Ned commented, as his dad wrestled a Newman's Cola out of its shrink-wrap.

'Eh?' Mr. Roach replied twisting his head inside the fridge to look at Ned. Mr. Roach's hearing wasn't the best and sarcasm was generally wasted on him in any case.

'Krystal's boyfriend' Ned repeated, nodding his head in the direction of the lounge room.

'Oh yeah, seems like a nice fella' Mr. Roach replied vacantly before shuffling back into the abyss. Ned remained in the kitchen, leaning cross-armed against the sink in solitary protest.

From around the corner he could hear Shane regaling the minutiae of his existence to Nath who he seemed to consider to be a superior troglodyte. He offered him a discount at the chicken shop through his connections and offered his newly acquired mixed martial arts skills to the BPT boys. Ned moved to the edge of the large archway that linked the two rooms and leaned against the wall, from here he could see his brother fawning over Nath like a giddy schoolgirl as he showed off his BPT tattoos while Shane quizzed him on the membership options. Ned's dad sat in his velour reclining cocoon seemingly absorbed in the game show on the TV. Shane rolled up the left sleeve of his *Limp Bizkit* t-shirt to show off his poorly considered and poorly completed southern-cross tattoo. Shane had commissioned his masterpiece after the regrettable, yobbo led, neo-nationalist race riots of late 2005, the same riots that inspired the welcoming bumper sticker on Nath's shitbox outside. Nath also displayed a southern-cross which he had embellished with a tribal design that ran the length of his arm.

'What tribe are you from?' Ned asked from the archway.

'What?' Nath replied confused.

'Your tribal tattoo. What tribe rocks those squiggles', clarified Ned who was now on the receiving end of a three pronged scowl attack from the sofa.

'Whatever.' Nath replied dismissively.

'Yeah, whatever Ned' parroted Shane, jumping to the defence of his new best mate.

'Fuck off and leave us all alone' followed up Krystal, concluding the trifecta of dismissals.

Ned redirected his gaze to the television and Nath continued his middle-class suburban gangster stories to the delight of Ned's attentive siblings. After a few minutes Ned felt he had stood his ground for a sufficient amount of time and retired to the toilet for contemplation.

*

The sky along the horizon was the colour of a sunburnt thigh as Ned paddled through 'Shark Alley' to the point. The sting was out of the sun and a light breeze had picked up, quickly drying any exposed skin and causing it to goosebump. Ned ducked below a wave and bobbed up beside Andy who was facing the oncoming swell.

'So how did they find out?' Ned asked, sitting himself up on his board.

'Facebook'.

'Dead set?'

'Yep' replied Andy, 'someone chucked some photos on there and some incriminating comments were made and now boom, he's fucked'.

'Have you seen him?'

'Nah, he's coming over tomorrow night, if you're keen to witness his breakdown?'

'Yeah, I might' Ned replied. Andy swivelled his board around and paddled onto a wave, disappearing down the face for a second before the tail of his board flashed across the lip and sent a rooster-tail of water into the air.

Ned sat low in the water to keep the wind at bay and scanned the horizon for the next set of waves.

*

'Give us a lift down the chicken shop' proposed Shane as Ned crossed in front of the TV spinning his car keys on his finger on his way to the front door.

'I'm only going as far as the beach' Ned responded as he continued out to the entryway.

'I'll pay ya' Shane shot back, even sitting up from his deep recline on the sofa.

'What, in biscuits and titty mags? I'll be right'.

'Nah, money', Shane insisted.

Ned's hand hovered above the front door handle as he considered the offer, 'show me'. Shane reached around his girth and plucked out his Velcro wallet, from which he produced a five dollar note. Ned's eyes narrowed as he looked at the money, 'righto' he replied and pushed open the door. Shane rocked himself out of his sinkhole and waddled out in tow.

'Got a hot date with the chicken princess?' asked Ned as Shane swung into the passenger seat, his weight shifting the needle on the fuel gauge. Shane ignored Ned's question as the car lumbered down Scarborough Street at a rakish angle.

'Since when do you have cash to throw around?' asked Ned, continuing with his questioning.

'I've had a few wins at the greyhounds' replied Shane, fiddling with the radio tuner, 'Mel's dad's been giving me some hot tips'.

'Just keeps getting better eh?' said Ned, steering the car past the bus stop and toward the main road. The gunmetal grey Pintara putted up the main road, its passenger side noticeably closer to the bitumen, until it came to rest opposite the Binnara Point Charcoal Chicken shop.

'We're here now; you can stop fiddling with that'.

Shane pulled his hand away from the radio and looked out through the driver-side window. Confirming that they had indeed arrived he flicked the fiver into Ned's lap and opened the door. 'If you want a lift back it'll be another five'.

'I'll be right', replied Shane heaving himself out of the car before slamming shut the door and following the scent of rotisserie chicken across the street. Ned stuffed the money into the ashtray and continued on up to the headland and along the beachfront to Andy's house.

'Fellas' greeted Ned as he strolled into the lounge room where Chris and Andy were watching a day-night cricket match on the TV.

'G'day mate' and 'Yo', Andy and Chris replied respectively.

'How's the cricket going?' Ned enquired.

'We're giving India a hiding' answered Chris, sitting up on the couch to make room for Ned. On the coffee table in front of the couch Ned noticed some loose sheets of A4 and leaned forward to take a look. Ned flicked through the sheets which were printouts of hotel and flight prices and travel information for California, Nevada and Mexico.

'You're getting serious about this trip mate, doing some research …' said Ned as he browsed the paragraphs.

'Yeah mate, gotta be prepared' affirmed Andy, wincing mutely in response to a body blow in the cricket, 'Chrisso's coming now too'.

Ned glanced up at Chris who was sitting in an armchair on the other side of the room. Chris was confirming this last statement with a slow, deliberate nod, eyes still glued to the TV.

'Oh…cool' said Ned, somewhat surprised. 'When did you decide this?'

'Today' answered Chris glumly.

'Have you heard anything about work?' Ned asked Chris, wary that he was probably not in the mood for discussion.

'I'm on paid leave at the moment while they investigate it' replied Chris 'but once they get my blood results from the hospital they'll give me the flick'.

'What did you have?' Ned asked.

'A couple of lines of coke…like four'.

'Where'd you get that from?'

'One of those posh tarts dressed as Harry Potter' replied Chris, who was looking down at his lap, transporting himself back to the night in question. Ned flashed a puzzled look at Andy whose wide eyes and pursed lips communicated that he had nothing helpful to add to the exchange.

'Well…. At least you've gotten a paid holiday out of it' said Ned, aware that this was a rather risky avenue to steer the discussion down since Chris's temperament can be best described as - in the kindest way - volatile.

'Yeah' Chris replied in a sad laugh, the kind only emitted by those who have begun to accept their residence at rock-bottom.

*

The tide was well out and an aura of pock-marked, dark, stinking mud lined the edges of the creek. As a youngster Ned, amongst many other local ragamuffins, would come down to the creek when the tide was like this and engage in epic mud battles. Today he was doing his best to avoid all unnecessary contact with the meconial sludge as he tip-toed his way along the bank with his fishing rod, doing his best not to snag himself on the spiny shrubs that lined the bank.

'Just walk through it you poof' mocked Big Jake overtaking Ned on his left flank, shin deep in the muck and wearing a Bintang singlet that looked as though it might blow away in a stiff breeze like dandelion spores.

'I'm alright up here thanks mate' insisted Ned, determined to continue along his chosen route if only to prove a point. The space between Ned and Big Jake grew as Ned was forced to negotiate his way over a fallen tree that was biting at his fishing rod and loose clothing as well as housing an army of sandflies that felt it proper to harass Ned long after he had passed the obstacle. Ned followed Big Jake's trail of sinkholes around a bend in the creek and found him leaning against a collapsed bank with his line slung out into the murk.

'You took your time princess' said Big Jake as Ned flopped down beside him swiping away at the few stoic sandflies that remained at his bother.

'Mate, you'll be picking that smelly shit out of your toenails for days and I will laugh at you' Ned retorted as he brushed the twigs out of his hair. Ned concertinaed a strip of squid onto his hook and flung it out into the brackish water.

'So what's the latest with you bro?' enquired Big Jake.

'Not much, I haven't been going to many of my classes at uni'.

'What have you been doing all day then, getting pissed in the student bar?'

'Nah, I've just been going to other lectures... science and medicine and shit, interesting ones'.

Big Jake replied with a shrug of the shoulders which loosely translated to 'whatever floats your boat' before hurriedly reeling in his line to find a fist sized toadfish croaking away at the end. 'I hate touching these slimy bastards' Big Jake muttered as he attempted to remove the fish by holding the top of the hook and helicoptering it free.

'I'm thinking about going overseas with Andy, Chris is goi....', Ned's comments were halted abruptly as the toadfish rocketed off Big Jakes hook and crashed with a wet slap into Ned's right ear.

'Sorry bro' Big Jake managed to gasp between bouts of laughter so overwhelming him that upon composing himself he felt it necessary to check his underpants in case he'd voided his bowels. Ned picked up the offending fish, which now lay croaking amongst the loose stones at his feet, and hurled it, like a slimy grenade, clear across the creek into the dense tea-tree scrub on the opposite side.

'Seriously bro, sorry' repeated Big Jake, still wearing a maniacal grin.

'It's alright mate' replied Ned who also found the incident rather amusing.

'Fucken hell, you launched that fish bro' said Big Jake, tracing the arc of its flight across the sky with his finger and adding his own impressive sound effects. Ned smiled in agreement and let out a rapid fire air giggle out of his nostrils.

'So what were you saying about going overseas?' asked Big Jake, returning a moderately serious air to the idyll.

'Oh, ah…. Andy's going over to the States, and Chris is gonna go too, now that he's off work indefinitely'. Big Jake nodded, taking in the information. He'd heard about Constable Bastoni's indiscretion via the small-town grapevine mutterings of Binnara Point. 'I'm thinking about packing it in at uni and maybe going as well'.

'Do it bro, you only live once, you're not gonna miss much here'.

'Yeah I know, it's just if I bail on uni I don't think I'd go back. It was a big deal for me to get into that course; I'm the first Roach to go to university'.

'First one to make it through your teens without a kid too' Big Jake added.

'It *is* an easy family to look good in' admitted Ned. He felt a few sharp tugs on his line and reeled it in expectantly, hoping for something worthy of the always empty bucket resting in the tree roots beside the creek. There wasn't a great deal of resistance as Ned reeled in his catch and his anticipation faded as he felt it drag through the mud. When Ned pulled the line out of the water a large mud-crab was dangling from the hook.

'Sweet bro, that's better than a fish' exclaimed Big Jake giving an enthusiastic thumbs-up. He then turned around and picked up the bucket and held it towards Ned, giving it a shake, 'pop him in'. This was the first edible critter Ned had pulled out of this creek for years. These expeditions had long ago become more of a social outing than any real attempt at food acquisition, and he knew Big Jake appreciated the adult male company.

As they walked down Scarborough Street with the crab and a 5 inch long mullet that Big Jake insisted would be not only edible but delicious, Ned spotted the white, douched-up Falcon parked in the street in front of the house.

'Looks like were blessed with the presence of Captain Cockbreath again tonight' said Ned, pointing at Nath's offensive vehicle.

'Better get used to it mate, he's moving in', Big Jake replied. This comment stopped Ned in his tracks.

'Are you fucking serious?'

'Yeah bro, he got kicked out of his place so he's staying here until he can find somewhere else. It's just for a while apparently'.

'That's what you said nine years ago and yet here you are' Ned replied cheekily. 'He's not going anywhere in a hurry'. Ned stared at the racist bumper sticker on the back window of the Falcon and made a decision.

*

Andy steered the ute up in his driveway and felt his mobile vibrate in his pocket as the loose bricks slid across the tray and banged up against the aluminium sides. After lobbing his boots up on to the decking and transferring the catalogues from the letterbox to the wheelie bin Andy checked the message.

'I'm coming too'.

'Sweet' Andy said aloud, to no-one in particular.

*

Ned, Andy and Chris sat on the balcony overlooking the greyhound track and discussed their upcoming jaunt. Chris had requested the Bulwarra Bay Greyhounds be their meeting place for the evening in an attempt to avoid the taunts, whispers and abuses the folk of Binnara Point enjoyed directing at him in recent weeks.

'Wow, this place is a real shit-hole' observed Andy, watching the patrons haunt the bar and poker machines. 'What time do the dogs run?'

'Dunno. Later on sometime', replied Chris expertly.

Shabby looking cars driven by shabbier looking people were arriving in the adjacent car park. Many of them were towing what looked like tiny caravans, containing the evening's entertainment who were muzzled, lean and as ugly as fuck.

'If horseracing is the sport of kings what do they call this?' asked Ned.

'The sport of small business owners?' suggested Chris.

'Where does it stand on the scale of racing sports? Does it go gallops, trots then greyhounds?'

'There's that horse hurdling too' said Andy.

'I think pigeon racing is above it. And camel racing' suggested Chris.

'And ostriches' added Ned, 'but it's above cane toad racing'.

'Ferrets'.

'It's between ostriches and ferrets' Chris declared with a confident nod and a surprising degree of certainty. Ned and Andy were satisfied with the assessment and returned approving nods of their own.

Over in the car park Shane spilled out of the passenger side of Nath's car, his arm draped in plastic wrap to shield his new tribal inspired tattoo from the elements. Nath emerged from the other side, resplendent in his flat-brimmed baseball cap and thick, braded gold chain draped on the outside of his t-shirt.

'So I reckon we write a list of places we want to check out and take it from there' suggested Chris, rising from his chair, 'I'll be back in a sec'. Chris walked inside and headed over to the betting area where he grabbed a tiny pencil and a betting slip. He returned to the balcony drumming the pencil against the slip, 'alright' he said with great enthusiasm as he sat down, 'hit me boys'. The three of them then exchanged ideas over several beers and a rudimentary list took shape.

L.A

Hollywood Blvd.

Venice Beach

Huntington Beach

The Wedge

La Jolla

San Diego

VEGAS!!!

Mexico

Chris dropped his pencil and slapped his now empty glass on the table, 'I gotta piss', and with that he scurried inside.

'He's chirped up', said Ned.

'Yeah, he's pretty pumped for the trip' replied Andy. 'I don't think his old man's speaking to him at the moment, I think he's pretty keen to get out of here for a while'.

'So, end of the month you reckon?'

'Yeah, I should be right to go by then'.

'So we're looking at about three weeks then, I'll have to get my shit together' said Ned. 'S'pose I should go pay my old Mum a visit'.

'Oh, that'll be good' replied Andy, his smirk undermining the enthusiastic tone.

Ned snickered out of his nose as he stared into his beer, swirling it around in his glass and thinking about the prospect of a visit to his mother's farmhouse in Collombindee and another first hand observation of her new, Roach free existence.

Below the balcony Shane was proudly showing off his newly needled on ink squiggles to his fellow greyhound enthusiasts and introducing his new alpha male superior to the finer points of trackside skulking. The pair sauntered about the totes with an unwarranted air of superiority which came naturally to Nath but to Shane it was surely inspired by the fact he was one of the few people there wearing pants with belt loops and shoes with laces. The fact that both men had girlfriends not purchased in a Thai brothel also elevated their status no end.

'There was a bloke in the toilet brushing his dentures' announced Chris as he planted himself back in his chair.

'Well at least he's brushing them' conceded Ned.

Chris stared blankly at Ned, seeming to have forgotten his train of thought. 'I'm happy to sort out the tickets and stuff, I haven't got much else on' Chris blurted after a pronounced blink and shake of the head which seemed to restore his focus.

'Happy for you to do it mate' said Andy who was rocking back on his chair and peering over the balcony railing. 'I see your brother and your new housemate are in tonight' he observed waggling a finger in the direction of the track. 'We might have to go down and buy him a beer for making you wake up to yourself'.

Chris turned around to glance over the railing, 'is your sister going out with Nathan Reynolds? That dude *is* a cunt Ned' he declared with a sympathetic look, before whispering 'you made a good choice' and reaching across to gently pat Ned's hand. Chris did not have a sympathetic bone in his body and was clearly imitating something he had seen on film.

Chris continued his makeshift note-taking with gusto, assigning set numbers of days per location and a series of sexual goals. Ned was intent on a more 'play it by ear' style trip but allowed Chris to scribble away like an excited preschooler. He half expected him to draw some stick figure scenes of the three of them on their trip and present them for display on the refrigerator, such was his childlike anticipation of the holiday. It must have been good for him, cheering him up and keeping his mind off the work and home issues that draped over him like a shit stained blanket.

This adventure would do them all some good, Ned mused. It would give them some perspective, make them grow up a bit, a journey of self-discovery and all that bullshit. For Ned it would be an opportunity to find some direction, take a step back from his reality and ponder it from a comfortable distance. For Chris it was an opportunity to drink strange beers and fuck new chicks, all in a place where nobody knew who he was. For Andy it was a holiday, and he likes holidays.

From below a crescendo of aggressive encouragement and abuse disturbed the relative peace of the balcony setting. All three boys popped up to observe the ruckus and witnessed the final few bounds of the evening's first race. As 'Sir Henry' crossed the line half a length clear of 'Don't Tell the

Missus' a chorus of cheers and profanities erupted. Shane held up his hand for a high five which remained there for an uncomfortably long time before he lowered it and attempted a complicated handshake with Nath. The dogs contesting the second race of the night were soon paraded before the modest crowd, Ned noticed that Melanie, the underage chip shop heiress and focus of Shane's affection was leading out the number four dog, 'Finnegan's Wake', waddling out in her best leggings and ugg boots.

'There's Shane's girlfriend' Ned announced as she joined the line of trainers behind the starting traps.

'Which one?' Asked Chris.

'The one whose mullet is tied in a ponytail' Andy slipped in before Ned could respond.

'Number four' Ned added dryly.

'The one on the lead or the one holding it?' Chris asked to nobody's amusement but his own.

*

The phone rang five times before Ned heard the familiar voice interrupt the trilling. ''Allo?' it said, the first consonant of the greeting absent.

'Hey Ma, it's Ned'.

'Oh Ned, How are *you* love?!' the former Mrs. Roach said in her parrot like shrill.

'Good thanks. Look, I'm going to go away for a bit, overseas, with a few mates and I thought I might come down and see you before I leave. Next week maybe?'

'Ohh, that'd be lovely Ned. Julian's here at the moment mind, but I'm sure you'll be fine'.

'Cool, well I'll let you know details later on' Ned said, not feeling up to a drawn out conversation about the goings on at the lettuce farm his mum ran with her new husband Daryl. Ned was particularly wary of visiting while Julian was about. Julian was Daryl's son and he was a rather unsavoury character.

*

In an Oral Pathology lecture Ned learned about pre-Columbian dentistry and tooth mutilation in Mexico. He wondered if this new knowledge would come in handy on his trip. Perhaps he could strike up a conversation with a Mexican dentist on his travels and impress him or her with his impressive knowledge. They could discuss the use of jade and turquoise to decorate the teeth and the early drilling technology used to achieve it. Later they could discuss if the shovel shaped teeth of the ancient Mexicans indicated their Mongol origins.

This was Ned's last week as a university student for a while, maybe ever. He dropped into a few of the engineering tutorials that he'd been skipping for the last few weeks in favour of the more interesting classes he'd been inviting himself to. After a tedious two hour review of Fluid Mechanics any lingering hesitation Ned may have felt regarding his exodus had been thoroughly quashed. There really wasn't a lot about the place he was really going to miss, it had served as an escape from the potentially contagious ennui of home that Ned feared would engulf him one day, and for that he was grateful. But as for it being a place of inspiration, it fell some way short. It was good practice for a life of tedium that a great many of its students could look forward to. If only Ned could enrol in a Bachelor of Interesting Topics, a degree that would qualify one for whatever the fuck one felt like doing.

*

Ned walked into the house and straight into the lounge room. The TV was on as it tended to be. The velour recliner chair was empty, which was unusual for this time of day. Ned leant over and touched the cushion, it was warm, his dad couldn't have been too far away. The front screen door hissed slowly and slapped back against the frame a second later. Rooster crept around the corner nervously, avoiding eye contact and with his head bowed, he was truly a dog with emotional issues.

'You know where Dad's gone Rooster?'

Rooster walked slowly across the lounge toward the kitchen, his head still low, flashing submissive upward glances at Ned, just trying to get to the backyard without upsetting anyone.

'What's up buddy?' Ned asked. Rooster trotted on toward the back door, offering a fleeting glance over his shoulder. He almost looked disappointed. Ned was the only person in the family that had much time for Rooster after his transition from cute puppy to ugly dog but they hadn't shared a great deal of time together recently. If bitterness was a canine emotion then Rooster was displaying it astutely and had made Ned feel quite guilty for his negligence.

As Ned followed Rooster out the door he was greeted with an unusual sight. Mr. Roach was standing shirtless in the backyard. A single whitish, well-worn George Thorogood, 1986 US tour t-shirt with a large, nuclear-orange wet patch in the centre hung from the clothes-hoist, inside-out and rippling gently in the warm breeze.

'What's going on here?' Ned asked from under the back awning.

Mr. Roach's torso slowly rotated, his feet remained planted into the forest of weeds. 'Eh?'

'It's not like you to be out in the sunshine'.

'I had an accident' Mr. Roach replied in a drawn out manner and with a slight smile, pointing to the shirt pegged to the clothes-hoist. 'It was this pricks fault' he continued, thrusting an accusing finger at Rooster.

'I'm sure he didn't mean it' Ned replied, clicking the fingers on his left hand, beckoning Rooster over for a pat. 'What did he do?'

'Got himself under the footrest on my chair. When I tried to sit it up he yelped and I spilt my drink'.

'You can't blame him for that… why you still out here, forgotten what that big yellow thing up there is?' Ned said motioning toward the sun while still trying to lure Rooster from under the caravan.

'I'm drying off. There's no towels'.

'Righto' Ned replied, all too familiar with such extremes of laziness. 'Well anyway, I wanted to let you know that I'm going to go away in a couple of weeks'. Mr. Roach remained silent, his hand was raised in a salute, shielding the sun from his unaccustomed eyes. 'I'm going overseas with Andy and Chris Bastoni'.

Mr. Roach looked at Ned without moving his head, 'Oh' he murmured with a slight up thrust of his head, 'that'll be good'.

'I'm gonna go and see Mum before I go'.

'That'll be nice' replied Mr. Roach who had uprooted himself and was now schlepping towards Ned, his hermit-white belly shining in the sun like a boiled egg. Mr. Roach continued on past Ned patting him on the shoulder on the way. This was an odd display of what Ned took as affection. He couldn't remember the last time his dad had touched him and it made him quite uncomfortable, which in turn, made him rather sad. Ned had been busying himself with a world of other worries and had spared little thought for the fact that his father had become a spectre, haunting the house and virtually invisible save for an occasional comment. He was just an extra in the background of everyone else's life. Ned walked over to the caravan and crouched down, offering his hand to Rooster who gave it a quick sniff before retiring further under the caravan to chew on his own arse.

*

Ned decided Thursday would be his last day at university. He checked the lecture timetable and decided to sit in on Introduction to Astronomy, Metaphysics and made an ambitious leap into Quantum Mechanics & Semiconductor Physics. Ned pondered what could have been as he struggled to understand the equations, but he knew he was going to be glad to see the back of the place. As he made his way home on the public transport journey that he loathed he paid extra special attention to the goings on, a last absorption of the mundane. There were the customary retirees, laden with shopping, prizes from the Bowling Club meat-raffles and the prescription medications that they seem to so love. The rear quarter of the bus was the usual rogues gallery of ne'er do wells in their finest tracksuits, bludging cigarettes from each other and rearing children irresponsibly. Ned couldn't imagine that there was any part of this routine he would miss, save from the old guys on the morning run who's lack of care for the opinions of their juniors he found inspiring. His last trip was highlighted by a conversation between a pair of fourteen year old crackers detailing their recent sexual conquests. The finer details of exchange made it clear that they were both lying and the resulting one-upmanship made for some quite ludicrous claims. The smaller and uglier of the two, whose receding chin and elongated face gave him a wormlike appearance, was adamant that he'd recently fucked a girl three years his senior in a men's toilet cubicle at the Middleton Plaza, and with such ferocity that he'd broken one of her ribs. This was despite the fact that he could have weighed no more than an average nine year old. Not to be outdone, his chum who was a lanky character with an adam's apple the size of a golf ball and the skin of a cane toad, had also scored on the weekend. This stripe of shit had apparently had his way with a French exchange student, and model no less, in some bushes down behind Middleton High School. The two lothario's alighted at the Plaza and Ned was left to divide his focus between the sights outside and his own transparent reflection in the bus window. As the bus turned off the highway and into Binnara Point it crossed paths with Nath's car which was speeding off northward towards Bulwarra Bay.

Ned dropped his bag off in his room, bypassed the lounge room, and trod his usual path directly to the kitchen.

'Just in time mate'. Big Jake was standing in front of the cook top coaxing some sausages out of a frying pan.

'Eh?'

'Krystal and Nath have just pissed off, you can have theirs' Big Jake replied, pointing at the row of empty plates with the wooden spoon he was using to dish out the snags.

'Oh, cool'.

'Grab a seat bro, it'll be ready in a minute'. Big Jake, with his hands full, motioned towards the lounge room with a backward thrust of his head.

Ned squeezed in beside Little Jake on the sofa which caused Little Jake to rise up several inches on the bulge of rubber foam created by the weight of Ned and his mother on either side.

'Jake says you've decided to go off with your mates' Jodie said, readjusting her substantial rump within the confines of the sofa, causing Little Jake to be tossed about on the ripple.

'What did I say?' asked Little Jake on his cushion peak.

'Not you, your dad' snapped Jodie dismissively.

'Yeah, I figured I might as well….. it's getting a bit cramped here'.

'When you going?'

'Couple of weeks, Andy's finishing up a job first. I'm gonna go down and see Mum tomorrow and stay for a few days'.

'Oh, good luck with *that*' replied Jodie cynically. Jodie had not taken her mother's leaving well. She felt that they had been abandoned and had sided strongly with her father. She hadn't been to visit her for years and had only attended the wedding to create an air of discomfort.

'Yeah, Julian's gonna be staying there too' Ned added with a cautious smirk.

Jodie responded to this with a shrill peal of laughter that was loud enough to send the galah's flying off the front lawn in a cacophony of shrieks and squawks and caused Ned and Little Jake to flinch. 'You'll have a real good time hanging around with that creep'.

Ned nodded with an expression of resignation, though he could see the funny side of it.

'Dinners up!' Big Jake called from the kitchen. This was met with a surge of activity on the couch that caused the cushions to surge and recede like a great ocean of dead skin, piss, mucus and twelve years' worth of arse-sweat. It stirred up the accompanying odour that had settled since its last disruption the previous evening; only now, it was one day's worth of sheddings stronger. This call up was the only thing that, aside from the occasional spider sighting, made Mr. Roach move faster than plate tectonics. Ned sank deep into the abyss left by the exodus of weight from the couch and rolled out onto the carpet below.

Ned chose to sit on the floor with his back against the wall beside the archway and left the Tuigamala's to battle for elbow space on the couch. The consuming of the volumous meal began in silence bar the sound of aggressive chewing and swallowing. Big Jake broke the silence with a proposition. 'We should have a Barbie before you go Ned, maybe get the boys around too?'

Ned nodded and made a muffled sound of approval through a mouthful of half chewed sausage.

'Yeah, haven't seen Andy for ages' Big Jake pondered out loud. Mr. Roach let out a long, guttural burp that wouldn't have been out of place at a zoo.

'Pop!' Little Jake giggled before following up with an impressive burp of his own, drawing a dirty look of disapproval from Jodie.

*

Ned's first petrol stop was at the 'Big Prawn' as he headed south on the Pacific Highway. It had once been bright orange but now sat mournfully atop the service station blotchy and faded like something had eaten its insides and left its shell in situ. Ned had raided the Bulwarra Bay op-shops for some cassettes to arm himself with for the 10 hour drive to Collombindee. Neil Young, Credence Clearwater Revival, Queen and Bob Seger would be keeping Ned company as he melted onto his vinyl car seat.

The long drive gave Ned time to mentally prepare himself for the upcoming week. His mother had left Binnara Point abruptly 5 years ago to take up with Daryl, a man she had met in an internet chat room. Daryl was a butcher in Collombindee, Central-West New South Wales whose wife had died a few years earlier from a brain tumour. After Ned's mum moved down Daryl sold his butchery and they bought a lettuce farm outside the town. Daryl's son, Julian, lived with them intermittently between sex holidays to South-East Asia.

Ned stopped to buy some pies from a shop called Freddo's and drove a little further to a park beside the Macleay River to stop and eat. He sprawled out on a bench to eat his lunch and watched the cars and trucks passing by on the bridge high above him. Below the bridge some swans were menacing some ducks that were eating the scraps of bread being thrown by some kids. After a good rest Ned returned to his car and opened the door to be greeted by a burst of warm air. Without thinking he dropped his shirtless self into the driver's seat and was sure he heard a sizzling sound as his bare back made contact with the super-heated vinyl seat cover. Ned let out a squeal and quickly sat forward before any permanent damage could be done. The steering wheel and seat belt buckle were also far too hot for human contact so Ned had to leap from the car without touching any part of it. He ran, like a man covered in ants, to find something cool to press his back against until the car cooled. He had to settle for shit strewn underside of the bridge where the shaded concrete pylons provided some relief.

300 kilometres further along, at the point where the Pacific Highway crossed the Hunter River, Ned made a right turn and headed west, away from the coast and towards the dry, flat inland, Collombindee was 3 hours away through an undulating sea of well fenced brownness.

Collombindee was not so different from Binnara Point. It was smaller, the bottom of the main street met the muddy Wauwe River rather than a vast ocean, but it served a similar purpose of entertaining the locals in a variety of ways. Further past the river, down a long, straight dirt road was where Ned's mum lived. As Ned turned off the tarmac and on to the dirt road he crossed a cattle grid which managed to shake the Bob Seger cassette out of the tape deck midway through the second chorus of 'Hollywood Nights'. In the rear-view mirror Ned watched as a plume of dust kicked up by his balding tyres obscured the grazing hills behind him. Ned pulled up behind Daryl's Land Cruiser and fished around behind him for his shirt. He pried himself off the car seat with a sound not unlike the tearing of paper as his skin unstuck itself from the vinyl. He emerged gingerly from the car stiffened by the long drive and took a minute to stretch his muscles and crack his joints. It was an orchestra of pops, groans and slams as he gathered his gear from the boot of the car.

'Allo doll!' Ned's mum sang out from the porch. She was dressed in a pink and white striped tennis shirt and cycle shorts. The sound of his arrival having clearly disturbed the serenity of her evening's television viewing.

Ned gave her a wave as he slammed the boot shut and limped over to the house.

'D'ya have a good trip?'

'Yeah alright….. Long' replied Ned walking up the porch steps.

Ned's mum nodded vigorously as she expelled a jet-stream of smoke from her puckered mouth, 'Yeah it is'. She flicked her cigarette stump over on to the lawn and moved forward to give Ned a hug. Her strong menthol cigarette odour caught Ned off guard and made him feel momentarily nauseous.

'It's good to see ya mate' Ned's mum mumbled into his chest as she gave him a squeeze, 'let's get you inside'.

Ned's mum led him through the door and into the cool, dimly lit kitchen. 'I've set up your room, it's down next to the laundry. Do you want something to eat?'

Ned looked about, reacquainting himself with the surrounds, 'ah, in a minute, I'll just dump this shit down first'. He flashed his mum a smile and then headed down the hall to the spare room. As he walked through the large open-plan living area he saw Julian sitting low in a big armchair, partially obscured by the computer sitting on his lap. His head was lowered displaying his wispy, strawberry blonde hair barely covering his freckled scalp, and his skinny legs hung limply from below the laptop. Ned threw his bag onto the floral bedspread that covered the spare bed and made a quick trip to toilet before heading back out in to the fray.

'We've got pies, nuggets, lasagna...' greeted Ned as he returned to the kitchen, his mother filing through the frozen items in the freeze drawer. 'Daryl's got a Lions Club meeting tonight, normally he cooks something nice'. Ned wasn't surprised by this. His mother had never been one for preparing meals with anything more than a microwave and a fork, seems nothing had changed. Good on her, Ned thought, if Daryl's happy to cook she should be happy to let him.

'I've already had a few pies today' Ned said, rubbing his belly, 'might have to go some nuggets'.

Ned's mum pulled a box of chicken nuggets and kicked the freezer door shut, 'go sit down love, I'll do this. You can tell Julian about your trip, he's travelled a lot' and she waved him away in the direction of the lounge.

Ned walked slowly across the room, not wanting to sit particularly close to Julian. He sat down in the corner of the long corner sofa that was against the floating wall that separated the kitchen from the main living area.

'How's it going?' Ned asked, not wanting to be rude, though he didn't much care what the response would be.

'Good thank you' came the reply in a nasal, slightly effeminate tone straight out of a horror movie. Julian's chin was resting on his chest as he sat slumped, zoned-in on the computer screen, no doubt trawling the internet with the worst of intentions.

On the wall behind Julian hung a garish rug depicting a stalking tiger emerging from long grass. The tiger was gold on a black woven background. The image was bordered with a gold repeating pattern and the rug was finished with a gold tasselled trim, it looked cheap as hell.

'I like your tiger rug' Ned called out to his mother jokingly.

'Oh yeah, it's nice innit?' came the reply, the sarcasm lost on Ned's mother. 'Julian brought it back from Thailand'.

Ned took the remote control from the coffee table and flicked through the channels; his mother went outside to bring in the washing and left the nuggets to cook in the oven.

A few minutes into the Friday night football game Ned's mum plopped down beside him on the couch. She sat side-on facing Ned with her left arm on top of the backrest and her left leg crossed in front of her.

'Sooo, 'ow is everyone?'

'Pretty much the same, Shane's moved into the caravan…'

'Oh yes, he mentioned that on Facebook'

'…and Krystal's new boyfriend's moved in…'

'Oooh, is he nice?'

'No'. Ned's eyes darted between his mother and the TV as he attempted to keep track of the game.

'Oh, well, tell me about this trip then'.

Ned gave his mother a brief rundown of his plans, leaving out all unnecessary information. As he described the trip to his mother Ned thought back to what Big Jake had said to him about it being good to see a Roach finally escape from Binnara Point and do something interesting. Looking around the house, the photos on the walls of his mother's new life, Ned realised it wasn't him, but rather his mother who had blazed the trail out of Binnara Point. For all of her perceived shortcomings, Ned's mum was actually pretty brave.

*

At 10.00pm Daryl arrived home from town, as with their previous meeting he greeted Ned enthusiastically.

'Hi Ned, good to see you buddy!' he said, thrusting out his hand for a handshake which he tuned into a back slapping handshake/hug combo after reeling Ned in. Daryl was a large man, tall and heavy set with thick, round fingers and a dense, though well groomed beard which was suspiciously dark for a man of his age.

The first few times they met, Ned had thought he was simply trying to get in the Roach kids good books, but it had continued on over the years and it seemed his enthusiasm was genuine. Ned didn't dislike Daryl, not any more. After the initial opposition and suspicion that went along with his mother's leaving, Ned had warmed to him. Daryl was good to Ned's mum and she seemed to be a much happier person now that she was with him. She'd trimmed down a bit, now she was active, working on the farm, she was outgoing, having made plenty of new friends in the community. And he'd weaned her off the pokies too. Her new hobby was collecting antiques, especially old jars and bottles.

*

Early the next morning Ned was roused by the barking of dogs. He looked out the window to see Daryl speaking to a man who was sitting in a beat up old ute with a couple of cattle dogs in the tray. The dogs were agitated by some goats penned up in the paddock next to the house. Ned checked the time on his phone, 7.49am. Normally, with the exception of the occasional early morning surf, Ned would tuck back down for another couple of hours kip. He left it five minutes but it was surprisingly noisy and bright. The section of awning outside his guest room window was Perspex and seemed to intensify the sunlight, directing it precisely onto the spot where his pillow lay. Ned got up at 7.54am and, after a quick trip to the bathroom, made his way to the living room. As he left the bathroom he could smell bacon cooking and hear the clattering of plates and utensils. As he rounded the floating wall he could see his mother doing her best attempt at a hot breakfast.

'Morning Ned' she said as she cracked an egg and sloppily dropped it into a frying pan.

'Morning' Ned replied, 'you cook breakfast these days?'

'Only on special occasions' Ned's mum replied, peering doubtfully into the pan. 'You ready for a trip out to Patterson's Gap? Big auction on out there today'.

'Ahh….yeah, OK'.

'I'll have to show you the collection before you go'.

Ned gave his mum a smile and a nod and wandered over to the couch to check out the Saturday morning sports updates on the TV.

*

'So your mum tells me you're off to see the world Ned' Daryl boomed as he vigorously rubbed his hands together in anticipation of the plate of bacon and eggs that was brought to rest in front of him.

'Yeah' Ned replied, echoing some of Daryl's enthusiasm, 'flying to L.A and then probably heading down to Mexico'. Ned's mother brought over two more plates of bacon and eggs and joined Ned and Daryl at the table.

'Great. You'll have to chat to Julian about that. He's a bit of a traveller, South-East Asia mainly, Thailand, Philippines, Vietnam, those sorts of places. He goes quite regularly', Daryl explained and he sliced and piled his breakfast.

Ned's mother raised the back of an opened hand to the side of her mouth 'we reckon he's got a girl over there' she stated hoarsely in mock whisper. The fact that Julian was a fairly obvious sexual deviant seemed to have evaded Daryl and Ned's Mum, whether it was through selective ignorance or not, Ned couldn't be sure. He just smiled and nodded.

'He stays up late doing business on the computer so we let him sleep in' Daryl insisted. By 'business' Ned assumed he meant 'frantically masturbating to snuff films'.

Ned's dislike of Julian was justified and it came about after overhearing a conversation at his mother and Daryl's wedding. Julian was seated at the same table as the Roach children. He was already in his early thirties at the wedding though his balding head and large tinted glasses made him look significantly older; this unfortunate head was teamed with the body of a malnourished 13 year old. A few hours into the reception Ned was standing at a table with his back to Julian who was describing his recent trip to Bangkok to another guest. He divulged how he had made a habit of finding a hooker early in the morning and locking her in his hotel room for the day while he gallivanted about in a way only an ugly white man can. He would return later in the day with a number of other girls that were 'lucky if they were 15', and invite them to do all sorts of unsavoury acts to each other and him. He justified this behaviour by insisting that it was 'part of their culture' and 'they'd always done that sort of thing in Thailand'.

'These eggs are delicious Deb' said Daryl as he wiped some yolk from his moustache, 'she doesn't usually do *this*, you're a lucky boy Ned'.

'Mmmm' Ned nodded, going along with sentiment.

After finishing up breakfast, Ned excused himself from the table and took himself off for a shower to get ready for the day's activities. When he emerged Julian was waiting by the bathroom door in a pair of clingy, grey-marl tracksuit pants through which Ned could clearly make out his evil little dick. His lurking presence startled Ned who withered away as he opened the door.

'Fuck me! Why are you standing there?'

'I need the bathroom' Julian replied robotically. Ned took leave of the hall and dropped his towel in the laundry before heading outside to look at the goats.

It was their eyes he found most interesting; their pupils were shaped like a keyhole. He tried to give them a fright to see if they were those fainting goats he'd seen on the internet, but it seemed they were not. Ned heard the window closest to the paddock slide up with a groan and a bang.

'We'll be going in a minute love, just waiting for Daryl to set up the big sprinklers down the lettuce patch'.

Ned gave his mum a thumbs up and carried on testing out the goats, attempting to feed them all manner of things hoping they would live up to their illustrious reputations as eaters of anything. The best Ned could get them to chomp on was some newspaper and the box the nuggets came in.

*

'....*the problem with these illegal immigrants isn't that they're black, or Asian or coming here and taking our jobs. It's the fact that there's a process for coming here to live and these bastards are jumping the queue ahead of people who are doing it properly. And don't get me started about whether they are in fact legitimate refugees, I know for a fact.....*'

'Can we turn this shit off please?' Ned asked as he sat between his mother and Daryl on the front bench seat of Daryl's ute, 'this bloke is talking absolute shit'.

'Ooh don't say that, Daryl loves listening to Bill Bennett'.

'Sorry Daryl but this dude is ridiculous, boat people are the least of our worries'.

'That's fine Ned, everybody's entitled to their opinions' Daryl replied as he reached for the scan button on the stereo.

'I know what you mean Ned' his mother announced, 'those poor people from Afghanistan, our army boys have been over there for years, still haven't managed to chase those wogs out have they'.

Ned wasn't sure which part of his mother's comment to correct first and in the end chose to let it slide, it wasn't the time for a lesson on politics and political correctness.

'Yes, the Muslims are becoming a problem?' Daryl added, 'they want to take over Australia now'.

Ned tapped away at the seek button hoping to find anything to end this painful conversation. He sat back, as much as was possible in the cramped conditions, when the stereo sprang to life with a static backed version of 'She Will Be Loved' by Maroon 5.

*

The ute pulled into a fairly non-descript driveway that was marked only by an a-frame placard with 'Auction Today' written in runny black paint. They travelled a few hundred metres down the drive toward a large old wooden building with 'Freestone's Sawmill' barely legible on one side, it looked as though it had last been painted about 80 years earlier. The grassed area on the far side of the building was being used as a car park and was quite full. As they entered the sawmill Ned was hit with the smell of sawdust and rust, though the tang of menthol cigarette still lingered as a result of the close confines of the trip. The space was filled with grey haired men in checked shirts and weathered ladies in denim shorts wandering amongst a sea of long disused and rusted machinery of all description, old electrical items and all variety of trinkets and treasures. At the end of the mill was a raised platform with a covered table and a lectern. Daryl placed his hands meaningfully on his hips and took his surrounds in with a deep breath. 'Alright then!' he said with a clap of the hands and headed off into the crowd, his checked shirt quickly blending in amongst the countless others. Ned's mum followed behind at a more leisurely pace, stopping to look at some old soft drink bottles in a crate. Ned wandered amongst the miscellanea, drawing the occasional 'tut' or frown as he touched or tried to operate some of the ancient shit on display.

*

The loud and constant rattling of the newly acquired items that filled the back of the ute meant that the trip back to the farm would be without music but it also mean it would be free of the nutty ranting's of talk radio. The steel typewriter that Ned was nursing was causing a fair bit of discomfort, particularly on the uneven stretches of road where it bit repeatedly against his thigh like a toothless metal crocodile. By the time they arrived back at the farm Ned's lap looked like a char grilled chicken breast with crisscross indentations battered into his pasty thigh flesh.

'We'll take all this stuff over to the shed' Daryl announced, 'you'll get to have a look at the treasure chest'. It appeared the junk filled shed beside the house had acquired a nickname.

'Young Ned, if you head over with the typewriter I'll follow behind with these bottles. Could you bring the keys over Deb?'

After a few false starts with the lock Daryl opened the shed door to reveal his pride and joy. The inside of the shed was fitted with ceiling to floor shelving on three sides. The shed itself was T.A.R.D.I.S like, it looked to be a standard double garage size from the outside but inside it seemed to double in dimensions such was the vastness of its contents. The shelves on the back wall were filled with scruffy bottles and jars of all shapes and sizes. Daryl took the crate over to the shelf and placed it on the ground

'We'll sort those out later'.

The front wall beside the door had a long work bench running along it. Ned dumped the typewriter on the bench and headed out to the ute to bring in the rest of the booty. He rolled a rusted up axle and wheels from an old cart down and an old iron sign for a long forgotten brewery up to the shed before the ute was empty.

'You've nearly run out of space' Ned commented after he dragged the sign in and left it wobbling against the work bench.

'We've already 'ad to move some stuff inside' Ned's mum replied, picking some spider web off a life sized ceramic rooster, 'I'll probably have to bring this in, very fragile'.

*

The next few days on the farm were spent relaxing. Ned helped out with odd jobs around the place and took his car for a bit a paddock bashing. In the afternoons he went swimming in the weir and hit golf balls across the dam.

The morning before he was planning to drive back up the coast Ned's mum knocked on the guest room door. He was reading the paper sprawled across the bed. She walked in carrying a ceramic statue of a horse the size of a labrador.

'Sorry mate, this girl's gunna have to live in here for a while, shed's full up'.

'What is that?'

'Worth a bit of money Daryl reckons' Ned's mum replied, not really answering the question. 'You feel like going out for tea tonight? Daryl's got a scout meeting; it'll just be us two'.

'Yeah, I don't mind'.

'I was thinkin' Chinese, whaddya reckon?'

'Sounds like a plan' replied Ned, who was transfixed by the statue who's practical application in any home was questionable.

There were two Chinese restaurants in Collombindee, The Golden Palace and the Good-Luck Chinese Restaurant. The Good-Luck was attached to the Collombindee Bowling Club; its food wasn't the best. The Golden Palace was reputedly delicious but its location beside the Collombindee Veterinary Surgery had led to many a nasty rumour about where they acquired their meat.

At 6.00pm Ned and his mum drove into town via the scout hall to drop Daryl off at his meeting.

'Golden Palace or Good-Luck?' Ned's mum asked as they reached the top of the main street.

'Golden Palace' Ned replied 'I'd rather eat a deliciously prepared cocker spaniel than shit tasting pork'.

The restaurant was empty when they went in which meant they could take the primo seat next to the tropical fish tank. The glare from the fluorescent lights bouncing off the vinyl tablecloths took some getting used to. After perusing the menu Ned settled for the number 18, Kung Po King Prawns with Chilli, his mum opted for the 23, Cantonese Sweet and Sour Pork. Their orders were taken by a school aged girl who was obviously the daughter of the proprietors, it was a wonder Julian wasn't skulking around here, she was just his type. The Golden Palace offered a far more authentic Chinese dining experience than the Good-Luck, where one could expect to be served by a woman named Janine who's closest affiliation with China is the mandarin character for 'family' she has tattooed above her left arse cheek.

'What's the deal with Dad?' Ned asked as he followed one of the Neon Tetra's as it darted around the fish tank.

'Your dad?'

'Yeah, Terry Roach'.

'What do you mean?'

'Like….who is he, I mean, he just sits there, he's like a fuckin' ghost most of the time'.

Ned's mum sat quietly for a moment. 'Well it doesn't sound like much's changed then. He was a lovely man once, but I think he gave up on life quite a while ago. It's sad really'.

'Why?'

'He had a hard time finding work after the chook plant closed down, all his mates left after that to work elsewhere and after a while he just gave up I s'pose'.

'Is that why you left?'

Ned's mum nodded, 'Yeah, that was a lot of it. But I hadn't been happy for a long time. We got married young, just did what everyone else was doing, never put a lot of thought into it y'know'.

Ned nodded.

'I just did what I thought I was supposed to do, before I knew it I was pregnant and that was it then, I was stuck'.

The waitress returned with their meals which didn't disappoint. Ned and his mum sat quietly for a while eating and watching the fish. Ned's mum asked about Little Jake and Shane's girls who'd sent her a birthday card a few months back. Ned told his mum about Shane's new girlfriend. They agreed to keep in contact via Facebook while Ned was away, at least once a fortnight, just to let her know he was alive.

Ned was fiddling with the radio dial in his car trying to find anything other than white noise as they headed toward the scout hall to pick up Daryl.

'Any of you kids could have come with me' Ned's mum said as the car rattled down the main street.

'Eh?'

'When I left, I only stayed as long as I did because of you kids. I wanted you to come too'.

'I know'. Ned replied with a nod.

*

Ned tore into the car park in front of the Sandy Hollow general store sending an up-current of dust into the air that filled his car, all four windows of which were wound all the way down. 15 kilometers behind him, Ned had made the grave error of trying to straddle a dead kangaroo in his car. He had mistakenly assumed that his car was high enough off the ground to clear the minced marsupial as it lay eviscerated in the middle of the highway. The kangaroo impacted the underside of the Pintara with a metallic thud and there it stayed for several kilometres before most of it came bouncing out from the back of the car after it had been sufficiently ground down by the road surface. The stench of the kangaroo had flooded into the car through the vents, causing Ned to close them and hastily unwind all the windows while dry-heaving. The open windows took the hard edge off the stink but it was still quite unbearable.

Ned was lucky in as much as the general store doubled as a service station and had a small selection of motoring paraphernalia. Ned purchased several car deodorisers in a variety of scents as well as a can of air freshener. Outside he took the watering can that sat on top of a bin next to the lone petrol bowser and poured water liberally through the engine housing where he could see chunks of furry flesh still clinging to the underside of the engine block. Ned hung the pine scented deodoriser from the rearview mirror and scattered the others, one of them bacon scented, across the dashboard and left the air freshener on the passenger seat for easy access.

As he hummed up the coast, Ned tried to breathe exclusively through his mouth. The smell of death was certainly less conspicuous but it had been replaced with a sickly mixture of fragrances that was only slightly better. Several kilometres spent stuck behind a cattle truck came as something of a strange relief. At every opportunity Ned would steer into puddles, hoping to rinse away the giblets that so offended him.

When he finally arrived back in Binnara Point, Ned wanted to drive his car into the creek and let it sink. By the time he pulled into the driveway it was 2 o'clock on Friday morning. When he opened the front door the hallway wall was awash with the light being projected by the unwatched television. The lounge room was empty save for Rooster who was asleep under the footrest of the recliner. Ned flopped onto the couch and watched a South African provincial rugby game that he stumbled upon as he flicked through the channels. After the sensory ordeal of the 11 hour car journey the usual sweaty stink of the couch was fairly innocuous.

The sliding, crashing and hydraulic strains of the garbage truck woke Ned at 5.30am. He was still lying on the lounge which he was able to smell again after the healing qualities of sleep had returned his sense of smell to normal human levels. As he sat up and wiped the sweat off his neck with his shirt he heard Big Jake tiptoeing down the hall toward the front door. Big Jake must have noticed the flashing echo of the TV because he made a detour to come into the lounge room to turn it off.

'What are you doing you weird prick?' Big Jake whispered as he spotted Ned on the couch.

'Hey mate. I got in late and started watching a bit of tele, must've crashed out'.

'You keen for that barbie tomorrow night mate?'

'Yeah why not'.

'Sweet bro, I'll catch you later' and Big Jake continued out the door and off to work.

*

'You should have seen this shed mate, I've never seen so much shit crammed in to one place in all my life. There was more stuff in there than in Ronald's shed'.

'Sounds like they're living the dream' said Andy.

Ned scooped up a handful of water and let it dribble out on to the nose of his surfboard 'You got everything packed?'

'Pretty much. I'm travelling light, just taking a backpack'.

'Yeah, I think I'll do the same. Is your old man still sweet to drive us all to the airport?'

'He was last time I spoke to him' Andy replied as he lay forward on his board to paddle closer to the point.

Ned paddled along side 'so Chrissy got done for gross misconduct?'

'Yeah' Andy giggled in reply, 'very grose'.

'He told me he's got all our trip itinerary sorted. Hope he doesn't lead us up shit creek'.

'We'll be alright' said Andy confidently.

*

It was quite a spread that Big Jake and Jodie put on for Ned. Certainly bigger than any birthday party or Christmas meal any of the Roach's had ever had. Perhaps it was the long flight, maybe they were worried that he might not make it back. Whatever reason, Ned really did appreciate it. Andy and Chris joined the Roach's and their affiliates for the barbeque which was a rather pleasant affair, all things considered. Shane had managed to squeeze himself in between Krystal and Nath, to his great delight, allowing him to talk endless shit without derision. Ned's dad made it out of the house to participate at his own limited capacity and even seemed to take interest in the discussion. Ned had planned to make a clean getaway, minimal fuss, this wasn't so awful though and he used the opportunity to bequeath his various possessions for use in his absence. Ned wanted his bedroom to be taken over by Little Jake, he seemed the most likely to keep it clean. The rest of his gear was to be divided between the Jakes as they saw fit. He entrusted his car keys with Big Jake, recommending that he give it a couple of weeks before going inside.

*

'Don't stick your dicks in anything dirty!' was Andy's dad's parting advice as he pulled away from the drop-off bay at Brisbane International Airport.

The three amigo's crawled through the check in one slow step at a time, weaving their way around the partitions at a putrefying pace before disappearing beyond the liquid confiscating barriers that lead to the air-side. After being deemed fit to travel and being appalled by the price of snacks, the boys killed the preflight tedium with a couple of extortionately priced beers in the artificially darkened airport pub.

Chris had requested the aisle seat for the flight due to him allegedly possessing a smaller than usual bladder and therefore being a more frequent visitor to the restrooms than the other boys. Upon hearing this Andy immediately claimed the window seat, he assured Ned and Chris it was because he liked watching out the window, but Ned knew better. 15 hours cheek to jowl with Chris could become an unpleasant experience. Chris wasn't the most considerate person and he became intolerably annoying when exposed to for an extended and unbroken period. This proved to be true after only a few short minutes. Shortly after settling into the seats aboard the 767 Chris began fiddling with every possible latch, switch and toggle, adjusting anything adjustable and taking up as much space as possible. Ned and Andy very quickly hooked into the headrest entertainment and Andy was able to watch uninterrupted save for the occasional visit by flight staff offering mini treats. Ned's viewing was interrupted by regular elbow nudges from Chris who was thrilling him with witty observations and informative comments.

'That stewardess with the brown hair is definitely keen on me, she keeps smiling at me'.

'She's smiling at everyone, they all are, that's what they do', Ned assured Chris.

'Nah, she's giving me the eye mate, I'm sure of it. Might be a chance for the mile-high club here'.

'Your best chance of that is if you go into the toilet and crack one off, but I don't think that counts'.

If Andy had genuinely intended on doing some out window gazing he must have been rather disappointed to find that his window was mostly obscured by the seat in front of his, and in any case, all he had a view of was the 'do not walk past this line' sign painted on top of the wing.

Chris hadn't been lying about his walnut sized bladder, his need to relieve himself was alarming. By the time the in-flight journey tracker had the plane located somewhere above Fiji, Chris had already made five trips to the toilet. Andy had managed to fall asleep and didn't stir until breakfast was served a few hours before they were due to land.

*

'Have things started to chill out a bit at home yet?' Ned asked Chris as he reseated himself after his 8th visit to the lavatory.

'It's just dad who's pissed really, I don't even reckon he gives a shit about my situation that much, he's just worried that I've made him look bad'. Chris replied, squirming in his seat, trying to find an un sat-upon piece of buttock.

'He's bound to get over it eventually. Are you pissed off about it?'

'Not really, I don't think I really ever wanted to be a cop, it was just put on me since I was young, family trade and all that bullshit. It was my old man's idea, not mine'.

Ned nodded.

'I would have liked to have left in a bit more dignified manner though' Chris added with a smile.

Andy was struggling to keep his eyes open to Ned's left.

'What the fuck is up with you mate?'

'I took a bunch of Valium, it's knocked me about. I don't think I'm gonna eat this'. Andy slid the aluminium tray to the back of his flight table and slipped back into his comatose state.

Ned helped himself to Andy'a breakfast and tried to get a glance out the window at the early morning light. He reattached himself to the in-flight entertainment and tried to maintain the circulation in his arse with rhythmic clenches.

The brown haired hostess came by to collect their discards and gave them a beaming smile. Chris gave Ned yet another nudge, just to make sure he saw it. Ned shook his head dismissively and continued with his viewing. The remainder of the flight was reasonably pleasant, Ned was able to find a movie that took up the remainder of the flight and Chris kept to himself, similarly occupied.

At what the pilot assured the passengers was 11.00am L.A time the entertainment came to an abrupt halt and the flight staff did the rounds asking the passengers to put their seats into the upright position and stow away their trays. Chris took the opportunity to put the hard word on the brunette stewardess. Ned saw Chris's lips move but missed out on the word as the headphones were still in place but the speed that the smile vanished from the stewardess's face, to be replaced by a stifled gurn of disgust, suggested nothing appropriate was said.

As they filed off the plane after landing, Chris avoided eye contact with the stewardess whose mouth was smiling as he filed past but whose eyes were sending invisible bolts of hatred.

'What did you say to her mate? She want's to kill you'.

'I asked her if she'd like to adjust my seatbelt'.

'Classy', Ned replied with a laugh.

Part 2

(International Time Travel)

After the excruciating LAX entry procedure the boys grabbed a taxi and headed for the hotel that Chris had booked over the internet the previous week.

The Buena Vista Hotel in Venice Beach was quite a place. It was located on the Pacific Coast Highway several blocks removed from the Venice beachfront and hadn't been updated since the mid 70's. The check-in clerk's skin looked like glazed pork rind and he had a moustache that seemed to be from a joke shop. He was wearing a net singlet and watching a Lakers game on a small portable TV. Anyone would have thought he'd been curing in this little cubicle since the day he was born.

'You boys from outta town?' he asked, rolling a toothpick along his top teeth with his tongue.

'Yeah, I made a booking, names Bastoni'.

'Sure. What accent is that? New Jersey?' the clerk replied sliding open a drawer filled with keys and plucking out a set.

'Australian' answered Chris.

The clerk looked puzzled and paused for a second before he handed over the keys, 'if you boys want any ladies just let me know, I got all kinds'.

'Ok...thanks mate' Chris took the keys, careful not to make skin contact.

'How much is this joint?' Andy asked as they made their way along the outside walkway to their room.

'20 bucks a night, bargain!' Chris answered proudly.

'As long as I don't catch syphilis from the bed sheets it's a bargain'.

As the door swung open they were greeted with a room that looked like it had hosted its fair share of illicit trysts and suicides. The smell of the room could best be described as uncooked egg. There was a double bed and a single bed separated by a small bedside table on which sat a lamp and a rotary-dial Bakelite telephone that looked like it had cracked a few skulls in its time.

'Have a look under this bed Andy' Ned called out from the other side of the room beside the single bed. Behind the frayed valance lay a thoroughly used condom curled up on the worn carpet like a forlorn ghost. Judging by the colour it had seen action in both barrels.

'That is *fucked*!' replied Andy recoiling in disgust.

Ned retrieved a wooden rod that was acting as a lock on the room's only window and prodded at the johnny before skillfully hooking it and running with it at arm's length into the bathroom and flushing it down the toilet in defiance of the sign on the back of the bathroom door asking guests to refrain from such actions.

By the miracle of west to east international travel, the boys had arrived an hour before they left which amused Chris no end. 'It's like the flight never happened, we've travelled through time'.

'I read about this, we're supposed to stay awake and get into the normal time routine to avoid jet-lag'. Andy commented as he peered out the dirty window to the street outside.

'Well, truth be told, I'm not that keen to spend any more time than is absolutely necessary in this room fellas', Ned added.

After a brief discussion and a whore's shower, the three headed outside and walked in the direction of the beach.

The boys were wholly unprepared for the reversed traffic flow and found themselves stepping in front of cars they were expecting to come from the opposite direction on several occasions.

The beachfront was something else too. It was late afternoon and the pedestrian boardwalk was busy with tourists gawking at the street performers and other oddballs lining the path. They followed the boardwalk north trying to avoid eye contact with the local vagabonds all the while being enthusiastically offered medical marijuana prescriptions every 45 seconds. Chris opened his backpack and produced a small notebook and a pocket map of Los Angeles.

'Is that your diary Chrissy?'

'This is the playbook fellas, I wrote down everything in here for the trip. We've got three days here before we get the bus out to Vegas' Chris replied waving the book in front of Ned and Andy.

'We can grab a feed here and then head towards Hollywood.'

Chris seemed to be confident about what he was doing and he was the only one who'd gone to the trouble of acquiring a map so Ned and Andy followed Chris's lead, hoping his confidence was justified.

They stopped for some tacos and continued north along the waterfront for a few minutes before arriving at Santa Monica Pier.

'We can follow Santa Monica Boulevard all the way to Hollywood' Chris surmised after perusing his map for several minutes.

'How far?'

'It doesn't look too far, a few K's I reckon'.

At Santa Monica Boulevard the boys headed east and walked for ages, passing through several suburbs, none of them Hollywood. As they reached

West Beverly Hills it was getting quite dark and Ned's tolerance for meandering had reached its limit.

'This is fucked Chris, we've been walking for ages, I'm getting a bus'. Ned received no opposition to his suggestion and the boys found a bus stop and caught the 2/302 which took them the rest of the way, which was still several miles, to Hollywood, via Sunset Boulevard through Beverly Hills.

'It's gonna be a mission gettin' home' Andy expressed as the bus crawled through the traffic.

'Better get good and pissed then' Chris replied as he gawked out the window at the bar's and restaurants filled with fame seekers and gold diggers all trying to climb to the top via the stairway of shattered dreams.

When the boys got off the bus they were at odds as what to do. Chris wanted to go back towards where he saw a bunch of scantily clad ladies milling about. Ned and Andy wanted to sit down somewhere with a drink. Chris was pleased when a decision was made to go back from where they alighted, at least they had seen what lay in that direction, to continue ahead would be delving into the unknown. After tramping along for a few blocks they disappeared into a busy looking bar called Begsy's Ballroom. It was dimly lit, bass heavy and filled with a wide variety of posers and maggots. The boys managed to acquire a table and treated themselves to a variety of American beers. The boys found themselves to be quite popular with some very sexually suggestive women who had engineered their garments to allow for maximum visibility of tits and arse whilst still maintaining a minimal level of modesty.

A girl, who alleged that her name was Charity, wedged herself onto the edge of the bench. Charity was sporting a substantial set of breasts that were being precariously contained within a flimsy strapless dress. The faint edge of her areola was peeking just above the seam of her bandeau, like the corona during a solar eclipse. It was this hint of a nipple that Chris had immediately taken a liking to. He'd already bought her several vodka and soda's, trying to woo her with tales of snakes and crocodiles, oblivious or perhaps naïve to the fact that Charity's affections required a deposit rather than charm. Charity would whisper into Chris's ear from time to time, causing the grin of a simpleton to spread across his face.

'These chicks work at a joint called Platinum down the road, we can get in for free if we go with them' Chris yelled across the table, straining against the rabble. 'Whadya's reckon?'

Ned and Andy both shrugged their shoulders.

*

The boys were escorted to Platinum by Charity, the halo of nipple still peeking over the horizon of her dress, and one of her cohorts who insisted that her name was Faberge. True to their word the boys were waved through the door by the two juiced-up gorillas providing security. Once through the doors they were greeted by a staircase leading below street level and lit from below, making for an eerie descent. At the bottom of the stairs the club was surprisingly vast with a raised runway running from the distant back wall to the horseshoe shaped bar in the centre of the space, giving the whole setup the look of a giant, horizontal phallus. The runway was also lit from below and housed three large poles than ran all the way to the roof; each one being attended to by a buxom young lady, two of whom were completely naked and one who was in the process of seductively removing her underpants.

'Do you guys want some drinks?' Charity asked in her best, well-practiced, sexy-voice which came across more patronising than arousing, like she was talking to a baby or a dog.

Chris responded with a silent nod, still absorbed in all the gyrating. Charity strutted toward the bar and Faberge led the boys to a table located under the arse of the girl dancing on the pole closest to the bar. The bar itself was attended by two semi-clad beauties under the supervision of a short, gruff, solidly built bald man who had the added attraction of having two old-style revolvers tattooed on his skull just above each ear.

Charity returned with three bottles of Coors Light which she placed on the table before taking Faberge by the hand, 'excuse us fellas, we've got a few things to do' she said with a wink before leading her partner away towards the back of the room and through the curtained doorway marked with a large 'staff only' sign.

The three boys sipped their beers in silence, mesmerised by the spectacle. The silence was broken by Chris who voiced his desire to get some one dollar notes. The beers went down quickly and the place was beginning to fill up with more and more gawking out-of-towners, all led in by pumped up tarts with promises of a good time.

Andy rose to his feet and temporarily ripped his gaze from the stage, 'another one boys?'

Ned and Chris both gave him a nod and Andy shuffled around to the front of the horse shoe. Ned looked on as Andy was greeted by one of the barmaids wearing a black thong and with black tassels over her nipples. After exchanging words that were lost in the thumping bass that boomed out of the speakers hanging from the ceiling, Andy's face contorted into a mixture of confusion and disbelief. After another short exchange the expression morphed into one of outrage. Ned leaned forward attempting to lip-read as Andy waved the barmaid away and stormed back towards the table. Andy's return from the short journey to the bar coincided with the arrival of Charity onto the stage which Chris greeted with an enthusiastic round of applause.

'Let's go fellas' declared Andy, 'no amount of nudity is worth 15 bucks a drink'.

'What!' spat Ned, nearly choking on his last mouthful of beer.

'Yep, these three are gonna cost us 45 bucks' snapped Andy pointing at the table.

Ned stood abruptly, knocking his chair over and joined Andy in looking expectantly at Chris whose eyes were darting between them and Charity's now fully exposed nipples.

'Fellas c'mon!' Chris pleaded, 'look at this place, from this table I can see like 12 tits, and that's not counting the ones being reflected in the mirrors. Plus I think Charity's keen for one'.

'I'm sure she is mate, but it'll set you back a shitload', Ned replied.

'She's already fleeced you for a mint' added Andy already leaning towards the front door.

'Nah, she's not a hooker, she's a dancer'.

Ned looked at Chris incredulously, surely he was not that naïve. 'Are you coming or what?'

Chris hesitated and the glanced over his shoulder where Charity's bare arse was orbiting a foot above his head 'Nah, I'll see you back at the hotel'

Andy stopped at the top of the stairs and asked the gorillas at the door where they might get a good feed nearby. The larger of the two, who looked like the type of bloke who ate on the toilet, recommended a place called Roscoe's a couple of blocks further on.

*

It was 11.30pm and Ned found himself sitting in a booth with an autographed photo of Bill Cosby above his head and the number 4 on a plate in front of him with a side of mac and cheese.

'This is an odd mixture of food' said Ned as he sat intimidated by the meal before him. 'Do you mix the chicken and the waffle together?'

'No idea mate' replied Andy who was wading blindly into his own number 4.

In the end Ned had little choice as the meal merged together after what seemed like an eternity of eating. He had to have a clearing bowel movement halfway through the meal in order to finish it. Andy looked a little worse for wear across the table as he sat slumped with mouth ajar and eyes glazed, battling to digest his meal with crumbs of chicken skin glued to his face with maple syrup. Through his open mouth Ned could hear Andy's stomach attempting to make sense of the mess it was presented with, groaning and gurgling menacingly. Ned's own stomach was fighting a similar battle, he could feel the hot mess dribbling into his intestine, it was going to make for an unpleasant fight for the toilet in the morning.

It was just after 1am when Ned and Andy staggered out of Roscoe's. They turned right onto Sunset and continued west back in the direction of Platinum and several miles further on, the Buena Vista Hotel.

'I don't think there are any buses coming' said Ned after they'd walked for nearly half an hour, 'let's grab a taxi'.

Andy nodded with a pained expression, he had started walking like a sick duck, clearly still struggling with his insides. A few blocks further on they came across a number of taxis lined up in front of a bar called Goosecock's. There were several groups standing alongside the taxis loudly and ineffectively organising themselves in the way only drunk people can. Ned and Andy weaved their way through the swaying and shrieking mob and slid themselves inconspicuously into the taxi at the head of the queue. Andy crawled across the back seat so as to position himself at the maximum possible recline with his head against the driver's side window and his feet tucked behind the passenger seat. Ned slid himself into the front seat, much to the surprise of the driver who leaned back and gave him the once over.

'We need to get to Venice mate' Ned announced, 'the big fella's not feeling too good' pointing over his shoulder to Andy.

'You guys from England?' the driver asked with his head tilted back, peering into the rear view mirror to get a look at Andy.

'Nah, Australia' Ned replied.

'No shit? You ever see that movie 'Croc Dundee' that's some funny shit' the cabbie continued. 'And that croc hunter, he's a crazy bastard'.

'Yeah' Ned replied out of politeness rather than enthusiasm, 'crazy'. 'The place is called Buena Vista Hotel, it's on the highway, I think I'll recognise when we're close'.

'Okay' said the cabbie as he pulled away from the kerb and carried on westward.

'My brother went to Australia once, with the navy, to Perth…you guys from Perth'.

Ned shook his head, 'no, not from Perth'.

The taxi was following a similar route to the bus they had caught earlier in the day, though at this time of the night the shine had come off the scenery significantly. The strutting of the pedestrians had degenerated into a swaying stagger or a hunched scavenging.

'That's not a knife' the cabbie blurted out in his best imitation, glancing over at Ned with a grin and a chuckle.

Ned humoured the cabbie with a loud fabricated giggle, 'not bad mate, not bad'.

'Sydney…Mel-bourne…The outback…You got them poison fish too'.

Ned nodded along as the cabbie rattled off his list of Australiana. He wasn't sure which fish the fella was referring to but he nodded along just the same 'yeah, you gotta watch out for them ones'.

In the back seat Andy was listening in with amusement, feigning sleep and struggling to fend off a smile.

The cab made a left turn near the end of Santa Monica Blvd. which took them in a southerly direction.

'Well this is the PCH buddy, what am I looking for?'

'Ah... it's the Buena Vista it's only small, there's a petrol station across the street called 76 maybe?'

The taxi continued along for several blocks, the road veering away from the beach and passing rows of similar looking concrete buildings. Ahead, Ned could see the red beacon that was the 76 sign, floating above the rooftops.

'I think that's the one just ahead mate'.

The taxi was stopped at a red light diagonally opposite the station, one building up from the corner the unlit, faded sign advertising the 'Bu n V sta Hotel' could be seen poking out from behind a miserable palm tree.

'We're here mate' Ned called out as he reached behind and slapped Andy's left knee which was resting behind the space between the front seats of the taxi.

*

Ned woke up early; out the window the sky was pink. He looked across to the double bed which was empty, as was the small sofa against the opposite wall. Ned sat up; he was stinging for a piss and looked over to the bathroom to see the door shut tight. He stood up and paced about the room for a couple of minutes, stopping to flick on the ancient TV. The set was old, it made an ultrasonic whine when Ned pulled to power knob and the picture gradually appeared as though one was coming out of a dark tunnel into the light. As Ned twisted the dial trying to find something worthwhile he felt as though his bladder was reaching rupture point, he scurried over to the bathroom door and knocked frantically. No response was received; Ned pressed his ear against the door and could hear the shower running.

'Andy…Andy!'

Nothing. Deciding he couldn't afford to wait any longer, Ned ran out the door and along the verandah walkway, as he bounded down the stairs each impact threatened to send a pulse of hot morning piss thundering into his shorts. He dashed across the car park and between two cars, relieving himself onto the shrubbery growing next to the fence that divided the hotel from the tyre shop next door.

He returned to the room thoroughly relieved and returned to the television dial, giving it a spin and settling for an early morning news show hosted by a toothy, large headed duo. Ned flopped back on to the single bed and waited for his comrades to return.

The shrill creak of the bathroom handle startled Ned as he was starting to drift off. The bottom of the swollen door dragged loudly across the floor tiles before Andy emerged from the steam like a rattled rock star, wearing only a towel around his waist and a look of exhaustion on his face.

Ned shifted up onto his elbows as Andy crossed the room and collapsed back onto the double bed.

'What's up with you?'

'It's carnage in there mate, I'm torn to ribbons'.

'Your soft little stomach wasn't ready for the onslaught of yank dining eh?' Ned joked.

'Apparently not. I've been in there since four o'clock'.

'Jesus…. shitting the whole time?'

'Pretty much.' Andy replied mournfully. 'I woke up with my guts killing me and bolted in there; I'd already followed through in my sleep so I chucked out my undies and just sat on the shitter. Every time I tried to go back to bed I had to run back in. I couldn't wipe my arse any more so I just squatted over the shower drain and let it flow'.

'That's really gross dude' Ned stated with a grimace.

'Mate, what could I do, if I wiped one more time my arsehole was going to fall out into my hand. The shit was spraying out of me like a fucking claymore mine'.

'I went to a few medicine lectures before we left and I'm pretty sure that can't happen.... So is the shower safe to use'.

'Yeah, by the time I went in there just liquid was coming out of me'.

*

The sky outside had turned blue and the toothy pair on the TV had been replaced by a man dressed as an alien asking the assumedly infantile viewers to do the alien dance. Ned plucked up the courage to hit the shower, and wandered into the bathroom to inspect the crime scene. Luckily the shower tiles were powder blue so any sneaky sliver of shit should be easy to spot. There were several inconclusive brown spots around the drain and between tiles that concerned Ned some, but he took his chances, shuffling about on his heels just in case.

The boys were hungry and keen to find some breakfast. Chris was still absent but they decided it wasn't necessary to wait around, fuck knew where he'd ended up and when he'd be back.

After a stroll down to the beach and a healthy breakfast at a vegetarian restaurant in an attempt to clean out their fragile innards, Ned and Andy got down to deciding how they would spend the day.

'I reckon we should go to Disneyland' Andy suggested.

Ned looked at Andy doubtfully, 'wouldn't it be a bit weird for two grown men to go to Disneyland without kids, or even girlfriends'.

'Who cares, you know you always wanted to go as a kid, I sure as shit did. Do it for Little Ned'.

Ned considered the argument for a moment, 'yeah ok, fuck it, let's go to Disneyland'.

The boys headed back to the hotel to grab some essentials and give Chris one more chance to turn up. Back at the room the boys grabbed their backpacks, there were no signs to suggest Chris had been back, and under the assumption that Disneyland would require a reasonably early arrival to make the trip worthwhile, the boys decided to leave. Although their previous meeting gave little reason to suggest that he would be able to provide any assistance other than as a pimp, Ned decided to swing by the hotel office and see if the leathery grub at the reception desk could help them out with a map or some directions. Ned pushed open the office door, the desk was unattended but Ned could hear chatter coming from the room behind. The door was open so Ned walked over and knocked before sticking his head around the corner. The clerk was sitting at a folding table with his back to the door, on the opposite side of the table sat Chris. The two of them were engaged in a game of dominos with a third man who was standing beside a fridge at the back of the room drinking a can of malt liquor.

'What the fuck are you doing?' Ned asked, stunned.

'Playing dominos with Gino and Dennis' Chris replied as though this were a perfectly normal thing for him to be doing.

'Why?'

'I came back and you boys were gone so I came down here and now I'm playing dominos'.

Ned shook his head, amazed, amused and confused. 'Well we're about to go to Disneyland, you gonna come?'

Chris stood up like a bolt, 'Yep'.

'We're going now…'

'Ok' Chris replied, not bothered by the strip club aroma that clung to him like a drowning skunk.

Gino spun his lizard head around, a pair of bifocals on a cord perched on his nose. 'You can get a bus to Disneyland from the airport, special Disneyland bus'.

Chris smiled, looking at Ned he held out two open hands towards Gino, intimating what a useful friend he had made.

'Where can we get a taxi?' Ned asked, giving Gino a chance to prove himself even more helpful.

Gino raised a dirty finger towards the character at the back of the room who was peering through the venetian blinds beside the fridge. 'Dennis drives a cab…. Hey Dennis! These guys wanna go to the airport'.

Chris's smile intensified, his face now resembled that of a cheap Buddha statue, his cheeks almost touching his eyebrows. He thrust his hands forward, 'Gino!'

*

The bus from the airport to Disneyland was filled with overweight parents and their overweight children sweating and squabbling. The three boys managed to acquire the back seat which they shared with a particularly enthusiastic Japanese teenager who was studying a map of the park intently. He had the misfortune of sitting beside Chris who remained unwashed from the previous night's shenanigans and smelt like a potent mixture of booze, perfume and shit.

'You fellas missed out last night' Chris announced for the third time. His first two attempts to start a conversation about his doings were shot down, firstly in the taxi and then at the bus stop but this time he didn't give them a chance as he barreled into his tale.

'The first thing you need to know is that I fucked her. Twice'.

'What did that set you back?' asked Andy, still clearly bothered by Charity's ruse.

'It wasn't like that mate. I paid for a lap dance but it was only because she would have gotten in trouble if I didn't, and she gave me a discount… and let me finger her. They don't normally let you do that'.

'I reckon every bloke gets told they're getting a discount' Andy replied without enthusiasm.

'I reckon every bloke slips a finger in too' Ned added dryly.

'Nah, she's not like that, she's saving for college, she want's to be a vet'.

This last revelation brought a chorus of laughter to the rear of the bus; even the Japanese kid was having a giggle.

'Serious', Chris continued insistently, 'she told me her real name and everything'.

'Oh, so her name wasn't really Charity?' Ned asked sarcastically.

'No, it's Suzy'.

'I wonder if Faberge was only a stage name too?' Ned questioned mockingly.

Chris sulked quietly for the remainder of the bus trip. He did turn sharply to his companions with mouth open and mind racing a couple of times seemingly ready to unload a ball-busting quip, but each time he thought better of it and returned to wallowing silently in his misguided sense of achievement.

*

By the time they had negotiated the entry to Disneyland and were strolling amongst the mobility scooters that seemed to be the standard form of forward momentum for the other visitors, Chris was back on speaking terms with Ned and Andy.

'It's not as magical as I'd expected' he observed as the three of them stood in line for Pirates of the Caribbean.

'Yeah, I reckon 'the laziest place on earth' would be a better tag line', Andy remarked as they shuffled slowly forward another few steps.

The cordoned off queues that had been originally conceived for the multitude of disabled children who visit the park were jammed with obese mothers shuffling themselves along in courtesy wheelchairs or whining along on scooters, cursing the little girl with cerebral palsy who was taking forever to get out of her wheelchair and into a teacup.

Ned grabbed the 'L.A and surrounds' map that was poking out of Chris's back pocket as they walked out of the Indiana Jones Adventure ride.

'We're pretty close to Huntington Beach here, we should head there after this'.

Ned passed the map to Andy who gave it a quick going over before handing it on to Chris, 'sounds good to me'.

Chris was starting to show signs of fatigue, leaning against or sitting on anything solid and dry.

'What d'ya reckon, couple more rides and then we'll head off?' Andy asked Chris giving him a playful pat on the back. Chris nodded drowsily in agreement as he sat slumped on a fiberglass rock.

*

In front of the main gate Chris and Andy sat on the kerb while Ned walked along the row of shuttle buses asking the drivers for travel advice. His enquiries were sated by the lady driving the fifth bus in the bay whose name tag informed Ned that she was Noreen from Santa Ana, CA. Noreen sent the boys to Harbor Boulevard to wait for the 460.

The bus ride to the coast took them through the L.A they recognised from rap videos and delivered them to the L.A they recognised from Baywatch. They walked across the vast, flat and rather featureless beach to the pier which had been made famous in Australia by way of numerous surf movies showing people 'shooting' it. After a short period of contemplation Chris lay down in the shade underneath the pier, succumbing to his lack of sleep and dignity. Ned, who had up until this point felt indifferent to Chris's weariness, began to feel a sudden surge of empathy for his friend.

'You want me to go and get you a Red Bull buddy?' Ned gave Chris a nudge with his foot.

'Yeah, get me three'.

Ned and Andy walked up to the beachside pathway and followed it north in search of refreshments.

After acquiring Chris's cans of pep the boys took a detour along the pier on the return trip, stopping to watch surfers and survey the coastline that was at once all too familiar and all too strange. The guys out in the surf and on the beach looked just like the guys back at home, the girls laying on the sand with their bikini-top strings untied pecking away at their mobile phones were identical. The pump jacks that dotted the coastline were something entirely unfamiliar, as was the broad and relatively featureless expanse of sand and concrete that flowed north, south and eastward from the shoreline. No sign of the grassy headlands that broke up the coastline at home.

By the time they headed back to Chris's day-nest they'd been gone for nearly an hour. As they walked across the beach alongside the pier Ned and Andy could see that Chris's curled up body was being attended by a pair of old, beach trawling good Samaritans. As they drew near, one of the blokes hovering over Chris looked up.

'This your buddy?'

'Yep' replied Andy walking over to join them.

'He drunk?'

'Nah, he's just a very special boy'. Andy crouched down and sprinkled sand into Chris's ear-hole, causing him to blindly lash out like a tantruming infant before sitting up and frantically shaking his head to disperse the sand.

'I guess I'll leave you to it then' said the stranger as he and his companion made a hasty, shuffling retreat.

'Thanks' called out Ned raising a hand in salute, before presenting Chris with his Red Bull's.

*

After 15 minutes the trio of cans had done the trick and Chris was back to his irritating self as the boys sat at a table in front of a 1950's themed diner waiting for their meals.

'The phone in there is the same as the one in our hotel room' Chris announced as he peered in through the front window.

'This place probably got most of its old shit *from* the Buena Vista, go give it a sniff' Ned suggested to no response.

A waitress dressed in a white poodle skirt and a red apron backed through the door carrying a tray of authentic 50's food for the boys. The leading edge of the white paper hat pinned to her head poked Ned on the cheek as she lowered the tray to the table.

'What's the plan for tonight?' asked Andy as he tried to gather up his authentic burger without spilling its contents onto the footpath.

Ned shrugged his shoulders, his mouth negotiating the oversized bun that were apparently all the rage after the war.

'I'm going back to Platinum' declared Chris, pointing at himself with the French-fry wedged between his greasy thumb and forefinger.

Ned and Andy shook their heads in simultaneous disgust. 'You'll have to go home next week if you keep throwing your money at hookers' opined Ned with a spray of chopped lettuce and breadcrumbs.

'I came here to party, I'm not on a cultural excursion'.

'Well, whatever, you're going on your own' Andy assured him.

'No I'm not, I'm taking Gino'.

'The girls'll love that eh', Andy retorted, 'creepy old Gino rubbin' his scaly old paws all over 'em'.

Chris responded with a dismissive spasm and focused in on his cold-war platter, leaving Ned and Andy to mull over their options.

After another duodenum testing feast the trio took to the streets of Huntington Beach to search for a city bound bus.

*

Back at the hotel, the room had been attended to, both beds were made with a fresh towel folded at the foot. Chris had spirited himself into the shower, his first since they'd left Australia, to pretty himself up for another night of premium priced debauchery.

Ned went through the operation routine with the antique television, finding a local news broadcast. He sat on the floor at the end of the bed and watched with little interest as the anchor rolled through some high school football scores. Andy filed through his bag doing calculations regarding his clothes rotation, now having to take into account the fact that he was one pair of undies down after last night's gravy leak. The news finished up with a piece about an outdoor concert on Santa Monica pier that was starting up for the evening.

'You wanna check that out?' Ned asked pointing to the TV.

Andy looked up from his bag and shrugged his shoulders, 'Yeah, might as well'.

The bathroom door bounced along the tiles as Chris came out looking flushed and smelling like a boys high school changing room.'Last chance boys, I'm leaving in a minute', he announced, adjusting his collar.

'No thanks filthbag' said Andy, cutting off the last syllable of Chris's offer.

'You've gone a bit over the top with the deodorant mate'.

'Nah. It's warm outside and it'll wear off a bit by the time I get there' Chris assured Andy as he gave himself a quick pat down.

A loud, two burst toot from a car horn radiated across the room from the car park in front of the hotel. It was a pre-arranged signal for Chris that it was time to leave. He gave his armpits a quick sniff and checked his pockets before strutting out the door.

'See you faggots later' he signed out in a poor American accent, flipping the bird behind his back as he walked out the door.

Ned shuffled over to the window on his knees and peered down into the car park where Gino stood beside the same taxi that had taken them to the airport earlier. From the 76 across the street Dennis came loping over with his hand to his mouth lighting a cigarette, the lank hair that that half-orbited the bald top of his head flapping with each dainty stride. Gino looked like an undertaker, wearing a black suit sans tie and with far too few buttons fastened on his shirt. In the company of Gino and Dennis, Chris looked like an Adonis and surely that was the point.

Ned turned away from the window and looked over at Andy, now reclined on the bed watching the television. 'What d'ya reckon Gino looks like? I reckon he looks like an Andean Vulture'.

'A cross between an iguana and one of those sick cockatoos with no feathers that they knit jumpers for' Andy replied without hesitation and without taking his eyes off the screen.

Ned nodded in agreement, he was right.

*

In the morning Chris was curled up awkwardly on the sofa, still dressed in his finery and covered in a greasy sheen like the couch had regurgitated him up onto the cushions. Ned checked his phone, it was 8.43am. Today was their last day at the Buena Vista.

'Andy…' Ned gave him a friendly nudge. Andy rolled onto his back and squinted as his eyes focused on the figure looming over him. 'I'm going down to the internet joint near that taco place we went to the other night, you wanna meet me down there in a bit?'

Andy frowned, still gathering himself, 'ah… yeah, ok'.

'Can you bring us down a towel; I might go for a swim after'

'Righto' replied Andy as he inched himself up onto his elbows, he looked over to the snoring mess on the sofa 'I see Dr. Love made it home last night'.

*

Ned planted himself amongst the rows of computers, most of which were attended by musty, unwashed travelers and transients much like himself. He compiled a brief email for his mother summarising his safe and uneventful transit and arrival. Ned then checked in on Facebook and was greeted by:-

Shane 'Big Man' Roach: is colecting scrap metal. will pick up for free

It seemed Shane was still trying to find a way to derive an income without having to work or pay tax. No doubt the back yard would start to resemble a sub-continental slum in the coming weeks. Ned hoped that Big Jake has managed to keep the Pintara keys away from Shane lest it become his scrap metal collection vehicle. It also appeared that Shane had decided to appoint himself a nickname. Ned was certain that nobody called Shane 'Big Man'. 'Fat Fuck', 'Fat Cunt', 'Fuckface', these were all names used in place of Shane Roach, never 'Big Man'. He may well have convinced, begged or paid Nath to refer to him by this ridiculous moniker, but that hardly counts.

Andy strolled in with a towel in each hand as Ned was flicking through some info on Las Vegas.

'You nearly done mate?'

'Yeah' Ned replied, 'Chris stirred yet?'

'He let out a fucking rank fart that I nearly choked on, but that was it'.

'Probably the smartest noise he's made since we've been here. At least we know he's still alive' Ned commented with a light chuckle.

'He didn't smell alive' replied Andy as he threw one of the hotel towels at Ned and turned for the door.

*

The water was cold enough to take Ned's breath away when he dived in under the modest waves. He tried to tough it out as Andy tip toed in, shrieking as water splashed up the inside of his board shorts with each surge of white water. After one last porpoise under the water Ned started marching toward the beach, scooping a hand-shovel full of water onto Andy's dry, cold-tensioned back. There was an absence of wind that made it possible to lay on a towel and drip dry in the sun without the risk of becoming a human sand-schnitzel.

On the promenade all the great Californian clichés converged. Musclemen, pumped and preened, strutted about while skateboards and bikes rolled past. There were even people roller-skating, something that had long been a frowned upon public activity back home for anyone over 12 and with a shred of dignity. There were outdoor basketball courts being used for basketball, something the courts at Binnara Point hadn't been used for since the initial excitement wore off a few short days after they opened. It was all very artificial as far as beaches go, but in its way it was nice. There was a certain lack of self-consciousness that made everyone more comfortable in their skin, you could always point at someone else and say 'at least I'm not as fucked as that guy'.

Andy was sitting up on his towel, shivers still winding down, facing away from the bulk of the crowd towards the ocean.

'My brother should come and live out here, he could be one of these blokes' Ned said, pointing to a man dressed as Spiderman and charging people to have their photo taken with him.

Andy glanced over his shoulder 'yeah, he wouldn't even need a costume'. He spun around and joined in observing the spectacle of the boardwalk. A dozen or so metres further down the boardwalk a man wielding a set of moose antlers was also posing for photos, though his were free of charge.

'You looking forward to Vegas?' Ned asked, eyes still glued to the madness in front of him.

'Yeah, I'm looking forward to a new hotel. I think it was a bad idea letting Chris take care of that stuff'.

'Probably' agreed Ned 'but I doubt we'll spend much time in the hotel'.

*

Back at the Buena Vista, Chris had vanished from the sofa leaving only crumpled velour and a damp patch of neck sweat on the arm rest. It was midafternoon and the sun shining through the window highlighted the dust that floated about the room and had settled on all the flat surfaces. A piece of notebook paper sat next to a patch of disturbed dust on the table between the two beds.

I've gone out for the day, don't know when I'll be back. The bus to Vegas is at 10

Tomorrow morning in Koreatown. I'll be back in time. Dennis will give us a ride.

Eat a dick, Love from Chris xxoo

Ned I've got your sunnies.

'Chris has fucked off for the rest of the day' Ned called out to Andy who was in the bathroom, 'apparently we've got to get on a bus tomorrow morning in Koreatown'.

The pipes behind the wall hissed as the toilet flushed, Andy walked out of the bathroom with a look of mild surprise splashed across his face 'Koreatown hey?'

Behind the wall the hiss narrowed to a shrill whistle as the toilet cistern filled at the speed of seasons.

*

Shortly after 5am Chris wobbled through the hotel door after a lengthy struggle with the lock. Charity, or perhaps it was Suzy since she wasn't on the clock, was pinned under his arm like a crutch. They zigzagged across the room in a spastic waltz before crashing onto the sofa.

'I hope you boys are all packed' Chris bellowed, with the goofy smile of a 10 year old who's seen his first tit stretched across his ridiculous face. Charity sat forward on the couch, well aware that waking two sleeping people in such a manner was, in most circles, considered rude.

Ned tilted his head forward from his pillow enough to see what was taking place across the room.

'What time is it?' Ned muttered through the concertinaed bed sheet in front of his mouth.

Chris looked at him with pupils like bathroom plug-holes, the goofy grin still frozen on his face. He shook his head slowly from side to side 'morning time'.

In the double bed Andy had now stirred, poking one eye out from under his pillow.

'It's ten past five' Charity whispered redundantly.

'I love you' Chris cooed, grasping Charity's upper arm and giving her a gentle shake which she responded to with a giggle straight out of a porno.

Andy sat up in his bed rubbing his eyes and yawning, 'Charity' he said, acknowledging their guest pleasantly, 'you still fleecing this dumb prick?' He then rose and walked into the bathroom, sneaking a glance down Charity's ample cleavage on route. Chris gave him a snarl and moved to speak but his brain wasn't playing along.

'We won't have to leave here until about 8.30' Ned carried on, still just a head resting on top of the sheets.

Chris's head flopped down, his chin resting on his chest and his eyes narrowed, 'D-Unit is driving us to the bus stop at 7.30, he has shit to do'.

'I can't believe your leaving me', Charity cried, like a z-grade actress.

'Don't worry baby, I'll be back, I'm gonna marry you!' Chris replied sitting up excitedly. Charity rewound her laugh track and let fly with another robotic, shuddering porn giggle.

'I'm gonna take her 'round the world with me!'

Andy exited the bathroom in time to hear Chris's last bold statement. He cast an exaggerated look at Ned and shook his head dismissively, 'you two need to shut the fuck up' he declared calmly before returning to bed.

*

Dennis, or 'D-Unit' as Chris had taken to calling him, drove aggressively up Venice Boulevard hunched over the wheel like a short-sighted meerkat that had been spat out by a hyena. The ash from the rollie burning between his orange fingertips sprinkled over his jeans as he jerked the wheel left and right. Between his thighs rattled a can of fruit punch flavoured Four Loko malt liquor.

'Chill out mate, what's the rush?' asked Andy with a hint of panic as he flopped about in the passenger seat like a crash-test dummy.

'I got places to be kid, things to do', replied Dennis, looking at Andy intensely and taking a drag from his rollie.

'Whatever mate, just keep your eyes on the road, please'.

Dennis flicked the remnants of his cigarette out the window and took a slug from his can before returning to his scoliotic driving pose.

The ride in the back seat, whilst frightening, was slightly less tumultuous. Charity was wedged between Chris and Ned and was absorbing much of the sideways momentum.

'You got my sunglasses Chris?' Ned asked during a lull in the swerving.

'Ah, I don't think I do mate, shit got a bit crazy last night, not sure where they are… I'll get you some new ones'. He gave Ned a consolatory pat on the shoulder with his hand that was stretched across the back seat, ensuring Charity was locked within his pheromone range.

The harrowing journey came to a halt at a set of traffic lights on the corner of Normandie and Venice where Dennis insisted they get out as this would be the closest he would be going to their bus stop. While the boys frantically threw their bags onto the sidewalk trying to get away before the lights changed and Dennis sped off into the smog, Charity stood by the roadside dodging bags and attracting the honks and hollers of the morning commuters. As Dennis tore off she blew him a cocked-knee movie kiss, the kind that the recipient would catch and put into his breast pocket. In Dennis's case it probably just gave him an uncomfortable erection that made his malt liquor can shift between his thighs.

Ned produced the map that he had dug out of Chris's dirty jeans before they left, 'if we follow this road north we should be right'.

The boys gathered up their bags and started trudging up Normandie Avenue, alongside Normandie Park and towards Koreatown, Charity fluttering behind them with black stilettos dangling from her hand.

'Are we gonna stop for some breakfast?' panted Chris, beginning to buckle under the strain of his bag and his three night binge.

'I think we should find the bus stop first, then grab a feed. The last thing we want to do is fuck this up and miss the bus'. Ned replied authoritatively.

Chris looked like he was going to cry, all the muscles in his face pushed to the centre so he looked like a foetus. He let out a sorrowful howl as he reluctantly trudged further up the road.

It took over half an hour for the group to reach the Koreatown bus stop on West 8th Street, by which time Chris was emitting a constant, feeble drone of self-pity and Andy had taken to kicking his bag along the footpath. Charity had remained quiet as she toddled along barefoot, now that the boys had reached their destination she was at a loss as to how to proceed. Ned consulted the map; they were still a good few miles from Hollywood.

'Chris, I think you're going to have to fork out for a taxi for your missus'.

Chris was slumped against a wall by the bus stop, hugging his knees and gazing up to the heavens in the throes of a substantial comedown.

'Chris' Ned repeated, jabbing at his thigh with his foot.

Chris's head rolled to the right and he looked up at Ned, 'Wha?'

'Charity needs money for a taxi'.

Chris propped himself onto his left buttock and pulled out his wallet then thrust it towards Ned, 'three-six-five-six'.

'Hey?'

'three-six-five-six', Chris shook the wallet, 'take it'.

Ned took the wallet from Chris's hand and scanned the immediate area for an ATM, spotting one in the wall across the street beside a key-cutters.

Ned withdrew twenty dollars and gave it to Charity. Chris mustered up the strength for a romantic farewell and it was all class, a tongue heavy kiss iced with a firm squeeze of the arse sent Charity fluttering off into morning sunshine.

*

It was when he reached the third step up into the bus that the sickly, stale assault of freezing cold recycled air backhanded Ned's sinuses and sent a searing needle of pain through his eyeballs. He led his team to the back of the bus, close to the toilet that all three of them were sure to be frequenting.

Ned threw his bag into the shelf above the seat and wedged himself into the back corner. Andy rifled through his bag and pulled out a towel. He sat down at the opposite end of the back row of three seats and wrapped the towel around his shoulders, 'it's fucking freezing in here, what's the go?'

Ned shrugged his shoulders, his arms crossed to fend off the cold, 'no idea mate'.

Chris collapsed silently into the two seats located directly in front of the toilet door oblivious to the cold. The bus gradually filled with a wide assortment of desperado's. A number of rough characters straggled aboard, intent on coming home rich or not at all, no bags, just a head full of shitty dreams. There were a couple of party groups on board, a bunch of forty and fifty-something women all the shape of frozen chickens and wearing shirts emblazoned with 'Patty's 50th' occupied the front few rows of the coach. The second party group consisted of eight bloated and balding Englishmen of indeterminate age on a stag week in the old colonies. The remaining seats were filled with a smattering of old, young, black, white, poor, quite poor and fucking poor, all keen to win the small fortune that they couldn't make in three lifetimes of minimum wage work.

When the coach finally grumbled to life the air-con kicked up a notch, Ned closed his eyes for fear that they would freeze over. As the bus rolled out into the brownness the bucks show hooligans let out an unruly cheer and began a chant based around the groom-to-be enjoying sex with ugly women.

As they drew further out of L.A County, the scenery got browner and the houses got further apart and eventually mobilised. The landscape was vast, hilly and for the most part, empty. It was not dissimilar from the desolate interior of the boys own homeland. Ned's head jack hammered against the window glass as the bus roared along the interstate 15 at seventy miles an hour and thirteen degrees Celsius. Andy and Chris had long fallen asleep as the bus crossed the border into Nevada and immediately past large, gaudy casinos built right on the state line to service those looking for one last gaming fix before leaving Nevada or those too impatient to wait for Las Vegas, half an hour further up the highway. After several more miles of mostly empty desert the exaggerated and insane skyline of Las Vegas erupted from the horizon like a shiny boil. The bus made its way through the low-rise fringes of the city and through the shimmering, heaving mess of the strip before releasing it's snap-frozen cargo in the middle of the old Downtown area.

The shudder that accompanied the bus engine winding down woke Chris and Andy, both of whom seemed rather surprised to find themselves in a rather unremarkable looking car park behind a battered looking brick hotel. The heat that greeted them as they disembarked the bus was a welcome relief; it was dry and came at them from all angles.

'This doesn't look right' said Chris as he scanned his surroundings through squinted eyes, looking for the glitter but seeing only dusty bricks and concrete. He cast a stern gaze at Ned, 'Where the fuck are we?'

Andy slid his backpack over his shoulders, 'this is Downtown Vegas buddy'.

'It looks shit'.

'It is shit'. Andy pulled a brochure out of his pocket and slapped it against Chris's forehead before handing it to him.

Chris looked down at the 'Vegas Baby' brochure in his hand, 'so where's all the fancy casinos and fountains and shit?'

'We drove past them, they're back that way?' Ned answered, 'it looked walkable, which one are we staying in?'

'Excalibur' Chris replied, unfolding the brochure and gave it an authoritative snap.

'Let's just get a taxi, I'm fucking sick of walking' Andy interjected, 'I'm gonna wear-out my thongs'.

*

The air conditioning in the taxi was a far more reasonable temperature, merely taking the edge off the heat rather than eliminating it violently. The taxi cruised southward and on to The Strip, the halting journey allowed Chris and Andy to soak up the sights they'd missed on the journey in. The man-made canyon of debauchery was packed thick with foot and road traffic, all taking up more of the space around them than they were entitled to. As they carried on further and further south, past all the landmark casinos, the view out the windscreen began to thin out.

'Where is this place?' asked Andy as he looked out the window to a gradually less spectacular Las Vegas Boulevard.

Down by the airport' came the reply from behind the safety-glass pod the taxi driver sat inside, 'we're gonna be there in a minute'.

It wasn't unimpressive. In any coastal town back in Australia it would have looked positively luxurious but here, in Sin City, in the shadow of the epic MGM Grand, it looked like one of the big resorts' red-headed stepchild;

hidden away, crying for attention, one snubbing away from a gun- massacre. The boys stood on the sidewalk looking at the hotel, imagining the magical things that might take place inside.

The room, which had a balcony overlooking the pool area, contained two double beds and was, compared to the Buena Vista, the height of luxury, on par with one of Saddam's palaces when it came to desert opulence.

Keen to explore, the boys dumped their bags and headed for the pool, via the casino floor. It was like a giant RSL. Seizure inducing poker machines trilled away in every direction. Old ladies shuffled about between machines, the buffet and the lavatory. And the carpet, which resembled a deftly arranged, repeating vomit, was perfect for masking the many spills and ejections that it would be in receipt of daily. They followed the backlit signs through a maze of hallways filled with gift shops selling a variety of branded shit, and chain restaurants also mainly selling neatly packaged shit.

The boys finally reached the pool area as the sun threatened to dip below the hotel rooftop. The pool was fairly empty save for a few kiddies and mums wallowing about and some beer-bellied middle aged men lying on the deck chairs like stranded whales.

Andy dumped his gear on an empty deck chair and dived into the pool, sending a merciful and relieving spray of water across the bloated whales drying out poolside. Chris and Ned took a more gentle route into the water, sliding in like a pair of crocodiles and making for the hot-tub in the centre of the pool.

'So what's the plan of attack?'

Ned held aloft a fifty dollar note 'I'm gonna gamble with this and then we'll head out to The Strip. Whad'ya reckon?'

'Sounds like a plan' nodded Andy, who was buttoning up his 'good shirt', having deemed the evening's outing worthy of long sleeves and a collar.

Chris was struggling to find something suitable to wear and resorted to giving the clothes he'd worn the previous night and all day today a dry clean with a can of deodorant.

'Aren't you gonna have a shower?' Ned enquired as the room filled with a scented mist that threatened to set off the fire alarm.

'Don't need to, that swim cleaned me up'.

'It didn't' Andy interjected, producing the only pair of socks he packed for the trip, neatly turned, out of his bag.

The boys psyched themselves up in the elevator down to the gaming floor and strode through the forest of pokies looking every part like confident and seasoned casino demons.

'I'm keen for a bit of blackjack fellas, whad'ya say?' proposed Ned.

'Yeah, cool' replied Chris with a clap of his hands and vigorous rub of anticipation.

'Fellas' said Andy calmly, 'there's something I'd like to do first, come with me'.

The mystery of this announcement took Ned and Chris by surprise, they followed quietly as Andy strutted between the rows of card tables and stopped at the first of two large roulette tables in front of the medieval themed bar area. He reached into his pocket and produced a rather thick wad of folded notes.

'What's that?' asked Chris, somewhat taken aback.

'Five hundred bucks boys, check this out'. Andy leaned through the ring of players and over the table, casually dropping his wad on the red diamond. Ned and Chris looked on in shocked awe as Andy took his place at the side of the table and waited for the spin. They could hear the ball purr along the rim for a short eternity before clattering into a pocket. Andy's eyes remained fixed on the wheel as it spun increasingly slower before revealing its prize. Ned and Chris stared at Andy in wide-eyed anticipation, waiting for a smile, a tear, whatever.

'27 Red' called out the croupier, Andy rocked around and gave the boys a double thumbs up accompanied by the kind of open mouthed grin that can only be aroused by free money or free pussy. He about-faced and waited as the croupier dealt him out $1000 worth of chips before smugly walking away from the table, chips aloft.

'Whatthefuckwasthat?' shrieked Ned rapid-fire, slapping Andy on the back.

'Just something I've always wanted to do' replied Andy still afflicted with a goofy-grin.

'You're my fucking hero mate' insisted Chris who was bounding around in front of Andy like a border crossing money-changer.

The boys marched back toward the blackjack tables to partake in some slightly lower risk activities. Andy was now exuding some sort of newly acquired alpha-male aura after his bold display and led the pack confidently as they passed the ten dollar tables and were on route towards the three dollar tables that warranted banner advertising at the front of the casino.

'Hang on fellas' Ned chirped, interrupting the procession, 'we should play on the five buck tables, those three buck tables are for pussies. If we each play fifty we'll get at least ten hands'. Ned eyes darted from left to right, Chris to Andy, as he waited for a response.

Chris just looked at Andy, ready to pounce onto his response like a spineless sidekick. Andy slowly began nodding his head in the affirmative, 'OK, I see what you're saying'. Chris joined in on the nodding, but far more rapidly like a neglected dog trying to please his master.

They spotted a table with three free stools and bought into the game. The dealer was a statuesque blonde who looked to be in her late-thirties and had been rocking the same glam-rock hairstyle since high school. Her name tag said that she was Jana from Yugoslavia. Ned stared at the name tag, he was certain that there was no country called Yugoslavia anymore, maybe she was from Yugoslavia, Ohio or Yugoslavia, Pennsylvania? Ned thought better of questioning this and instead concentrated on the cards. Ned sat in the centre of an arc of five stools, to his right sat a thin, little Asian woman with a salt and pepper bob and wearing a foam-rubber visor on her head like she'd just come in from a game of tennis. To her right sat a heavily built man rocking a solid beard and a sleeveless t-shirt, he looked like a more hirsute, Roseanne-era John Goodman. Unfortunately for the boys their novice status became abundantly clear when they were scolded after the first deal for putting both their hands on the table. Jana corrected them in an accent straight out of a vampire movie, thus answering Ned's earlier musings.

'You must only place one hand on the table sir, also no cell phones on the table'.

'Sorry' all three boys replied in a staggered round.

'It's our first time' Chris added with a nervous giggle.

'Is ok' Jana replied with a hint of a smile.

After a couple of poorly played hands Jana and the little Asian lady took pity on the boys and began offering advice in clichéd accents.

'You stay, you sixteen, she only twelve' the Asian lady offered.

When Andy attempted to hit on an ace and a nine Jana politely informed him that he had twenty and should probably stay. A waitress came by and took some orders, when informed that all drinks were complimentary Chris was visibly moved and immediately mentally filtered through all the drinks he was afraid to order all of his life up until this point.

'Johnny Walker, Blue Label,' his excitement was barely containable as he continued, glancing over to the others to make sure they were noticing how cool he was, 'two ice cubes… and a dash of water'. The waitress, her best years well behind her and no longer seeing the need to be pleasant, wrote down the order with a look of contempt, adding 'asshole' to the end. Ned and Andy's requests for beers were much more graciously received.

'Y'all from Australia or New Zealand?' boomed hairy John Goodman from the end of the table, having just ordered himself another beer.

'Australia' replied Ned, nominating himself as international spokesman for the evening.

'I been to Australia, and New Zealand, in the Navy' added John Goodman, pointing to a messy tattoo on his shoulder.

'You don't happen to have a brother who-s a cab driver in LA do you?' Ned asked.

This drew a confused look from Hairy John Goodman who continued, 'Perth then Melbourne, Brisbane, Auckland then we went up to the Philippines. You guys are crazy out there in Australia, crazy...' his spiel was halted by Jana dealing out another lot of cards.

'Stay' the little Asian lady waved her hand over her cards.

'Stay?' Ned repeated in the form of a question.

'Stay' Andy parroted confidently.

'Hit me' Chris declared, slapping the table.

'You must take your hand off the table sir' Jana replied before dealing another card

'Sorry' Chris replied sheepishly

'Bust' Jana announced nonchalantly before scooping up Chris's cards.

By the time the waitress had dispensed the order Chris was down to his last five dollar chip. He took a slug of his top shelf specification and threw down his lonely red disk.

Jana scored an ace and flipped over a king, clearing the table, offering a shrug of the shoulders and a smirk as way of an apology.

'Fuck this, how much longer are you boys gonna play?' Chris snapped frustratedly.

'Chill out buddy' Ned reasoned, 'there's no rush, we've got free drinks, these guys are cool' Ned pointer over his shoulder with his thumb, drawing a nod of acknowledgement from John Goodman.

'What am I supposed to do, I don't have any more money?'

'Go for a walk mate, sit in the bar' Andy suggested, 'we won't be long'.

Andy's dominance from the roulette was still pervasive and Chris slunk to the bar like a naughty dog.

Chris's departure coincided with the departure of Jana who tagged out, to be replaced by Jenny from Henderson.

The boys had a good run with Jenny, winning quite a few hands while Chris watched on forlornly from the Galahad Bar. Chris's place at the table was now being occupied by an intense looking Indian man who was pounding back the Red Bulls with reckless abandon. He became agitated with Andy a number of times when he received a bad card after Andy had hit.

'Come on man, we're supposed to be playing as a team' the Indian man snapped, somehow managing to perspire in the ultra-fresh climate of the casino floor.

'Chill buddy, how many of those Red Bulls have you had?' Andy demanded calmly.

'Too many, I've been awake for like three days, I'm down six grand!'

'Jesus' Andy replied under his breath, raising an eyebrow to the rest of the gang at the table.

Aside from the Indian guy, the rest of the table was enjoying incredible luck, Ned was up over $200 and Andy was in the same ballpark as they slugged back their third free beer.

In the middle of another promising hand Chris's head appeared between Ned's and Andy's.

'Seriously boys, I've been waiting for ages, let's go party somewhere', his brow, furrowed in sadness and frustration, protruded like that of a great ape.

Ned checked his phone, careful to keep it well away from the table and the ire of Jenny, who unfortunately for all, was drawing near a dealer tag-out. It was getting on for 11pm, they'd been down here for several hours but the lack of clocks and windows had distorted reality quite successfully. Ned could now understand how Mr. Intense sitting beside Andy had managed to lose three days, six grand and part of his mind in this never ending, psychotic funfair.

'A few more games mate, look' Ned hammered his pile of chips on the table to emphasise his success.

Chris looked hopefully at Andy, hoping for a more pleasing response from his liege.

'Couple more mate'.

Chris's shoulders sank and he trudged back to the bar, his shoulders remaining slumped and his head bowed like a man being hoisted unconscious from the sea.

'You fren look sad' the little Asian lady whispered to Ned, pointing over to Chris, staring at them from the corner of the bar.

'He is sad' Ned whispered back.

Jana tagged back in and the waitress returned for another order and collected the empties. Mr. Intense ordered another Red Bull and sat twitching, impatiently waiting for a change of fortune, his knees bouncing away under the table like a jackhammer.

'You fella's been to San Diego?' John Goodman asked after Jana wiped everyone out with a twenty.

'Nah, just around LA so far'.

'You fren still looking at you'

'You should check it out, I've lived there twenty years. You got Tijuana just across the border...' John Goodman gave Ned a wink, and then cupped a pair of invisible breasts in front of his own ample chest.

'Look you fren!' the little Asian lady said louder, slapping Ned's arm with the back of her hand. Chris was sitting with his head on the table like he'd been taken out by a sniper.

'He's ok, he's just having a sulk' Ned assured her.

After a few more deals Ned and Andy were in possession of some freshly arrived beverages and Chris stormed towards them with an ultimatum.

'I'm out of here now, are you cunts coming or what?' The unexpected dropping of the c-bomb caused a halt to proceedings at the table as all in attendance looked on slightly taken aback.

'Not yet mate' Andy replied. Ned shook his head.

'Fuck ya's then'. Chris stormed off towards the exit, destination unknown.

*

Several hours in, Ned and Andy had fallen victim to the mindfuck tactics of the casino. They'd imbibed an endless stream of free booze and they'd forgotten that the coloured plastic disks in front of them represented currency. Ned was now placing bets based on colour patterns of chips, forgetting that the green ones were worth twenty bucks each. Fortunately his luck was in and his once modest pile was now rather impressive. Mr. Intense had made two runs to the cash machine and was starting to succumb to his distress and the countless stimulation drinks as he sat, a quivering mess at the end of the table, reacting to each hand as though they were electric shocks fired straight at his scrotum.

John Goodman looked to be faltering, his head dropping from time to time and his grip on his beer bottle becoming more and more fragile. The little Asian lady was still rock solid, guiding Ned to a small fortune as her own pile grew, perhaps it was her visor that somehow made her impervious to the constant distractions and trickery that the house flung about freely. The cause and effect nature of the drinking had sent Andy on to a toilet break that had gone on for quite some time. It must have been twenty minutes since he staggered off with his chips rolled up in the front of his shirt like an infant marsupial.

It wasn't long before Mr. Intense was down to his last few chips; he made the bold move of placing all of them, four in total, onto the table in a last desperate flail at salvation. He landed a five and a six, Jana, in her third stint at the table sat on eighteen.

John Goodman, who had taken to non-verbal cues when requesting cards, knocked on the table and scored a king.

'Twenty four, bust'.

Mr. Intense made a noise like he was trying to swallow a nail.

The little Asian lady was sitting on 19 and waved Jana from Yugoslavia away. Ned looked blankly at his ten and seven, unable to comprehend its total.

'You hit, she eighteen already'.

Ned looked up at Jana and gave her a nod. Six.

'Tventy three'.

Jana scooped up Ned's cards and looked at Mr. Intense who was already frantically motioning for her to sling him a card, his knees pumping up and down like F1 pistons. Another six. Mr. Intense swallowed another nail. Seven.

'Fuck my life! Fuck! My! Life!' He stood up and paced about in a three foot circle. A man in a satin backed waistcoat came and informed him that language of such nature was not welcome at Excalibur Resort and Casino. Mr. Intense stopped pacing, looked at the gentleman in the waistcoat and turned about, arms crossed across his chest, and walked away with a face that looked like his skull was trying to burst out.

'He crazy, too stress out' the little Asian lady said nudging Ned with her elbow.

The ruckus had rattled John Goodman out of his pre-slumber and after a taking a moment to reacquaint himself with his surroundings he took a sip from his beer and swirled it around in his mouth.

*

Ned looked at the empty stool beside him; it must have been at least an hour since Andy left for a toilet break. He was left at the table with the little Asian lady and a wobbly couple who'd taken Mr. Intense's stool at the end of the row. Another beer arrived, and Ned sat, a blurry eyed passenger outside of time.

When John Goodman stood up and clumsily gathered his chips Ned glanced at his phone, 4.08am. He'd been perched at the last five dollar table for nearly nine hours; even the little Asian lady was starting to look weary. Ned stood up and for a second, the casino spun around him like time-lapse film footage, it had been hours since he'd last been on his feet. When his eyes regained focus Ned grabbed his chips by the fistful and poured them into his jean pockets. He wove his way toward the cashier, following the spatter pattern of the carpet as it meandered across the floor. At the counter, behind a wall of Perspex sat a goblin-like creature in a waistcoat and bowtie, maybe he was a man once but the graveyard cashier shift at the Excalibur had devolved him. Rodrigo from Fountain Valley CA. looked on blankly as Ned pushed his pile of plastic through the slit between the counter and the enclosure. Rodrigo totaled the chips robotically and counted out $435 onto the counter-top which Ned balled up and jammed into his jeans.

*

Ned opened the door to the hotel room to find it undisturbed. It seemed nobody had been back in since they had left the room nine hours earlier. After a quick shit Ned headed back down to look for Andy. As he exited the lift on to the ground floor Ned caught a glimpse of the 24-hour all-you-can-eat buffet out of the corner of his eye and decided to swing by. At half past four in the morning the buffet was fairly empty, there were several boisterous characters gorging on fried food after a long night on the tiles and a hyper-obese man who could well have been in Las Vegas on an eating vacation. Ned piled his plate high with a variety of golden-brown coloured foods and took his place at a table with a view of the rotisserie. After getting his fill of deep fried everything Ned took his greasy digits out on to the gaming floor. He did a lap of the room which was still disturbingly busy. Elderly, partially mobile couples sat side by side at the slot machines, some were the stereotypical early risers no doubt but a great many must have been lost, confused and bewildered by the endless arctic summer provided by the casino.

Ned scoured the rows of slot machines with a deep-fried chicken drumstick in his hand, looking for a straight spine and skinny legs. It was the row of machines closest to the main entrance where he spotted him, sitting with his shirt unbuttoned and a crust of vomit on his right cheek that looked like an uncooked omelet. As Ned drew nearer he saw that Andy was barefoot, his shoes and socks were sitting on the floor in front of him. More raw omelet sat drying on the crotch of his jeans.

'What's going on buddy?'

Andy turned slowly, 'hey mate'. His breath smelt like the warm water at the bottom of a bin.

'What happened here?' Ned asked, waggling a finger over the mess.

'Shit got crazy man, I went in there for a bit' Andy croaked, pointing to Camelot, the Excalibur's attempt at a nightclub, 'and now', he looked down at the bedraggled mess below his neck.

'Carlos?' Ned asked knowingly.

Andy nodded and tapped the spin button on the slot machine.

'Did you see Chris?'

'Nah', Andy sent the icons spinning again.

'What did you do with the cash?'

Andy pointed to a plastic cup sitting between his slot machine and the one beside. Ned peered in; there was what looked like about 4 bucks in quarters, a whistle and some stray vomit.

'Where's the rest, you know, from the roulette?'

Andy fired a finger pistol at the pulsing screen in front of him.

'Fuck *off*… All of it?!' Ned replied in shock, the kind of shock that surfaces as a giggle.

Andy nodded again, his lips pursed and eyebrows raised like he didn't really believe it himself.

'Fucken Carlos eh', Ned gave Andy a slap on the back. 'I've gotta get some sleep, you coming?'

Andy spun through the rest of his credits, picked up his shoes, socks and cup and followed Ned towards the lifts.

*

The trill of the telephone rocked Ned out of his brief, deep slumber. The clock radio beside the phone said 8.33am. Andy was lying face down on the other bed and remained motionless. Ned looked at the phone for a moment, skimming through the possible scenarios he might be presented with on the other end of the line.

'Hello?'

'Good morning sir, this is Jeremy calling from reception. I'm calling for a Mr. Dobson or a Mr. Roach?'

'This is Mr. Roach'.

'Sir I have a gentleman down here who says his name is Mr. Chris Bastoni, ah… he doesn't have any photo ID, or a room key, he insists he is Mr. Bastoni…'

'It could be' Ned replied, 'he's not up here'.

'Could you maybe come down…?'

'Yeah, I'll be down in a bit'.

'That would be great, thank you'.

At the reception desk stood Jeremy, his artificial smile beaming as he greeted some fresh victims to Lady Luck's fetid bosom. Leaning against the reception desk stood Chris, shirtless, covering his modesty with a price banner from a car yard wrapped around his waist like a bath towel. $2999 Low Mileage A/C.

'What the fuck is this?' chuckled Ned as he zigzagged through the partition in front of the reception desk.

'Mate, crazy story' Chris replied, shuffling his way forward.

'So he *is* with you?' Jeremy chimed in, the disgust faintly veiled by his cheesy perma-smile.

'Yeah mate, unfortunately'. Ned escorted Chris back to their room past a myriad of bemused onlookers, 'You got your wallet, or any money?'

Chris shook his head and held up his bank card with his free hand, 'just this'.

Ned opened the hotel door; Andy was still lying prone and rather lifelessly on his bed.

'Andy…Andy!' Ned bellowed across the room.

'Mrrrphm' came the muffled reply deep from within Andy's pillow.

'Mate, there's something you need to see'.

Andy slowly rolled over and looked at Ned, his face frozen. Ned stepped aside, revealing Chris in his paper skirt which he kept in place with his left hand. A vertically oriented smile spread across Andy's face.

*

'You just got greedy mate', mumbled Andy through a mouthful of waffle.

The all-you-can-eat buffet was in full swing now; there was a queue all the way around the bay Marie for the fresh pancakes being flung out by one of the breakfast cooks at the end of the buffet.

'I thought you were in love with Charity mate, why did you feel the need to fuck those two chicks?'

'Ned, are you fucking serious? Firstly, only a psycho would turn down a threesome and secondly, I was checking two more milestones on my fuck-list, a black chick, or two in this case, and a chick who can dunk a basketball' Chris replied as though it were the most obvious thing in the world.

'So one of your lifelong goals has been to fuck a chick who can dunk a basketball?' asked Ned bemusedly.

'Well they don't have to be able to literally dunk, just really tall, like 6'2'.

'Could they both dunk?' Andy asked, rolling up some bacon in another waffle.

'The shorter one was 6 foot easy, the other one was like 6'3, 6'4 maybe'.

Ned cracked open a banana that had somehow snuck into the fried food bonanza, 'so they both fucked you?'

'At the same time' Chris added proudly.

'And then they said that they had another friend who would fuck you too, but she was in a different hotel?'

'Yep'.

'Then they took you out to a car and... were these guys in the car?'

'Nah, I got in and then the chicks got in and then like 5 seconds later these two massive mothers got in and one of them whipped out a gun'.

'What kind of gun?' Andy asked, stretching out in his chair to aid his digestion.

'Like a Beretta, a cop's gun, like my old one'.

'And they drove you to a cash machine' Ned continued his analysis.

'Yeah, up the other end of town, near where we got off the bus' Chris confirmed.

'How much?' asked Andy.

'I could only get out $800, you know how there's a limit'.

'So why did they drive you out into the middle of nowhere after that?' Ned asked, desperate to sate his intrigue.

Chris shrugged 'to get away I s'pose, so I couldn't dob them in'.

And they left you in just your undies, and with your bank card? Weird'.

'They were gonna take my bank card too but I asked them to be cool and give it back. I asked for my wallet as well but they said no 'cause of the prints' Chris explained with a waggle of his fingers. 'They said they'd chuck it out of the car somewhere and someone might hand it in to the cops if I was lucky'.

'You're lucky they didn't just shoot you in the head' Andy remarked as he pushed his greasy plate to the middle of the table.

'Nah, they were cool, they wouldn't have killed me. I tried to get them to give me a lift back to The Strip but they just bailed'.

Ned and Andy could only laugh at Chris's naivety.

'At least you got those ticks on your list eh mate' Ned reasoned.

'Was it worth 800 bucks, and all of your shit?' asked Andy.

Chris shrugged his shoulders, 'mmm…. Maybe, more like 450, 500'.

By midafternoon all three boys were in their hotel room feeling the full brunt of the previous night's escapades. The room looked like a First World War field hospital; three bodies lay limply, strewn and groaning amongst a dank mess of blankets and clothing. The air was thick with the stench of piss, sweat, bile and regret. Sometime after 4pm Ned attempted to leave the room to acquire some sustenance. He made it as far as the elevator landing before feeling a simultaneous uprush and down rush towards his north and south orifices, sending him scurrying back to the room for an exhaustive evacuation. Ned hadn't done a solid shit since he stepped off the plane in LA. Toilet paper was no longer his friend and his days of quiet contemplation seemed a distant memory.

No-one moved again until nearly 8pm. Andy got up and flicked on the TV, he found the casino's program of events and watched, hoping to see some sort of dinner special or time reversal option where one could have their losses reimbursed.

It seemed that the all-you-can-eat buffet was still the only real option food wise without having to venture outside, thus taking them an uncomfortable distance from a soft surface to collapse onto or a quiet corner in which to throw up. The sound from the TV roused Ned and soon he and Andy were discussing their options. They decided to volunteer Chris for a food run down to the buffet and woke him up to deliver the news, he didn't put up much of a fight, he knew he owed Ned a solid after the mornings events.

After another bowel distressing feed of fried abattoir sweepings Ned set the clock radio's alarm for 9am, tomorrow they would be bussing out of Vegas and back to California.

*

It was another clear desert day, the sun was hot but the heat was more intense from below, radiating off the concrete and bitumen like a convection oven. Ned was starting to regret his decision to walk to the pick-up point downtown. He had concluded that since only Chris had managed to set foot outside the hotel during their brief spell in Sin City, they should walk to the bus, taking in the sights along the way. They had a few hours to kill anyway, and 'the best way to see a place is on foot' and numerous other motivational clichés managed to convince Chris and Andy that this wasn't a shit idea as they were preparing for departure back at the Excalibur.

The sidewalk of The Strip was littered with colourful escort calling cards that were being dispensed dutifully by several migrant workers interspersed along the roadway clad in high-visibility jackets. If you didn't look too closely the scattered cards looked like rainbow confetti, almost decorative, closer inspection revealed censored tits and bright phone numbers trodden into the ground and fading in the sun. There was a large amount of foot traffic, heads flipping from left to right, marveling at the various gimmicks meant to lure them in and relieve them of their money. Everyone was gawping, taking photo's and fanning themselves with fast food coupons and discount show vouchers as they watched the rockets of water firing out of the fountain in front of the Bellagio. It didn't seem like anyone who lived in this city came out in the day time, not in this part of town anyway. Several down-and-outs had taken to selling hyper inflated bottled water to the sweating land-cows from the mid-west that waddled by in their rarely aired summer kit, parting with 3 dollars to briefly replace the fluid that they were permanently mopping from their wobbly necks.

'I already walked past all this bullshit this morning' Chris muttered, trailing a few paces behind Ned and Andy, 'let's just get a fucken taxi'.

'Your dressed this time so it's different' Andy replied as he absorbed the human and non-human marvels that surrounded them.

'We're probably like halfway there anyway' Ned added hopefully.

'We're not' Chris snapped back under his breath. 'So much walking!'

*

Chris was right; it took them nearly two and a half hours to get to the Windsor Hotel in downtown, where the bus back to LA would collect them. When they arrived at the hotel there was still an hour before the bus would leave. Andy and Chris decided to wait in the shade in front of the hotel while Ned went for a walk around downtown. In this part of town you could tell you were in the desert, the buildings were mostly low rise, you could see the brown hills in the distance and the fine brown dirt showed through between the buildings and on the worksites. The stains on the parked cars hinted that you didn't have to go far to be amongst the stones and the dust. Ned found this end of town more interesting than the overt indulgences of the main drag. This end of town had the wedding chapels he'd seen in the movies, the casino's here were plain in comparison to the behemoths further south, their gimmicks were cheap, bordering on sad, like if the guy who lived next door to the Taj Mahal put a plaster gnome and an inflatable pool in his front garden. What they were though is *real*, the grimness of what happened inside these places was visible on the outside. No-one went into these places under false pretenses, they were like cigarette packets with photo's of cancer on the front. It was here that Ned saw the real people of Las Vegas going about their routine, petrol stations, hardware stores and pawnbrokers lined these streets and the fountains here trickled without an audience.

*

The ride back to LA was a different beast to the ride in three days earlier; it had a 'morning after the night before' feel to it. There were no groups in matching t-shirts, though there was a boisterous group of college students who were still riding high after their weekend of pool party shenanigans and a few hours away from the inevitable greying comedown they would fall victim to once the chemicals thinned out. When the bus pulled in to a truck stop at Barstow, Chris inserted himself into this group of frat boys, feeling the need to impress anyone willing to listen with the heroic tales that no longer impressed his travelling companions. By the time the bus arrived back in Koreatown Chris was being celebrated as a foreign dignitary, his tales of misadventure were on their way to becoming folklore.

The arrival back in LA meant that the boys were now playing it by ear, no more of Chris's pre-arranged hotel bookings.

'What's the plan?' Andy asked, watching the bus pulled off into the afternoon.

'Not sure… we could try and get to San Diego, old-mate at the casino reckoned it was worth a look', Ned replied with a shrug of the shoulders.

'Yeah, could do'.

'We can go find an internet joint and find out about getting down there'.

Chris traipsed across to Ned and Andy and away from his new fans, 'these guys said we can crash with them if we want'.

'We're thinking of heading down to San Diego, just gonna head to an internet café to find out about it'. Ned replied, not contemplating the suggestion for a second.

'Oh, ok', Chris replied crestfallen.

Ned and Andy started off for the shopping plaza a block up from the bus stop.

Andy stopped and turned back towards the bus stop 'You coming?'

Chris was still stood at the bus stop deep in thought, he looked up at Andy 'ah, yeah' and followed along.

In the shopping centre they found a mixed business that offered internet, mobile phone repair, snacks and herbal medicine. The place was empty aside from a man leaning against the counter chatting in Korean to the proprietor.

'Are we right to use these mate?' Ned asked the man behind the counter, motioning toward the four computers set up against the back wall of the store.

The man glanced over momentarily and gave a quick nod before returning to his conversation.

'I need to make a phone call, I'll be back in a minute' said Chris as Ned and Andy started making for the back of the store. Chris walked over to the counter, 'is there a phone nearby buddy?'

The man behind the counter looked at Chris for a second and then whipped a skinny arm towards the entry 'outside, phone is near bathroom'.

Chris followed the spindly limb out into the thoroughfare of the mall and disappeared around the corner.

A few minutes later the chair beside Ned's slid out from under the computer desk and Chris flopped down into it. Ned peered across at the neighbouring computer screen as Chris hammered away at the keys.

Send Email 18/04/11

Dear Mum, how are you? I am fine. I lost my wallet in Los Vegas yesterday so if the American cops or something call, you don't have to worry. Could you please ask them to send it to 7 Parkside apartments 1266 North Normandie Avenue Los Angeles California 90027. Don't tell dad.

Love Christopher.

'We're gonna get a train down to San Diego mate, you good to go in a minute?' Ned asked as Chris clicked his email away.

'Huh?'

'We're getting the train, the stations a couple of minutes away'.

'Oh, ah, fellas.... I'm gonna hang up here for a bit, see if my wallet turns up and stuff'.

'Really?' Andy quizzed, thoroughly unimpressed.

'Yeah' Chris nodded, eyes at the floor, 'I can catch up with you guys later on'.

'Where are you gonna stay, with those dudes from the bus?' Ned asked with a hint of concern.

'Um nah, actually I'm gonna crash with Suzy' Chris replied sheepishly.

'Charity?!' Andy blurted, drawing disapproving head shakes from the Korean's by the till.

'Yeah'

'You sure?'

'Yeah'

Ned and Andy looked at each other exchanging doubtful facial arrangements before turning to look at Chris with the same expressions.

'Fuck.... Well we've gotta take off mate, are you heading over there now?' Ned asked.

Chris nodded but kept his gaze low, he knew the boys thought he was a dickhead.

All three headed out to the front of the shopping centre to get a cab to their destinations. At the taxi rank Chris stood quietly observing the oncoming traffic.

'Chris, it's cool mate, we're sweet' Ned said reassuringly, 'right Andy?'

'Yeah' Andy replied tersely.

'Ok' Chris mumbled with a doubtful smile.

A cab sidled up to the rank and the driver leant across the seat and looked at the boys through the passenger window, he pointed down at the seat and mouthed something that ended in cab or car or maybe cap. Ned gave the driver a thumbs up. 'Chris, you grab this one mate, we'll get the next one'.

Chris cast Ned a hesitant look, 'you sure? Nah, I'll grab the next one'.

'Get in mate' Ned insisted, flashing a forefinger at the back door of the cab.

Chris stood motionless for a moment looking at the taxi.

'Man's waiting'.

'Alright', Chris opened the back door and slung in his bag. 'I'll be in touch, we'll meet back up soon once I've got my shit sorted'.

Ned gave Chris a pat on the shoulder, 'righto buddy'.

'Have a good one' Andy added as Chris closed the rear passenger door behind him.

Chris wound down the window and threw out a peace sign to Ned and Andy as the taxi pulled away.

'That was slightly unexpected'.

Andy shrugged 'yeah I s'pose, he's hardly the most predictable prick in the world though'.

Another cab rolled in after a few minutes and Ned and Andy were on their way to Union Station and the southbound rail.

*

'25 bucks seems a bit steep, I only want it for a couple of hours'.

Ned pigeoned his head in agreement, 'it is a bit'.

The boys stood under the awning of Bluey's surf shop at Mission Beach where the waves were rolling small but neat.

'I could probably buy one for this price in Mexico', Andy muttered to himself as he inspected the dinged up old board.

'The bloke might hook us up with a deal if we only want an hour or two' Ned reasoned, taking a quick glance over his shoulder to make sure Bluey wasn't listening in.

Ned and Andy waded in to the shop to find the boss in an attempt to knock down the surfboard hire price. The shop was deserted, Ned walked all the way around the shop once and Andy cut through the rows of clothes in the middle. On his second circuit Ned came across a fellow who may or may not have been Japanese crouching down below a rack of wetsuits.

'Excuse me mate, do you work here?'

The man hurried to his feet, catching himself amongst the neoprene tendrils hanging from the rack.

The guy untangled himself and turned to face Ned, he was definitely Japanese.

'Yeah, sorry buddy, what can I do for ya' he panted rapid-fire in a thick SoCal accent.

'I wanted to borrow a couple of boards for an hour or two, it says all day hire out the front…'

'Yeah, yeah that's cool man, which ones do you want?'

Andy managed to follow the voices through the maze and find Ned mid negotiation.

'Just the old twinnies mate, yeah?' Ned replied, deferring to Andy who nodded in confirmation.

'Sweet, well the boss ain't here boys so if you just leave your ID's you can take 'em out for free'.

'Yeah?... Thanks mate' Ned replied with a beaming smile.

'No problem, I might see you guys out there…. I'm Mike by the way', he offered his hand.

'Ned'.

'Andy'.

'Right on' Mike replied, nodding enthusiastically.

The spray sizzling off the back of the waves stung Ned's face like a swarm of mosquito's as he and Andy frantically paddled through the break. The water was cold and the boys were out in board shorts and feeling every chilled atom kicked up by the wind. Neither of them were especially accustomed to toughing it out in the cold and after nearly an hour Ned's teeth were chattering like a wind-up toy. As Ned looked towards the shore preparing to call it quits he spotted Mike paddling towards them. He raised an arm to Ned and Andy as he popped over a fat face.

'You guys look cold' he said as he paddled up alongside.

'It's fuckin' freezing mate' replied Andy hugging himself, hunched and shivering.

'Yeah man, springtime, not many guys out in shorts this time of year', Mike sat up on his board and swung around to face the waves. 'How long you guys in town?'

'Dunno' replied Ned through chattering teeth, 'probably not long, we're keen to check out Mexico'.

'Mexico's awesome dude, me and some buddies are heading down to Tijuana tonight. Gonna party for a few days'.

Ned and Andy nodded stiffly, the cold gaining the upper hand in the battle.

'Mate, I think I need to head in, it's not good enough to put up with this' Andy said to Ned motioning at the water with a tilt of the head.

'Yeah' Ned replied looking over his shoulder at the beach, 'do we just leave these out the front of the shop Mike?'

'Yeah, just let the guy inside know, your ID's are in the register'.

'Thanks mate' Ned and Andy replied almost in unison.

The boys began paddling for the shore, keen for a reprieve from the chill.

'Yo!' Mike called out from behind them 'I'll leave you guys my number and the name of my hotel in Tijuana at the store, swing by and grab it if you decide to head down'.

'Yeah cool mate, might catch you later then' Ned called back, lifting a pallid hand out of the water and giving a trembling wave.

'Peace!' Mike bellowed two digits raised aloft as Ned and Andy willed themselves ashore.

*

The rest of the afternoon and evening was spent at La Jolla checking out the sights and spotting the moneyed Californians strutting on the waterfront.

On the balcony above them sat tables of middle aged women who looked like they'd been fingered by King Midas, tittering about all manner of shit, pushing out the fake tits, and jangling the fancy jewelry that will never quite make up for the lack of attention they got in high school.

Andy appeared from beneath the balcony with a plate of nacho's and a couple of cans of Pepsi, 'the bloke in there says we can walk across the border'.

This piece of information was quite an insight for two young men who had grown up on a continent that housed a single borderless nation.

*

Ned and Andy arrived at Bluey's just after it opened for the day. Like their last visit the place was empty, all the space that might have been taken up by customers was taken up by rack after rack of clothes, t-shirts, board shorts, wetsuits and towels creating impenetrable curtains of fabric across the space. At the back of the store, behind the counter stood a heavy set gentleman who looked to be in his 60's at least, he was wearing an old pair of Okanui shorts and a stretched out t-shirt that allowed tufts of grey hair to sprout from below the collar. This guy had to be Bluey.

'Hey mate, did Mike leave a bit of paper here for us?' Ned asked trying not to stare at the impressive thatch of hair poking up from between Bluey's shoulder blades.

'Mike, yeah. You the Aussie guys?'

'Yeah, we took a couple of your boards out for a paddle yesterday'.

Bluey lifted up the cash register and slid out a folded receipt, 'here you go fellas, off to TJ huh?'

'Thought it might be worth a look' Andy replied looking at the receipt.

'That it is', Bluey replied knowingly with a faraway look in his eye.

'If it's not too much trouble mate could we bum your phone to call a taxi?'

Bluey's hands disappeared below the register and rattled around a bit before he plonked a phone onto the counter.

The cab dropped the boys off at the parking bay nearest to the border at San Ysidro.

'This is exciting hey? Never crossed a border before' Ned commented, grinning excitedly.

'You've been to Queensland' Andy replied dryly.

'International border smartarse'.

After a short walk, a flash of a passport and a quick unzip of the bags the boys were in Mexico. A great many taxi's greeted them on the other side, sedans, beetles and vans in varying conditions and colours.

A sketchy looking character in an old Seattle Supersonics jersey approached them as they stood looking at the scenery with little idea of how best to proceed.

'Hermano's, hermano's, where you going? You want a ride?' he peppered as he walked toward them open armed.

Andy pulled the receipt out his pocket and read it's scrawling out 'Hotel Posada Tiburon, Emiliano Zapata, Zona Centro. You know where this is?'

'Zona Centro. Jes, you need to take a taxi' the man assured them ' I take jou'.

Andy looked at Ned for guidance; he was met with a shrug and a tilt of the head.

'Righto then', Andy handed the receipt to their new friend and the boys followed him to a beaten blue Nissan Tsuru.

'I have a car like this back home' Ned said quite surprised by the universal nature of vehicle ownership. He liked this guy much more now.

'Jeah man, is a good car. Get in, get in' the taxi man replied as he opened the rear driver's side door.

'Are you Schrempf or did that come on the singlet?' Andy asked as he threw his bag into the back of the car.

'Wha?'

'Is that your name?' Andy repeated, pointing to the back of the jersey.

'This? No. My name is Javier'.

'Harvyay?'

'Jes Jarvier'.

Javier jumped into the front seat and looked at the receipt before balling it up and throwing it on the floor in front of the passenger seat, he was heavy on the horn as he made his way through the sluggish traffic.

'Jou guys here for a party?'

'Ah, just having a look around really mate, not sure what'll go down', replied Ned craning his neck to get a look through the windscreen.

Javier flicked open the glove box, pulled out a card and bent his arm back between the front seats, 'here, jou take my card, jou want girls, weed, coke, seubertia, dog fight, cock fight.... guys if you like?', Javier looked at Ned and Andy in the rear view mirror to gauge the reaction to this last suggestion, 'whatever you like, I hook jou up hermano's'.

They hadn't gone more than a mile before Javier pulled over.

'This is it, Posada Tiburon'.

Ned looked out the window and then at Andy who was fixed on the hotel which looked like something out of Scarface.

Ned nudged open the passenger side door and slid out tight to the car to avoid the intimately passing traffic before arriving as the comparative safety of the sidewalk. Andy gave the roof of the car a drum, 'thanks mate'.

'Don forget' Javier trumpeted through the driver's window, miming an invisible phone to his ear and then taking a toke from an invisible joint before returning, horn blazing into the traffic.

'Fucken hell, we could have walked that in about 10 minutes' Ned exclaimed as he watched the Tsuru disappear up Emiliano Zapata.

'Yeah, better to be safe than sorry though eh. Plus now we've got a hook-up for a cock fight'.

Ned flung Andy a concerned look, 'Serious? You wanna see that shit?'

Andy shrugged, 'when in Rome'. He took a look at his surroundings and a big deep breath in, as though the scent might give him guidance. 'S'pose we better find a phone and give Mike The Jap a call'.

Ned slammed his hands into his pockets like they were on fire, 'Fuck! The taxi driver's still got the bit of paper', a pained expression formed on his face 'also, Mike The Jap? Racist'.

'Sorry. Well let's just check-in here we might spot him and if not, oh well'.

'Righto' Ned replied eager to get out and about.

*

After dumping their gear and taking a key attached to a key ring the size of a house-brick the boys pushed through the heavy steel door out of the hotel and Ned prepared for his first taste of the developing world.

The boys embarked on an intuitive, meandering, walking tour of the area around the hotel. Ned slipped off the footpath into a tourist trap, emerging a couple of minutes later with a 4 dollar pair of Ray-Bans and a Spanish phrase book and dictionary.

'This bad boy might come in handy' Ned stated proudly waving the book in front of Andy.

As they walked up and down the calles and avenidas Ned practiced the recommended phrases in his handy, pocket sized interpreter.

'Donde esta el baño?'

'Cuanta cuesta?'

'Como esta?'

'Gracias'.

'Por favor'.

'You sound just like a real Mexican' Andy quipped sarcastically.

'Thanks mate', Ned replied, returning the sentiment.

*

After their invigorating and eye-opening stroll, Ned and Andy returned to the hotel. As they approached from the eastern end of Emiliano Zapata, a loud American voice filtered through the horns and car engines.

'Yo! Guys!' On the narrow wooden first floor balcony above the hotel entrance Mike stood in a Christ pose with a bottle in each hand. 'Get up here!'

Ned signaled back with an overhead thumbs-up as they passed under the balcony and into the building.

'You guys just get here?' Mike asked as Ned and Andy made their way on to the balcony where Mike and his buddies had set up for the afternoon with an ice-box filled with Tecate and deck chairs at the ready.

'Nah, we've been here for a couple of hours, we lost your number in the taxi but we've got a room here so it's all sweet' Ned replied, checking out the view from the balcony and stepping over the empty bottles.

'Having a big one tonight boys?' asked Andy as he stepped out onto the balcony and made himself comfortable against the flaky wooden railing. He dished out nods of acknowledgement to the other guys present who raised their beers ever so slightly in reply.

'Always' Mike answered before reaching into the ice-box to dish out some fresh beverages, 'what about you guys?'

'Not sure' said Ned shrugging his shoulders, 'maybe…'

'We're gonna try and track down a cock fight' Andy insisted enthusiastically, 'you boys keen?'

Mike and his buddies looked at each other seriously for a moment before a contagious smile did a Mexican-wave around the balcony that said 'fuck yeah we are'.

*

Javier announced his arrival with a car horn recital of the first bar of 'La Cucaracha'. Ned and Andy filed out the door with Mike and his two buddies, Travis and Teeth.

The five of them managed to jam themselves into the Tsuru, which sank half a foot under their weight and groaned as it crept out into the street.

'I fine jou boys a good cockfight, is in Flores Magon' Javier boasted.

'Are you coming the fight too?' Ned asked struggling forward from the crammed back seat.

'Jes, mi senora, her fadder he coaches de chickens'.

The journey out to the cock-ring took half an hour, through the suburbs, gradually thinning out to the southern fringe of Tijuana. Javier pulled up beside a nondescript block of land that was mostly surrounded by a frayed and worn chain-link fence. The last of the daylight had disappeared and a dim light and a small scattering of silhouettes was all that could be seen beyond the wire.

'Is this it?' Andy asked doubtfully

'Jes, here is the pellea de gallos'.

'It looks pretty dodgy' Ned said to the others as they uncrammed themselves from the back of the car.

'Come in, come in. Is fifty pesos'. Javier led the group to a gap in the fence around the corner from the dusty road where the car was parked. On the other side of the gap two young girls, maybe 10 or 11 years old were collecting the entry fee in a bucket. They were being supervised by a boy of about the same age and size who was chewing on a bit of chicken. Perhaps it was one of the losers Ned thought as he deposited his pesos and walked into the sparsely grassed lot. The boys marched on towards the light that was being filtered through a tightly packed crowd twenty metres ahead of them. As they reached the edge of the huddle Ned could see over the caps and cowboy hats into the square, concrete walled enclosure from above which the light was emanating. Three dapper looking Mexicans stood in the square having what appeared to be a light hearted discussion. The floor was covered in dirt highlighted with blood spatter, feathers and shit.

'This place is fucking nuts' said one of the Americans watching over Ned's shoulder.

In front of Ned against the outside of the concrete wall sat several important looking men at a table with clipboards, stopwatches and small wooden boxes. A woman carrying a bucket of beers and soft drinks was doing laps of the ring, 'bebidas, cervesas, frescas' pouring out of her mouth in a cartoonish, monotone loop. Mike followed her through the crowd and returned with a bunch of Pacifico's dangling from between his fingers.

'Looks like the next fight's about to start' Andy noted loudly over the rabble of the crowd.

Two birds were handed over the wall at diagonally opposite ends of the death ring. One diagonal was painted red the other green and after observing the chooks briefly strutting about the ring the men gathered around, began placing bets with each other and with the official bookmaker set up beside the table of officials. The officials, it seemed, were in charge of the time keeping and the spurs to be attached to the feet of the gladiatorial fowl. A third bird was brought into the ring and took a turn stirring up each contestant with chicken smack-talk and aggressive shadow pecking like some sort of pre bout fluffer.

Andy leaned over and shouted in Ned's ear as the crowd banter escalated, 'are you gonna put on a bet?'

Ned kept his eyes glued to the pre-fight show, 'I might watch this one first, get a bit of a feel for it'.

The trainers began plucking feathers from the chickens arse to angry them up before the fight and then it was on. The birds would strut around, eyeing each other off and then launch into a brief flurry of feet and feathers and then repeat the process, it was not nearly as graphic as Ned had feared, in fact he found it quite comical and a tad exciting. After several flurries the chook from the red corner lay on the sand maimed or exhausted, it was difficult to tell. To the great surprise of the five guerros, the trainer of the incapacitated chicken picked up his charge and began administering aggressing mouth to beak resuscitation and plucking more feathers from around the birds cloaca. Even more surprisingly it worked, briefly.

Mike's head appeared between Ned's and Andy's, 'this is some crazy shit dudes, fucking nuts'.

The revived avian was good for a few more furious flutters of aggression before succumbing to some unseen injuries hidden beneath its feathers. The referee, who it seemed was also a vet, called it, time of death 20.25pm. The fighter out of the green corner had been victorious and would live to fight another day while the red corner would end up on a skewer, marinated in chilli oil.

'I'm gonna go and grab a quick feed before the next fight' Ned told Andy as the ring was being cleared for the next bout. He followed the smoke signals towards the neighbouring property where a portable barbeque was set up beside a trestle table. The drink-bucket lady was there making a pit-stop and small children were running about in the dim light shrieking and laughing. As he approached the table Ned attempted to recite the appropriate greetings and phrases in his head.

'Hola'.

'Hola, buenas noches' came the reply, step 1 complete.

'Uno taco por favor'.

'Pollo o carne?' the little woman asked.

'Ummm...' Ned looked at the woman puzzled, 'Ahh...'

The little senora pointed first at the chicken sizzling on the hotplate and then at the dark meat, 'pollo, carne'.

'Oh, ah, carne por favor'.

The lady began building a taco at an impressive speed, 'salsa?'

Ned was pretty sure he knew what this meant, 'si, gracias'.

With that, Ned's first fully Spanish transaction was complete. On the way back to the ringside Ned was intercepted by Javier.

'Ayy, Hermano! Jou like it' he asked enthusiastically, his big smile making his thin moustache invert.

'Yeah man, it's ok', Ned replied with a reassuring smile.

' Ey man, dis is my senora, Nancy', Javier presented a short plumpish woman in heavy make-up standing shyly behind him.

Ned racked his brain, trying to remember the correct greeting, a couple of quiet seconds passed, before bam, 'much gusto', Ned offered his hand.

Nancy softly shook his hand and mumbled something, her eyes flicking between Ned's feet and face.

'She don speak no Eenglish, no worry' Javier blurted dismissively, 'we go see de nex fight'.

Back at ring the fluffer was doing his job on a large majestic looking rooster, gleaming white with a puffed out chest and confident strut. The fans seemed encouraged by this impressive specimen and began waving colourful peso bills about. Ned squeezed back in amongst the guerros where he was able to get a look at the other contender. In the green corner stood an entirely different looking bird, it had fuck all feathers and some epic looking scars where it had been stitched up after previous battles; it was also a lot smaller than the glamour chook at the other end of the enclosure.

Andy noticed that Ned had returned 'looks like everyone's getting on the big fella' he remarked.

'I'm getting on the dinosaur' Ned declared through a mouthful of corn tortilla and donkey meat, 'check him out, he's been in a million fights, that other chooks just a poser. That haggard one looks like a velociraptor, he'll win'.

Ned, Andy and the gringos were shuffling their pesos ready for a bet, they were all quickly pounced on by locals eager to shark the clueless visitors. A young looking fellow who couldn't have been more than 16 or 17 rapped on Ned's arm holding up some notes, 'Quarenta, si? quarenta' he pointed to the big bird in the red corner and then to himself 'quiero el rojo'.

Ned pointed to the velociraptor 'me?'

The young man nodded and held up two sky blue twenty peso notes. Ned nodded and gave him a thumbs up. The two then shook on the agreement. The young bloke had a girl under his arm and was whispering in to her ear, probably about how the stupid guerro had just bet on the sick looking bird in the green corner Ned thought. Andy was negotiating with a chubby middle aged man in a straw hat and Mike, Travis and Teeth were exchanging notes with a group of men standing by the neutral corner on the other side of Andy. After the fluffer was removed and the spurs were selected and affixed the rumble began. There was the standard posturing and shadow strikes before the flash rooster attacked, the velociraptor, true to Ned's theory, was crafty, ducking and weaving to the rear of his opponent then delivering a telling blow. The velociraptor kept his head low and sniped away at his opponent whose once radiant white tresses were soon dirty, stained with blood and dust. Before the first round was complete the larger bird lay dead in the middle of the ring, his trainers frantic attempts at resuscitation came to nothing. The ugly little dinosaur was returned to his cage with a few new war wounds and five new fans.

'Told ya mate' Ned gloated to Andy, 'that cunt had technique'.

Andy nodded with a grin 'it was an impressive display'.

Ned turned to the young fellow with whom he'd made his wager and shrugged 'beginners luck'.

The kid pulled out his forty pesos and handed it over, Ned gave him a pat on the back, 'next time mate'.

'Que?'

'Ah… mucho gusto'. Ned saw the drink lady passing at the edge of the crowd and squeezed himself out, purchasing three beers. He returned to his spot and gave the young bloke and his girlfriend a beer each. Ned held his beer in front of him 'cheers'. The young couple looked at their drinks and then at Ned's, they held their drinks towards him. 'Cheers' Ned repeated.

'Cheese' the young man echoed with a smile.

*

Three quick raps on the door then nothing. Ned raised his head slightly off the pillow before it collapsed back down. Three more raps.

'Guys' came a muffled voice through the door.

Ned started to roll of the bed but heard Andy's feet hit the wooden floor on the other side of the room and rolled back to the centre. Andy opened the door enough to stick his head out.

'Do you guys know where Mike went to?' It was Teeth standing at the door with his bag.

'Nah, not sure mate', Andy pulled his head back inside the room, 'Ned you know what happened to Mike?'

Ned lifted his head off the pillow again, this time with slightly more success, 'Ah, no I don't think I do'.

'Nah mate' Andy doubly confirmed to Teeth, 'are you off?'

'Yeah we should be, I mean he can probably get back on his own but I thought I should check'.

'Yeah right, well if I spot him I'll let him know'. Andy closed the door and returned to his bed, 'so it looks like Mad Mike's gone missing'.

'He'll be alright' Ned replied, looking at a large brown stain on the ceiling above his head.

'Yeah' Andy agreed and lay back on the bed with his feet still on the floor.

They boys eventually headed out for some breakfast and saw Travis and Teeth sitting in the reception area.

'Any luck?' Ned asked.

'Yeah, he ended up in Rosarito with Javier, he woke up on his kitchen floor this morning' Teeth replied with a grin.

'He's on his way over now, fucking tripper' Travis added, looking at his watch.

'Good news I s'pose'.

'Yeah' the Americans replied in unison.

'Alright, well we're off fellas, catch ya later'. Ned and Andy gave the yanks a farewell wave and headed out the door. They were a few dozen metres down the street when Andy stopped 'hang on, I'll be back in a sec', he turned about and headed back to the hotel. After about 30 seconds he popped back out the door and jogged up to Ned, 'Teeth'.

What?'

'Teeth, his last name's Teeth, Jeremy Teeth'.

'So?'

'I've been wondering since yesterday why the fuck the dude was called Teeth, now I know, it was really bugging me'.

*

Shane 'Big Man' Roach: taking bets, best odds, any sport 0431324636

'Fuck me' Ned muttered under his breath, 'Andy check this out', he swiveled the computer screen to the right.

Andy looked at the screen for a few moments and had a chuckle 'I can't see that lasting long'.

Ned had also received an email from Big Jake.

Inbox 23/04/11

Hey bro, hope you're having a good time over in the states. Nothing new here, Shane got hold of your car keys for one of his scrap metal runs but I made him clean it out and I've hidden them now. The silly prick's got a pile of shitty metal under the back awning and a suitcase filled with old TV leads, he's been going around cutting them off the back of old TV's, dickhead. Little Jake says g'day and wanted to let you know that he's started back at footy again, they've got their first game this weekend. Anyway, let us know how you're travelling bro, keep in touch.

'You found anywhere you like the look of?' Ned asked Andy as they scanned the internet for a new destination.

'Yeah looks like there a few spots worth checking out' Andy replied sliding a notepad across the table to Ned with some names scribbled on it.

'You heard from home?'

'Yeah, the old man's scored another job up in Bulwarra Heights, Nana's killing it down at the bowling club, same old shit really'.

'Yeah, same here'.

*

Three days. They were probably the longest three days of Ned's life. When they arrived at the hostel in Sayulita Ned collapsed on to the bunk and didn't move for a long time. He lay there in a confused state of half waking, half sleeping delirium. His sheets smelt like mint mixed with lawnmower fuel. It was midafternoon when they arrived and when Ned came-to the sun was just peeking over the hills behind town. He and Andy had spent two nights trying to sleep either on a bus or at bus terminals on hard seats or hard floors. The first leg of their journey took them from Tijuana to Hermosillo, it was nearly 13 hours but it was pretty luxurious as far as buses go. Plush, cushioned, reclining seats and entertainment by way of small overhead TV's showing the entire Twilight series dubbed over in amusing Spanish voices. Unfortunately, like their previous coach experience, the air conditioner was set to blast freeze. Ned disembarked from the bus in Hermosillo wearing every item of clothing from his bag, he had a pair of jeans on his legs and his arms threaded through his second pair. The temperature change from inside to outside was about twenty degrees, Ned thought his bones might shatter like a car windscreen due to the violent suddenness of the change. The next four hours were spent in the Hermosillo bus terminal trying to ration the bathroom pesos for the remainder of the journey and sneakily dispose of some unwanted baggage in a binless environment. Ned had a couple of books that he no longer had the will to carry and was keen to get rid of them while he was relatively unconfined and he supposed that some other weary traveler with time to kill might appreciate some free reading material. Ned left the books on an unattended table beside a cafeteria that wasn't yet open for the day and wandered out into the waiting arena a few hundred grams lighter. The waiting room housed numerous rows of molded plastic seats, in front of which, behind floor to ceiling glass, the buses sat in a long row. Above each, hanging signs notified passengers of the destinations. Ned made himself a little nest on one of the rows and began doing what the room was built for. A few minutes later an unintimidating security guard wearing a uniform that made him look like a pilot, sidled up to Ned in his nest.

'Disculpe Senor'.

Ned looked up at the security guard with a look of weary confusion. The guard pointed towards the doorway leading back into the main terminal area, 'Olvidas dos libros?'

Ned looked at the door and then blankly back at the guard.

'Eeh, two…' the guard mimed page turning 'book?'

'Oh' Ned replied, 'books, yes, si, um.. I don't want them', he gave the guard a smile, shaking his head.

The guard hurried out into the terminal and returned proudly with the two books. He held them out thrusting them at Ned, 'Jes, jes'.

'I don't want them' Ned repeated, waving his outstretched hands and shaking his head.

'Jes' the guard persisted, nodding enthusiastically, seemingly very proud of his sleuthing skills, keen to justify his grand uniform.

Ned, deciding it wasn't worth breaking the poor bloke's heart, took the books, 'Gracias senor' and put them back into his bag.

Andy had managed to spend the majority of his time in Hermosillo asleep, curved around the armrest between two segments of a waiting pew. His brief period of consciousness allowed him a 4 peso visit to the restroom and a 6 peso packet of luminous corn snacks.

The bus from Hermosillo to Los Mochis was 2nd class. No TV, no toilet, it was an old passenger bus from Bumfuck, Idaho that was spending its twilight years rattling over the dusty roads of north-west Mexico. The ticket in Ned's hand had 10.45 scrawled on it in pencil; at 10:35am Ned gave Andy a nudge and walked outside to row of buses. The overly helpful security guard was leaning against the glass window smoking; Ned decided to give him another problem to solve. He approached the guard and presented him with his ticket.

The guard looked at the ticket briefly and with his cigarette pointed over Ned's shoulder 'Los Mochis, quatorce'.

Ned looked behind him and then back at the guard 'quatorce?'

The guard dropped hid cigarette and twisted it into the ground under his impressively shiny boot. He then licked his right index finger and drew a big number 1 and a big number 4 into the dust on the window beside him 'quatorce' he said smiling.

'Ah, gracias, gracias' Ned said nodding. He walked back towards the doors and banged against the glass, Andy looked up as Ned motioned towards the buses and began walking towards bay 14.

There was an empty wooden bench in front of bay 14 and there was the bus from Bumfuck but that was all. There were no people, no driver, nothing. Ned and Andy sat on the wooden bench looking at the bus waiting for something to happen. At 10:41am one of the undercarriage doors popped open ever so slightly, a few seconds later it opened all the way. Two bare feet appeared from inside the buses belly, followed by two hands that proceeded to dress the bare feet in a pair of socks. Ned and Andy sat transfixed on this rather unexpected development. Two leather shoes fell onto the ground and the feet slid forward revealing a pair of grey slacks and untucked white shirt. Once the shoes were attached a full human was birthed from below the bus. The man tucked in his shirt and looked up, spotting the boys sat staring at him on the bench in front of the bus.

'Los Mochis?'

The boys both nodded.

'Salimos en un minuto' the man said, he then proceeded to open the bus door and jump behind the wheel, there was a short crunching sound before the bus whinnied to life like an old mule.

The driver stepped out of the bus and stood by the door, he waved Ned and Andy over, 'boletas?'

The boys presented two frayed squares of paper that resembled bowling club raffle tickets and boarded the beast.

The bus left the terminal, Ned and Andy were the only passengers for two hours before an elderly couple, each carrying a bucket of eggs joined them. Not even Andy could sleep on this bus, the jarring vibrations made it impossible to rest a head on any part of the interior, every so often a sharp pain would shoot up a nerve bundle in a leg or up the spine after a particularly tremendous pothole or speed hump. The vibrations also managed to shake all and any shit into the lower colon making for a panicky trip. At some point during the ride some of the old couple's eggs were shaken loose and made a sticky mess in the aisle. The highlight of this leg of the journey was the appearance of a small musical troupe on the bus a few stops before the Los Mochis terminal. They boarded the bus and entertained the passengers, who had grown in number as they drew closer to the town, for 10 minutes, scoring a handful of Ned and Andy's pesos for their trouble.

Though still struggling to regain their land legs after the endless vibrations of the 6 hour journey, the boys decided to hop the first available bus south and try to make it to Mazatlan, the next major town along the pacific coast route, thus avoiding the cost of overnight accommodation and hastening their arrival in Sayulita. It was another 2nd class bus and by the end of its run the boys would have spent 24 hours on the road. On the way out of

Los Mochis a lady boarded the bus between stops selling drinks and snacks. Ned purchased some tortilla chips and a bag of orange drink. Andy, ever sensible, bought a packet of pumpkin seeds and a bottle of water.

*

43 minutes. That's how long it took from finishing the bag of orange drink to the first concerning groans escaping from Ned's tortured stomach.

'I feel a bit weird mate, you feel okay?'

'Yeah bud, I'm sweet' Andy replied reassuringly, picking bit of pumpkin seed out of his teeth.

'I think there was something wrong with those chips'.

'Hmmm, it was probably the bag of juice you drank. You shouldn't really drink from bags sold on the street'.

'What?' Ned queried, a gurn of discomfort forming on his face.

'Yeah, I got really crook in Bali from drinking a bag of cordial that some dude was selling on the roadside. It's the water'.

'Why didn't you say anything?'

Andy shrugged his shoulders and continued his dental preening.

Ned's duodenal contractions condensed until it was a constant, hollow churning, like his stomach was sucking on a straw from an empty bottle. Ned shrunk in space over the passing minute and miles, retreating into the foetal position, trying to ride it out. The time between stops seemed to slow down and the time on his phone went metric, stretching out the minutes. He burrowed through his bag and unearthed his Spanish phrasebook and dictionary and filtered through the pages.

Stop.

1. *(halt) (taxi/bus)* parar.

Stomach

1. *(organ)* estomago

   (before n) - pains dolor *m* de estomago

Ned memorised this routine 'parar por favor, dolor de estomago; parar por favor, dolor de estomago'.

Outside the bus the scenery was quite spectacular, the road was cut into a hillside overlooking the ocean, the houses of the villages, whilst modest and often ramshackle, were lovingly decorated and individual, certainly not the boring and unimaginative tract housing of Australia and America. The bus rattled to a halt in one of these villages where a group of old timers mingled by the roadside. Ned took this opportunity to evacuate briefly; he hurried to the front of the bus, 'Donde esta el baño?'

Ned was confident with this phrase, it had thus far served him well.

The driver pointed out the window to some buildings on the other side of the road, 'en la tienda'.

The words meant nothing but Ned dashed across the street in the direction the driver's finger had described. In front of a nondescript concrete dwelling a small sign advertising ice cream identified it as a shop. Inside Ned encountered a sweaty teen sitting behind a small counter beside the door.

'Baño por favor'.

The teen raised a sweaty left arm to the back of the store 'en la parte trasera'.

Ned feigned comprehension and followed the line of the limb to the back of the shop; there was a door next to a shelf filled with cans. Ned opened the door, it was dark, and he couldn't find a light, he felt his way along a wall and found amongst the discarded packaging a sink, he stuck out a leg and felt the cool, redeeming porcelain of a toilet. Ned lowered his head into the bowl and for the first time in his life he made himself sick. His finger went down further than he thought it could ever go, he wretched, this must be how it's done, he wretched again but they were blanks, only thick saliva dribbled into the toilet. Ned took his hand from his mouth and instead just started coughing and straining until eventually a hot, stinging gush poured into the bowl and another and another until he lay on the dark, cool floor, empty like a discarded pool toy.

Back on the bus Ned sipped from Andy's water bottle, trying to erase the brittle, chalky feeling ever present after a hearty up gush. His breath smelt like the bottom pub's piss trough.

The second 6 hour bus trip of the day ended at the glorious Mazatlan bus terminal at 11.35pm. The timetable suggested that there wouldn't be another bus until 7.45am.

8 hours and 10 minutes. That's how long Ned and Andy spent in the Mazatlan southbound bus terminal. The terminal was a massive awning open to the road on one side with rows of wide aluminium seats with plenty of room to lie down. Although it was exposed to the elements the temperature was pleasant enough and crashing here would save them the hassle of looking for a hotel room for 7 hours that would probably be scarcely more comfortable than the metal pews that were their current option. There was an unattended toilet which meant the peso coins could remain in the bag and a 24

hour shop across the street for any snacking requirements. Ned and Andy constructed themselves some quite comfortable beds out of towels and t-shirts whilst a folded over backpack made for quite a comfortable pillow. Andy was snoring away a minute after his head hit his makeshift pillow, while on the bench opposite, the ordeals of the previous days travel meant Ned was soon asleep too.

'Ptt, ptt', a wet slapping sound woke Ned from his desperate kip. 5 or 6 times a minute, 'ptt' then silence, then 'ptt'. It wasn't the sound of rain, it was too irregular and too volumous, more like a leaking pipe, only the sound was moving around the shed, close then far, from in front and then from behind. Ned opened one eye but saw nothing obvious to explain the patter. Andy lay facing into the bench with his back to Ned, on the sleeve of the t-shirt he was using as a top sheet Ned noticed a whitish smudge about the size of a 10 peso coin, Ned opened his other eye, it was bird shit. Ned knew this because a warm, sloppy wad of it just made a 'ptt' on the bench within splashing distance of his face. Above them, attached to the girders of the station roof hung a mesh of chicken-wire Ned had earlier assumed was to stop bats from roosting inside the terminal. It was now acting as a fecal sieve, dropping the nutty shitblobs of the resident birds that had colonised the Mazatlan south bus terminal onto everything below. Ned saw that shit was falling from the roof like slow motion rain; he bundled up his belongings and sprinted to the footpath outside the awning. Andy lay oblivious to the shitstorm as the pitter patter continued around him.

'Andy!' 'Andy!'

Andy opened his eyes, through the perforations in the bench he could see Ned standing out by the taxi-rank with his clothes balled up in his arms. He sat up and looked around, the terminal was empty, the clock above the ticket counter said it was 5.15am. 'What the fuck are you doing?'

'Have a look at the ground mate'.

Andy scanned the floor, he noticed it was now dotted with shiny, wet blobs. He looked at his shirt and his backpack; both were sporting similar, milky stains. 'What the fuck? Where did all this shit come from?'

'Above' Ned replied, poking a digit skyward through his clothes bundle.

Andy scooped up his nest of garments and zigzagged to the safety of the open air like he was outmaneuvering a sniper.

'How long did you leave me there for you prick?'

Ned shrugged his shoulders and said nothing.

'We're even now' Andy muttered, wiping his backpack along the grass beside the footpath.

At 6.30am a man with a mop and bucket arrived and began the daily task of cleaning up the carnage of the pre-dawn deuce blitz. Every bench, countertop and turnstile as well as the whole floor required a thorough mopping before it could be safely used by a public averse to avian droppings. He noticed the boys with their belongings polka-dotted with excrement and had a little chuckle; they obviously weren't the first to be caught out.

7.45am came; the terminal was gleaming clean and open for business. Ned and Andy boarded another American reject for a 5 hour wind to the town of Tepic. The boys tried to use this trip as an opportunity to catch up on some sleep after they were rudely interrupted in Mazatlan, unfortunately Tepic was a kilometre above sea level and so for a good portion of the trip the bus was groaning and straining to climb and with the prime sleeping location of the back seat sitting directly above the engine, it was mission impossible. The ascent also meant that to lie down was to risk rolling off the seat onto the worn and dirt heavy bus floor. On the approach to the town, spruikers boarded the bus, hidden amongst the passengers. A very enthusiastic man had boarded the bus and began aggressively extolling the virtues of some sort of citrus based skin cream, doling out pungent samples to the middle aged women on the bus, promising miraculous rejuvenation, or so Ned assumed, much of the dialogue was lost on him. He did recognise some words - young, excellent and beautiful were being splashed about with reckless abandon. A tiny old lady came aboard selling bags of something that looked like yellow Cheetos's. Ned and Andy decided that these would make a suitable breakfast given the circumstances; they looked tastier than the beauty cream at least. Tepic was a different creature than the other towns they'd stopped in on their way down the coast. It was up high, the air was cooler, they were deep in the jungle now, the arid north long left in their wake. Their arrival in Tepic also signified their arrival in the state of Nayarit, on whose coast lay their final destination. Sayulita was now just 3 hours away, Ned felt as though he could smell it, assuming Sayulita smelt of hot bus engine.

 Down-hill. It matters-not how fast you're travelling, when you go down-hill you feel like you're getting somewhere. The bus that was escorting Ned and Andy on their final leg certainly wasn't going fast as it wound its way down to the coast, but the knowledge that the bus odyssey was almost over seemed to iron out the corrugations and potholes and turn the violent vibrations into gentle massaging fingers. Even the sound of a lady throwing up into a hastily emptied shopping bag failed to dampen the sense of relief and achievement that cloistered Ned.

*

Ned looked in the grubby mirror and noticed that he had a contour map embossed into his skin from the wrinkled bed sheet he'd lay prone on for the preceding 14 hours. His head was like an over-ripe pumpkin. Undeterred, he wobbled out of the hostel and went in search of some bread and eggs, looking like something just escaped from a sarcophagus.

The hostel was located near the edge of town close to the highway. The boys had made a beeline for it when they had arrived the previous afternoon; this walk to the shops then, was Ned's first look at the town. Many of the buildings were brightly coloured and the town was surrounded by lush greenery that snuck into the gaps between the buildings and repossessed any free ground. The town square was a couple of blocks back from the beach and provided a shady social area where children played on beat-up old scooters and skateboards and locals gathered to gossip and giggle at the conspicuous tourists. Ned stopped at a tiendita a block from the beach to pick up his supplies and then continued on the waterfront. The section of beach directly in front of the town was fringed with small restaurants and shops and a surfboard hire place was set up on the sand. Aside from this small interruption of civilisation, the rest of the beach was fringed with forest and rounded off at each end with a rocky, green-topped headland. Where the road ended and the beach began several locals were setting up small stalls selling home-made trinkets and souvenirs and in the shade of the last row of buildings, fisherman were laying out their catch and relaxing after their mornings work; a brave few were already slugging down their first tall Pacifico's of the day. It was a lovely beach and already, at this early hour, the weather was more than agreeable.

The small courtyard behind the hostel had a large gas barbeque where Ned was waiting for some eggs to slowly fry and some bread to slowly toast. He watched on from a safe distance away, seated on a suspect chair belonging to a rusty patio setting. Andy had scored the prime location on a hammock hung between two beams that supported the awning that covered the cooking area.

'The beach looks nice' Ned remarked as he lifted an arse cheek off the patio chair and craned his neck to check the condition of his eggs.

'Yeah, I know. I went down there yesterday arvo when you were passed out' Andy replied, 'the waters warm too'.

'Right. What else did you get up to while I was asleep?'

Andy shrugged, 'Not much. Had a wash, washed some clothes, had a few beers down at the beach...'

A thin plume of smoke spiraled its way up from the bread that was arching away from the hotplate, Ned heaved himself out of the chair and tended to his fare.

*

Send Email 28/04/11

Hey Jake, what's the latest? All good here mate, just chillin in a joint called Sayulita down in Mexico. Just me and Andy at the moment, Chris lost his shit up in America, haven't heard much from him for the last week. Say hi to Jakey for me, hope his footy's going well. Keep Shane away from the car if you can. Catch you later.

Ned x

*

The boys spent the best part of a week re-energising after the self-inflicted toils of the previous weeks. They rotated between the sand the surf and the beach cantina, fattening up on fish tacos and tamales. At the hostel there had been very few others in residence, Ned and Andy had been the only occupants in their six-bed dorm room the whole time they'd been there and they had the run of the facilities until the weekend.

On Saturday morning Ned woke to see a long arm hanging from the side of the vacant bunk perpendicular to his own and furthest from the door. At the foot of the bunk was a large rucksack slumped against the wall from which erupted some unidentifiable garments and a strong, damp, grassy odour. An intruder had infiltrated Ned's sanctuary. His name was Mauricio.

*

'Have you guys been here long?' Mauricio asked inspecting one of the knots securing the hostel hammock.

'A week or so', Ned replied, assessing his eggs from a safe distance.

'Where had you come from?'

'Tijuana…. By bus'.

A pained expression of empathy appeared on Mauricio's face, 'Ooh, tough. All at once?'

Ned and Andy both nodded, eyes glazed like they were there again, their spines vibrating on their own.

'Crazy'.

'What about you?' Andy asked, adjusting himself in the hammock

'I drove down last night from Guadalupe' he pointed skyward 'up in the mountains'.

'Yeah right'.

'I've been working up there with these people, the Huichol's, they're a native tribe from this area but there's not so many left. They're really cool. I just came down for a break for a few days'. Mauricio sat back in the aluminium chair with his skinny arms behind his head and his skinny legs resting on a milk crate. 'So what are you guys up to today?'

*

'So what's that accent?' Ned asked Mauricio while they walked through the square on the way to the beach. It had been playing on his mind since Mauricio had uttered his first few words in the courtyard that morning, it sounded a bit American, a bit something else, like Spanish maybe or French. His appearance gave few clues, he looked like a fairly standard, lanky dude of no specific background, he was darkish, sort of, Mediterranean perhaps.

'Ah, it's a mixture I guess' Mauricio replied ' I'm from El Salvador but I went to school in Canada, my father sent me away because of the war'.

'So where do you live now?'

'Nowhere in particular, I'm just trying to be useful. I bought some land in El Salvador, I want try and use it for good. My father he was not such a good guy for my country'.

'Oh', Ned replied, happy to leave the line of interrogation there.

'What did he do?' Andy asked enthusiastically.

Ned shot him a look of subtle deterrence, trying to tell him to shut the fuck up with just his eyebrows.

'Killed thousands of people' Mauricio replied quite matter-of-factly.

'What!?' the boys shot out in stereo.

'Well not personally' Mauricio clarified, 'but his government did'.

*

Mauricio's mastery of both English and Spanish came in very handy for Ned and Andy, it allowed them to freely communicate via proxy to anyone they pleased and order food that didn't come with pictures. He also cooked enthusiastically and treated the boys to a lobster dinner one evening after picking up a couple of crustaceans cheaply from a local fisherman who'd had a few too many early morning Pacifico's.

'Do you guys want to come up to Guadalupe for a few days? I think I will probably go back there tomorrow' asked Mauricio over a plate of Ned's barbeque eggs on toast, a dish he had mastered during his Sayulita hiatus.

'Whad'ya reckon?' Ned smacked at Andy between mastication's.

Andy nodded, his cheeks puffed out with food like an autumn chipmunk as he made an approving noise through his nostrils.

'Sounds like a plan' Ned declared with a clap of his hands.

The boys spent their last day in Sayulita like all the others, wallowing by the tide line, wetting and drying cyclically. They took a couple of hire boards out for a paddle and downed a belly load of fish tacos to round off a pleasant stay.

The next day Ned and Andy loaded their bags into the tray of Mauricio's pickup, excited about the trip up into the mountains, the memories of the arduous journey down to Sayulita pushed to the back of their minds.

'There's a ceremony in the village tonight, have you guys tried peyote before?'

Ned and Andy shook their heads.

'It's an important part of their religion, to speak with their ancestors. You should try it, it's some crazy shit. The first time, I spent 5 hours up in a tree; I thought it was talking to me'. Mauricio smiled as he said this and giggled to himself. The pickup bounced heavily over the corrugations on the road and the bags were performing somersaults in the back, the sound of them crashing down onto the tray reverberated through the cab like a gunshot. A fine dust from the road surface had worked its way through the vents and was floating about the occupants in a fine display of Brownian motion, glistening in the sunlight like a million tiny stars.

'If you don't mind me asking mate, what's the story with your dad?' Ned asked after plucking up the courage over the preceding miles of bumps and bangs.

'Well, to put it simply, there was a long civil war in El Salvador between the government military and the rebel guerillas. The rebels were fighting for the poor people; they were very popular because most of the people of El Salvador *were* poor. My father was an important man in the military and they virtually ran the country. They were killing thousands of people, in the whole war it was like 70,000. It was dangerous for me because I could be a target for the guerillas, a prize, so I was sent away when I was small. I mean, when I was a kid I didn't give a fuck, I thought my dad was a hero, you know, I had everything I wanted'.

'What happened to him?'

'Nothing yet, he's chilling out in America. Some of the guys he worked with have been arrested but not him'.

'Fuck' Andy spat, shocked by Mauricio's story.

'Yeah, I didn't know anything about it until I started researching it when I was in my junior year at high school. I wanted to find out about my country and started finding all this shit about the war from the other side, you know, unfiltered, it was pretty shocking'.

Ned pressed on with his questioning, 'What does your dad say, do you talk to him?'

'Yeah, he says he was doing the right thing for the people, trying to modernise the country, share the wealth but obviously he went a fucked up way about it. Plus he was looking after number one first; we were loaded really…so obviously there are some disagreements there'.

The quality of the road degraded with the rising altitude, it felt as though they were driving on square tyres as they bounced around the pickup like astronauts. They'd long left modern amenities behind in a plume of dust and were now bouncing through the scrub high above the coast with scarcely a building in sight.

'This place is very basic but it's cool, the volunteers have a hut but I've been staying in a tent, we can find a tent for you guys' Mauricio announced as they encroached on Guadalupe.

The village consisted of small houses made of wood and stone that blended in with the barren, scrubby surrounds, making them near invisible from a distance. The harsh landscape had kept them safe from invaders and allowed them to remain in a time-warp. Ned, Andy and Mauricio shook the thick layer of dust off their packs and wandered towards the centre of the village. In front of some of the houses children played in the dirt while their mothers and grandmothers went about their daily activities, some preparing food, some making handicrafts, all dressed in fantastic and brightly coloured costumes. Mauricio was intercepted by a weathered man in well-worn work attire who began conversing with him in rapid Spanish and gesticulating in the direction of the volunteer huts. Mauricio nodded as the man spoke and then pointed at Ned and Andy before shaking hands with the man who gave Ned and Andy a quick wave and continued on his way.

'That man is Jorge, he is one of the main guys around here, he built the new huts for the volunteers'.

'What did he say?'

'He was telling me that some new people arrived the day before yesterday, you guys will have to stay in a tent, I told him that you wouldn't mind'.

The volunteer hut was pretty cool, rooms were built around a central kitchen and eating area that had a few comfortable chairs and a computer off to one side, it was open on all sides with a thatch roof and short walkways leading to the rooms that surrounded it. A sign informed guests in English and

Spanish that the computer area would be locked between 10.30pm and 8.00am, as would the fridges.

'The tents are in room 5, I'll go and get them and we can put them up near to the bathrooms'. Mauricio headed towards the room while Ned and Andy sat in some non-resonating seats for the first time in a good few hours.

'Looks alright for a few days eh?' Ned exhaled while picking wet dust out of his nostrils.

'Yeah, the bird on the computer over there looks a good sort too' Andy replied looking past Ned.

Ned removed the digit from his nose and turned to take a look. A dark haired young lady in a singlet and chino's was sliding herself in front of the computer, 'could be onto a winner there mate' Ned agreed. The girl turned her head away from the screen and caught Ned and Andy mid leer, the boys quickly turned around and feigned interest in the zippers on their backpacks. After a few seconds of embarrassment Ned snuck another peek over his shoulder, she was still looking, then she smiled, much to Ned's relief. He returned the smile and attached a dainty wave that he immediately regretted.

'They have only two-man tents, it might be a tight squeeze' Mauricio said apologetically as he dumped the tents on the floor in front of the boys, 'maybe you can keep your bags in my tent?'

The toilet and showering facilities were in an old shipping container that had been painted white and adorned with rather tasteful murals to identify the male and female ends of the facility. The ground around the toilet was hard, but from what Ned was able to survey in his short time in Guadalupe, all the ground here was hard, hard or wet. Eventually the tent pegs went in with the persuasion of a couple of large stones and the boys new temporary home was arranged to their satisfaction. Next door, Mauricio was having similar issues and had also resorted to bludgeoning the tent pegs into submission.

'Fuck... That was some hard work' Mauricio grunted, wiping the sweat from his forehead with the back of his arm. 'When Jorge comes back we can go and meet some of the old people who are doing the ceremony tonight'.

'Yeah cool, I might duck back into the hut and check in on my emails and shit' Ned replied, admiring his handiwork for a moment before heading for the hut.

*

Inbox 06/05/11

Hey buddy, glad to hear you're all good, Jakey and the girls say hello. I saw Chris this morning, what the fuck happened there? He had some yank chick with him, I didn't speak to him long, he said he ran out of money and had to leave, the chick was a bit of glamour though, massive tits. Anyway, stay cool bro.

Jake.

Hi Ned, hope you're having a lovely holiday, any exciting stories? Nothing much happening on the farm. Darrell bought a 12 foot rooster at an auction last week, it used to be on the roof of a co-op down in Junee, it's leaning against the shed now! Julian's off on another trip, just to Bali not like you all the way over there.

Stay safe, Love from Mum and Darrell.

Meanwhile, on Facebook:

Shane 'Big Man' Roach: No more bets

Nathan Reynolds: Dont wory mate me and the boys will sort those cunts out

*

Ned slid his feet across the loose stones that covered the ground all around the village as he walked from the hut back to the tents. As he rounded the front of the hut he could see Andy and Mauricio talking with the girl they had been admiring earlier. Andy spotted Ned approaching from over the girls shoulder and gave him a cheeky wink. The conversation stopped as Ned turned the triangle into a square, six eyes looking at him.

'So Chris is at home apparently' Ned said breaking the silence.

Andy nodded, taking in the new information coolly. 'This is Adi' he replied, leaning in the direction of the girl standing between Ned and Mauricio.

'Hello', Adi said with a nod of her head.

'Hi' Ned replied, mirroring her action.

'We were just talking about tonight' Mauricio piped up, getting the conversation rolling again to everyone's relief. 'Adi arrived here yesterday so she hasn't met any of the old guys yet either'.

'Are you going to join in?' Ned asked trying to be polite, cool and slightly mysterious all at once and unsuccessfully.

'I might just watch for now' Adi replied with smile.

'Are you from Mexico?'

'Israel' Adi replied.

'Oh…cool'. Ned rifled through his memory banks for some sort or Israel related quip but drew an unfortunate blank.

'Yeah, sooo I was actually just on my way to the bathroom' Adi said holding up the towel in her hand as evidence, 'so I'll leave you guys for the moment'. She excused herself and slowly backed away from the scene towards the shipping container.

By the early evening Mauricio had acquisitioned some camp chairs and the boys had themselves a quaint little set up beside the potties. They relaxed as the heat of the day ebbed away, sinking contentedly into their chairs.

'So did Chris tell you that he'd bailed home?' Andy asked rocking back.

'Nah, Jake ran into him. He said that he had an American bird with him'.

'Old Charity eh, she's living up to her name'.

'Yeah, I'm not sure who's the parasite in that relationship' Ned mused, hopping about in his chair, trying to find some even ground.

Jorge came shuffling up the path that ran through the middle of the village carrying several plastic bags filled with miscellanea and beer. He made his way up the slight rise towards the boys' encampment.

'Necesita para poner esta lejos. Vuelvo en dies minutos y le llevara a reunirse el Mara'kame' Jorge said with an exaggerated smile raising the bags he held in both hands.

Mauricio nodded and gave Jorge thumbs up while Ned and Andy offered polite smiles of perplexion.

'He's coming back in ten minutes and he'll take us to meet the shaman' Mauricio translated without missing a beat, having now become well accustomed to Ned and Andy's Spanish struggles.

Jorge led the boys to a hill behind the village; it was the highest point in the immediate area and provided an impressive view over the village and the lake as well as the green and brown mottled mountains that ran to the horizon all about them. An old man dressed in white linen adorned with brightly coloured woven and beaded motifs was building a sort of shrine out of stones, branches and other bits and pieces that seemed fairly innocuous to Ned's untrained eye. Jorge called out to the man who replied to him in halting and rapid sentences. Mauricio looked on silently, Ned and Andy waited for him to slide into his role of team interpreter but he looked to be as ignorant of the exchange as they were.

'What's he saying?' Andy asked as the discussion between Jorge and the shaman carried on.

Mauricio turned to Andy and shrugged his shoulders, 'I don't know, they're speaking in the Huichol language'.

Jorge waved the boys over to the half built shrine, 'this is Ramiro, he is the Mara'kame of this village, he gives his blessing for you to participate in the ceremony'.

Ramiro gave a little bow to the boys and said a few mysterious words before returning to his work while Jorge looked on.

'Do we need to give him a hand?' Ned asked, watching Ramiro shuffle about, grunting, moving rocks and sorting through the items from Jorge's bags.

'No, we need to go back to the village and come back here after it's dark' Mauricio replied.

The boys left Ramiro and Jorge and walked and slid down the slope toward the volunteers hut at the bottom of the hill.

*

Adi was in the kitchen cooking eggs when the boys strode into the hut, her hair was damp and shiny and spiralled down from her head like two minute noodles. The boys stretched themselves out on the soft furnishings.

'Do you guys want something to eat? There are more eggs in the fridge, or beans?' Adi asked without looking up.

Ned, Andy and Mauricio exchanged triangular glances and facial contortions that resulted in Ned offering to assist with the preparation of some eggs and bread, he had, after all, mastered this combination over the previous week. He took his place behind the hotplate and got to it while Andy and Mauricio kicked back.

'Did Jorge take you up to meet the shaman?' Adi asked as she watched Ned's egg whites creep across the hotplate towards hers.

'Yeah, he's up there setting up his gear'.

'Well it should be interesting, don't you think'.

'Yeah…probably….. I guess, maybe' Ned replied without answering.

Adi gave Ned a confused look and let out a little snicker. Ned became very interested in the eggs.

*

A small fire burned in front of the shrine that Juan Jose had put together. The shrine consisted of large and small stones stacked in a pile, from which protruded 5 long thin sticks adorned with coloured trinkets. The boys, Adi and Jorge sat around the fire with several other members of the village while Ramiro conducted the ceremony. His words filtered through like Chinese whispers, Jorge translated the Huichol into Spanish and Mauricio translated the Spanish into English.

'He is asking the ancestors for their blessing' Mauricio whispered after being instructed by Jorge.

Ramiro was singing, almost droning-like, a call to prayer. His eyes were closed but his lid's fluttered.

'He is communicating with the god Tatewari, he is the main guy, the peyote god' Mauricio whispered as Jorge spoke softly beside him. Ramiro threw some tobacco leaves and some cactus into the fire and wafted the smoke around the human circle with a large feather. He then took some more cactus which had been sliced into flat rings and ate them. A ceramic pot was produced, almost like a miniature cauldron and a steaming liquid was poured into several small bowls which began to make their way around the circle. Each participant took a long, deliberate sip from the bowls as they moved around the group. Ned gave the brew a quick sniff, which gave little hint of flavor, before taking a gulp. It tasted like boiled dishwater.

*

Ned followed the sound of waves until he reached the sand. He found himself walking along a familiar stretch of sand. It looked just like Binnara Beach but somehow different. The tree line came right to the dunes, the creek was wider and there was no park or surf club to be seen, in fact there was no sign of civilisation of any kind. It was twilight, the brightest stars were already shining in the sky but a fringe of light along the eastern horizon suggested that the sun was on its way. In the damp sand that was drying as the tide fell, Ned came across some boot prints that led off towards the northern headland where, if this was Binnara Point, Ned had his thinking spot. Ned followed the boot prints which disappeared at the base of the headland where large metamorphic rock took the place of sand. Ned walked a path that he had walked a thousand times before up through the miniature canyons and chasms to the bald green temples of the headland. This was definitely his spot, the view was the same, but overgrown, or yet to exist, or something.....it must have been a lucid dream. Ned sat in the spot and surveyed the landscape, he looked south, focusing on the southern headland and followed the beach northward, spotting where the houses, public barbeques, benches and surf club weren't. As he looked down at the foot of the headland he traced its jagged edge eastward into the water. Below, and further around the cliffs from where Ned sat, a figure stood to attention on top of one of the large rock cairns that rose clear of the surf in all but the wildest cyclone swells. The figure was facing away from Ned staring out into the vast and empty ocean. Ned looked around but saw no one else; he called out loudly to the solitary figure.

'Hello! Excuse me! Oi!' but his voice disappeared into the ether as the figure remained still, unaware of any incursion into its solitude. Ned rose from the spot and made his way down the headland, scampering over the exposed rock towards the cairn at the front of the promontory. As he scrambled over the hard edges, moving closer to the water, the form on the cairn began to take on a familiar shape. In the dim light Ned could see that the figure was dressed in a matching blue tracksuit, black curly hair sprouted from below a green baseball cap.

'Ronald?!' Ned called out as he climbed up to the base of the cairn.

Ronald looked over his right shoulder, down to where Ned stood thoroughly confused a few feet below him.

'What are you doing down here mate?' Ned asked, concerned.

'I should ask you the same thing' Ronald replied, without the hesitation and robotic aloofness he typically expressed himself with. He even smiled.

It was Ned who's response was hesitant, 'yeah…. I don't know really, I thought I was dreaming but it feels pretty real'.

Ronald turned around to face Ned, his heels firmly planted on the rocks below him. This was another thing that Ned had never seen Ronald do, he was forever on his toes, his heels always floating above the ground. Ronald's eyes narrowed, 'how did you get here?'

'I don't know… wha'dya mean here?'

'Where were you before you're where you are now?'

'Mexico' Ned replied vaguely, none of this really made sense, he was confused, certainly, but he felt calm and Ronald didn't seem to be distressed in any way.

'Mexico, so that's where you disappeared to. I thought I hadn't seen you for a while' Ronald replied to Ned whilst also satisfying his own curiosity.

'How did you get here? Where is everything? This is Binarra point right?' Ned enquired hoping at least some of his confusion might be abated.

'Yeah, it's Binnara Point' Ronald confirmed, 'everything's not here yet, I got here by my machine'.

Ned stood puzzled by the vague responses and Ronald hopped down from the cairn and joined Ned on the rock platform supporting it.

'What machine?' Ned asked.

'My time machine, I built it out the back of my house, you must have noticed it'.

Ned laughed nervously, 'nooo, you got that thing working? The greatest minds in the world can't even come up with a plausible theory and Crazy Ronald just knocked one up in his backyard out of scrap metal and old toasters'.

Ronald stared blankly back at Ned, he said nothing.

'Sorry mate, I didn't mean to call you that, but this all seems pretty fucking insane'

'I suppose it is'.

*

'So... tell me...' Ned looked around, his arms outstretched, 'what's going on?'

'I can go back in time, but I can only go to the spot I left from' Ronald explained as he and Ned sat on the sand in front of where the Surf Club would one day stand. The sun was now inching upward, its pale disc now wholly above the horizon. 'Each time I end up where the machine is in the future, in the bush over that way' he pointed to the south-west into the dense coastal scrub.

'How many times have you done it?'

'Quite a few... while I'm here, or, wherever, in the past I mean, no time goes by in the future, so when I go back it's less than a microsecond of time, no matter how long I spend in the past'.

'What about the future, can you go forward?'

'No, I can't go to the future because it hasn't happened yet. I guess it's like the end of a cassette tape, I can rewind to anywhere along the way but I can't go past the end of the tape, which is our present.'

'Am I the first person you've seen?'

'The first on this trip, but other times I've come back I've seen people. One time I came back it was 1921, there was a big jetty here with a train on it, the pub was in the same spot, the Surf Club was up closer to the headland. Another time there were Chinese people here. Did you know Chinese people discovered this country, after the Aboriginals I mean'.

Ned was enthralled, he was starting to believe it, the more Ronald spoke the more believable it became. But it was the fact that Ronald spoke, so clearly, spoke at all, that still bothered Ned.

'Mate, I hope you don't mind me asking, but... you seem a bit different, with your talking and... you're walking more...normally'.

'Yeah, I'm still trying to figure that out. Maybe because I'm not born yet, I'm just what I would be, the conditions that I have in the present don't affect me here?'

'Oh, well it's cool for you I guess'.

Ronal nodded, 'yeah, it's different; I get around a bit faster'.

'What's it like when you're back, in the future I mean... inside your head?'

'It's mostly the same, I can just express my thoughts more clearly here, and I can focus on what's happening around me a bit more. I can't concentrate as well here though; I don't think this version of me could have built a time machine'.

The air was beginning to warm up now as the sun lit the sky blue and the pink faded away. Ned sat quietly, admiring the uncorrupted scene, it was his favourite view but without, the sounds, the traffic, the people, the ships lined up on the horizon, just the nature, just the best bits, and Ronald.

'Would you like to see where our houses will be one day?' Ronald asked, briefly interrupting the serenity.

Ned lifted his chin off his knees and sat up, 'yeah mate, that'd be cool'.

Ned and Ronald strolled southwards along the edge of the dunes toward the creek; a light breeze was blowing in off the ocean, accompanying the sizzle of the waves disappearing into the sand.

'Have you come across any locals on any of your visits?'

'Not around here' Ronald replied, 'they seem to prefer to stay a bit further north, up near Bulwarra Bay, they're friendly though, I walked up there last time and they just watched me from a distance'.

When they reached the creek Ronald stopped to take off his boots and socks and roll up his tracksuit pants, 'it's easiest to walk through the water, the bush is too thick and the creek runs quite close to where the houses will be, they must have diverted it at some stage'. Ronald waded along the creek edge, the water just covering his ankles, Ned followed behind, he was already barefoot, the water soothed his feet which ached from his earlier scrambling over the rocks under the headland. The creek seemed cleaner; the dark mud that Ned had so often battled with on his fishing dates with Jake was nowhere to be seen. It was definitely wider but the sounds were all too familiar, black cockatoo's shrill squawks pierced the serenity and the intricate songs of the finches sprang forth from the dense undergrowth.

'Have you hidden something or marked something and then checked to see if it's still there in our time?' Ned asked as he trailed Ronald further up the creek.

'It was one of the first things I did'.

Ned waited, expecting Ronald to continue. 'And...?'

'And nothing, there was nothing there. I carved numbers into some rocks and trees and when I checked back in 2011 they weren't there. I don't think we are able to affect the future, not the future we live in anyway... or I might have just not looked in the right place'. Ronald gave Ned a smile and stepped up onto the bank. They were a good distance down the creek now, it was cooler here and the noise was much louder, it surrounded them. The sound of cicadas and flies had joined the chorus, making a multi tonal drone to back the sporadic bird calls.

'It's just a little way up here' Ronald said, sitting and shaking the water from his feet before putting his shoes and socks back on. He rocked up to his feet and pushed back the stiff, sharp Melaleuca branches and motioned for Ned to follow. The dry, fallen leaves and twigs under foot were torture on Ned's bare feet.

'I saw a snake last time I walked through here, it was about 300 years later than it is now, but still...' Ronald pushed on for another few minutes, the scrub thinned out and became interspersed with grasses and the sun's heat kicked up a notch as it reached the surface unfiltered. Ronald and Ned wandered a few hundred metres before Ronald called a halt to their procession.

'Here we are' he announced, he pointed with both hands to the ground beneath him, 'this is where my machine is in about 800 years, your house is just there' Ronald pointed over Ned's shoulder.

Ned turned around and tried to imagine his house standing there, guessing where the caravan and clothes hoist would be. He walked across and stood where he thought the Roach's lounge room would one day stand. The view was certainly better now, no unkempt lawn, no scattered and discarded household shit, just trees, all the way up to the ridge that would become Bulwarra Heights and all the way to the beach.

'I like it better now'.

Ned and Ronald made their way back to the beach and sat down by some ancient palms growing beside the mouth of the creek.

'So how do you get back?'

'The battery runs out'.

Ned flashed Ronald a quizzical look.

'The amount of time and the distance into the past is dictated by the amount of power I put through the machine. I've gradually been using more and more which sends me further back in time but I've been keeping my trips short, the longest I've been back is 20 hours. I'm about halfway through this one'.

'How did you figure it out?'

Ronald picked up a long smooth stone and dug at the sand between his feet 'Thinking, I've just been thinking and reading since I was a kid. I'm sure other people have come close, there might even be other people doing it. Once I figured out...'

Ned could see Ronald's mouth moving but all he could hear was a dull hum, like someone had turned down the volume of the world around him. He kept his gaze fixed on Ronald who continued to mouth words that Ned could not hear. The sky behind Ronald began to lighten, the blue got paler and paler until it was white. The whiteness marched forward, engulfing the two of them like a milk cyclone until there was nothing.

*

Ned's eyes crept to the right where Mauricio sat transfixed on Ramiro who sang and wept, accompanied by Jorge who was playing a homemade fiddle cut from a single piece of wood that produced a sound that was more police siren than concerto. Andy sat cross legged beside him with a half-smile and glassy eyes, like he'd had one too many cones. Adi was smiling too; her smile was one of admiration, the smile you see at an art gallery or at a concert. Several of the Huichol men were shuffling about to Ramiro's song, kicking up the dust around the ceremony ground. Across the fire a couple of other volunteers watched on and whispered to each other. The dust floated amongst the fire-smoke in slow motion, it reminded Ned of the trip up to Guadalupe in Mauricio's ute. Every time Ned had a thought it seemed to last an eternity, he was in his own slow motion world outside of which time was moving in fast forward. He was careful not to look at any one person or thing for more than a second, because to everyone else it may have been a short eternity. The fire, people stare at fires, Ned would stare at the fire.

*

Ned was looking straight up. It was blue, but it wasn't the sky. A bit of dust danced across Ned's eyeball but it was soon lost as his focus was drawn to a threatening drop of condensation that dangled from the blue polyester that hung a few feet from Ned's face. At the foot of the tent a mass that smelled like Andy was balled up in a sleeping bag. Ned reached up and smeared the condensation droplet across the tent fabric which it soaked through cooperatively. He then sat up and unzipped the tent flap letting in a gentle waft of cool air.

Two dirty feet hung out from inside Mauricio's tent and were being attended to by a pair of dueling flies. Ned hobbled towards the volunteer's hut, the stony ground giving his bare feet a thorough going-over. Ned slipped as he reached the wooden step that led into the hut, catching his shin on the edge. He persevered and waited until he'd secured one of the comfy chairs before inspecting the damage. Halfway down his right shin Ned observed, what he had learnt in one of the medical lectures he had attended, was a second degree abrasion. It had already begun to swell and a jagged line of blood, like a fork of lightning, had pushed its way to the surface. Ned lifted his leg up on to the arm of the chair and laid back in an attempt to distract himself from the pain.

Adi entered the common area through the same door as Ned. She was dressed in combat trousers and a singlet with her hair wrapped in an impressive towel-turban, managing to make her truck drivers outfit look as glamorous as any ball gown. She glanced over and saw Ned's feeble form lying pathetically across the armchair.

'Everything okay?' Adi asked with just a hint of sarcasm.

'I just bashed myself on the step outside' Ned replied with a pained giggle.

Adi strode towards Ned; his wound was now bleeding with a bit more substance and was slowly weaving its way through his leg hair, downhill towards his knee.

'What did you do?' Adi asked without a hint of sarcasm and a smattering of actual concern.

'I slipped onto the step, my shin cracked against the edge'.

'I'll get the first-aid kit, don't touch it'.

Before Ned had a chance to dismiss her concern and put on a show of toughness, Adi jogged over to the room where Mauricio had procured the tents and emerged moments later with a large green box that looked like it should be filled with fishing tackle. She placed it on the floor beside Ned and rifled through it, placing several items on the chair behind Ned. She twisted the cap off a small vial containing a clear liquid. As she began moving in the direction of the wound she must have noticed the look of slight concern on Ned's face.

'It's saline solution, to clean the wound, it won't hurt' she said with gentle, matter-of-factness.

'Oh, yeah' Ned nodded assuredly, 'I'm not worried'.

Adi squeezed the saline over Ned's shin and then placed a square of cotton gauze on top of the wound, 'hold this' she said as she dug back into the green box. She produced some plasters to hold down the gauze, 'you'll need to put some ice on this too, it's swelling already'.

'You done this before?' Ned asked.

'Yes. I'm a medical student; I've practiced on a lot of silly boys like you' Adi replied, snapping shut the box and Ned's mouth simultaneously before returning the first-aid kit and retreating to her room.

Ned hobbled across to the fridge to get the water that had been his original motive for coming to the hut and grabbed some ice from the freezer, tying it to his leg with his shirt.

Ned limped back to the tent where he was confronted with Andy emerging from his sleeping bag like a shy crab. Mauricio's feet had disappeared inside his tent, or possibly outside. Ned eased himself into one of the camp chairs and lifted his leg up onto the other, making himself rather comfortable.

'What happened to you?' Andy asked, his head protruding through the open tent flap.

'I ate shit over at the hut, smashed my shin on the step' Ned replied as he adjusted the makeshift ice pack on his leg.

Andy had a little chuckle and trod his way out of the sleeping bag, shaking it off onto the floor of the tent. 'Did Jorge sort you out with the bandage?'

'Nah, Adi. She's a medical student'.

'Is she?' Andy drawled with a raise of his eyebrows, 'too bad you didn't injure your balls'.

It was a clear day, a cool breeze blew up the hill in gusts with just enough chill to raise a few goosebumps on Ned's arm. Mauricio came striding out of the toilet container and greeted the boys enthusiastically.

'Are you guys ready to work today?!' he bellowed clapping his hands together loudly.

'Ned's had a little accident mate, he might struggle' Andy joked, pointing at Ned's raised leg.

'Oh no!' Mauricio cried with comedic exaggeration, 'shall I call in a helicopter?'

'I'll be alright mate, what are we doing?'

Mauricio pointed down the hill to the far end of the village 'we're building some classrooms down there'.

*

'I came here to get away from this shit, look at me', Andy called out to Ned as he pushed a wheelbarrow towards the partially built classroom they'd been assigned to.

Ned looked up from the pile of stones he was shifting out of his own wheelbarrow and gave Andy a wink, 'it's for a good cause mate, and they're putting you up for nothing'.

'I want to make bracelets with the old ducks up the other end, this shit's hard. I'll make bracelets all day if they want'.

The boys had been given the task of moving a large pile of quarried stones that had been left by the side of the track that parted the village up to the site of the classrooms where they were being used for the foundations. Mauricio was overseeing their efforts with an uninhibited display of shaudenfreude, taking great joy in the smart comments, as well as the thatch spears, he was firing at them from the roof of the adjoining building.

'Come on guys! I thought that you Australians were meant to be tough, you work so slow!'

Mauricio's jeers were met with well intentioned, middle finger salutes. The boys, between them, managed to get through six barrow loads of stones before Jorge arrived with a 25 litre pot filled with rice and beans.

'Comemos!'

Inside the almost complete classroom that Mauricio sat atop, Jorge set up his pot with a canteen of orange cordial and some tortilla bread and let the workers loose on the makeshift smorgasbord.

Ned and Andy sat against the wall with their lunch, the sun shone through the space in the roof where the thatch hadn't been laid and illuminated the concrete floor beside Ned's outstretched legs. He slid his right leg across, exposing his wound to the stream of light. Adi floated into the room, still immaculate, free of all the sweat and dirt that plastered the rest of the lunch crowd. She grabbed a plate of rice and sat down against the wall beside Ned.

'So, how's my patient?' Adi poked Ned's leg with her fork.

Ned pointed to his full cheeks and he powered up his chewing and swallowed an uncomfortably large lump of rice and bean tortilla before coughing out his reply, 'good thanks'. Ned gave Adi a reassuring smile, 'you're looking a bit clean, what have they got you doing?'

Adi gestured across the room with her fork, 'I'm doing some health advice with the mothers and girls up in the finished room. I'll be doing the same work as everyone else in a few days though'.

'How long are you staying here' Andy asked, swiveling around to face the others.

'I'm not sure' Adi shrugged, 'a few weeks maybe'.

'Do you have to go back to university soon?' Ned asked between tortillas.

'No, I've deferred my studies for a year, I wanted to see some of the world, you know?'

Ned nodded; he knew well what she meant.

'I went straight from school to the army and then my studies, I just needed a break. A lot of people from Israel do this'.

'When were you in the army?' Andy asked, surprised by the offhand remark.

'For two years after I turned 18, it's compulsory in my country, national service'.

'Like, the proper army? Did you get to shoot bazookas and throw grenades and shit?'

'Yes' Adi replied casually, 'everyone does it'.

'Fuck, I'm glad we don't have that shit, 2 years in the army, pfft', Andy looked at Ned waiting for an enthusiastic concurrence.

'You would have to do 3 years' service because you're a boy'.

Andy shook his head with a disbelieving grin. Ned maintained the neutral ground.

'Israel is a very dangerous country, most people are happy to do their service, to protect the people'.

'Sounds a bit like brainwashing' Andy retorted.

Adi's eyes narrowed, 'you don't know what you're talking about' she replied dismissively before changing the subject, directing a question at Ned. 'How long are you here?'

'Um, not sure really. We didn't really know we were coming here until the day before yesterday, we just tagged along with Mauricio?'

'Oh, have you been in Mexico long?'

'Couple of weeks, we started in Tijuana….we were in America before that'.

'Oh' Adi nodded and carried on eating her lunch.

Jorge started black bagging the scraps Mauricio dropped through the space in the thatching, his shoes slapping the concrete in front of Adi's feet.

'Wow, you guys are really lazy, get back to work' Mauricio laughed as he leapt across the room and grabbed the last tortilla before Jorge could toss it away, 'and you ate all the food you assholes!'

*

Ned took a sip from his bottle of Pacifico and placed it down on the dirt beside his camp chair.

'It felt real man, I seriously think it could have happened'.

'Maybe it did' Mauricio reasoned, rocking back in his chair 'science doesn't know everything, crazy things happen every day'.

'What did *you* see?' Ned asked.

'I still saw what was happening, the ceremony I mean, but it was just more...' Mauricio mimed an explosion with his hands '...intense, like it was the only thing happening, everything else kind of disappeared for a while'.

'Well it was one wild trip', Ned declared clasping his hands in his lap and looking skyward.

'You know, I've done a bit of reading about the Huichol ceremonies. They are sometimes called 'portal' ceremonies, the shaman perform it to visit with their ancestors and gods. Maybe it's true?' Mauricio mused.

'Yeah, it just seems weird, he *was* building a time machine before I left but it seems a bit insane to think he actually did it. I don't think he can even tie up his own shoe laces'.

'Crazy things', Mauricio repeated reaching down for his beer.

Andy emerged from the volunteer hut where he'd been making use of the computer before lockout time and made his way up the hill towards the tents. Ned took his foot down from the empty camp chair that Andy had earlier vacated.

'What did that peyote do to you last night?' Ned asked as Andy crunched up to the tents.

'Huh?' Andy snapped, dragging his chair forward.

'Did you see any weird shit?'

'Yep'.

'What was it?'

'I was chilling out with Piglet. Remember Piglet?'

Ned nodded and had a little chuckle. Mauricio looked on, confused.

'Piglet was a dog I had when I was about seven' Andy explained 'he ran away, allegedly'.

'Ah' Mauricio sighed, 'and you saw him last night?'

'Yeah, he was playing around between my feet but instead of barking he made this weird whiny screech. I think it might have been Jorge's violin getting mixed up in there'.

'Why, did you see something weird?' Andy asked.

'Ronald'. Ned replied with a grin.

'MacDonald?'

'Yep, at home, but back in time. His time machine works apparently'.

'Fuck eh; I feel a bit ripped off with my Piglet encounter'. Andy took a beer from the plastic bag that was flapping away like a wounded seagull on the ground between Ned and Mauricio.

'What's the latest from home?'

'Dad's asking when I'm coming home' Andy replied morbidly, 'he's got a big job on in Binnara starting in a few weeks'.

'What did you say?'

'I said I'd get back to him. I checked my funds, they're not looking the best' Andy stated with a frown 'it might be worth checking Facebook in the morning though mate, looks like Shano's been busy'.

'Whad'ya mean?'

'I won't ruin the surprise mate'.

*

Inbox 13/05/11

Hey mate,

What's the latest? Nothing major going on here. Me, Jodie and Jakey are heading up to Borongil Caravan Park for three nights, there's a teachers strike on Friday so we're gonna make the most of it, haven't been away for a while. Shane got himself into a bit of strife with a few hard nuts down at the pub, they gave him a flogging for taking bets, that'll learn him. Brown Snakes are killing it this year, five from five to start the season, Jakeys carving up too, bagged a double last week.

Have you been getting many waves?

Check ya later bro.

Jake.

Shane 'Big Man' Roach: is engaged to Melanie Hodges

Barnesy Barnes: Congrats mate!
Melanie Hodges: Love ya babes xxx
Dane Wilson: Sucker lol.
Tenille McCarthy: Fuck you Shane you fucking pedophile
Shane 'Big Man' Roach: Fuck off tenille
Melanie Hodges: You're a psyco Tenille.
Tenille McCarthy: You've got it coming too bitch
Barnesy Barnes: Jesus!

*

'Did you see it?' Andy called out as Ned marched toward the stone pile. A big, silly grin plastered across his face.

Ned gave a reluctant nod and stopped to pick up his wheelbarrow.

'Funny hey?'

'Not really' Ned replied, marching off towards the pile.

The boys got stuck-in and managed to shift the whole pile before lunch, taking time to admire their achievement from the shady wall of the nearly complete classroom that had housed the lunchtime smorgasbord the previous day. For the first time since their arrival there was an absence of breeze and the lake at the bottom of the village was beginning to look inviting. Ned inspected the two days' worth of dirt stuck in his pores; it gave him a fetching tandoori hue like a suburban tart. He knew Andy was thinking about going home, it was just a matter of how long.

'Comemos!'

It was beans and rice again, taste wise it was doing very little for Ned but it was good for his constitution after his torrid introduction to foreign cuisine and Jorge provided enough salsa picante to make a handful of Guadalupe grit taste alright. Mauricio came and joined Ned and Andy as they ate quietly in the shade, overlooking the lake which reflected the clear, blue sky like a giant mirror. It was a beautiful day.

*

Adi was reading a book at the lake edge with her feet in the water. Ned could see her from the track as he tied up his last bundle of thatch, the task he had been given for the second half of the day. He decided he would go down to the lake and wash his hands, despite the fact that it was substantially further away than the toilet container. He'd been meaning to all day anyway, it was just a coincidence that Adi was down there, he wasn't a creep.

Ned crouched down a couple of dozen feet away from Adi and dipped his hands in the water, pretending not to notice her. He scooped a handful onto his face and peeked across to see if Adi was looking. She wasn't. Ned's cool act had failed to make much of an impact thus far; perhaps it was time to abandon it altogether. Maybe Adi wasn't even that attractive. Maybe Ned had developed jail-eyes over the last couple of weeks, he hadn't really seen many girls since they crossed the border, maybe she was just the best of a bad bunch, slim -pickings and all that shit.

'All done for the day?'

She'd spotted him. Ned looked across, all his previous thoughts vanished, this was not a case of jail-eyes.

'Yeah, finally'. Ned rose from his haunches and strolled towards Adi, 'good book?'

'Yes thank you, do you know it?' she held it up, it was a battered copy of The Little Prince.

Ned shook his head, 'no'.

'It was one of my favourites when I was little; I found it in a hostel in Guadalajara'.

'That was lucky' Ned replied as he sat himself down and scooped up a handful of stones.

'Yes' Adi agreed, returning to the book as the conversation fizzled out.

Ned sat quietly for a few minutes, flicking his handful of stones into the water one at a time.

'Sorry if Andy was a bit rude yesterday'.

'Huh?'

'At lunch, when you were talking about the army'.

'Oh, never mind that. I hear that a lot, I can understand his opinion, it's a very strange thing for someone who's grown up in a safe country to understand'.

'Yeah, it doesn't seem like the most appealing thing to do when you're 18, go off and join the army for a few years. You think you're finally free and then boom, bossed around all over again'.

'Yes' Adi concurred, 'but if you know it's coming then it's not such a big thing, plus all of your friends, everybody, is starting with you so it's not so bad'.

Ned nodded gently, giving an impression of agreement. He didn't really agree, his studies of the Middle East conflict had him erring on the side of Palestine in all matters political, but this didn't seem like the time or place or person to be unloading his views upon. Not just yet anyway.

Ned threw the rest of the stones into the water and stood up, 'I better go and see what those other clowns are up to'.

'Okay' Adi replied with a smile, shading her eyes from the halo of sunlight behind Ned's head, 'I'll let you borrow this book when I'm finished, if you like?'

Ned smiled, 'Yeah, that'd be cool'.

*

Ned saw movement through the gap under the tent door flap. A balled up shirt parted the flaps at speed and hit the back wall above his head. The top of Andy's head followed shortly after as he crawled into the tent and flopped down on top of his sleeping bag. 'It's gonna cost me a fucking fortune to get home'.

Ned rolled on to his front and waited for Andy to further vent his frustrations.

'I'll have to either get back to LA or down to Mexico City, it's gonna be nearly two grand either way'.

'So what's the plan? Ned asked wriggling up unto his elbows.

'I reckon I've got enough for a couple of weeks max if we can bus it down to Mexico City for cheap'.

'Righto then, we can have a word to Mauricio; see if we can sort out a lift to a town in the next couple of days'.

*

Jorge's old truck made Mauricio's ute look like the queen's royal carriage. The dashboard was dressed up like a Catholic altar, the hymns blasting from the tape deck written and performed by Michael Jackson. The springs under the bench seat sang in time with the bumps in the track as the rusty beast grunted and snorted it way to Ixtlan Del Rio and national highway 15. Jorge chain smoked for the length of the journey, donkey rooting life into a fresh cigarette as the one in his mouth was in its death throes. Ned had to be satisfied with looking at the pictures in the book Adi had given to him before they left, the constant rattling making reading impossible. On the inside cover of the book were Adi and Mauricio's email addresses in case he got lonely after Andy had left. Jorge gleefully tooted his horn at the passing vehicles that became more frequent as they drew closer to the highway. The horn had lost its vigour over the years and sounded a bit like an emphysemic wheeze that finished with a modest squeak that caused Jorge to smile and look at the boys, taking his eyes off the road for an uncomfortable amount of time. Each time Ned and Andy would force out a laugh and give him a thumbs up to assure Jorge that they too found the sad horn endlessly amusing.

The truck rattled up to an unassuming looking building that didn't seem to serve any specific purpose. Half the building was an empty, doorless garage, while behind some flimsy bars that covered a large window, a young man sat alone in a mostly empty room watching a small TV. A couple of old women and small children sat under an awning at the front of the building amusing themselves as they saw fit. Jorge went to the window and spoke to the young man before returning to Ned and Andy who stood by the back of the truck awaiting instructions.

Jorge held both his hands up with fingers outstretched, 'dies minutos, colectivo para Ixtlan, jes?'

Ned nodded 'yes, Ixtlan, ten minutos' mirroring Jorge's pose.

'Jes, very good' Jorge replied and motioned for the boys to go and join the crowd under the awning.

Ned and Andy grabbed their bags from the back of the trucks and headed for the shade.

Jorge gave them one last salutary cough of the horn, 'tank jou, adios!' he yelled as he pulled out onto the highway and back up into the hills.

'He didn't mind throwing a bit of English around at the end there' Andy snapped while constructing himself a seat out of his backpack.

'It was hardly Shakespeare mate' Ned replied in Jorge's defence.

The old ladies snuck occasional glances at the skinny foreign interlopers, careful not to stare. The kids cared not for such politeness and stared to their hearts content.

It wasn't a bus that turned up after dies minutos, rather, a truck similar to Jorge's rattled to a stop in front of the awning. It's tray was covered with a blue tarpaulin stretched over a flimsy frame and three sweaty people were squeezed into the front alongside the driver. The bench cleared as the old ladies waddled towards the rear of the truck along with several of the children. They all moved to the back where a hand appeared from within the canopy and hauled the women aboard as the children scrambled up unassisted. Ned looked into the building through the grate and interrupted the viewing of the young bloke inside.

'Excuse me senor' Ned pointed to the truck 'Ixtlan?'

The man eyes lifted to observe the shape in the window and nodded subtly 'Ixtlan'.

Ned waved a 20 peso note under the grate, 'we pay you?'

This was met with a shake of the head and an arm flung in the direction of the collectivo.

Ned looked at Andy, shrugged and picked up his bag, 'guess we get on'.

*

The boys found themselves sat beside the tail-gate of the truck, the road whizzing by a few feet below them. The back of the truck held a surprising number of passengers; Ned counted 21 by the time the bus arrived in Ixtlan. The system seemed to be that payments were made upon alighting. The collectivo would stop and a man would emerge from the front end and assist anyone so requiring, as well as collecting the fare. The arrangement of the canopy meant Ned was only able to observe where the truck had been rather than where it was going, saving them from the frightening close encounters with oncoming traffic. The boys sat by the tailgate, hoping that Ixtlan was the terminus and not merely a stop along the way as they had given up asking the other passengers if they were in Ixtlan after every stop.

Eventually something resembling a large town began appearing and disappearing into the distance and the collectivo drew to a halt that saw the entire compliment of passengers exit the vehicle.

Ned paid the truck conductor, feeling the need to cover Andy's fare due to his current financial stresses.

They had been let out on a dusty shoulder, with nothing that screamed 'big bus station' within sight.

'Excuse me mate' Andy spoke slowly to the conductor, 'where is the bus station?'

The conductor looked at Andy apologetically 'no hablo Ingles'.

'Fuck!'

'We go to Guadalajara' Ned sounded out waving an outstretched index finger between Andy and himself.

'Guadalajara?' the offsider repeated.

'Si, si, Guadalajara'.

'Necesitian el terminal de autobus, es recto, uno kilometros', the conductor replied, pointing further down the road.

'Ah, gracias' Ned replied with a smile, acting as though he understood more than he did, which was that they had to walk along the road until they came to a bus station.

'Looks like we're walking again' Ned said to Andy as they picked their packs up from the ground. The boys waved to the conductor and gave him a thumbs up as they set off up the street. They had gotten all of 10 metres before the collectivo pulled up beside them and gave a healthy toot of the horn, the driver waving them aboard, and in the luxury of the front seat. Ned and Andy jumped in and were kindly delivered to the roadside opposite the station.

'Terminal para Guadalajara' the conductor proudly announced.

Ned handed over some more small pesos and gave the bonnet a hearty thump of appreciation as he exited the vehicle.

*

45 minutes doesn't leave a lot of time for sightseeing. As Ned sat in the luxury coach that would deliver he and Andy to Mexico City he contemplated whether that length of time qualified as a visit. Do you need to actually spend a night somewhere to say that you've been there or does just physically being somewhere for any length of time, no matter how brief, count? If someone asked 'have you been to Guadalajara?' was Ned within his rights to say 'yes'? He and Andy had spent their three quarters of an hour in Guadalajara in

queues. The queue at the ticket window was short, the queue for the toilet was just one other guy so it hardly counts but the queue at the taqueria next to the bus station was long and slow so any future discussions about the visit would be restricted to in an around the bus station and the sights Ned was able to see on the road in and out of the city. One thing was for sure, the place was huge, the city disappeared off into the horizon in every direction. The impressive skyline took Ned by surprise; it was a world away from the stones and thatch of Guadelupe.

*

'This has to be the fanciest bus stop in the world' Andy said as he looked around awestruck. 'It's bigger than Bulwarra Plaza'.

Mexico City's western bus terminal was vast; the polished tile floors reflected the light from above like a calm beige lake. Within its walls it housed all manner of fast food options, putting most shopping mall food courts to shame. Many of the people milling about and spreading out on the benches carried plastic shopping bags in their hands though they contained items brought from home rather than items to take home.

Ned had a list of directions he had copied from various online sources that would hopefully lead them to their accommodation. A short ride on the subway would take them from the Western Bus Terminal to the Insurgentes metro station and the Zona Rosa where their modest hotel was located.

*

Ned had a new favourite band when he stepped on to the rubber wheeled, safety-orange metro train. On the platform a choir of blind men accompanied by a blind accordion player were putting on a fine performance, all dressed immaculately in white shirts and black slacks, the men sang Mexican folk songs with gusto, hoping to hear the ting and patter of coins landing in the accordion case laid open in front of them. Ned had emptied the few remaining pesos out of his wallet into the box before he boarded and tried to play the few songs he heard over again in his head for future recollections.

It seemed that the inside of city trains were much the same world over. Hands of different sizes, colours and states of cleanliness gripped shiny bars above expressionless faces all avoiding eye contact with each other. The only noteworthy difference was the appearance between stops of men, women and children using the carriages as captive marketplaces selling CD's, stickers, chewing gum and themselves. A man blasted Christmas carols from a homemade backpack stereo, skipping through the songs and selling his pirate CD's for a very reasonable price. Two young boys stood at one end of the carriage and sang acapella to little reaction. Another small boy walked up and down the carriage placing stickers cut from a roll onto the legs of seated passengers, hoping to collect a few coins on the return trip down the aisle in exchange for his wares. The boys seem to have mastered the sad-face in an attempt to broaden their appeal by means of sympathy. It was entirely possible that they actually were sad and it was just their regular face, Ned wasn't sure which of these scenarios was the more heartbreaking and he was unable to assist anyway having already parted with his pesos back at the platform.

Many youngsters very much like the ones plying their trade on the underground scooted about the public space at the station entrance on street level. Adults, whom Ned assumed to be the parents of at least some of these children sat or stood around the station entrance selling socks, shoes, hats, underpants, chips, crickets, pirate cd's and dvd's, mobile phone cases and all sorts of other cheap shit. Amongst the traders, sitting against walls and trees, others begged for the money of the passing crowd, able to offer only a forlorn face and a surge of guilt.

Ned and Andy's experience with begging had been mainly restricted to drunken school mates at the top pub asking for a beer after they'd run out of cash. They decided not to feign interest in the cut priced crap and took advantage of their lack of Spanish to ignore the pleas, calls and comments without offence and head towards the hotel using Ned's hand drawn pirate map. They wandered across a busy road and soon found themselves on a paved pedestrian street flanked by bars and restaurants, who's clientele spilled out onto the footpaths and enjoyed the sunshine. The hawkers selling their shit in front of the station were replaced by hawkers proffering cards and pamphlets extolling the virtues, or lack thereof, of the local titty bars and gay bars. The avenue was adorned with a row of sculptures and the whole place had a pretty cool vibe, certainly not the intense and violent city they had expected. The hotel, according to the map, was a few blocks down and went by the magical name of Rosa Hermosa Hotel. Upon entry it was clear that Rosa Hermosa had enthusiastically embraced, perhaps even pioneered the 'run-down 1970's bordello' theme. It smelled of bathroom deodoriser sprayed over an ashtray and had stains on the roof that resembled bruises. Ned followed Andy down a dimly lit hall towards their room with a colourful map of the city in one hand and a small bar of soap in the other, both courtesy of the front desk.

'Fuck eh, we've definitely done the grand tour of cheap hotels of the Western Hemisphere' Andy commented as he dumped his bag on the queen sized bed in the middle of the room.

'I'd say more than one porno has been filmed in here' Ned replied as he surveyed the dim, deep tone surrounds, browns and reds dominating the décor. Good for hiding expulsive stains Ned thought.

'This bedspread does seem familiar' Andy quipped as he headed for the bathroom.

Ned sat down on the dubious bedspread and unfolded the map, an arrow drawn in pen with the words 'esta aqui' scribbled next to it, helpfully indicated their current location. They were fairly centrally located as far as cities go and just a few blocks from a large expanse of green that contained lots of little icons suggesting they were places of interest.

'Looks like we're pretty close to most things' Ned declared, holding the map aloft as Andy exited the bathroom and using it as a fan to push the toilet odours away.

'Good' Andy replied, 'I don't think I'd really want to spend more time than necessary in here'.

*

They managed to find their way to the vast Chapultepec Park. The park housed the city's zoo as well as a colonial palace high on a rocky outcrop. The paved walkways that meandered through the grounds played host to market stalls, though the whole place had something of a carnival atmosphere. Some of the stalls offered temporary tattoo's and face painting and in one clear area a man was performing stand-up comedy to a large and adoring crowd. A large, sickly green artificial lake was filled with colourful pedal boats being steered around by excited children and loved-up couples. Ned and Andy wandered about the park taking it all in and enjoying the open space. After a pit-stop at a mobile taqueria the boys headed across the park from the market area to the palace. At the bottom of the long and steep hill that lead up to the palace a miniature steam train was offering lifts to the top for a premium price. Ned and Andy being adults and not in any particular hurry, chose to make their way by foot. The palace was an interesting enough place, and its garden balcony offered an excellent view on the multi-faceted monstrosity that is Mexico City. After a short rest the boys headed back down the hill and towards the market which would lead them back out into the city proper.

*

Inbox 16/05/11

Hi man, hope you guys are enjoying the big bad city.

I'm heading back down to my camp next week, are you interested in coming along? I could pick you up somewhere along the way. Let me know soon if you're interested. Check out the pyramids if you get a chance, you can catch the metro most of the way.

Mauricio Montano

Hi Ned,

How are you enjoying Mexico? Not drinking too much Tequila I hope?! As long as you're having a better time than Julian, he got attacked while he was over in Bali, can you believe it? He came home all black and blue, even lost a tooth poor fella. You wouldn't think those little Balinese would be capable would you? Anyway he's recovering here with us. Daryl say's for you to stay away from the donkey bars, not sure what he means but he's having a chuckle over there. Anyway got to go. Stay safe.

Love Mum.

'Any luck mate?' Ned asked after browsing his emails.

'The best I can find is via L.A for twelve hundred, might just have to go for it' Andy replied with a hint of frustration.

'When does it leave?'

'Four days'.

The reality that their buddy adventure would soon be over dawned on Ned; in four short days he would be all alone in a strange land. 'Right, better make the most of it then'.

Send Email 16/05/11

Hey Mauricio,

Count me in mate. Let me know the best place to meet you and what day, I'll be there.

Ned.

*

It was pissing down when the boys exited the Indios Verdes metro station. Across the expanse of cluttered, potholed bitumen that served as a marketplace and a car park Ned could see a long row of green and white buses, at least one of which should be headed to Teotihuacan. The boys scurried between stall tarps, dodging the moonscape of potholes filled with caramel coloured water. Water poured from the edges of the hastily assembled tarps which meant ducking in and out of the rain and getting quite wet instead of soaking wet walking between tarps. After a convoluted journey Ned and Andy arrived at the first of the buses, the sign on the windscreen read Toluca. Ned jumped on to the bottom step.

'Pyramids?' Ned sculpted a head-sized invisible pyramid in the air between himself and the driver. The driver gestured backwards with his thumb and mumbled something unintelligible that Ned pretended to understand. Ned stepped off the bus and motioned for Andy to follow as he began jogging along the row of buses that lined the roadside. Indios Verdes was the end of the metro line and so a sea of buses lined the streets to deliver commuters to the outlying areas.

'Oi! Is this the one?' Andy called out to Ned who was jogging half a bus length ahead. Ned stopped and turned.

'What's the sign say?'

'Pyramids'.

Ned jogged back to the front of the bus and he and Andy jumped on. A look down the aisle told them that this was the right bus, mixed in among the mestizos were several very out of place heads attached to backpacks and clutching guidebooks. The boys shook off the sheen of water that clung to them and found a seat near the back of the bus.

'It's gonna be shit day if the rain keeps up' Andy declared flicking tiny balls of mud from his jeans.

'They'll sell those ponchos out there I reckon, plastic ones'.

'Yeah maybe. You know I haven't seen a single fucker wearing a poncho the whole time we've been in Mexico, it's false advertising, sombrero's too'.

'It's true' Ned agreed, 'I've seen guys dressed like cowboys, and the rest are just dressed like ratbags from back home'.

'Next time there's some sort of Mexican dress up party I'm just gonna wear an old soccer shirt and some leather shoes, I'll be the only authentic one there' Andy announced with a grin.

The rain slowly cleared as the bus drove out of the fringes of the city. The buildings thinned out and the mountains that ringed the city came into view. The paved road deteriorated and slums popped up between permanent dwellings and the sewerage filled streams that ran alongside the roadways. The houses blended into the cleared hillsides, both stained the same dusty brown. After passing through several more of these fringe, dust towns the bus pulled up in a well-kept parking bay. The fence surrounding the bay funneled the visitors towards the entry gate where after paying the modest admission the boys were released into the vast open spaces of the ancient city. The sun had broken through the clouds and lit up the puddles on the paved roadway leading to the pyramids. Small souvenir stalls lined the roadway selling traditional handicrafts as well as shit like tea towels and aprons. The roadway led onto a vast square surrounded with low stone buildings, behind the square stood a small pyramid dwarfed by two massive pyramids standing to the left, the Pyramid of the Sun and the smaller though equally impressive Pyramid of the Moon. The boys headed down the avenue that lead from the entry courtyard towards the pyramids. The stone buildings were adorned with carved heads of animals and deities, the largest having long central staircases that were covered in sightseers cautiously struggling up and down the steep and narrow steps.

Andy pointed at the pyramid directly ahead of them 'you wanna head up there?'

Ned looked up at the massive pile of stones, squinting against the glare darting up from the wet paving stones of the square, 'might as well'.

The base of the narrow stairs that led up the Sun Pyramid was clogged with eager tourists keen to scramble up. A troupe of Canadian Girl Guides were gathered in front of Ned and Andy, clad in blue uniforms adorned with blue and red striped neckerchiefs. The troupe masters were all of an advanced age and advanced girth, their comfort built bodies seemed wholly unsuitable for the ascent. To nobody's surprise at the top of the first modest set of stairs the huffing and heaving troupe leaders sent their girls ahead, citing the need for their belongings to be supervised at the bottom by responsible adults as their reason for stopping.

*

'I definitely saw one of those fat old birds pull a whole cooked chicken out of one of those bags' Andy insisted as he and Ned found themselves an empty spot at the top of the pyramid. From the top of the Sun pyramid the smog layer that hovered above the City was put into spectacular perspective. A thick brown band hung below the high clouds like a skid mark across the southern sky. From here the factories that that hugged the outskirts of the city could be seen, dumping their filthy load skywards, while poor people scraped a living in and around their dusty foundations.

Ned and Andy sat down on the stony top of the pyramid and soaked up the view of the sprawling old city below.

Ned stretched out his legs, shuffling his backside to find a comfortable groove, 'pretty impressive eh?'

'Yeah, sure is a lot of rocks', Andy replied wryly, the shit smear across the sky reflected in his market Wayfarers.

'What do you want to do for your last two days?'

Andy shrugged his shoulders, 'dunno, nothing in particular, just kick around the city I s'pose. What are you gonna do when I've fucked off?'

Ned traced the mortar around the stones under his knees, 'I'm gonna meet up with Mauricio on his way back down to El Salvador, go and chill down there for a bit'.

'Hmm' Andy nodded, 'that should be alright, has he got some boards down there?'

'Yeah I think so; I could probably pick one up somewhere if he doesn't.

'Yeah' Andy exhaled in agreement. He then picked up some small scattered pebbles that had come loose from the mortar and flicked them down the side of the pyramid and quietly watched them bounce down the slope.

'Are you pretty bummed about going home?' Ned asked after a few silent minutes watching the pebbles skip down to the ground.

Andy remained silent for a moment, looking back over the grounds and the day trippers, 'yeah I s'pose I am a bit, it's gone by pretty fast, it wasn't what I expected but it's been good'.

'Do you think you'll stay in Binnara forever?' Ned asked Andy, not for the first time.

'Nah, maybe for a little bit longer but I can't see myself there long term'.

'I don't think I'm gonna go back'.

'No?' Andy replied with slight surprise.

'Nope'.

*

Ned was disappointed to arrive back to Insurgentes without having seen any sort of blind choirs or similar entertainment, just backpack boom-boxes blasting Christmas carols and Shania Twain and some shoeless kids selling chewing gum.

*

Before Andy's departure the boys managed a trip to the Zocalo square in the middle of the city where they saw an Aztec dance troupe of dubious authenticity and a lineup of unemployed tradesmen who had turned themselves into breathing advertisements for themselves. Andy took exceptional excitement at the way the city centre services were so specifically ordered. He was full of praise for a city that was sensible enough to have product specific streets as he wandered down the avenue of perfumeries, across the library lane and down a street of spectacle shops and optometrists.

'This is ideal, no fucking around, "what are you looking for?" "A computer". "Well you should try the street where every shop is a computer shop". Common sense, that's what that is'.

'I've got a soft spot for the trains, 20 cents a pop and free entertainment' Ned added.

'Yeah' Andy mused, 'if you ignore the murders, smog and shantytowns they're on to something here'.

*

On the trip out to the airport Andy's cold heart briefly melted and he purchased a small sticker and two packets of chewing gum from the juvenile carriage spruikers. He assured Ned it was to get rid of his pesos before he left but Ned knew better.

*

Inbox 19/05/11

Awesome, I think the best place to pick you up would be near the border in Chiapas State, it would save driving through the city which would be a big hassle. If you can get down to Tapachula I can pick you up on Thursday afternoon or Friday at the absolute latest.

Mauricio Montano

Ned had made use of the airports internet facilities and now had a challenge to distract him from the fact that he was now flying solo. He had two days to get to Tapachula and no real idea about how to do so. He needed to get as far south as possible, ideally all the way to the border. Ned decided to take his chances and get the metro to the south bus terminal and try his luck.

*

The bus to Tapachula was very fancy indeed; the seat reclined back about 45 degrees and no passenger was more than a few feet away from a fold-down mini flat screen TV, and all for only 25 bucks. The bus traversed a mighty path, from Mexico City to Panama City. 3 days and 7 countries it gobbled up on its run. Ned was a passenger only for its first leg, a 20 hour jaunt to the Guatemalan border, though the faces of many of the passengers suggested they were going to be in this bad boy for some time longer. Ned shared his row with three members of a family travelling home to San Salvador, consisting of a tiny little woman clad in black with a colourful scarf on her head who was escorting her two granddaughters that Ned guessed were about twelve and eight, one shorter and one taller than their petit grandparent. His arrival instigated a reshuffle; the shy younger girl who had been occupying the seat beside where Ned was to sit became rather uncomfortable upon his arrival and insisted that her older sibling swap in. After a heated discussion, grandma made an executive decision and sent the older sibling across the aisle to sit beside the funny looking stranger. It wasn't long into the trip before Ned began to reap the dividends of his temporary adoption into this little family. Every time grandma cracked out the treats Ned was given his choice. Every so often he would catch the littlest member of the family analysing him, looking at his funny clothes, wondering what sort of freak her family had in their midst.

After an hour or so of travel the screens flashed to life and presented the passengers with another overdubbed edition of Twilight that brought a tiny shriek of delight from Ned's young neighbour. Ned reclined his seat and observed the film for the second time, enjoying it even less on this trip despite the superior comfort. Every so often he was invited to make a selection from the packet of sweeties that grandma produced from her bag, offering her a beaming 'gracias' with each dig.

The movie ended only to be replaced with the second instalment of the series, delighting the little girls flanking Ned and drawing sighs and groans from some of the more senior males aboard. Halfway through the movie the expressions were reversed when the screens went blank as the bus pulled off the highway and wound down by the roadside. Outside Ned could see the driver opening up the luggage undercarriage; he was being supervised by several uniformed men carrying some fairly heavy-duty firearms. A single hard looking soldier who didn't look to be any older than Ned boarded the coach and strutted down the aisle with the coach pilot in tow. They passed by Ned's row, heading for the back of the bus, the muzzle of the soldier's rifle passing uncomfortably close to his head as it swung a little with each pace down the aisle. Ned wasn't sure what was going on and so kept his focus ahead, not wanting to draw any attention to his foreignness. The soldier passed by again on his way to the front, the pilot still in tow and a third person had joined the procession. The guy had to be a yank, his grey-blond hair cut into a long, lank bowl and a pair of old acid wash jeans cut into shorts certainly made him stand out from the rest of the passengers. The soldier lead the gringo off the bus where the other uniformed, gun toting teenagers waited for them. Out the window Ned could see the Yank talking very expressively with the soldier who had dragged him off the bus; he seemed to be the senior member of the troupe and the only one older than seventeen, and not by much. The Yank opened a large tan suitcase and a smaller brown one parting his clothes and other possessions so the soldiers could inspect the cases. The soldier then pointed to a large cardboard mass wrapped in about four miles of masking tape to which the Yank responded with a very expressive pantomime that eventually seemed to either satisfy or bore the soldiers sufficiently enough to let the journey continue.

Ned observed the Yank in detail as he returned to the bus and strode back down the aisle. 'Rosiszky Family Reunion, Ozark Mountains, 1998' was written on the front of the Yanks t-shirt above a black and white photo of an elderly couple that looked like it was taken in the early 1900's. The couple in the photo bore a striking resemblance to each other and to the Yank. Ned's eyes flicked between the living face and the screen printed ones amused and disturbed. To his horror his gaze met that of the Yank as strode down the aisle towards his seat; Ned quickly turned his head towards the window and pretended he had something in his eye.

*

'Is this your girlfriend?'

Ned turned to see two unnervingly intense eyes looking at him. The crazy Yank from the back of the bus was leaning down beside Ned's seat; his eyes stated darting between Ned and the 12 year old girl sitting beside him reading a comic book.

Ned glanced briefly at his neighbour and then back at the Yank, 'No'.

'Well if you want someone to speak English with I'm sitting at the back here'.

'Yeah, maybe later on mate' Ned replied, hoping this would usher the nut back down the aisle.

'Ok' the Yank replied and shuffled off.

Ned hoped that the Yank would become otherwise occupied or maybe arrested at the next checkpoint allowing him to travel in peace. Each time Ned detected movement from the rear of the bus he closed his eyes and let his head flop down, hoping this ruse would prevent any further incursions.

After a peaceful couple of hours the bus pulled into a terminal and all the passengers disembarked after the driver called out something, part of which Ned understood as 'half an hour'.

Ned stood on the bitumen between the bus and a large stall selling fruit, snacks and sweets that a number of other passengers were sizing up. As Ned looked on he became aware of a mass looming to his left.

'You wanna learn 100 Spanish words in under a minute?'

Ned turned to see the Yank, 'how do I go about that?'

'Anything ending in 'a b l e' or 't i o n' in English, like vegetable or vegetation, you can use in Spanish, you just gotta get the pronunciation right, *vegetahblay*, *vegetashione*'.

'Really?'

'Yeah man' the Yank assured Ned enthusiastically.

'Thanks'. Ned looked back over at the stall, he wasn't quite hungry enough to buy anything to eat now, but how long would it be until they stopped again and how many more corn snacks could he eat before he became one.

'You taking this bus all the way?' the Yank asked interrupting Ned's contemplation.

'Huh?..Oh, nah, just to the border'.

'I am' the Yank continued proudly, 'all the way to Panama City. I'm actually going all the way to Argentina but Panama City's as far as I can get by bus, then I gotta get a boat, can't cross the Durian Gap you see, into Columbia, too dangerous they say'.

'Oh right'.

'Yeah, get a boat to Arboletes on the coast, then more buses to Buenos Aires, gonna take me a week'.

Ned nodded feigning interest and politeness.

'Yeah, got me a lady down there, moving down there, that's why I got so many bags' the Yank declared, pointing towards the understow of the bus. 'The checkpoint guys keep hauling me off because I got a big ol' saddle under there, makes me suspicious'.

'That's no good' Ned replied automatically.

'Yeah but those guys are all corrupt anyways, I could just slip them a few dollars if I was haulin' drugs anyway you know, they're just kids most of 'em'.

Ned raised his eyebrows, 'yeah probably'. He didn't want to upset this bloke; the best thing to do was just go along with his theories.

'My old lady, she's got horses down there, that's why I got the saddle, it's an antique….. Yeah, met her on the internet a year ago but I had to sell my house in Thailand before I could move down'.

'Thailand eh?' Ned's ears pricked up, 'You know a guy called Julian Mather?'

The Yank took this off-hand question very seriously, rubbing his chin and tilting his head as he scoured his acid-decayed brain.

'You probably don't, it's my step-brother, he spends a fair bit of time over there' Ned insisted, trying to save the Yank any unnecessary brain strain

'Yeah, yeah, the name rings a bell. Anyway, yeah had to sell the house, I was married to a Thai lady ya see and then the government said foreigners couldn't own property in the area anymore, they were gonna take my house so I had to sell it. The wife wasn't planning on leaving so that was that, goodbye and good luck'.

A lot of information was coming at Ned, information he didn't really want. Being seen talking for an extended period of time with a suspicious character also put him ill at ease, he wasn't really in the mood to be negotiating his freedom in words ending in 'a b l e' and 't i o n' at the next checkpoint because he was too polite to walk away from an, at best, eccentric gringo unloading his recent life history. Much to his relief Ned spotted the driver getting back onto the bus and decided to make a move.

'Looks like we're off in a minute, I'm gonna go and grab some food' Ned declared pointing to the bus driver hanging out of the door.

The Yank looked over at the driver and Ned jogged over to the food stall with haste. Ned browsed the food for a good couple of minutes, giving the Yank an opportunity to get on the bus. When he'd decided upon a few bananas and packet of pumpkin seeds and paid for them there was a queue tailing out of the bus and slowly shortening. Ned joined the end of the line, the immediate area free of any noticeably unhinged characters.

The cast aboard the bus seemed to be mostly unchanged, the El Salvadorians Ned was sharing his row with were present, although the younger sibling was taking her turn at sitting beside the strange güero with his hand of bananas. The seats behind were empty, Ned contemplated taking them but assumed that they would soon be filled by new arrivals, that and he didn't want the little girl to think there was something wrong with her. A few stragglers scrambled aboard as Ned was tucking into his first banana. They wandered down the aisle, ticket in hand scanning the rows for their allocated seats. One of the seats behind Ned's was snapped up as the stragglers merged into the rows. The undercarriage doors slammed shut and the latch locked in with a loud clunk before the bus rattled out of the terminal.

'You like the Asian ladies? The Orientals?'

Ned didn't turn around, he didn't have to, the Yank had procured the vacant seat behind and his head was now hanging over Ned's right shoulder.

'Um, not especially, I mean, no more than any others'.

'Good, good, they'll take you for everything you got, that's why I got me a Latino woman now, much more appreciative'.

'What about Americans' questioned Ned, 'that's where you're from?'

'You get your good one's, just like anywhere, but I can't live in the States, too many rules'. The Yank paused briefly to see if Ned had anything to offer before carrying on tangentially. 'I had a bunch of stamps, inherited them from my Dad, where I got the saddle too. Now you might not know this, but stamps are legal tender, if I want to buy something, a can of beer say, well I can pay for that with stamps, the can costs a buck I give the guy five 20 cent stamps, that's a buck. I had, altogether, five hundred dollars' worth of postage stamps, I sure as shit wasn't gonna send a thousand letters'.

'You could have posted the saddle maybe?' Ned suggested.

The Yank paused for thought, a very long pause though his head still bobbled about beside Ned's.

'Yeah, I guess. Anyway I tried to buy a plane ticket with the stamps, no go. I went right on down there and told the son of a bitch at the office that he damn well had to accept my stamps, they're legal tender! Anyway to cut a long story short, the police got involved and I won't live in the Fascist States of America that's for sure'.

'Yeah, that's fair enough I s'pose' Ned replied, baffled by the story though somehow entertained.

As they crossed into Chiapas State the bus was stopped by a federal checkpoint. Ned looked out the window to see several soldiers looking at the luggage under the bus, another under-fed looking soldier strutted down the middle of the bus, his machine gun slung low, bouncing against his skinny thigh as he strode down the aisle. He stopped in front of Ned and motioned for him to open his backpack giving the corn snacks and dirty undies half a glance before carrying on. Outside, the Yanks saddle package sat on the roadside, a soldier lifting up a corner with the toe of his boot. The Yank, having grown used to the procedure got up from his seat and exited the bus to partake in an animated discussion with the federales. Wild gesturing ensued with The Yank at one stage playing the part of air-jockey as he mimed riding a horse. The exchange took a very long time; Ned assumed that the federales were on the receiving end of a long and unnecessary tale. They would have to weigh up if it would be the safer to let him carry on regardless of his cargo than expose their senior officials to this bizarre human. Eventually The Yank returned to the bus, now certainly, if not already the topic of conversation for the rest of the travelers after another delay.

The Yank returned exasperated and plonked himself down once again behind Ned. 'Damn checkpoints, I tell ya back in Thailand I didn't have this trouble'. The Yank gave Ned a tap on the shoulder, 'I'll give you a tip, if you're ever trying to smuggle something, not that I think you would, but if you do, here's the trick. When I used to get hassled at the border in Thailand the officers would always ask "why are you coming to this country, what is your purpose?" blah, blah, blah, I started telling 'em I had AIDS. I said "Why, I'm here for my AIDS treatment", you never seen someone get waived through so fast, that's the trick'.

This ridiculous piece of advice brought a smile to Ned's face, 'yeah, sounds good' Ned muttered in reply, stifling a laugh.

'I wish I could remember how to say AIDS in Spanish', The Yank mused, leaning back in his seat, much to Ned's relief.

'SIDA' a voice from across the aisle announced, 'AIDS is SIDA'.

Ned and The Yank both flicked their eyes across, the man sitting across the aisle from The Yank looked back at them with a grin unencumbered by too many teeth.

'SIDA! I'll have to remember that', The Yank boomed gleefully, 'you hear me telling...' he paused as leant forward, just behind Ned's left ear 'sorry, what's your name?'

'Ned'.

'Ned? That short for Edward?' the Yank asked with a look of concern.

'No, just Ned'.

'Oh. Well I'm Doug'. The Yank leant back and carried on '...yeah, so you hear me telling young Ned here about my saddle?...'

It seemed that Doug had found a willing set of ears upon which to regale his epic, Ned thought maybe the rest of his trip might be a peaceful one. Just to be sure he dug around in his backpack and took out the copy of 'The Little Prince' that Adi had given him, hoping it would both entertain him and shield him from craziness.

Ned inhaled the book; Doug's booming, absurd anecdotes disappeared into the distance as Ned read. When his eyes lifted after he'd read the last line it was dark outside and his El Salvadorian family were all fast asleep, the littlest one having commandeered the centre armrest as her pillow. With the ultra-recline available on this luxury liner of the highways Ned stood a chance of getting some sleep, which would be ideal considering they were due to arrive in Tapachula at 6.30am, further checkpoints notwithstanding. The hum of the engine and the vibration of the road made for a rather soothing sensation when filtered through the coach seat, a kind of mechanical lullaby.

*

The hum became a rumble and Ned felt hard ground pressed against the bare soles of his feet. Ned turned his head towards the rumble and saw a bulldozer bouncing across the gravel towards him. The driver, sporting an impressive moustache under his scuffed white helmet, signaled for Ned to move out of the way. Ned jogged across the gravel to an adjoining dirt road dotted with gravy coloured puddles and dark brown splash stains. Ned followed the road away from the machinery, towards the tree line where it disappeared into the scrub. When he felt that he was far enough away Ned stopped to have a look at where exactly he was. At first it appeared to be a non-descript worksite, a vast, flat expanse of dirt and gravel crisscrossed with dirt tracks. The hills gave it away, they were the same ones he'd seen a thousand times before, the dirt track beneath Ned's feet was Scarborough Street. Ned carried on along the track, beating the familiar path towards the beach through unfamiliar surrounds. The bush eventually gave way to bitumen and Ned was on Ocean Parade. He strolled towards town passing by Andy's house, currently occupied by his grandparents. The paint was stuck fast to the exterior walls and was a brighter shade, the splinters yet to take hold of the veranda and the rust on the gate and letterbox was in its infancy. The pre-fab mansions were nowhere to be seen, the length of the street occupied by modest weatherboard houses all similar to the Dobson's at number 22.

The foreshore was slightly more rugged, free of the brick barbeque areas and picnic tables on slabs. There were a few people about as Ned strolled north; their attire led Ned to believe this might be the 70's, some of the garb seemed familiar to him from his visits to the local charity shops, though now on their first showings.

The top pub looked pretty much the same, aside from the outdated hoarding advertising long forgotten brands of beer it was just a different shade of yellow and a couple of coats thinner and inside Ned was sure it would have smelled the same. The buildings on the main drag were the same, most of the shops were different though and the cars were way more awesome.

He was standing in front of the doctor's surgery when Ned saw him; it was the same then as it is now.

'When are we?' Ned called out across the road.

Ronald looked across the road trying to attach a body to the voice, he took his hands from his pockets and cupped them around his mouth and checked no-one was paying too much attention, '1976!'.

*

'How long since the last time?' Ned asked.

'Not sure, probably around 600 years'.

'Ok, but I mean in real time. Was it 8 days ago?'

Ronald though for second, rubbing his chin for effect, 'yeah, that sounds about right'.

'Do you think you might be sucking me along somehow?'

Ronald shrugged, *'it's possible, I guess, I can't really explain your being here'.*

'Have you figured out what you're doing yet?' Ned asked, careful to be polite.

'I've gotten more accurate with the power, I can get to within about 20 years on a long trip and about 3 or 4 on a short one, like this'.

'What was the idea coming back to 1976?'

'I've been trying to travel back but within my own lifetime, after 1987' Ronald explained, *'As you can see I missed by a bit'.*

'How close have you gotten?'

'1984. Even with the lowest amount of power that will make the machine function I still always end up earlier than my own birth'.

'Maybe you can't be in two places at once eh?' Ned suggested in an attempt to be helpful.

'Yeah, more like three places at once, I'm in two places at once now, I'm still at home in the machine and I'm here, if I visited myself I'd be in three places at once. Probably you just can't be in the same time at the same time, if you know what I mean?' Ronald cast Ned a confused glance. *'I'd like to know if someone else could travel within my lifetime, if it's restricted to the traveller or the builder of the machine'.*

'Seems like it's pretty complicated'.

Ronald snorted in response to Ned's understatement.

'I mean, I guess it makes sense. I guess any plans to travel back and kill Hitler are out of the question' Ned added, uncertain if he understood or not.

'Yeah' Ronald concurred, seemingly missing Ned's attempt at humour. *'Unless I can get a portable machine that's super accurate, and do some very*

detailed research and even then I don't think I can change history, I haven't yet. Maybe it would create a different future, but the one we live in stays the same because it's all already happened. If I did kill Hitler I might not be born in that future'.

'Yeah, I get that.' Ned declared assuredly. 'So have you seen anyone you know?'

'I don't really know many people' Ronald replied dryly.

'Oh...Were there workmen when you arrived?'

'No, it was still dark'.

The light seemed to intensify, Ned squinted but everything around him started to turn white, like clouds, then like milk then like nothing.

*

The sound of the luggage bay doors popping open startled Ned into consciousness. Dim light filtered in through the windows of several other buses parked along the front of the terminal. Ned's left leg was immobile, tingling painfully from toe to arse as it woke. Most passengers had begun moving stiffly from their seats, shuffling wearily towards the exit like a chain gang. Ned levered his seat out of its deep recline and gave his dozing leg a blood pumping shake.

The gummy hombre from across the aisle squeezed past giving Ned a close encounter with the worn, saggy arse of his jeans, though Ned couldn't help but admire his belt, a brown leather number embroidered with white roosters around its entire girth and fastened with a large, shield sized leather buckle that sported a very majestic rooster silhouette.

The staleness that had surrounded Ned for the past 20 hours became abundantly evident when Ned finally escaped the confines of the coach and took a long drag of the fresh Chiapas air. The stale, bodied stink of the bus still clung desperately to his clothes and Ned felt as dirty as a vet's finger. A large metal clock on the terminal awning said that it was 6.20am. Ned was hopeful that Mauricio would arrive at some stage during the day, saving him another night in a dodgy hotel. Inside the terminal a few of the ticket booths were in the process of opening and passengers were gathering for the first buses of the day. A large map of the city was hung on the wall beside the glass exit doors. Ned scoured it, looking for the terminal which didn't seem to be highlighted on the map in any way. It seemed to be a decent chunk of a place if the map was to be believed, so at least he should be able to keep himself amused until Mauricio turned up. Perfectly on cue, a hand with its index finger extended appeared from Ned's left and tapped at a spot near the top of the map.

'Aqui'. One of the ticket booth attendants had noticed Ned's fruitless map gazing and had come over to help. 'Aqui' he repeated, pointing his finger from his map to the floor.

'Aqui...here?' Ned replied copying the attendant's gestures.

'Si, si' the attendant nodded with smile.

'Gracias'. Ned gave the attendant a thumbs up as he headed back to his post.

After quickly scribbling a map Ned headed out in the direction of the town centre. The air was damp and heavy, it was much warmer than it had been in Mexico City and Ned hadn't gotten far before his shirt showed the telltale marks of a sweaty backpack. The main road that passed in front of the bus terminal bypassed the town and bent straight for the border. After 20 minutes of walking along the main road Ned turned off down a perpendicular street lined with pale, pastel coloured houses. Ned was intending to turn down a street named 'Cinco de Mayo' but the lack of signs meant he had to make a best guess. The area he found himself in seemed to be mainly residential with the odd small business repairing whitegoods or selling groceries. But not being in any hurry he ambled along, turning right and left sporadically, weaving his way towards where his map suggested the town centre would be. The smell of shit slowly began to fill Ned's nostrils, shit and raw meat. As he rounded a corner he was confronted with a large covered outdoor market in the act of being set up for the day. He wandered through the fresh kills being strung up between stalls selling, toys, watches and sunglasses and picked up a couple of fresh tamales for breakfast. Ned emerged from the market back into the sunlight and found himself opposite the town square which was serving a similar purpose, holding stalls selling books, backpacks and less fetid delicacies.

Ned sat down on a raised section of lawn bordering the edge of the square to chow down on his tamales. He watched on as the stalls filled up with their various goods and the townsfolk began to emerge from the peripheries of the town centre. Shutters rolled up and gates slid and swung open as the permanently housed businesses prepared to open for trade.

After a feed and a stretch Ned felt moderately invigorated and trawled the town centre in search of an internet café and hopefully an update from Mauricio. After a fruitless amble around the centro Ned tried his luck in the suburban grid that merged into the town on its northern edge. On the third zag of his street scan Ned happened upon an unadorned shop front attached to the side of a family home. The open glass doors in front revealed 5 computers inside with a teenage girl sitting in attendance behind an empty glass display cabinet. After a serious of hand gestures and monosyllabic exchanges Ned sat down at computer 3 between a couple of middle aged Mexicanos pecking away at their keyboards like they were killing ants on a countertop.

Inbox 21/05/11

It's 7.00am on Thursday, I think I should be in Tapachula by 6pm hopefully, not too much later anyway. Pick a place for me to meet you and email me back. You can call me on 044576856743221 if you're unsure of anything.

Peace. See you soon.

Mauricio.

Send Email 21/05/11

Hey mate I haven't had a good look around so it's probably best of we just meet at the bus station, it's on the main road into town as far as I could tell, should be easy enough to find anyway.

See you there mate.

Ned.

Hey Jake, I'm on my way down to El Salvador, I know how thick you are so you might have to crack the atlas out. Andy had to bail so I'm flying solo from now. Should be down there in the next day or so, I'm going to help out on a building site with a bloke I met here, should be cool.

Ned.

*

Ned headed back to town and found himself once more at the covered market. It was now in full swing, trading under a chorus of chatter and a scented zephyr of life, death, raw, cooked and everything in-between. Along the front edge a string of traders displayed their wares by the roadside attempting to ride the coat-tails and catch the overflow of their more formally arranged neighbours. One of these remora stalls had, amongst its piles of macho libre masks, football shirts and sunglasses, a rack of elaborately decorated belts much like the one Ned had earlier admired on the bus. After a quick dig Ned found a fetching belt adorned with a strutting rooster on the buckle and a strap emblazoned with a poultry themed pattern intermittently interrupted by a proud white rooster. Ned purchased and immediately adorned the belt with pride, discarding his comparatively plain and ugly belt to the nearest rubbish pile, disturbing the resident flies and startling the scavenging street mutts.

Ned killed the remaining hours with experimental snacking around town and a slow and particular sweep of the Tapachula Histographic Museum. He was back at the bus terminal by 5.30 in anticipation of Mauricio's arrival. He planted himself conspicuously by the large roadside terminal sign to minimise any delay due to confusion.

Ned amused himself by throwing stones at the A-framed Esso placard rusting away on the other side of the road. He hit it 64 times, as well as this he clipped his finger and toenails and set a new personal best of 1 minute 44 for holding his breath before Mauricio rumbled to a halt on the opposite side of the road at 7.30pm.

*

'Sorry man, I got stuck behind some trucks and…. it was fucking slow man'. Mauricio's head protruded from the open driver's window as he shouted across the street.

Ned leapt to his feet and dusted off his shorts, 'No probs mate'. He scampered across the street between vehicles and lobbed his bag into the dusty, flaking tray as he ran around the back of the truck to the passenger side. As Ned reached for the handle the door flung open, giving his fingers a bash on the way through. Ned took a step back to avoid any further collision as Adi leapt out of the truck.

'I'm not sitting between two sweaty men, you're in the middle' she declared, ushering Ned into the cab.

Ned began to squeeze past and then paused, 'what are you doing here?'

'Why not?' Adi replied giving Ned a light shove, 'in you go'.

Ned slid across the warm, perished vinyl until he was rubbing shoulders with Mauricio, the door slammed hard as Adi hopped in behind him.

'You got your passport' Mauricio asked, 'we're going to be crossing the border soon.'

'Yeah, it's in my bag somewhere… I'm pretty sure' Ned replied with a sudden feeling of nervousness.

The sound of stones flicking up against the underside of the truck blocked out all other sound as Mauricio hauled it back on to the road in a plume of dust and scattered gravel.

'You have a good time in the big city?'

'Yeah, pretty good' Ned confirmed, 'went and had a look at the pyramids'.

'Pretty cool huh?!' Mauricio replied vigorously

'Yeah, it's a cool city; I'd like to check it out again sometime?' Ned glanced across at Adi who was staring out the window, 'have you been'.

'Yes, but only for a day when I flew in, I will get there eventually'.

She sounded tired; they had travelled even further than Ned and without the luxury but Mauricio seemed unusually chirpy.

'So what's the plan, are we stopping for the night?' Ned asked as they bundled down the highway like a frightened dog.

'Nope' Mauricio replied confidently, slapping the dashboard. 'I can get this baby back by 2am I think'.

'How long have you been driving today?' Ned asked with concern.

'About 12 hours, I got these', Mauricio reached down to the foot well and produced a plastic bag filled with cheap Mexican energy drinks, several empty cans clattered around his feet and sat flattened below the windscreen.

'I had a mate who tried to survive on those things, it didn't end well'.

Mauricio just chuckled and carried on down the highway as fast as his grubby old beast could manage.

'So you finished all the work at Guadelupe?'

'Yeah, I mean, pretty much, they had a bunch more people arriving so I decided to bail', Mauricio pointed across at Adi who was now asleep, a clump of her hair flapping out the window, 'she said she wanted to check out my camp so… why not'. Mauricio shrugged and took a slug from the can pinched between his thumb and forefinger and pulled a face like the can had been filled with hot piss.

*

Adi woke with a start when Mauricio slid the truck to a halt at the border crossing. In front of them stood a short, wide bridge that straddled the Suchiate River that acted as the border between Mexico and Guatemala. The sun had settled for the evening and the bridge was floodlit dimly from its four corners. Ned, Adi and Mauricio peeled themselves off the vinyl bench seat and stepped out onto the dusty frontier. Ned rifled through his backpack eventually unearthing his passport from inside a damp towel to his eternal relief, and the three of them made their way to the immigration office for some stamps. The bridge was being patrolled by a troupe of Guatemalan youths offering their services as guides, porters, interpreters and beggars while older Guatemalans acted as unofficial money changers. One youngster insisted that Ned give him his passport and after being refused ran along in front of him pointing out menacing looking cracks and insects on the bridge as Ned walked toward the corresponding office on the Guatemalan side. Ned was keen to be rid of the boy and shooed him off with a handful of small denomination pesos. Milling around the immigration office the money changers held up handfuls of Guatemalan Quetzals and calculators, punching in made up numbers and imaginary exchange rates. It was a relief to be back in the truck and back on the road, bombing through the Guatemalan countryside and having the shit shaken out of them as the cans of pep juice piled up around Mauricio's feet.

Part 3

(The Diary of a Bum)

6th August

Ned slumped down in his seat and slid the headphones down around his neck and stared out the window thinking about the party he'd been to a few short days ago. Isabela's 5th birthday party put all the 18th's and 21st's Ned had ever been to shame. The whole village had turned out and she was stoked. Dani had put Ned's money to good use filling one bucket with cheesy corn snacks and another with some sickly red cordial. A pig shaped piñata briefly hung from one of the trees in front of Dani's house before being shredded by the enthusiastic birthday girl in an explosion of flour and sweets. Dani's brother arrived dressed as a clown and entertained the children with his routine, aided by an 8 rack of San Lucas lager. The boom box from the cantina was brought across and played a fine selection of latin rhythms long into the night. The last place Ned thought he'd be today was on a plane back to Australia.

*

22nd May

...I was born in the United States, my family left when I was seven years old.

How come?

My Dad...... he had a bit of a crisis I think...... he decided we needed to start a new life. My mother says it was because he lost his job and we couldn't afford our big house anymore.

Had he been there before?

No but my mother was born there.

Were you scared?

Not really, I didn't know much about it. I was excited to see my grandparents and my cousins, it was okay.

What did your Dad do?

He was a trader, stocks and things, finance I guess you call it. He still is, his crisis wore off after a few years.

My dad lost his job and had a bit of a crisis too.

What did he do?

For a job you mean?

Yeah.

He worked in a chicken factory, getting the bones out.

.....What does he do now?

Nothing.

He's retired?

No, he just never got another job, he gave up...... on everything pretty much.

What about your mother?

She doesn't live with us anymore; she lives on a farm with a guy called Daryl.

My grandparents live on a farm, they grow flowers.

Where do your parents live?

Tel Aviv.

Just the two of them?

Yes, my sister lives in London. Do you have any brothers or sisters?

Yeah, a brother and two sisters, they just live at home....well my brother lives in the backyard.

Are they younger than you?

One of my sisters is, the other two are older.

Oh...

Is your sister older?

Yes..... So what were you doing before you came here?

I was studying.... I studied civil engineering.

Why did you stop? Didn't you like it?

Not really, I can't say I found it especially inspiring, I couldn't really see myself doing it every day with much satisfaction. Different to you I guess, I reckon medicine would be cool. I started studying engineering because I didn't know what I wanted to do and it sounded important. I didn't get the marks to do medicine, not that I would have.

Well at least you realised it now instead of when you're 40... We're not so different, you and me.

Yeah... What are you doing here?

Kind of like you, I''ve been in a routine my whole life, school, the army, university; I just wanted to do something that was my choice. I do want to complete my studies, I think being a doctor is a pretty useful thing but I feel like it would be more useful somewhere like here and not in some city hospital, you know?

Definitely.

I like it here.

Me too….I really liked the book you gave me.

Oh you did? It was my favourite when I was little.

It struck a bit of a chord.

Yeah I know what you mean….. so, what do you think of this place?

Seems pretty cool, I think he's on to something here, I'm looking forward to getting in to the water.

Don't let me stop you.

I thought maybe I should wait for Mauricio to get up.

I don't think that will be any time soon, it was a long day for him yesterday.

Yeah, this is ok though….. How long do you plan on staying?

I'm not sure, just taking it day by day, it is pretty here.

…..I could see myself spending a fair amount of time here, I can't imagine going home for a while, I know I'd get there and wish I was back here again. I think Andy was pretty bummed that he had to go home.

I would worry about my family I think, I would probably be forced home by guilt.

I don't think that would be a problem for me.

*

23rd May

'There's a store about a mile up the road with a computer and there's the cantina on the other side of the road down there but otherwise this is it'.

Mauricio had led Ned and Adi to the highest point of his property where the long-drop toilet was located. Through the trees there was a sweeping view over the ocean and behind them a gentle slope led down to the tiny village consisting of a few small houses and the concrete block cantina. The cantina was little more than a covered slab with some tables and chairs and a home-made barbeque, the houses were only slightly more enclosed.

There was a three bedroom cottage on Mauricio's site and several slabs that would be the foundation of several more arced around the edge of the property on the flat ground at the bottom of the rise.

'There's a guy, Dani, that lives next door with his family, he's going to be the cook when I get this place running. You could probably borrow a surfboard from him; I can take you guys to meet him'.

Ned nodded and smiled enthusiastically, from what he could see he was in a place as close to paradise as he had ever been.

By the gate that separated Mauricio's block from the roadway stood a hastily assembled shack that according to its signage acted as both a fish restaurant and a bus stop for the once daily bus that linked Santa Sarita to the outside world. It was Dani's Fish Shack.

*

24th May

With the toilet door wide open, watching the waves roll into the bay, Ned enjoyed shitting like never before. The trip had taken its toll on Ned's digestive system and after a few days of good fresh food and clean water Ned had hardened up in more ways than one. It had been a week since he'd arrived in Santa Sarita and Ned had found the place very much to his liking. He'd been able to acquire a surfboard from Dani and had spent the past few mornings fishing with Dani out in his small boat bringing in dinner for the village. It was these early starts that allowed Ned the freedom to shit with the door open, confident in the knowledge that the others would be asleep for a while yet.

*

Inbox 25/05/11

Made it home chump, shit trip, I was in the airport in LA for 12 hours, fucking nightmare. Took me nearly 50 hours to get home from when I left you in Mexico City so I was feathered for days after I got back. Apparently Chris has fucked off up north fruit picking with the stripper, his old man still seemed pretty filthy on him when I spoke to him at the pub. I'm already back at work. Saw Shane and his jailbait missus down on Beach Street yesterday. Nothing good happening here mate, stay put I say. What's Mauricio's joint like?

Andrew Charles Dobson

*

28th May

A lot of families from this area lost people during the fighting, that's why there's not so many old men around here.

What happened?

The soldiers came and took all the men down to the river and shot them.

Why?

They thought that this village was helping the guerillas. They did the same thing all over the country. Dani's father and uncles were all shot.

Does anyone around here know who you are? Who your dad is?

I don't think so. I'll tell them one day, once I feel like I've been helpful.

What does your dad think about what you're doing? Does he know?

He doesn't know… it's his money but he wouldn't interfere, he is still a proud Salvadoran, he wants this country to be great.

Do you think he regrets what happened here?

If he doesn't then he's a bad man, I think he does. Either way I'm going to try and make up for it.

*

1st June

In front of each building stood a neatly dressed man with a shiny new shotgun slung across his front. It seemed that San Salvador had enthusiastically taken on all the modern conveniences that the western world indulged itself in. Shiny beacons of saturated fat were dotted through the city, some sporting additional 'local' specialties on their standard menu to endear themselves to the people. Amongst the fast food bonanza stood large prefabricated concrete cathedrals supplying groceries, hardwares, homewares and electronics in bulk. Mauricio pulled up in front of one painted a lurid orange and going by the name of Handi-Mart. Ned and Mauricio had come into the city to order some building materials and pick up some bulk essentials. As they headed into Handi-Mart, the gunslinger at the front door greeted them with a broad, welcoming smile as he tapped his fingers on the butt of his shotgun. Inside they were greeted with the abrupt drop in temperature that Ned had become accustomed to in this part of the world.

'So this is your hometown huh?' Ned asked as Mauricio scanned the large signs that hung above the aisles.

Mauricio let out a puff of amusement 'Yeah, I guess, it's different now though, now we have Handi-Mart' he declared raising his arms triumphantly.

'Where did you live?'

'A few miles from here, in the north of the city, my grandmother still lives up there' Mauricio replied, before heading off to his left 'we need to go to aisle 8'.

*

5th June

Ned and Adi strolled along the beach to where the river trickled out of the jungle. From the shadowy, sun spotted gully they could hear the shrieks and laughter of children around the bend in the creek, just out of sight. It had rained for the preceding few days which meant there was enough water in the creek for the kids to leap in from the high parts of the bank and use the rope swings that had been there since their parents were children. Dani had shown them this place the day before the rain, telling them it was a good place to swim. Ned and Adi approached quietly and found a place on the bank from where they could watch the kids as they swung into the water and splashed about. After a few minutes they were spotted and a few brave youngsters came over to question the visitors. The kids stood in front of Ned and Adi whispering and giggling amongst themselves, apparently nominating a spokesperson for the group.

Adi broke the ice, 'Hola niños como estan?'

The three dripping wet kids all giggled, 'bien' came the staggered reply.

Adi playfully poked the girl standing closest to her 'como te llama?'

The girl smiled and swiveled at the hips, 'Isabela', she then reached out and touched Adi's curly hair and let out a giggle. The other two kids joined in on the laughter, all reaching forward and touching Adi's hair. Isabela started asking Ned and Adi questions that neither of them could translate with any success, soon the other two joined in and Ned just nodded and said 'si' to everything which caused the children to stop out of confusion. With the kids staring at Ned, who they must have assumed was some sort of foreign idiot, he whipped out one of his most used and useful Spanish phrases, 'no entiendo, solo hablar Ingles'.

Isabela proudly stepped forward and announced, ' yes, no, happy-face, sad-face, es Ingles'.

Ned and Adi raised their brows simultaneously, impressed with what they heard.

Isabela was not done, 'one, two, three, four, five, six, seven', to which Ned and Adi gave a round of applause.

By now the rest of the children had arrived and Ned and Adi sat before quite an audience. Ned leapt to his feet and marched over to the rope swing where he swung ungracefully into the water, much to the kid's amusement.

*

Inbox 09/06/11

Hi Ned, haven't heard from you in a while, how's it going? We've still got Julian here, he's still very shaken up after what happened to him over there in Bali. Everything else here is good, haven't had much rain though which as you know is bad news for the lettuce, anyway, stay safe.

Love from Mum.

Send Email 09/06/11

Hey Ma, sorry for the lack of contact, I'm quite far away from the nearest town so I can only get online once or twice a week, I'll try and write more often. All good here, having a good time. Hope you get some rain soon.

Ned.

*

12th June or Circa 1832

There was a full moon overhead, visible through a break in the silver backlit clouds. The bright moonlight bounced off the slick, wet leaves that surrounded Ned. His feet were soaked, he could feel the mud rising up between his toes and spreading over the tops of his feet. Ned pulled his feet out of the mud and headed in the direction of the crashing waves he could hear in the distance. At the edge of the dunes Ned wiped his feet on the tufts of grass that sprouted from the sand and flicked out the stubborn mud that clung to the skin between his toes. The sand on the beach was dimpled with the rain drops that had fallen earlier in the night and in the distance Ned could make out a faint flickering light through the trees at the northern end of the beach. As Ned made for the light he could smell smoke and as he drew closer the sound of voices. Ned crept slowly towards the voices trying to stay in the darkness. From a safe distance he knelt down and watched a group of uniformed men chatting and drying off by a large fire. There were a number of canvas tents set up in the vicinity and further away several other fires burned. The uniforms looked like those that Ned had seen in historical re-enactments put on for school kids and tourists. Close to where he knelt 5 horses were tied to a tree. The men around the fire spoke with British and Irish accents, as they discussed the terrible time they'd had crossing the range in the rain and what they thought they might encounter when they set off in the morning. Ned wondered if Ronald was nearby doing the same thing as him. He wanted to call out, to ask Ronald more questions but his fear of the unknown, about what might happen if he were to be seen kept him hidden and silent until the whiteness washed over him.

*

13th June

'The logs are coming today, hope you got a good night's sleep' Mauricio announced as he emerged from the bathroom, steam rising from his head like winter cow shit.

'What time?' Ned asked, looking up from his cornflakes.

Mauricio shrugged his shoulders as he finger-combed his wet hair, 'they'll just dump them down by the front gate, we'll hear it'.

While Ned was midway through mid-morning shit when the metronomic chirp of a reversing truck broke the serenity. Muffled instructions were carried up the hill towards the long-drop on the easterly breeze. The chirping stopped, replaced by the sound of six tons of treated pine hitting the dirt as Ned and the tilt-truck dropped their loads simultaneously at opposite ends of the property.

When Ned made it back down to the bottom of the hill the truck was nowhere to be seen and the dust clouds around the timber pile had all but settled; Mauricio stood atop the pile, assessing the mass of wood glancing up occasionally to imagine them arranged more formally around the mostly empty block.

*

14th June

'Do you think we'll be able to get much done, just the three of us?' Ned asked as he placed his end of the pine stack onto the dirt beside the slab furthest from the gate.

'We'll have to' Mauricio replied wiping his brow, 'Dani and some of the other guys will help too, and once we've finished the first one we can maybe get a few volunteers, they can stay for free and help out'.

Ned exhaled loudly through pursed lips, looking wearily at the site and the unshrinking woodpile down the hill.

'There's no rush though' Mauricio added with as reassuring smile.

'Do you definitely know what you're doing, these cabins aren't just gonna fall down one day are they?'

'Sure I do' Mauricio boasted, 'I'm an engineer'.

'Well I'm most of the way to being an engineer and I sure as shit couldn't build a house' Ned replied doubtfully.

'Trust me man, they'll be solid'.

*

Inbox 19/06/11

Hi Ned, Hope all is well, any interesting stories? Daryl and I have joined the local historical society, Daryl thought it might give us a bit of a headstart on the other collectors in the area. It's been very dry, the dams are really low, looks like we might have to buy some water. Julians on a disability pension at the moment, psychological trauma you see, poor kid, make sure you stay out of trouble, you don't want to end up like him.

Love from Mum.

Send Email 19/06/11

Hey Ma, I'm doing fine, nothing too much happens here so no exciting stories unfortunately, lots of swimming, fishing and working. Bad news about the rain, hopefully it all sorts itself out. Historical society sounds good. I won't end up like Julian, you don't need to worry, I'm a good boy.

Ned.

Shane 'Big Man' Roach: Anyone kean to put in to a greyhound sindicate? Hit me up.

Jimmy Miller: How much do you want?
Shane 'Big Man' Roach: 200 buck minimum, I've got a hookup for a real good dog, so far it's me and Nath
Jimmy Miller: Who's gunna train it?
Shane 'Big Man' Roach: Me and Nath are gonna train it, I got a book.

*

20th June

Ned and Adi strolled along the beach to where the river was trickling out. They had made a habit of coming down here a few afternoons a week to swim with the kids. It had been dry for a while so the water was low, limiting the activity to splash fights and wallowing.

'I wish we had a place like this where I grew up' Adi said as she sat hugging her knees, watching the children splashing and shrieking.

'There's a creek like this one where I'm from' Ned replied, 'it's a fair bit muddier and smellier though. We used to have some pretty intense after-school mud fights down there'.

Adi smirked, resting her chin on her shoulder as she turned to look at Ned. 'Sounds like fun. We had a pool at our place in LA when I was really small but in Israel we just went down to the beach every now and then'.

'I wonder if these guys' parents played down here when the war was on, they might not have been allowed out?' Ned mused, 'did Mauricio tell you what happened down here?'

Adi nodded her head, 'Yes, it was horrible, and in such a beautiful place'.

Ned and Adi watched quietly as the children began racing folded mango leaves down the current, filling them with stones and seeds to play the part of passengers.

'What do the kids do for fun in the bad parts of Israel, where all the trouble is?' Ned asked as he watched the kids chase their boats towards the beach.

Adi's gaze moved from the creek to the dirt between her feet, she shrugged her shoulders, 'kid's always find something to do, they play football and games like normal kids, but some…' she hesitated, 'you see some dressed up like the men, playing shooting games in the street, copying the crap they see'.

'Do they ever get mixed up in the fighting?'

Adi kept her eyes fixed on the ground, tracing shaped into the ground with her fingers, 'sometimes… on both sides'.

'You?' Ned asked hesitantly looking at the trails in the dirt Adi was making.

'No' Adi replied dismissively, shaking her head before looking up the creek, facing her head away from Ned.

'Sorry, I didn't mean to upset you…'

'It's ok, just…' Adi paused and forced a smile, though Ned could see her eyes glazed, fighting back tears, it was the first time she had shown anything other than an air of absolute confidence and assuredness. 'It just reminded me of something…. Bad'.

'Sorry, you don't have to tell me'.

'No, I want to' Adi replied, straightening herself up in the dirt. 'In my second year with the army, we were in Gaza City, there was this little boy, there had been some trouble and we were enforcing a curfew. This little boy came from around the corner into the laneway we were checking and this guy, he called out and the boy froze, he was holding a wooden gun, a toy, and he shot him, he was 5 years old'.

'Fuck' Ned muttered under his breath.

'The guy who shot him was only 19, he just did what he'd been trained to, it's just a shame, for both of them, just two kids stuck in a bad situation, just kids'.

Ned remained quiet; Adi's sadness had become frustration by the end of her story. It was dawning on him that he really didn't have a lot to complain about back at home.

'Adults definitely fight about some dumb shit; the kids just sit in the middle wondering what the fuck all the fuss is about'. Ned put his arm around Adi, she leaned in and rested her head on his shoulder, Ned wrestled with a smile and maintained a stoic rigidness whilst he celebrated internally, his frustrations with the adult world abandoning him for the moment.

*

Send Email 24/06/11

Hola Dickhead,

How's home treating ya? Still all sweet here, just getting into the swing of things now, starting to slap up a few buildings. Could do with you here, we need a work site know-it-all to kick a few bits of timber. Waves are alright here too.

Peace, Ned.

*

29th June

Adi strode into the kitchen and dropped a small handmade envelope on the table in front of Ned.

'Look what I've got for you' she giggled as she dragged out the chair opposite Ned and sat down.

Ned picked up the envelope, which was unlabeled and gave it a shake, 'what is it?'

'Open it' Adi replied, rocking back on her chair with a wide grin.

Ned peeled apart the envelope and tipped a folded piece of notebook paper onto the table. Ned unfolded the note which revealed a short direct message scrawled scrappily across the sheet in lime-green crayon, " ned you are nice I love you from Isabela and Maria".

'Looks like you've got some fans' Adi joked.

'Great' Ned replied, squirming uncomfortably in his seat, 'nothing like having a couple of five year olds on your case'.

'Aww it's cute' Adi cooed, 'you should be flattered'.

*

3rd July

'Are you feeling a bit sick' Mauricio asked Adi, giving her a playful pat on the head as she sat at the rear of the boat looking pallid and pained as she hugged her knees and stared at the wet panels in front of her feet.

Adi lifted her head to look at Mauricio, 'I don't know why I let you stupid boys talk me into coming out here, we're all going to die you know, this boat is not seaworthy' she snapped before letting her head flop back down.

'Don't be silly, this is a very good ship' Mauricio laughed in reply.

Ned had gotten to know the run of the boat rather well and was steering it towards a spot that he and Dani had been successful in most mornings, 'I think you're s'posed to look at the horizon or something, stops you from being sick so I've heard'.

A pained groan came as a reply from the general area of Adi's knees.

As Ned guided the boat as it cut through the slight windchop, Dani and Mauricio checked the gear and prepared the bait, the smell of which only added to Adi's nauseum.

The fishing was good this fine morning; Dani had pulled in an impressively sized Albacore and Ned had a couple of plate sized Snapper on ice. As the sun crept higher into the sky so the swell increased and a couple of hours in, the boat was swaying nicely with an occasional thud coming from the hull when the boat found a bit of air. Mauricio, who had earlier bragged that he could catch a fish with his hands, was lying across the bow, dangling a bit of bait into the water from his fingertips.

'Guys' Adi whimpered from the back of the boat, 'I need to go to the bathroom'.

Ned looked around to see Adi sitting rigidly on the rear bench tightly gripping it on either side of her. 'You'll have to go over the side'.

'I will not!' Adi replied sternly.

'It will take like half an hour to get back, can you hold on?' Mauricio asked, his head still hanging from the edge of the boat.

Adi gave no reply and sat scowling at the sea to her right. She remained defiantly quiet for several minutes before eventually breaking the silence, 'and how exactly am I going to go over the side?'

'You could hop in, or someone could hold on to you while you dangle over' Ned suggested.

'I don't think so'.

'We could tie some rope to the front and you could hang onto that, like abseiling' Mauricio chimed in, throwing his bait away and sitting up on the bow.

'I have rope' Dani declared, pointing to the storage space below the console.

Before long Mauricio was giving the toilet rig a test run, dipping his backside into the chop and giving the rope a good tug, 'seems ok to me' he declared, giving Adi a cheeky wink.

'I want all of you to go to the front and look away until I say' Adi commanded with the stern gaze of a drill instructor, 'if anyone turns around I will kill them.... I'm serious, I know how'.

I bet you do' Ned replied.

'What is that supposed to mean?' Adi snapped.

'I've seen "Munich" and "Don't Mess with the Zohan" I know they teach you moves over in Israel'.

Ned, Mauricio and Dani stood shoulder to shoulder facing the western horizon, giggling at the muttering and cursing coming from behind them.

'This is the worst day of my life!'

*

7th July

Is Adi short for something?

No, why do you ask?

No reason, I've just never heard it before.

I was named for my grandmother; we have the same name, Adi Sarah James.

I was named after a murderer.

A murderer? Why would your parents name you after a murderer?

Well he was like a folk hero, like Billy the Kid or something, but he did kill a bunch of people. Ned Kelly.

How strange.

Yeah.

*

Inbox 12/07/11

Hey Ned, what's the latest mate? Roosters gone missing, he might of kicked it, any ideas where he might have taken himself? Jakeys a bit upset about it. Hope alls well bro.

Jake.

Send Email 12/07/11

Hi all, just a general message to let you all know that I am alive, well and disease free. We've been building the first cabin for a few weeks now, it looking good. Having a good time with the locals and keeping out of trouble. Hope all is well at your end.

Cheers, Ned.

Send Email 12/07/11

Hey Jake, I wouldn't worry too much, he's wandered off before, if he's dead try under the house.

Ned.

*

16th July or Circa 1947

'Long time no see' Ned called out. Ronald was sitting at the end of a bench with his back to a pair of men in overalls deep in discussion.
Ronald brought his index finger to his lips and made a slight head movement towards the two men. Ned tried to soften his stride and stopped a couple of metres short of the bench. He waited silently as Ronald

eavesdropped on the two men before rising to his feet and walking away towards town.

'What was going on there?' Ned asked as he caught up to Ronald.

'Just seeing if I could learn anything, sometimes I hear some pretty good stories' Ronald replied.

'Right. What were they talking about?'

'They want to organize a strike at the mine'.

'When are we?' Ned asked, trying to get an idea from the surroundings.

'I haven't had a chance to check yet, probably after the war I think, 1947 or 8 judging by the cars over there' Ronald replied, pointing out a row of parked cars on Beach Street.

'Any theories yet on how I'm turning up here?'

Ronald shook his head, 'not yet, maybe it's magic' he said almost laughing.

Across the street a dapper couple strode over to one of the cars, they looked like they'd stepped straight out of an old photo.

The glare coming from the car windscreens started to intensify, the sun seemed to be growing in the sky.

'I think my times about to run out mate, the lights are going up'.

'That's how I know too', Ronald said, 'before you go, your dog's been in my shed for a week, I've fed him a couple of times, maybe you should tell someone to come and get him'.

'Thanks mate, this was a short one eh' Ned replied as Ronald and everything else disappeared into the fog.

*

Send Email 17/07/11

Hey mate, ask next door to have a look in their shed, Rooster might have gone in there I reckon.

Ned.

*

23rd July

Ned strolled into the cabin with a couple of fish and threw them into the freezer, 'feel like a trip into town?' he asked Mauricio who was fiddling with a calculator and a notepad at the table, a half-eaten bowl of muesli in front of him.

'You run out of money?'

Ned pressed his back against the cool steel of the fridge, 'it's getting a bit low but Dani wants to give Isabela a birthday party next weekend and he hasn't got any'.

'That's good enough for me' Mauricio replied pushing his notepad away and springing to his feet.

The dry spell had left the road super dusty and it flowed into the car freely through the many gaps in the cabin. Ned and Mauricio had taken to wearing their shirts over their faces like a couple of bandits as they bounced along the road toward San Salvador.

'What was the stuff you were doing this morning, with the calculator?' Ned asked through a mouthful of t-shirt.

Mauricio tucked the bottom half of his makeshift mask above his top lip, 'I'm a bit worried about how much it's going to cost, I want to get a few machines in, to speed it up a bit, but they're not cheap. If I ask my father for more money he might start asking questions'.

'I have some money' Ned replied, 'it's just sitting there in the bank, maybe I could chuck a bit in'.

'You want be my partner?' Mauricio asked, sounding surprised.

'Maybe' Ned shrugged, 'strictly business though, no shenanigans'.

Mauricio laughed, 'please, I'm way out of your league, besides, Isabela is my friend and I would never steal you from her'.

At the super bodega the boys stocked up for the party with a bag of cheese snacks and a bag of pork rinds both the size of couch cushions and enough cordial to sweeten the Dead Sea.

'We should get a cake too' Ned suggested as he and Mauricio found themselves in the bakery section.

'Sounds like someone's got a soft spot for little Isabela, her love letter must have worked'. Mauricio picked up a pink, heart shaped cake and held it out for Ned, 'something like this perhaps'.

Ned flipped Mauricio the bird and picked up a chocolate cake.

*

27th July

Ned floated on his back looking up at the clearing sky. Overnight it had rained for the first time in several weeks and now the water in the bay was stained brown by the creek. Ned felt like he was in one of his mum's dams, the water around his backside cooler than the water washing around his ears. After a good soak Ned headed for shore swimming until the water was too shallow and then propelling himself with his hands, wary of the creek debris that littered the sand below him.

At the table in front of the fish shack Adi sat with Isabela and her chums making a piñata for Isabela's birthday party. On the other side of the road Mauricio and Dani sat in the cantina with a couple of Dani's cousins staring at a pile of mysterious meat burning on the cantina barbeque. Ned pretended not to see the girls and made a beeline for the cantina.

Ned dragged a chair over to the barbeque and joined in on the meat viewing, highlighted with an occasional prod, burp or comment in Spanish that Ned could half understand with a three minute internal translation delay.

Ned was lost in the hypnotic blackening of the meat when Adi's voice, swam aggressively across the gravel road, 'you guys are missing out on some serious fun over here!'

Several heads turned in the direction of the fish shack momentarily before quickly returning to the hotplate, only Ned's gaze remained on the piñata party.

'Maybe later, when you're a bit closer to being finished and I won't have to help' Ned called out across the gap.

'Come on!'

'We don't need fun Adi' Mauricio added, not diverting his eyes, 'we have meat!'

*

1st August

The festivities were winding down and Ned and Adi found themselves sitting alone amongst the bent and empty San Lucas cans in front of Dani's fish shack. Ned had decided between his seventh and eighth tin that tonight he was going to plant one on Adi, just as soon as it was appropriate. Ned glanced at Adi out of the corner of his eye, she was staring into the middle distance, she seemed relaxed, maybe she was tired, she might have been thinking about going to bed, eep. It had only been about ten minutes since Mauricio had staggered off into the darkness, plonking his way towards the house. Ned hadn't yet psyched himself up sufficiently to make his move; he hadn't mentally rehearsed his play. Ned shifted himself a couple of millimetres closer to Adi on the wooden bench, he didn't want to give his game away just yet, and a subtle shift to his left was just fine. Adi was facing slightly away from him, still staring into the darkness. Ned decided a predatorial reach around sucker kiss was not in his best interest, he needed her to face him.

'Adi'.

Adi turned her head and looked at Ned, waiting for him to continue.

'ah…. That was a good party huh?'

Adi furrowed her brow, slightly confused, causing Ned some concern, she must think he's drunk, drunker than he actually is, 'yes' she nodded, furrowed brow intact, 'it was fun'.

'Yeah' Ned echoed, nodding his head, realizing he was coming across particularly smoothly

'Everything ok?' Adi asked, looking at Ned as though he were a patient.

Ned lurched forward like a retarded ninja, a million disjointed thoughts racing around in his wobbly head. He could feel the cold tip of Adi's nose touching the skin beside his left nostril, straightening up his thoughts, she definitely seemed to be giving some back, she wasn't pushing him away or recoiling in horror. Ned opened his right eye just to check everything was legit, satisfied that it was, he began to relax into the kiss that had occupied his mind for the last couple of months. After what seemed like both an instant and an eternity Adi slowly pulled herself back, she looked like she was trying to smother a grin. Ned quickly repositioned himself so as to obscure the semi that was brewing inside his board shorts and pushing up through the fabric like a Halloween spectre.

'I was wondering when you were going to do that' Adi said with a giggle, 'I thought maybe Mauricio was going to get a kiss before me'.

'Yeah right, well he was my first choice but apparently I'm too ugly for him' Ned replied with a smile.

Adi took Ned's free hand and slid hers inside, 'it was about time'.

*

Inbox 03/08/11

Hey Ned, could you please give us a call at home mate, as soon as you get this, very important.

Jake.

Ned, I've just had Jake around here, they're trying to get hold of you, give him a call ASAP.

Andy.

Hi Ned, you need to give home a call or even me, bit of sad news I'm afraid, I'd rather you hear it over the phone though rather than in an email, please call as soon as you can.

Love from Mum.

Part 4

(Taking care of business)

The two Jakes stood near the exit door of the arrivals hall. Ned spotted them quite quickly as he ambled across the tiles dodging the flailing luggage of the other new arrivals searching the space. Little Jake waved excitedly as Ned approached, signaling their location flamboyantly.

Big Jake thrust his hand out at Ned, 'good to see ya bro, was the trip ok?'

'Yeah, long - but ok'.

'That's good… you want me to grab ya bag?'

'I'm alright mate'.

'What did you see in America Ned?'' Little Jake asked placing a hand on Ned's forearm.

'Oh lots mate, I went to Disneyland'.

'*Ohh coo-ool*! We should go to Disneyland Dad'.

'Yeah Jake, I think you should pay though'.

'Ok!'

They stepped out into the grey afternoon and into the teeth of a howling wind, customary in an Australian August.

The journey back to Binnara Point consisted of family friendly banter, Ned and Jake each aware not to talk details until Little Jake was out of earshot. Little Jake fired questions at Ned about monkeys and airplanes and food until his thirst for knowledge about the western hemisphere was sated.

Jakes van scraped onto the driveway behind Ned's blue demon just as the last strip of purple light vanished from the evening sky.

*

Ned dropped his bags on the floor of the room he had bequeathed to Little Jake and took a deep breath that smelled of dirty socks with a hint of week old lunchbox apples. Ned kicked off his shoes and wandered out to the back patio. Jake joined him after a few minutes with a couple of cans and a packet of Newman's own brand chicken chips.

'So what happened?' Ned asked, cracking open his drink.

Jake took a long slurp from his can and wiped the fizzing residue from his top lip, 'Well... I came back from work and he was sitting in his chair like normal but he looked kinda grey and his mouth was hanging open a bit, I gave him a nudge and he didn't feel right so I chucked him down on the floor and started doing the moves, you know, fifteen and two and all that but I think he'd been gone a couple of hours'.

'S'pose it was good you found him and not Little Jake or one of the girls'.

'Bro, Shane was sitting on the couch the whole time, all fuckin' day, didn't even notice his old man was dead in the same room for half the day' Jake exclaimed with half a chuckle before pulling himself up.

'What?!'

'Yep, dead set. Said how was he supposed to know, he was always just sitting there on the chair without talkin' or movin' much'.

'Fucken hell', Ned exhaled with a shake of his head. 'How have the girls been?'

'Ok, Jode's been trying to organize everything, the funeral and all that, plus there's solicitors and shit to deal with for the house and all that'.

'Right'.

'Krystal's been quiet, had a couple of days off work, Nath's been away so she's just been in her room on the blower most of the time'.

'What about Jakey?'

Jake gave a smirk and fiddled with the ring pull on his beer, 'he's been real good mate, he had a little cry but he has a book about a kid whose grandpa dies and he's been really good, it's made it easier on Jodes'.

Ned returned the smile and gave a nod.

'Haven't seen much of Shane, he's just been waddling between his shitbox and the pub, he hasn't been in the house for a couple days'.

*

Over the horizon of the mattress Ned could see the crescent of Little Jake's pot belly rising and falling like an uncertain sun. His hips ached from a night spent on a thin roll of foam on the floor of his former bedroom. The sun was streaming in through the venetian blinds and laying a trail of warm and cold along his body and over his face that was not going to let him get back to sleep.

Ned wandered out into the kitchen where he could see Jodie's ample buttocks protruding from behind the pantry doors. Ned's bare feet made a wet tearing noise as he padded across the sticky kitchen lino, loud enough to prompt Jodie to pull her arse in and poke her head out from behind the particle-board door.

'Sorry matey, did I wake you?'

'Nah, nah, I didn't even know you were out here' Ned replied with a wet sniff.

The floor beneath Ned's feet vibrated as Jodie strode over before wrapping Ned up in a tight bear-hug; it was the closest she had been to him since pinning him to the ground as a primary schooler and dangling strings of thick spit menacingly above his little face.

'Sorry I wasn't here last night when you came home, me and Krystal had to close the shop'.

'Yeah, Jake said', Ned managed to gasp with the last vestiges of air remaining in his evacuated lungs.

Jodie released her grip and held Ned by his shoulders at arm's length, her left hand smelled like unwashed potatoes and soft carrots, her right hand smelled like cigarettes, 'so you got home okay, did you have a good trip?

'Yeah, all good' Ned replied, standing rigidly still in slight shock.

'Are you ok? Jake said you guys had a chat last night'.

Ned nodded, looking over Jodie's shoulder out the kitchen window towards the MacDonald's backyard.

'The funeral's going to be Friday, I've already told everyone. Luckily Mum had gotten him one of those funeral plans from the tele before she left, so it's not costing us anything'.

'Did you invite Mum?'

Jodie dropped her arms and pursed her lips, she stared intensely at Ned for a few second, 'She's not invited Ned' came to curt reply, 'and I don't want you inviting her, she made her choice 5 years ago'.

Ned walked past Jodie and towards the pantry,

'I'm serious matey'.

'Ok'. Ned made himself a bowl of cereal and ate it standing by the sink, looking over the fence at Ronald's time-machine which stood exactly as it had when Ned left.

*

'That's pretty fucked up, how did he not notice'.

'Yeah, I dunno'.

Andy folded his torso around the kitchen wall and waggled a banana between his thumb and forefinger.

'No thanks mate, I only just had brekkie'.

'Suit yourself'. Andy sauntered into the living room and stretched himself out across the sofa opposite Ned's armchair. 'So Friday huh, where are you having it?'

'There's like a chapel thing attached to the funeral joint, it's all very convenient. Roseborne Gardens, you can scatter the ashes there too, it a package deal'.

Andy nodded as he smacked on a chunk of banana, 'they've covered all the bases'.

Ned turned in his armchair to face the window from which he could see the street outside and across to the green area and the beach in the distance. 'So what have you been up to since you've been home?'

'Fuck all, I was back on the bricks a day after I got home, just been working'.

'You seen Chris?'

'Yeah I did actually, he came back for a couple of days to pick up some of his shit, he still got Razzle or whatever the fuck her name was hangin' off his arm'.

Ned let out a chuckle, sitting back here in Andy's place he felt like it had only been yesterday that he was last here, like the last four months never happened.

*

When Ned returned home Shane was slumped in their father's armchair. It was the first he'd seen of him since he'd been back. He seemed fatter than when Ned had left, like a land-whale wrapped in a 2pac t-shirt. His gaze was fixed on the cage fight taking place on the TV. Ned stared as Shane sat transfixed, ignorant of Ned's presence. His chubby fingers stroked the armrests like a blind man reading, slowly and deliberately feeling all the bumps, crusts and bare patches. In the snippets of silence between the slaps of sweaty man-flesh and over-zealous commentary Ned could hear Jodie shouting commands to Little Jake out in the backyard.

*

Daryl's ute was parked at the end of the road that led up to Rosebourne Gardens. Ned spotted his Mum leaning against the passenger door; Daryl was in the driver's seat reading something on his lap. Ned motioned for Andy to pull up alongside and wound down his window.

'What are you guys doing out here?'

Ned's Mum looked over her shoulder and peered over her sunglasses, 'Hi Neddie.... is that you Andy, how're you love?'

'I'm well thank you Deborah', Andy shouted out through the passenger window.

'Are you heading up?' Ned asked with a thrust of the head in the direction of the crematorium.

'Yeah.... I just thought I'd wait, ya know, until everyone else was in... I don't want to cause a scene'.

'Don't worry about Jodie, she does have some tact, she won't have a go at you until afterwards'. Ned gave his Mum a smile, 'jump in with us, Dazza too'.

*

In front of the chapel Tenille stood looking like a sun-shrunken balloon, all lumps, sags and puckers in a pair of leggings that were stretched to within an inch of transparency and an ill-fitting blue cardigan that cut her belly in two.

'Hello Tenille' Ned's mum said unenthusiastically.

'Hello Deborah' Tenille replied, equally disinterested.

'How are the boys?'

'Good' Tenille grunted, 'they're in there with your son, could you give them these please', Tenille handed Ned's mum two caps with flaps on the back. 'Tell him there'll be shit if he lets the boys get burned again, I'm sick of finding peeled skin around the house'.

'Ok' replied Ned's mum who continued on to the chapel door without another word or a backward glance.

The chapel was predictably decorated with neutrality, unable to offend and unwilling to surprise. There were twelve rows of pews on either side of a central aisle and to his credit Ned's father had managed to fill the front three on either side with a smattering of other guests dotted around the remaining rows.

'You go sit with the others up the front; I think it's best if I hang back here'. Ned's mother whispered as she peered in to the chapel.

Ned paused and turned to look at his mother who gave him a reassuring nod and waved him away.

Ned took a seat beside Big Jake in the row behind his sisters and a smattering of relatives he hadn't seen for varying degrees of time. Nath had arrived and sat between Krystal and Little Jake, he'd courteously removed his hat though its imprint remained firmly embedded in his scalp fat. Above the collar of what he assumed to be Nath's court suit, Ned noticed a barcode tattooed onto one of his neck rolls. His father's coffin sat plainly on a raised stage at front and centre. The basic funeral cover that the Roach's were entitled to provided them with a plain raw pine casket with nylon rope handles and a tasteful bouquet to place upon it. Ned's sisters had jazzed it up somewhat with a couple of photos and a drawing Little Jake had done. The coffin was being addressed and referred to by a member of staff who pretended to give a shit.

As Ned had assured his mother the service passed uneventfully, Krystal and Jodie both spoke briefly and Uncle Douglas had a brief attempt at a humorous anecdote before scarlet curtains were drawn across the platform and the assembled mourners proceeded outside to George Thorogood singing 'Kind Hearted Woman'.

*

'You coming back with us or with Andy?' Big Jake asked Ned as they filed out into the sunshine.

'Um… with Andy I think, I'll see you guys back at the house. Do you need me to get anything?'

'I think we're right mate'. Jake followed Jodie toward a cluster of Roach's gathered below a whirling cloud of cigarette smoke.

Ned found his mother and Daryl standing at the front end of Andy's car with Andy reclining on the bonnet.

'You guys coming back to the house?' Ned called out as he strode across the car park towards the car. Ned's mum gave him a faint smile as he approached, 'I don't think so love, I don't want to cause any problems. I just came to make sure all you kids were ok, I think we're just gonna head back to your auntie Janine's place and head home in the morning.

'You're more than welcome to come back with us tomorrow, I could use a hand with the lettuce', Daryl added with a chuckle.

'Well why don't we go for a drink at the pub before you go to Janine's?'

'You don't have to Ned; you should go with the others'.

'Nah, it's cool, I told Jake I would be a little bit'.

Andy slid down from the bonnet, 'you want a lift back to your ute?'

'I think we'll walk mate, I'll swing by yours on my way back home'.

'No worries, catch ya later then'.

Andy eased himself into his car and rolled off leaving them with a toot and the tympanic clatter of gravel bouncing off his fuel tank.

*

'It's been a while since I've been in here, glad to see they've tidied it up a bit' Ned's mother commented as they passed through the bar area towards to beer garden of the top pub. 'Plenty of familiar faces though'.

Ned escorted Daryl and his mother outside where they found a quiet spot by the back fence.

'Now I know that you'd like a sparkling Rose Deborah, what will you be having young Ned?' Daryl asked with his hand hovering over his back right pocket.

'Whatever you're having Daryl, make it two'.

'Alright then, I'll be back shortly', and with that Daryl strutted off toward the bar.

'I'm glad you came, I'm sure Krystal and Shane are too… I think Jodie's just putting on a front, she would have said something if she didn't want you there'.

'Yeah maybe, I think she's still very hurt, she took on a lot of responsibility when I left, I still regret that' Ned's mum lowered her head a little and was quiet for a moment 'it was good to see Little Jake, he's getting so big!'

'Yeah, in every direction, he'll be rolling to school soon'.

'Oh Ned... you leave him alone, he's a good boy'.

'I know, he's great, just a bit fat'.

Ned's mum flashed him a look of playful disapproval and had a little laugh. 'You seem to be handling it all very well, it must've been a bit of a shock... it was for me'.

'Yeah, I don't know... I know I'm supposed to be sad but nothing's changed really, I feel bad, I want to be upset, it seems like the normal thing but....' Ned shrugged his shoulders.

'Everyone's different mate, you're not bad' Ned's mum reached across the stained pine table and placed hand on Ned's forearm.

'So do you think they've still got your photo in the pokie fiend book behind the bar?'

Ned's mum let out a roar of laughter, 'maybe, don't think they'd recognize me though' she replied waving a handful of long grey hair in Ned's face.

'Now they didn't have a great selection of dark ales in there Ned so I've gotten us both a Piper's Black'. Ned looked up to see Daryl tiptoeing towards the table holding three glasses between his two thumbs and forefingers. He lowered the glasses toward the table, bending at the knees and keeping his upper body comically rigid, lowering himself to nipple height with the table before placing the drinks and scooting around beside his lady. Daryl picked a glass of what looked like water from the bottom of one of his farm dams and plonked it down in front of Ned.

'Well this is a lovely spot you've got here Ned'.

Ned flashed his mother a wry smile, while she did her best to disguise hers.

Daryl took a sip from his schooner of Piper's which left a caramel coloured boomerang of foam clinging to his moustache.

'So from all reports, your trip overseas was good'.

'Yeah it was' Ned replied 'I hadn't really planned on coming home'.

'Well it's a lovely little town you've got here; you'd do well to better it'.

'Well it's not for everybody Daryl, it wasn't for me'. Ned's mother turned her gaze from Daryl to Ned, 'I think you should do what you want, you don't have to stay here, but if you do it doesn't mean you're going to turn into your dad'.

Daryl became very interested in the goings on inside the pub and politely pretended not to listen.

'Your dad got a few bad breaks and just threw it in, he gave up. He was different once, he had plans, he wanted out of Binnara Point but he was lazy, his life could have been very different; mine too, all of ours'. Ned's mother gave Daryl a reassuring pat on the back, 'sorry love, you're still the best thing that happened to me.... aside from my kids I mean'. Ned's mum laughed nervously as she simultaneously patted her husband and her son, 'you're all wonderful, I'm a lucky lady'.

*

Ned, his mother and Daryl stood on the footpath outside the pub.

'Well it's about time we got over to Janine's place; it was good seeing you Neddy'. Ned's mum leaned in and gave him a big hug that smelled like shampoo and vinyl, 'I love you buddy'.

Daryl offered Ned a firm handshake and walked to the driver's door.

'Have a look up the top of the linen cupboard Ned, there's some old photo albums up there, you might get a different impression of your dad'.

Ned nodded and waved to his mum as she hopped in the passenger seat and the ute pulled away down Beach Street.

*

Andy was sitting on his verandah wearing just his suit trousers when Ned reached number 22 on his way home.

'How'd you go?' he asked as Ned opened the gate which let out a rusty groan.

'Yeah, good, had a couple of beers and a chat' replied Ned, flinging the gate shut behind him. 'You keen to come down to the shindig at mine?'

'Yeah I'll come with you mate, I've always enjoyed watching your ratbag cousins do weird shit'. Andy got up and went inside to get a shirt, Ned waited outside and watched the beach, thinking of all the different versions he'd seen on his time-freakouts.

'Ready?' Andy asked kicking his front door shut and rolling a t-shirt down his torso.

'Yeah' Ned replied diverting his gaze from the beach and making for the gate. 'Thanks for this mate'.

*

'I got it last week, if the bloke down at the bottle shop scans it, it comes up as a bottle of Bundy Rum…', Ned and Andy pushed through the from door, interrupting Nath as he told a couple of feeble-minded, once removed Roach's about his neck barcode. The group stopped their discussion and observed as the boys wandered through the middle of their cluster and out into the kitchen. The back screen door was open and Ned could see Jake sitting at the patio table with Little Jake on his knee chatting with a group of aunties and uncles. A small collection of empty beer bottles, some acting as ashtrays cluttered the middle of the table. It seemed a good a place as any for Ned and Andy to plant themselves. On the steps of the caravan Shane sat cradling a beer and watching Kobe and Shakur perform karate maneuvers on the fragile fence palings. Rooster was observing from beneath the caravan keeping himself out of reach and out of trouble.

'We'll go out and sit with the Jakes' eh' Ned suggested to Andy, motioning towards the backyard.

Andy nodded in agreement and followed Ned outside where they joined the throng at the table.

'What are your plans for the house?' Ned's Uncle Douglas asked Jake, tapping the ash from his cigarette on to the patio concrete.

'Haven't given it much thought mate' Jake replied, 'been a bit busy'.

'You gonna sell it?' Uncle Doug continued, 'you might get a decent price for it'.

'We haven't really discussed it mate' Jake replied unenthusiastically.

'If you sell it you should put in a pool first, that'll bump the price up'.

Jake shook his head, glancing toward Ned and Andy for help.

'Maybe we should put in a spa too' Ned added with a chuckle, drawing a dagger laced stare from Jake.

'Mmph' Uncle Douglas grunted, pulling the beer bottle away from his mouth and pointing it toward Ned, '*that* is a good idea, it's a wonder your old-man never got around to any of this'.

*

The last of the mourners vacated the house shortly after 11pm. There was a decent mess that nobody intended to see to until the next day or maybe the day after. Ned sat at the patio table and contemplated his plan of action amongst the pile of discarded beverages. Mid contemplation he remembered something his mother had mentioned earlier in the day and headed inside.

At the top of the linen cupboard pushed to the corner sat a brown document box behind some bed sheets that looked like they'd sat there unmolested for 15 years. Ned recognized the patter on some of the sheets to be the same as the ones his mum used to cover the sofa in years gone by. Ned dragged the box down from its lofty locale and onto the floor. It was heavier than he'd expected and the box top was covered in a thick layer of grey dust held together by long abandoned spider webs.

Inside the box Ned found four large, ring binder photo albums with a small pile of loose photo's at the bottom of the box. Ned carried the box out to the back patio and cleared a space on the table.

Ned took the top album from the stack and placed it on the table in front of him. Ned opened the album, the first page had a couple of old Polaroid photos of people he didn't recognize sitting on the bonnet of an ancient looking station wagon. The plastic film that held the photos onto the cardboard back has lost its tack and as Ned turned the page the photos slid out of their place and piled up in the binding. On the next page there were photos of a couple Ned recognized to be his parents at a party or maybe a barbeque looking young and happy and a little drunk, his dad wore a beaming smile, his head planted on the shoulder of Ned's mum who leaned back into him, her lit cigarette held a safe distance from both their faces.. As he flipped through the pages Ned saw more and more pictures of the young man his father had once been, photos of him playing cricket, on holidays smiling with his arm around Ned's mum, photos of him with his mates and without a care in the world. These pictures could have been photos from Ned's own life, if the faces were changed these were pictures of a young man with the world at his feet. As Ned stared at the pictures he felt a warmness gradually building behind his eyes, a hot wet tear dropped onto the page in from of him. Ned mourned the man in the pictures not the man that was buried today. Somehow, Terry Roach had managed to die twice.

*

It was baking hot, 50 degrees easily; around Ned was a flat barren landscape strewn with rocks and little in the way of shade. From behind him Ned heard the rapid scuffing of boots on gravel, he turned to see Ronald running towards him.

'Finally' Ronald panted as he crouched down in front of Ned, sweat dripping from his jaw and disappearing into the dust.

'What's happened here mate?' Ned asked, 'Have you worked out how to travel to other places?'

Ronald shook his head and looked up at Ned, still on his haunches. 'No this is the same place as always, just way, way back, a couple of million years'.

'We're not gonna get harassed by any T-Rex's are we?' Ned asked looking around a tad nervously, a hand across his brow to shade his eyes.

'No, we're not that far back, you might spot Homo Habilis if you walk far enough' Ronald replied, rising to his feet.

'How long have you been here? It's fucking baking!'

Ronald looked skywards taking off his cap and wiping a sleeve full of sweat from his forehead. 'A couple of hours, I've been waiting, hoping you'd turn up somewhere'. Ronald gave his cap a shake and put it back on his head. 'I noticed that your back home, in Binnara Point'.

'Yeah' Ned replied, 'I had to come back, my dad died'.

Ronald responded hesitantly, 'sorry to hear about that.... Well, the thing is. I was wondering if you could maybe help me out. I would have asked the normal way, over the fence but, you know, it's a bit of a struggle, I can talk a lot more freely here'.

Ned gave Ronald an understanding nod, 'what do you need?'

'Do you remember how I said that I was trying to travel within my own lifetime but I could never do it?'

'Yeah' Ned replied.

'Well, I want to find out if someone else can do it, I want to know if someone can travel to a point after I was born. I need someone younger than *me to go into the machine'. Ronald looked nervously at Ned, waiting for a response.*

As Ned looked back at Ronald, considering his subtle proposal a smile spread across his face, 'yeah, I'm keen, let's give it a go'.

This brought a smile to Ronald's face.

'I'll pop around tomorrow, or....whenever this ends, you know...' Ned continued, 'I'm excited to be time-travel pioneer'.

The sunlight seemed to intensify as Ned and Ronald discussed the plan, the already pale sky grew lighter and lighter, it seemed to be falling, lowering towards them, the glare became almost unbearable, Ned knew what was about to happen.

'What day were you born?' Ned asked, squinting to see as the whiteness enclosed.

'February 27, 1987, I think it was at about....'

Nothing.

*

A warm beam of light sat across Ned's face like a luminous bandit mask. It turned the insides of his eyelids pink and refused to let him sleep any longer. He could hear the noisy, snotty breathing of Little Jake on the bed and he could feel the crumbs that had worked their way to the surface of the carpet during the night and now stuck to his arms and back where he'd rolled off the foam mat that was acting as his bed. Ned slid his mobile phone out from under Little Jake's bed, it was 8.18am. He waded through the sea of dirty clothes and out of the bedroom, where he waded through a second sea of dropped food and empty beverage receptacles that floated amongst the general household mess until he was in the backyard. The box of photo albums was still sitting unmolested beside the patio table which had shed some of its mess onto the floor during the night. Ned tiptoed across the dew-damp overgrown Couch to the fence and hopped up on the bottom railing. Ronald's machine sat gleaming in the MacDonald's neat yard, the sun reflecting off the morning-damp like glitter.

*

Ned walked out of Aaron's Solicitors and Conveyancers with a sense of relief. He knew he was doing the right thing and it meant he was now free to do whatever the fuck he liked. He strode down Ocean Parade with a plan, or at least enough of a plan to build on. He opened the gate of number 22 and flopped down on the verandah bench seat.

'How'd you go?' Andy asked through the flyscreen of the kitchen window.

'Really good mate, the bloke seemed to think it could be sorted pretty quick, just need to wait for the documents to be done up'.

'That's good news' Andy replied as he kicked open the screen door and sat at the other end of the vinyl bench, 'keen for a wave in a bit, maybe a pub lunch?'

'Yeah, sounds good mate, I'll just have to duck home in a minute and take care of something first, won't be long though'.

Andy nodded thoughtfully and chewed on a piece of toast as Ned stared out into the ocean, all the way to El Salvador.

*

Ned jumped over the fence and landed on the soft, manicured grass on the MacDonald side. He walked over to the machine and gave it a consultory rap with his knuckles. The machine gave a hollow rattle in reply followed by the sound of a small seed rolling down one of the corrugations on its roof and falling silently onto the lawn. Ned looked over to the house; a neat row of plants lined the bottom of the back wall breaking rank to allow for the back door, he walked across and peered in to the house, his face pressed against the flyscreen. Inside there was no movement, a large stainless steel fridge stood opposite the back door about 4 metres away between the two sat a shimmering redwood dining table decorated with a brightly painted vase atop a lace doily. The sound of a latch rattling pulled Ned's head away from the back door. From the side access Ronald emerged, tiptoeing towards the machine with a battery from a fishing boat.

'Ronald', Ned called out as he turned and walked toward the machine, offering a friendly wave.

Ronald looked at Ned, pausing briefly before continuing on towards the machine. Ned followed behind and watched quietly as Ronald opened the door and disappeared inside for a short time.

'Hello', Ronald said when he emerged from inside the machine holding a small car battery, his eyes fixed on the ground to Ned's left though looking at nothing in particular. Around his neck hung a particularly impressive looking gold chain with a large gold adornment dangling from it.

'Hey mate' Ned replied, 'I wasn't sure if you were home…. is it ready to go?'

'Yes' Ronald nodded, bending down and placing the battery on the ground.

'Do I go in?' Ned asked, trying to sneak a peek inside.

'Yeah' Ronald replied, opening the door allowing Ned a glance.

It looked like a mixture of an outdoor pit-toilet and a hot water heater. Panels of sheet metal were riveted together rather haphazardly and a coil of copper tubing ran around the inside. In the centre was a wooden bench that sat atop a small pile of vehicle batteries.

Ned looked at Ronald and pointed hesitantly at the machine, 'now?'

'Yeah' Ronald replied briefly glancing at Ned before diverting his gaze elsewhere.

Ned stepped into the machine and sat himself down on the wooden plank. Ronald kneeled down in the open doorway and reached between Ned's legs, linking the batteries to the copper piping with modified jumper-leads. After attaching all but one of the clips Ronald backed out of the machine and stood up, holding the last unattached clip in his right hand, 'you have to do it' he said, handing the lead to Ned and pointing to one of the laps of pipe before closing the door.

Inside the machine it was dark aside from some slivers of light sneaking in between some warped sections of sheet metal. It provided enough light for Ned to make out the copper piping in front of him and the jumper-lead clip in his hand. Ned hesitated for a moment, looking at the clip, nervous and excited; he took a deep breath, winced and bit the clip down on the pipe.

It was suddenly light again, Ned stood in the same spot but the machine and Ronald were gone. Ned did a quick self-assessment and looked up to see the back door of the MacDonald's house open. A head popped out from around the door and looked straight at him.

'Can I help you?' asked a younger and hotter Mrs. MacDonald in a passive aggressive tone.

'Ah....yeah....I think, maybe.....' Ned rattled his brain for something plausible, '...I think my Frisbee came over your fence, I think it was this fence...' he replied, slightly impressed with his sharp thinking.

'Well I can't see it, what colour is it?' Mrs. MacDonald replied, stepping out into the yard.

'Um, it's a red one, a Coke one'.

Ronald's mum scanned the yard and then gave a shrug of the shoulders.

'It might have been that one' Ned suggested, pointing to what would in the near future be the Roach's yard, 'I'll check over there'. Ned jogged across to the fence and grabbed the top of the palings in readiness to leap over.

'Don't do that' Mrs. MacDonald called out, 'go around'. She started walking towards the side access and motioned for Ned to follow. Ronald's mum opened the side gate and ushered Ned through, 'you don't want to give the old girl next door a fright, knock on the door'.

'Thanks' Ned replied, giving the younger Mrs. MacDonald a smile and a thumbs up.

'Okay' she said closing the gate behind him and giving a little wave.

Ned strode out onto the footpath and began looking for something that would inform him the date. There was no telling how long this trip would last so he thought it best to get a move on. He stopped in front of the house that would be his and admired it for a moment, the lawn was cut and free of mess, the driveway was unstained and uncluttered and no screaming, either live or televised could be heard from the kerb, it was like looking at a before photo from a high school anti-drug lecture. Ned glanced at the letterbox and noticed that a copy of the Bulwarra Advocate was hanging wrinkled from the slot. Ned wriggled it free and checked the date at the top of the front page, Thursday June 19th 1986. The paper couldn't have been more than a couple of days old, Ned reasoned as he peeled the pages apart and perused the news items. Ned counted on his fingers and decided he'd popped up around eight months before Ronald's birth. Mrs. MacDonald couldn't have been more than a few weeks pregnant, she definitely wasn't showing. It seemed the mission brief had been accomplished without a great deal of fuss, now he just had to wait. Ned didn't really know what to do except tread the well-worn path up to Ocean Parade and kill time in the usual way. Scarborough Street looked much like it did in 2011, just a bit shinier and a bit less tired, the houses we're all the same aside from the odd colour change or missing extension, some of the cars were even the same, albeit with a lot less rust. Along Ocean Parade the houses were starting to show wear and ahead, towards the top pub Ned could see the first of the double story flash joints in the making, its wooden skeleton looming above its modest, weary neighbours.

When Ned reached the pub he heard music and rabble washing over the beer garden fence. He peered over and saw a sizeable crowd of locals sitting about, making the most of the winter sunshine. Ned decided it might be a bit *of fun to pop in for a look and headed around to the front of the pub. Inside a meat raffle was taking place, old paper notes were changing hands as the raffleers weaved their way through the crowd. On the old wood paneled TV that sat heavily on a shelf above the bar a footy game was being shown with the sound off. Ned ghosted to the bar and grabbed a horseracing form guide that lay spread out across the countertop. Saturday June 21st, 1986 was printed in small bold letters at the bottom of both pages.*

Ned wandered out into the beer garden to wait for the inevitable recall back to his own time. He found a spot in the sun on the edge of a table occupied by a couple of young fellas who probably still sit in this spot on Saturday afternoons in Ned's time only with a lot less hair and a lot more to complain about.

Ned sat quietly observing the crowd when his eyes were drawn to a familiar object a few tables away. Amongst a group of non-descript twenty-something's Ned spotted a George Thorogood, 1986 US Tour t-shirt. Hovering above the shirt was a head of dark, shaggy hair and skinny, tanned arms emerged from its sleeves, arms that gesticulated as he held court with his tableside audience. Ned casually sauntered over to the Ocean Parade fence where he could subtly observe the group whilst pretending to be looking over the fence at the beach. Sitting in front of Ned was the man he saw in the photos, the original Terry Roach. Ned watched quietly from the beer garden, meeting his real dad for the first time. He felt a sense of pride, he wasn't a great man, just an average man, but that was much more than he had been for all of Ned's living memory.

Ned stepped away from the fence and walked towards the table where his dad sat, he hurried, not wanting to give his brain time stop him. He walked up behind his father and tapped him on the shoulder; his dad twisted around and looked him up and down.

'Terry Roach?' Ned asked as he looked down at his father.

'Yeah' his dad replied, with a look of confusion.

Ned thrust out his hand, 'I thought it was you, I just wanted to come over and say g'day'.

Ned's dad shook his hand and gave a quizzical smile, 'have we met?'

'Ah, not really, we're kinda related' Ned replied.

'How's that then?'

Ned scratched his head, 'um... it's a bit difficult to explain really'.

'Yeah right?' Ned's dad replied with a furrowed brow, 'so what's your name mate?'

'Ned Roach'.

'Well, we must be related, not too many Roach's about', Ned's dad took a sip from his schooner; 'you want to join us for a beer?'

'I can't really stay mate, I just wanted to tell you, not to give up', Ned replied, to the great confusion of his father.

'What?'

Ned reached out and placed his hand on his dad's shoulder, 'don't give up'. Ned turned and headed for the door of the pub. Before leaving the beer garden he turned and glanced back at his dad, who was looking back at him, confused, enlightened or indifferent.

Ned began making his way towards the headland to wait it out. It didn't take long, as he started up the path toward his spot the sky started changing, the grass below Ned's feet faded to yellow then to white, the clouds reached down to touch the white earth and it was over.

*

Ned's eyes slowly adjusted to the sudden darkness, he could see the copper piping an arm's length in front of him. He stood up and pushed open the door to see Ronald turning to face him, having only been out of the machine for a few seconds himself.

Ned stepped out and clamped his hands on Ronald's shoulders, causing him to flinch, 'June 21st 1986, sorry mate'.

Ronald stood silently looking at his machine as Ned jumped over the fence and on to a white Rooster shit hidden in the long grass.

*

'Mate this is a pretty big deal, I don't know if I feel right about it' Big Jake said with a shake of the head, pushing himself away from the table.

'I'm positive mate, I really want you to have it' Ned replied insistently, pushing the contract towards Jake. 'You and Jodie have been running this show for years now anyway, you deserve it, and this way you guys can decide what happens'.

Jake picked up the papers in front of him and read them, glancing over the sheets at Ned every so often for reassurance which Ned provided with winks, nods and the occasional gayface.

Jake flipped over the last page of the document and placed it back on the table, 'maybe you should give it a few days mate, in case you change your mind'.

'Just sign it you pussy, I'm not gonna change my mind, and it means I can fuck off and leave you kids to it' Ned piped back, flicking the pen across the table at Jake.

Jake picked up the pen and tapped it on the table looking blankly at the contract and then up at Ned, 'you're sure?'

'Do it!' Ned snapped with a giggle.

'Alright' Jake sighed, initialing the first page before flipping through the others doing the same and signing where required.

'Well done buddy' Ned applauded as Jake signed the last page and flung the contract and the pen into the middle of the table, 'you're a homeowner now'.

Jake pointed aggressively at the screen door behind Ned, 'get the fuck out of my house!' he screamed menacingly before collapsing into a girlish giggle fit.

The back door flung open and Jodie wobbled out, obviously disturbed by the minor commotion. 'What on earth is going on out here?'

Jake pointed to the pile of paper in the middle of the table, 'your brother's signed his share of the house over to me'.

Jodie stared at Ned, a dumbstruck look slapped across her face, 'Ned…. You didn't have to do that'.

'I wanted to, I want you guys to have this place' Ned replied with a smile.

Jodie's eyes began welling up as she leant down and she and Ned had their second adult hug.

*

Ned's eyes struggled to focus on the saturated road in front of him as sheets of water ran across the bitumen making it look like a fast flowing river of motor oil. The rain fell so heavily it felt as though he was wearing someone else's prescription glasses, everything was distorted and visibility was only a few metres.

'Do planes still take off when it's like this' Andy asked, hunched over the steering wheel like Quasimodo.

'I think so' Ned replied, wiping the inside of the windscreen with his sleeve.

*

Ronald's cap hung from a branch a few steps in front of Ned; 'Headland' was scratched into the bark below it. Ned grabbed the cap and followed the sound of crashing waves to the beach. When he reached the shoreline Ned could see a set of footprints, slowly being eaten away by the rising tide, leading northward towards the familiar pile at the end of the beach.

'Waiting for me again mate?' Ned called out as he climbed up the rocks towards the cairn where Ronald sat cross-legged with his back to the beach.

'Sort of' Ronald replied turning his head, 'I leave a message when I can, just in case'.

Ned climbed up and sat on a large rock just below Ronald, 'sorry the experiment didn't really work out'.

'What do you mean?' Ronald asked, looking down at Ned.

'Trying to get me to a time after you were born, in the machine'.

'Oh, no, that worked out fine, the 21st of June '86, I was there'.

Ned looked up at Ronald confused, 'you were born in 1987 you said'.

'I was' Ronald confirmed, 'but I was conceived on the 4th of June 1986, I wasn't born the day you traveled to but I was alive'.

'No shit?' Ned replied, surprised, 'how do you figure that'.

'A bit of maths, plus my dad had a pretty fixed work routine, it had to be that day' Ronald declared, 'I could work out what day you were conceived, give or take a few'.

'No thanks' Ned replied with a chuckle, 'I don't really want to think about it.... So any way, you found out what you wanted to know, that's good'.

'Yeah, that much anyway' Ronal replied with a shrug.

'What have you been up to?' Ned asked as Ronald gazed out to sea.

'I've been collecting things'.

'From back in time?' Ned asked.

Ronald nodded his head with a slight smile of his face.

'I thought you couldn't bring stuff back?'

'I don't' Ronald replied, 'I just listen and watch, you'd be surprised how much stuff is buried about the place. Back in the day people were always burying things and then forgetting about them or just not ever getting back to dig them up again'.

Ned was stunned and impressed, 'really?'

'Yeah, some stuff I haven't been able to get to, under houses or the road, but there's still plenty'. Ronald pointed to the gold chain hanging around his neck, 'I got this from behind the Charcoal Chicken, it was in an old biscuit tin with a bunch of coins and rings and things, a man buried it there in the 30's, during the depression, I heard him telling his son'.

'Doesn't anyone wonder what you're up to, in the now I mean, with you digging around everywhere?'

'Not really', Ronald replied with a shrug and a smile, *'they just think I'm a retard'.*

*

Ned rolled out of bed and staggered to the door, rubbing the sleep out of his eyes and picking the dry crust out of his nostrils. He pulled the door open quietly, unsure of the time, not wanting to disturb anybody.

'Wow, you must have been really tired' Adi declared from the kitchen table as Ned wandered out of the bedroom, 'you've been asleep for about 20 hours'. She gave him a beaming smile and tapped the seat beside her at the table, 'sit down, Mauricio has just gone to pick up some eggs'.

Ned sat down at the table and smiled at Adi, 'how's things?'

'Really good' Adi replied, 'The girls have been asking after you…'

'Oh, right' Ned replied with a chuckle.

'I'm glad you're back'.

'Me too'.

*

Shane 'DJ Ninja' Roach: DJ-ing at Binnara top pub, 9.00pm Friday, be there!

*

THE END

Printed in Great Britain
by Amazon.co.uk, Ltd.,
Marston Gate.